Douglas Lindsay was born in Scotland in 1964. It rained.

The Cutting Edge of Barney Thomson

Douglas Lindsay

F/483414

PIATKUS

For more information on other books published by Piatkus,
visit our website at *www.piatkus.co.uk*

First published in Great Britain in 2000 by
Judy Piatkus (Publishers) Ltd of
5 Windmill Street, London W1
email: info@piatkus.co.uk

The moral right of the author has been asserted

A catalogue record for this book is available from the British Library

ISBN 0 7499 3158 2

Set in Times by
Action Publishing Technology, Northgate Street, Gloucester
Printed and bound in Great Britain by
Mackays of Chatham, plc

To Kathryn

A Chronologically Disadvantaged Prologue

The Sad Tale of Brother Festus

Brother Festus. An honest man. Weird name; honest nevertheless.

They used to call him a variety of things in school. Foetus. Fester. Fetid. Fungus. One Horse, although that's a completely different story. He was not strong either, the schoolboy Festus, and so he was teased and bullied. Every aspect of his character remorselessly picked apart, exaggerated and turned into an object of ridicule. Hair too long, hair too short; wearing school uniform, not wearing school uniform; gunk in his ears, food in his teeth, gloop in his eyes, Y-fronts too big; no pubes, then later a thick forest of wiry agriculture; voice like a girl, voice like a moron; good at art, bad at tech; chipolata penis, hairy arse, breasts too big, testicles like peas, tongue like a Spam sandwich. Everything.

Somewhere there's a queue, and it's populated by comedians just waiting to tell another queue of talk show hosts that their comedy comes out of being bullied at school. A defence mechanism, etc. . . . Festus tried that too, but he didn't have the jokes. And so they had some-

1

thing else about which to tease him.

Humour having failed, he retreated to that place in the head where everyone goes, but only the sad and solitary remain. And he has never left.

And so time and bitter experience brought him to the Holy Order of the Monks of St John, in north-west Sutherland, fifteen years prior to his soon-to-be untimely death. An austere existence to go along with his austere thoughts, for life has taught this man never to attempt to expand his mind. A place where no one teases him, and no one cares about the idiosyncrasies which plague his personality and his appearance. He has found his home. A job to suit his underdeveloped intelligence, people with whom he can associate. Brother Festus is in his element.

He arrived in the mid-eighties, and so easily missed the events of Two Tree Hill. He has heard about them, of course. Low whispers in dark corners, though there is always much that goes unsaid. Two Tree Hill; the very name still causes Festus's stomach to churn at the personal memories it induces – the world's injustice against one man. A man alone, cast from society, as Festus has been himself. He has never dug too deeply into the story.

And so, at this time of murder and terror, heartache and horror, the dichotomy of faith against reality, and the continuing serial of corpulent bloodshed, Brother Festus is about to be another victim. Not, however, of the man who wreaks vengeance for the iniquities of Two Tree Hill. Festus will fall victim to that other great serial killer – the accident.

Festus sweeps the stairs. A small flight leading down into the main part of the abbey church. His brush moves ponderously across the cold stone, his eyes never straying from the work he is about. He must wash them next. Not

2

his job normally, but the new floor cleaner, Brother Jacob, has vanished. Festus is happy to sweep the floors and the stairs. Happy, in his own way.

The storm rages outside and every crack and joint and bolt and buttress grinds its teeth in strained agony. Stained windows stand tight against the wind, and inside the church nothing stirs. Not a draught blows, not a mouse roars, not a spider waves a forward leg, not a dog has his day. The strained quiet of the grave, statue and sculpture looking down on the back of Brother Festus as he bends to his work. God's work.

Sculptures of holy men, whose names have long since been dumped into the damned sepulchre of time; the Virgin Mary, sanguine and resigned to her place in history; a strange, lonely, bemused Jesus at the Last Supper, with the disciples nowhere in attendance, while the Son of God tells his best parables – *There was this bar, right, and in walked a Sadducee, a Pharisee and an Australian* – and no one listens, but for a detached foot, the foot of Judas; the angel Gabriel, a good-looking guy, bearded and sad, eyebrow raised to some melancholy contradiction, a seraph's question as to the corruption of man and all that lies before him, a sculptor's vague musing on the limits of consequence; a bitter St Francis, the mad monk, scattering bread, a statement of his sexual desperation, his face lined with pain, his eyes scarred by the decades of frantic do-gooding, defying the black heart which lies within us all; and a substantial collection of gargoyles, fine figures, their heads no more grotesque than comic caricature, the classic 1400s, pre-Reformation, Gothic Götterdämmerung. One of these, it will be, that kills poor Brother Festus. By accident, indeed, or perhaps by the hand of God. For God's hands are, to quote some Italian gangster somewhere, pretty

3

fucking big, you know what I mean?

Brother Festus moves slowly down onto the floor of the church. Cold stone, under which the bodies of buried Crusaders still lie, their names long since worn from the tombstones of opprobrium, so that most of the brothers are no longer aware of the bare skulls which stare up at them as they walk across the floor.

Men who died on the most unholy of Holy Crusades; men for whom the bell tolled – a dagger in the guts, a scimitar drawn swiftly across the neck, hot oil poured into a tortured open mouth. They all watch Brother Festus, waiting to welcome him to their eternity of torture.

Festus sweeps the floors.

What does a monk think about when he's sweeping the floors?

God? The existence or otherwise? Deities in general? Some petty infatuation with one of the other monks, or with a long-remembered girl in a photograph which he keeps secreted beneath his mattress? Sport, perhaps, a metaphor for life which once tugged at him and gave him something to live for, so that years later he still remembers the missed birdie opportunity or the dropped catch at silly mid-wicket; the missed smash from the back of the court, the mistimed tackle; the perfect goal unbelievably ruled offside. Or maybe the average monk thinks of nothing as he sweeps the floor. His mind is a blank, random visions and thoughts flickering a minute distance below the surface, yet never seeing the light. Yes, who is to say that a monk thinks of anything as the brush moves methodically across the cold stone?

Brother Festus is different, however. Here is a man clinging to the only dream he has ever had, a grotesque sexual parody created in his early teens, from which his

4

limited imagination has never allowed him to progress. He is off in some nether world, inhabited by strange-shaped women dressed in black leather, various parts of their bodies oiled and on display, ravaging Festus's body as he gaily snorts cocaine off the three breasts of another. And all the while, he imagines that he slips farther and farther into damnation, and he loves every minute of it.

And so it is that he does not see the gargoyle, strangely misplaced from its perch upon high, where it has rested for over five hundred years. Resting and waiting; waiting for the opportunity to fall on an unsuspecting monk and to pierce his very flesh. A monk like Brother Festus.

Festus sweeps the floor. Mind a long way away, running the gamut of adolescent depravity, oblivious to his surroundings. The gargoyle breaks away from its base; the stone cracks noiselessly, a precise split. The sort of clean break that you would think only a master craftsman could achieve.

The fall is silent and swift. Ten seconds earlier and it would have smashed into the floor in front of Festus; ten seconds later and it would have missed him to the rear. But the timing is meticulous and, from on high, from the roof of the church, from the midst of the elaborate super-sculpture, from the gods, it comes.

It is an interesting gargoyle, based at the time on a local farmer with a nose like a parsnip. Long, corrugated and mild to the taste.

The gargoyle spins in free-fall, like a high-diver completing some elaborate octuple somersault, before the fall is sharply arrested as it thumps into Festus and the nose embeds itself in the back of his skull. And stays there.

Festus collapses to the floor, the gargoyle impaled upon him by the nose, so that he looks like a man with

5

two heads. The blood seeps out slowly, running down his pallid cheeks and onto the floor; blood from Festus's head mixing with that from the gargoyle's bloodied nose.

Festus is dead. The Crusaders lie in wait below, anticipating the arrival of their brother. The abbey church is quiet. Not a mouse roars, not a dog has his day. And somewhere, somewhere, there may be the sound of the architect of Festus's timely accident going about his business.

Chapter 1

That Old Dead Cow

'Whit'd'ye dae at the weekend, then?'

'I can't believe the lift isn't working. Twelve sodding floors.'

'You don't think the cooncil's got better things fur tae dae wi' their money than spend it on poor bastards like the folk who live here? Whit did ye dae at the weekend?'

'No wonder these places are riddled with low life. They build these sodding great monstrosities bloody miles from the nearest shop or pub. They've got nothing.'

'That wis thirty-five year ago.'

'That makes it worse. They've had all that time to improve things and they've done bugger all. Even the sodding lifts don't work. Imagine you're some single mother with three weans and ten bags of shopping.'

'The single mother's probably about sixteen, and the stupit wee tart went an' shagged some wank-arsed fifth-year wi' a foosty moustache, jist so she could get pregnant an' get her own cooncil hoose. So whit wis she expectin'? A bloody bungalow in Bearsden wi' mair rooms than shite? Whit did ye dae at the weekend?'

'Nothing. I did nothing at the weekend. Same as every other weekend. You, however, have presumably got a story to tell, the way you're going on.'

'Did a bit o' shaggin'.'

'The audience gasps. Who was it this time? Did you have to make do with Aud, or did you play away from home?'

'Well, ye could say Ah played a home leg an' four away legs at the same time.'

There is a brief pause in the conversation. They plod past the third floor.

'What are you saying?'

'Whit does it sound like?'

'You slept with your wife and four other women at the same time?'

'Aye.'

'Bollocks!'

'Pure right Ah did. Bloody brilliant.'

'You slept with five women at once?'

'Aye. Satisfied the lot o' them 'n a'. Orgasms a' o'er the shop.'

'And what did Aud have to say about this?'

'She had the screamin' thigh sweats fur it. Loved every minute.'

'She loved it?'

'Aye.'

'She said that?'

'Aye.'

'Really? Aud? Actually said that she loved it?'

'Well. Nae in so many words, ye know.'

'What did she say?'

'Well, she didnae actually say anythin' as a matter o' fact. But Ah could tell.'

'Right. So what did the four women you weren't shagging at any given moment do while they were waiting their turn?'

'Got stuck intae each other, ye know.'

'And Aud did that?'

'Aye.'

'Aud? As in Aud?'

'Well, she might no' have, Ah'm nae sure. Ah wisnae exactly lookin'. Ah wis surroundit by heavin' piles o' sweaty female flesh. D'ye 'hink Ah gied a shite about who wis doin' whit tae whom?'

'And who were they?'

'Who?'

'These mythical four women that your wife was so delighted for you to sleep with that she joined in?'

'Just a bunch o' wimmen, ye know.'

'What do you mean, just a bunch of women? Four women off the street? Four women you met in a bar? Four women you got out a Malaysian catalogue? Your cousins? Robert Palmer's backing band? The Bangles? All Saints? Who?'

'Jist a bunch o' wimmen.'

'You're going to have to do better than that if you're going to retain the credulity of your audience.'

'Ah don't know, dae Ah? They were jist wimmen. Ah didnae get their names. Whit, yet 'hink Ah wis botherin' aboot whit they were called, an' a'that?'

'So where did you meet them?'

'In town.'

'In town? So, you were just walking down Argyll Street and you and Aud stumbled across four compliant women who all wanted to go to bed with the two of you?'

'Aye.'

'On Argyll Street?'

'Whit? Well, it wisnae Argyll Street, but it wis somethin' like that.'

'What then? Sauchiehall Street? Renfield Street? Fantasy Planet Street? Walt Disney Street?'

'Piss off, Mulholland.'

'How often have you given evidence in court, Sergeant?'

'Whit are ye sayin'?'

'There weren't any four women at the weekend. You're making it up.'

'No Ah'm no'.'

'Aye, you are.'

'No, Ah'm bleedin' no'. There were pure four women wi' me an' the wife.'

'Bollocks.'

'Whit?'

'You're talking pish. You always talk pish when it comes to sex. Every time. You could talk pish for Nike, you. You're full of it. I can just see the advert for the new line of Nike sportswear for talking pish in, with you standing on some Brazilian beach, cheesy music in the background, and talking the biggest load of pish anyone's ever heard.'

'OK, OK, so it wisnae four.'

'How many?'

'Three.'

'How many?'

'Three. Ah'm tellin' ye it wis three.'

'How many?'

'Awright, it might huv been two. But Aud wis there 'n a', so that makes three.'

'Bollocks. How many?'

'Christ's sake, awright. It was jist the two o' them an' Aud didnae know anythin' aboot it.'

'You're full of shite, Ferguson. Who were they?'

'Well, ye know, a couple o' birds, 'n nat. Jist a couple o' birds.'

'They were prostitutes, weren't they?'

'Naw.'

'Weren't they?'

'Naw. Ye 'hink Ah cannae get a lumber wi'oot goin' tae a prostitute?'

'Aye, that's exactly what I think. Even your wife doesn't go anywhere near you.'

'Bloody hell, aye, awright. They were prostitutes. It still counts, though. It's still sex, an' they still get added tae the list.'

'Brilliant. So what did you do? Did you pay for it, or did you threaten to arrest them unless they did you a turn?'

'Whit dae ye take me for?'

'Well?'

No answer. They get to the twelfth floor, walk with silent footfalls along the hall to the graffitied door. A cold wind blows in through the broken window at the end of the landing. A dog has left its calling card on the floor; a toy car with all the tyres removed waits patiently near by.

'You've got to get a grip, Ferguson. One of your superiors finds out about that kind of thing, you'll get your balls rapped.'

'You're my superior.'

'Aye, well, lucky for you I don't give a shit. You ready?'

'Aye.'

'Right.'

Detective Chief Inspector Joel Mulholland knocks on the door. Somewhere inside, a glass is dropped on the floor.

✂

'Get out o' ma face, ya numpty-heidit eejit.'

Ferguson pushes the man in the chest, forcing him

11

back against the wall. Doesn't get out of his face. An ugly face it is too; pockmarked, like wet cement which has been attended to by a child on a pogo stick. Lips like thin broken biscuits, moustache the neatly clipped hair of a German woman shotputter's armpits.

'Numpty-heidit eejit, Billy? Can ye no' dae better than that? Is that as rude as that minuscule little napper o' yours is gonnae allow ye tae be? Disappointin', Billy, very disappointin'.'

Billy McGuire grits his teeth and stares at the ground. Ignores the hand still pushing at his chest and drifting towards his neck.

'Come on, Billy, ye know where the Big Man is. Ah know ye know, and you know that Ah know ye know. So why don't ye just gie us a' a break, save us a lot o' time, an' tell us?'

McGuire says nothing. Lips are sealed. Not any criminal code of conduct, however. If he remains silent, he'll get hassle from the police and possibly convicted of a minor offence or two. If he does open his mouth, at some stage he'll get his lips and nose nailed to the floor, followed by other unsavoury acts which won't leave him much blood to be going on with. He is constantly reminded of the fate of Wee Matt the Helmet, whose flaccid penis was squeezed into the jaws of a double hole punch. These are not men to wrong.

'Sod it, Sergeant,' says Mulholland. 'Bring him in and we'll see what we can get. No point in hanging around here too long.'

Ferguson grabs McGuire by the collar and leads him to the front door. Out onto the landing and then the slow trudge down the stairs, strange smells drifting up to meet them. They both know this is just another pointless arrest in another pointless day of crime prevention and detection. They know that McGuire will not talk, they know that this day will see them no nearer the heart of the drugs operation they have been chasing for the past three months. Some day, some time, they might get a result, but neither of them holds out any hope. Going through the motions.

'See that shite on telly oan Saturday night?' says Ferguson.

'What shite might that have been?' says Mulholland. 'The shite where some guy brags about having sex with eight hundred women at the same time, when in fact all he did was cut a hole in a melon while watching some low-grade porn flick on Channel Five?'

Unabashed. 'The Rangers. Load o' pish. See a' they bloody foreigners. If ye're gonnae sign shite, ye might as well sign Scottish shite, ye know, instead o' a' that foreign keich. Just cause some idiot's got a name like Marco Fetuccini or Gianluca Spaghetti doesnae mean they're automatically gonnae be able tae kick a ba'. Load o' pish.'

Mulholland trudges down another flight of stairs before he answers. Thinking about the weekend. Another series of arguments; irrelevant, vapid and senseless. Just like the irrelevant, vapid, senseless day which he is enduring, and the entire week which lies before him. He knows he's feeling sorry for himself. Thinks he can justify it.

'Didn't see it,' he says eventually. Ferguson grunts in reply, but doesn't ask why. He knows all about Mulholland's domestic problems, and is not going to air them before the likes of Billy McGuire.

'Cannae even beat soddin' Dundee,' he says instead. 'Absolute shite. Bloody St Johnstone at the top o' the league. Whit a joke. We used tae be one o' the best countries in Europe, for Christ's sake. Used tae win things.

Now we're lucky if we can beat one o' they mince sides fi' Latvia, wi' names like Locomotive Tallinn and Rice Krispies 1640.'

'Tallinn's in Estonia,' says Billy McGuire.

'You shut yer gob,' says Ferguson. 'Ah wisnae talkin' tae you. Whit dae you know aboot fitba', anyway, Heid-the-ba'?' Gives him another push down the stairs.

'Fitba',' says McGuire, 'wherein is nuhin' but beastly fury, an' extreme violence, whereof proceedeth hurt, an' consequently rancour an' malice dae remain wi' them that be woundit.'

Ferguson stops and looks at him. Mulholland, a few steps ahead, turns back.

'Whit?' says Ferguson.

'Thomas Elyot,' says McGuire.

'Thomas Elyot?'

'Aye.'

'Listen, sonny, ye think Ah gie a shite aboot Thomas Elyot. Ah'll gie ye Thomas Elyot, ya bastard. Any mair o' that an' Ah'll stick soddin' Thomas Elyot up yer arse. Now, shut it.'

✂

They arrive at the station, pushing McGuire in front of them as they go. Ferguson walks in without a thought. Work is work, each day is just another day; a means to an end. Mulholland's heart sinks every time he walks through the door. Dreams of the day he can clear out his desk for the last time and retire. Get to spend every day with Melanie.

Some dream.

'Book him, Sergeant, will you? And if he quotes any more literature at you, you can kick his head in.'

'Stoatir.'

Mulholland goes to walk past the front desk. Up the

14

stairs to his office is his intention. A cup of coffee, a few minutes with his feet up, before he has to consider the other eventualities of the day. It is still morning, with the day lying ahead of him like a huge rotting animal in the middle of the road. The customary dead cow of a Monday morning.

'Chief Inspector?'

Mulholland stops and turns.

'Yes, Sergeant?'

Sergeant Watson, the ugliest man ever to front a desk in a police station in northern Europe. Cheekbones like slabs of meat, Brobdingnagian nose, garrulous moustache wandering at outrageous tangents across his face; a face which has seen its share of excitement. Lips like slugs.

'M wants to see you,' he says.

Mulholland stares at him. At his nose, in fact. Takes a second to stop himself. Sees the few minutes with his feet up quickly vanish.

'When?'

'Soon as you got in.'

Looks at his watch. Not yet ten o'clock, but it doesn't really matter. His days have become one bloody chore after another.

'Wants me to take that stunning wife of his to the Christmas night out next week, does he?'

'The catalogue babe? 'Fraid he's already asked me to do that.'

'An' me 'n a',' says Ferguson loudly, as he disappears into the bowels of the station.

'Brilliant,' says Mulholland. 'Thanks, Bill.' Thanks for bugger all. And so he heads up the stairs, mood plummeting like a rollercoaster which is permanently on a downward drop. Crap job, crap marriage, crap life. Looking for someone to take it out on. Better not make it

15

the Superintendent, but once he's finished with him he can have a go at McGuire. Kick his backside for him if necessary.

He walks through CID, the usual bustle of activity. Phones ringing, people talking, paper piled high on desks. In the midst of it all, an oasis of calm; one of the sergeants with a magazine open in front of her. Cup of coffee in her right hand, left hand drumming out a beat on the desk. Reading an article on 'Why Men Are Crap at Sex', although he can't see it. Instant resentment. Why should she get to do what he is being prevented from doing? He stops beside her desk.

'Nothing to do, Sergeant?' he says.

Detective Sergeant Proudfoot raises her eyes. She doesn't work for Mulholland, doesn't need to give him any attention. Has, on the occasion of station ladies' nights out, placed him in the top three of her list of guys on the force she wouldn't kick out of bed for sleeping in Gromit boxer shorts, but it doesn't mean she has to listen to him.

'It's getting done,' she says. Manages to leave the insult off the end of the sentence.

He stares at her for a few seconds; shakes his head finally and walks on by. It's like being a schoolteacher sometimes, he thinks. Without the endless summer holidays. People like Erin Proudfoot did nothing for the force and nothing for its reputation. No good whatsoever. Ferguson might be a bigoted Philistine with even fewer brain cells than he has sex organs, but at least he gets the job done.

Worse than that, of course; he feels all the more annoyed because he finds her attractive. And a lot more attractive than the bitter Melanie Mulholland, twisted wretch of his home life.

He stops outside the Superintendent's office. Gives himself pause. Breathes in, then lets out the long sigh. What kind of mood will he be in today? How ridiculous is his Bernard Lee impersonation going to be? How many times will he use the phrase 'national security' when talking about shoplifting from Woolworths in Partick?

Christ, there must be more than this, he thinks, as he opens the door and walks into the tepid cauldron of point-less imagination.

A Bloody Supper

Late Monday night, and the monastery sleeps. Long before the death of Brother Festus, it begins. While Joel Mulholland staggers home from the pub to an unhappy marriage; while Erin Proudfoot sits alone, crying her way through *Fried Green Tomatoes. . .*; while the monks lie secure in their beds, and while shepherds watch their flocks, one sheep is led astray and put to the sword.

A particularly gruesome death, this one, the first at the monastery. The blood pulses from the severed artery for some minutes after the deed; it runs along the cold stone corridor; reaches the worn, grooved steps in such volume that the first trickle grows and swells until it has become a miniature, ensanguined cascade, the warm red liquid tumbling gaily down the stairwell, turning it into a cruel and bloody parody of the Reichenbach Falls. And all the while, Brother Saturday lies with eyes open, body limp, becoming colder, the sensation still there although the first stroke of the knife has killed him.

The killer watches the blood flow, taking some plea-sure in the cardinal flourish, the rich harvest of his revenge. His second victim, this, his second plunge of the

17

knife into the velvet crust of human flesh, and the fevered excitement which he felt that first time, so many years ago, is a little greater now that he is closer to the object of his desire. The sweat still beads on his lip, the hairs still rise excitedly on the back of his neck, the purple vein pulses in his forehead; and the buzz electrifies his body. He is not yet some high-roller of the serial killer brigade, in this for the heart-thumping indulgence of it all, and he is not yet ready to change his modus operandi; to dance with some other form of death. His motive is revenge, and the gratification should not be in the deed but the outcome.

But all that might change.

Twelve men must die. Ten remain, although only the names of three of those ten are known to him. He has come to the end of his search, and yet the rest are hidden. It might well be time to take a greater vengeance than he had at first anticipated. But he has not made any firm decisions. Not yet.

Lifting the body by the legs, he begins to drag it backwards along the corridor. He reaches the stairs and starts to clump silently down. The body limply hugs the decline until the head arrives and then slowly, step by step, it thuds into the hard stone, and the skin around Brother Saturday's skull quickly bruises.

Chapter 2

Another Contender for Crap Day of the Year Award

Tuesday morning. Another lousy day. Mulholland sits before his Superintendent, for the second day in a row, listening to nothing at all. The rain against the window, maybe; the beating of his heart. There is a disgusting taste in his mouth and his head throbs extravagantly; the result of four hours of gin during a pointless night in the pub with Ferguson and another couple of police goons.

Detective Chief Superintendent McMenemy closes the file he has been reading and looks up. He engages Mulholland's eyes for a while without saying anything. The usual routine.

'Late night?' he says eventually.

'Aye,' says Mulholland, and it comes out as a hoarse croak.

'Understand you had a little too much to drink?'

Mulholland laughs and nods. Brilliant. How did he manage to work that one out?

'Gin,' he says, and leaves it at that.

McMenemy shakes his head. 'Girl's drink, if you ask me. Can't you drink whisky, laddie?' he says, then grumbles some more. Mulholland grits his teeth.

McMenemy, the man who would be M, sits back in his chair and stares at him, across the great gulf of the desk. There's no way the old man has brought him up here to tell him off for drinking gin instead of whisky, no matter how much it pains him. It's probably going to be some pointless rebuke for all the time he's been spending on the drugs case, with nothing to show for it.

'Have you been speaking to Ian Woods much?' McMenemy says.

Mulholland shrugs. This is different, he thinks, and immediately feels uncomfortable.

'Woods? No more than usual. Had a few drinks with him last night, but there wasn't much conversation. All he wanted to talk about was this Barney Thomson business. Kept muttering about how it was Thomson who was committing every crime that's currently being committed in Scotland, and how everyone blames him because he hasn't caught him yet.'

'Mmm,' says M. 'How do you think he's really getting on with the case?'

Mulholland hesitates. He has begun to see the minefield he might have wandered into; or been ordered into. Can't say Woods is doing a brilliant job, because he hasn't caught the guy yet and everyone knows he's an idiot; however, it doesn't look good to denounce him either.

'All right, I think,' he says. 'But Thomson just seems to have vanished.'

'Exactly,' says M. 'He's doing all right, but he hasn't found him. The press are whipping themselves and everyone else into a frenzy. You see the *Record* today?'

Mulholland shakes his head, and M lifts the paper from beside the desk and tosses it across to him. 'Lock Your

Doors, as Barber Goes on 20 City Crime Spree.' After that he tosses across the *Sun*. 'Police Flounder as Vicious Murderer Kills Two More.' Finally he tosses over the *Scotsman*. 'Barney Thomson Shagged My Mum, Claims Medical Student.'

'It's getting ridiculous,' McMenemy says. 'People can't go out at night – the entire country's living in fear.'

'It's all a load of mince,' says Mulholland.

'I know that. You know that. There are a heck of a lot of other people who know that, but the press love this kind of thing. We have to put a stop to it, and the only way we're going to do that is by catching the man.'

Mulholland nods, but doesn't say anything. Has begun to see what's coming.

'I'm taking Woods off the case,' says M. 'I want you to head up the investigation. We need results on this.'

Mulholland nods again. Thinks, Of course, I'm the man who's been after the same drug barons for over three months now without so much as a sniff of evidence.

'It'll be hard on him, but there's no place for sentimentality on this. We have to have it cleared up before Christmas, if possible.'

'Right,' says Mulholland, deciding it's time he contributed to the conversation. 'Ferguson and I'll get on to it this morning. Go over everything Woods has done, see what he might have missed.' He could shake his head as he says it, knowing that Woods, for all that he's the Albion Rovers of criminal investigation, probably won't have missed anything.

'Actually, I'm splitting you and Sergeant Ferguson up on this one,' says M. 'We don't want to lose sight of the drugs case the two of you have been on, so I'm leaving him on that. See what he can come up with on his own. Give him Constable Flaherty to work with.'

21

Michelle Flaherty? Ferguson's going to be gutted, he thinks, but it is a side issue. How much of a censure to himself is it that Ferguson's being left to the case himself is what he begins to think about. However, the thought does not get far before it becomes bogged down in the sludge of disaffection which dominates his head. And it might be good to work with someone other than Ferguson for a change.

'So I'm putting you together with Sergeant Proudfoot. I'm sure you'll make an excellent team.'

'Good,' says Mulholland instinctively. Thinking, Bloody hell, the dozy, layabout idiot. A bloody woman to nursemaid through the investigation, that's all I need.

'Right. I don't like to put undue pressure on my officers, but we need a positive result, Chief Inspector. You've got ten days.'

A Load of Balzac

Detective Sergeant Erin Proudfoot spoons another sugar into her tea, then slowly stirs. She has almost come to the end of the article she is reading in a two-month-old *Blitz!* magazine – 'How to Spot a Millennium Lounge Lizard'. She considers that she has encountered a few of them herself and doesn't need an article in a magazine to point her in the right direction. Still, it is slightly more informative than '51 Ways to Have Sex in a Helicopter'.

The frenetic bustle of the station on a Tuesday morning continues around her, following a typical Glasgow Monday night. Six stabbings, two rapes, fourteen break-ins, thirteen car thefts, one defeat for Partick Thistle. She has been allocated one of the less serious stabbings, and is waiting for the woman in question to be brought in by a couple of uniforms. Senga-Ann Paterson, seventeen. Rejected by her boyfriend, the father of her two children – a rejection she dealt with by stabbing him in the testicles with a knitting needle. While he'd been hospitalised the previous evening, the police had let her go because there was no one else to look after her children, and they weren't sure if the boyfriend would be pressing charges. One operation, and one removed testicle later, there is no doubt. She is being brought in.

Besides that, Sergeant Proudfoot has four phone calls to make following up an alleged insurance fraud, plus fourteen reports to complete from ongoing investigations. Her in-tray is piled high.

She turns the pages of her magazine. Past the adverts for generic perfume to express your individuality, and wafer-thin sanitary towels. Stops at the picture of a stick-like figure with blond hair and legs which go all the way up: headline, 'Gretchen Schumacher – The New Eastern Uberchick on Why She Prefers Men to Strudel'. Shakes her head, tosses the magazine onto her desk. Another five minutes gone. She lifts the phone and dials the number for Lloyds insurance in London. Curses the crime insurance fraud as she does so. As if they don't have better things to do.

The phone rings. She prepares to wait; rummaging through her in-tray, she can see the people at Lloyds doing other things. Reading magazines. She lets it go a few times then cuts it off; dials another number. Scotland Yard. Might actually be someone answering the phone there. Pulls another file from her tray, the easiest one to deal with. Indecent assault, a guilty plea.

A phone rings elsewhere in her office, is immediately answered. Why can't Lloyds and Scotland Yard be like this? she thinks. Doesn't like the phone; prefers turning up unexpectedly on doorsteps.

'Haw, Erin?'

She turns towards Ferguson and raises her eyebrows.

'Yer knitting needle wummin's downstairs. Room Three.'

Right.

She shrugs, closes the file and sticks it back in her tray. She lifts her tea and heads downstairs.

✄

'Now, you're sure you don't want a lawyer present?'

Senga-Ann Paterson raises her eyes and stubs the butt of her cigarette, smoked all the way to the filter, into the ashtray. She emits a pained sigh.

'Ah says Ah didnae, did Ah no'?'

Proudfoot nods, studies the paper in front of her. Tries to stop herself looking at the three safety pins which dominate Paterson's nose.

'Very well, Senga.'

Here goes, she thinks. Maybe I don't enjoy interviewing any more either. In the wrong job, but what else could she be doing? An artists' agent, maybe. Sign that sexually deprived idiot Ferguson up as her first act. He could be a stripper or something. The Polis Plonker. The Dangling Detective. Sergeant Sausage.

'Do you know why you've been brought in?'

Senga-Ann Paterson chews some Wrigley's Juicy Fruit. Proudfoot gets a whiff of it, mingled with tobacco. Delicious.

'Tae gie us an award fur fightin' back against the tyranny o' evil men?'

Proudfoot taps her pen. Nice try.

'Not as such. You're here because James McGuiness has had to have his right testicle removed . . .' – pauses for the ejaculation of laughter – 'as a result of the injury

24

he received from a knitting needle yesterday evening.'

Paterson laughs: Proudfoot taps her pen on the desk.

'It's a serious business, Senga. You're facing a charge of aggravated assault. You could be looking at up to seven years in prison.'

'Nae chance, missus. No' wi' ma two weans tae look after.'

'They can be taken into care, Senga. Found foster homes.'

Laughter is replaced by indignation. Desdemona and Monrovia are all Senga-Ann Paterson has.

'Christ. It's no' as if the bastard didnae deserve it. He's lucky Ah didnae get them baith. If he hadnae put up such a performance after the first wan, Ah would have.'

Proudfoot holds the pen upside down between her second and third finger. Taps. Has 'The Girl from Ipanema' playing in her head; stops tapping before she has to arrest herself.

'Did you stab James McGuiness in the testicles with a knitting needle on Monday evening?'

'Whit? Whit are ye askin' me that for? Yese know Ah stabbed him. An' Ah'd dae it again 'n a'.'

You might not want to say that to the judge, Proudfoot thinks. Doesn't care. She has had enough of people like Senga-Ann Paterson.

'Why did you do it, Senga?'

Paterson fumbles another cigarette from the packet. Her white fingers shake. Nervous; bitter. She lights up, thin lips sucking. Hollow cheeks.

'Why dae yese think? He's a pure bastard, so he is. Ye know whit he went an' done?'

'What?'

Paterson opens her arms in an expansive gesture. Almost sets fire to the curtain behind with the cigarette.

25

'He went an' shagged Ann-Marie.'

'Oh.' Should have known. 'And she is . . .?'

'She wis ma best pal. Still is, Ah suppose. Ah mean, Ah'm nae blamin' her, or nuthin'. James is a brilliant shag, an' a' that, ye know. It's every cow for hersel' out there, Ah know that. But that bastard shouldnae huv shagged her. Ye know.'

'When was this?'

'Saturday night. Ah'm stuck in wi' the weans watchin' the telly, an' Ah'm thinkin' that he's doon the boozer wi' a' his mates. Ye know, Arnie the Baptist an' Bono an' No Way Out an' a' that lot. But no', he's no' doin' that, is he? He's doin' the bare bum boogie wi' ma best mate.' Shakes her head.

'And how did you find out?'

Long, nervous draw on the cigarette. Hollow cheeks. The chewing gum smacks inside her mouth. As she exhales, Proudfoot can see it through the smoke, passing between tongue and teeth.

'Wid ye credit that Ann-Marie phones us up tae tell us aboot it? Pure neck, so she's got. Jist gies us a call. Haw, hen, see yon man o' yours, he's a pure brilliant shag, so he is. That's whit she says. Ah mean, Ah know that already. Whit did she think Ah wis doin' wi' the bastard? Ye think it's fur his looks? Cause it isnae. Ye seen him?'

'Not yet.'

'Pure stank, so he is. Looks like yon eejit on *Beauty an' the Beast*. Ye know, the big ugly bastard.'

Proudfoot nods. She still can't get 'The Girl from Ipanema' out of her head. Starts tapping the theme from *Mission Impossible* to try to shift it.

'So, you confronted him with this?'

Paterson rolls her eyes.

'Pure right, Ah did. An' ye know whit he says? Ye

know? He says, "There is nae infidelity when there has been nae love." Ah mean, can ye believe it? Quotin' Balzac of a' people. Cheeky cunt.'

There is a knock at the door. It opens. Proudfoot turns.

'Up the stairs, Sergeant. Two minutes.'

The door closes, and Mulholland is gone.

Proudfoot turns back to Paterson and shrugs.

'Got to go, Senga. We'll continue this later.'

'That you gonnae get yer arse kicked?'

Proudfoot smiles. 'I doubt it,' she says, although she wonders what he could be wanting with her. Maybe she could sign him and Ferguson up as a double act. The Delinquent Dicks. The Bratwurst Brothers.

She stands up. Says, 'Interview suspended at nine twenty-five' and switches off the machine. Senga-Ann Paterson draws deeply on her cigarette. The two women look at each other.

'Balzac, eh?' says Proudfoot.

Paterson nods. Thin face; a slight movement of the safety pins. Pink hair.

'You might get off yet.'

Barney Thomson - the Return of the Native

She sits across the desk from Mulholland, trying not to look at him. She is annoyed at herself for finding him attractive. Has never gone for authority figures, but he is young for his position, as she is herself. Beneficiaries of the vacancies caused at the station by the slaughter of four detectives the previous March.

He looks up. Eyes that change colour with the light.

'Busy?' he says. This is work, and he can't sit here feeling stupid just because he dislikes her and fancies her

27

at the same time.

Daft question, she thinks, although it is probably pointed, seeing as he caught her in the middle of one of her five-minute breaks. She can't remember the last time she wasn't busy.

'Usual crap,' she says. 'Insurance fraud, assault, knitting needles in the testicles. The normal stuff.'

Mulholland winces, says, 'Aye, I heard about that.'

He lets out a sigh. Stares at the file in front of him. Taps it. The poisoned chalice.

'Something come up?' asks Proudfoot.

Mulholland raises his eyebrows and nods slowly. A slight movement of the head. You could say that, he thinks.

'Barney Thomson,' he says.

Oh. Barney Thomson. She bites her lip, her heart beats a little faster. She knows all about Barney Thomson. Everyone in Scotland knows all about Barney Thomson. The Barber Surgeon.

'What about him?'

'He's ours.'

Ours?

'How do you mean that, exactly? Ours?'

'Ours. Yours and mine. You and me have to go after him. The two of us.'

But we're not a couple, she thinks. Ferguson's going to be pissed off. And Masterson as well. Hates it when one of his DS's gets dragged away.

'What about Ferguson?'

'The Chief Super wants a woman on the case. We all know he's anal about the fact that he's got no female DCIs. You're the closest he's got. So you're on it. With me.'

'And what about Woods? I thought it was his case?'

Mulholland breathes deeply, stares at the floor. Feels a certain amount of pity for Woods. He is a bit of an idiot, but you have to give people the chance. He shrugs.

'Well, you know what he's like. Woods has had two weeks and he hasn't found anything yet. The boss is like a football club chairman whose team fail to win either of their first two league games. So he's out on his ear, and I'm next in line.'

Proudfoot nods. No surprise. She considers Woods a nice enough bloke, but effectively brain-dead. Everyone knows it. Woods couldn't find a criminal if you gave him two years and stuck a homing device up the guy's back-side. So the chances of him finding some nefarious mastermind like Barney Thomson are virtually nil.

'And Masterson? Is he not going to be pissed off at you taking me off his hands?'

Mulholland shakes his head. 'Doubt it. He'll probably get Jack Hawkins or someone like that to order around for as long as it takes. You know he's a misogynist bastard anyway. He'll love having a bloke to play with instead of you.' He tries not to think about that as he says it. Has always had his doubts about Masterson. 'Right, so this it. The Barney Thomson file. Pop quiz, Sergeant. Thirty seconds; everything you know about the man.'

She breathes deeply; gathers her thoughts.

'Right. Killed his two colleagues. Don't remember their names. May have killed six others, but there's some talk of it having been his mother. Not sure.'

Mulholland taps the file again. 'The mother's looking favourite. Least, that's what Woods has come up with. The man might be a moron, but he's done some decent work on this. Just hasn't found the guy. Anyway, if it was the mother who killed them, it was the son who disposed of the bodies.'

She nods, presumes she is expected to pick up the story. 'He made it look as if one of the guys he worked with was the killer. Porter, that was his name. Left all the other bodies to be found, disposed of his. The investigating officers at the time all thought they were looking for Porter. And they all ended up dead.'

'Aye, bloody right they did. Besides Loch Lubnaig . . .'

'Which is where Porter's body turned up two weeks ago.'

'Exactly. So, did those four officers shoot each other as was thought at the time, or did Barney Thomson do it?'

She shakes her head. Stares at the floor. She'd liked Robert Holdall, had had a brief thing with Stuart MacPherson. Good men, both of them.

'It's all circumstantial though, isn't it?' she says. 'Has Woods come up with any proof?'

Mulholland shakes his head. 'Everything he's got is in here, but I doubt any of it's solid. But let's face it. The guy did an O.J. Simpson the minute Porter's body was found and Woods pitched up to interview him. The actions of a guilty man.'

She nods. Sounds right. You don't run unless you've got something to run from. She's been avoiding reading all the stories about Barney Thomson in the papers, avoiding talking about him at the station. She's got enough crime in her life without adding to it. But she can't hide from such a major investigation, and Barney Thomson should not be able to hide from the police.

'So, where do we start?'

Mulholland pushes the file towards her across the desk.

'You start by having a look at this. Take your time. Later on this morning we'll go and talk to the wife. Agnes. See what she's got to say for herself today. You never know with these people. She might have thought of something new. After that, we're going to Inverness. Thomson withdrew money from a machine up there on the first evening he went missing. That's just about all we've got.'

'But Woods must have gone up there. The locals must have looked into it.'

Mulholland sits back and shrugs his shoulders. 'But not the Chief Super's latest star crime-fighting duo.'

'Brilliant. Batman and Batgirl.'

'Yep.'

They stare across the desk at one another. Try to ignore the singular mixture of contempt and attraction. Enough complications in life without that kind of thing getting in the way.

'Right then. Get back to the Batdesk and read up on this guy before we go after him.'

Proudfoot lifts the file and their eyes meet across the desk. A moment, nothing said, and she turns and walks from the room.

The door closes and Mulholland is left alone in silence. A crap job; a miserable wife; dumped with Barney Thomson; landed with Erin Proudfoot. He sits in the same chair that a year earlier was occupied by Robert Holdall, and feels Holdall's ghost crawl slowly down his spine.

Chapter 3

Drama at Patagonia Heights

'But, Bleach! Surely you knew that Wade was married to Heaven before he fell in love with Summer? That was why Solace left Fox for Flint before she ran off with Lane.'

Bleach staggers; her hand covers her eyes. Oh, what a fool she's been! All these years loving Wade; all these years denying Zephros, finally forcing him into the arms of Saffron. Only to discover that Dale had been lying about his relationship with Lalage and that Moonshine had given birth to River's baby, Persephone.

Bleach leans back against the hard kitchen table – the table where once she had been loved by Bacon. Her eyes glaze over and suddenly she starts sobbing. Her chest heaves, her lips contort; the late morning sun, shafting in through the ornate New England window, highlights the grey hairs in her fringe. Tears stream down her cheeks – great rivers of water – turning her face into a cruel burlesque of Angel Falls.

Through the flood, she stares at Taylor, the bearer of bad news. Never shoot the messenger, isn't that the cliché? Well, damn them, thinks Bleach. Damn all messengers!

Slowly, with unbearable tension, she pulls the .7mm Beretta from her pocket. She aims it directly at Taylor's heart. Taylor gasps.

'Why, Bleach!' she exclaims. 'This is so unlike you. Have you seen your therapist lately?'

'Hah!' says Bleach. 'Eat dirt, Bitchface!'

And as the credits begin to roll at the close of the most exciting episode of *Herniated Disc Ward B* in living memory, and the gun shakes in Bleach's trembling fingers, the doorbell rings. Agnes Thomson stares at the door and lets out a long sigh.

'Jings tae crivvens,' she says. 'Huvnae had a moment's peace in two weeks.'

She presses stand-by; the television blinks and fizzes to the dead grey screen. It is another twenty minutes before the start of *Patagonia Heights*; but as in all the other shows to which she is addicted, the magic has evaporated from what used to be an ecstatic forty-three minutes.

She opens the door and stares at the two strangers. A man in his late thirties, woman a little younger. Polis. Written all over them. The latest in a long line. The man holds out a badge.

'Chief Inspector Mulholland. This is Sergeant Proudfoot. Mrs Thomson?'

Agnes Thomson nods. Has long tired of telling these people where to go. Understands the only way to get rid of them quickly is to co-operate. The quicker they realise that she knows nothing of her husband's whereabouts, the quicker they move on.

'Yese want tae come in?' she says. Voice weary. Agnes Thomson's life has changed in ways she could not have dreamed. Not in her worst nightmares.

Proudfoot and Mulholland follow her into the flat, through the small hall to the lounge; a room smelling of a warm and dusty television. Agnes Thomson sits down, indicates the sofa. They look around them as they take their seats. An untidy room; dust on the tables, a collection of cups and plates beside Agnes's seat. The seat from which she sits and watches soap opera after pointless soap opera; *Catastrophe Road* blending into *Bougainvillaea Plateau* which blends into *Penile Emergency Ward 8*.

Proudfoot feels immediately depressed. She rarely fails to be depressed when she visits someone else's house in the course of her duties. She's read the reports. Believes that Agnes Thomson tells the truth; that she knew nothing of her husband's murderous activities and that she knows nothing of his present whereabouts. This is a duty call.

Mulholland looks around the room; recognises a life in tatters. He is not to know that this was an empty life even before Agnes Thomson discovered that her husband butchered human flesh.

'I realise that you've spoken to many of our colleagues, Mrs Thomson,' says Mulholland. 'But we've just been put on the case and we need to follow up every lead for ourselves.'

Agnes shrugs. Has a rare moment of insight. 'Cannae find him, eh? Kicked that eejit Woods aff the case? Nae surprised. Yon bastard couldnae find shite in a sewer.'

Mulholland stares at the carpet; Proudfoot looks at the blank television screen, tries not to laugh. Woods in a nutshell.

'Could you tell us about the last time you saw your husband, Mrs Thomson?' says Mulholland. Still doesn't look her in the eye. Is picturing Iain Woods up to his thighs in water, wearing industrial gloves and a gas mask, searching for elusive faeces.

Agnes has answered this question many times; has moved on from getting annoyed about it. Only doing their jobs, she has finally reasoned with herself.

'That Tuesday morning. About eight o'clock, Ah

34

suppose. No' sure, like Ah've telt a' yer colleagues. Ah wis eatin' ma breakfast an' watchin' the telly. It wis the final episode o' *Calamity Bay*, ye know. Ah'd taped it fi' the night afore 'cause Ah wis watchin' *Only the Young Die Young.*'

'Oh, aye, I saw that episode,' says Proudfoot. 'The one where Curaçao had the sex change operation so she could impregnate Gobnat.'

Agnes nods. Doesn't smile in recognition. Hasn't smiled in a long time.

'Barney?' says Mulholland, attempting to reclaim the conversation.

Proudfoot shakes her head. 'No, Barney wanted to marry New Orleans, but she was engaged to Flipper.'

A pause. Pursed lips. A raised eyebrow.

'Oh,' says Proudfoot.

'Your husband, Mrs Thomson?'

Agnes doesn't need to think. Has told it many times before. Just refuses to tell it to the newspapers, and finally they have given up camping on her doorstep.

'We didnae say much at breakfast,' she says. Thinks about it. 'In fact, we didnae say anythin' at breakfast. Never did. Jist didnae talk much, ye know. That wis us.'

Go and see the wife again, M had told him. Woods might have missed something.

Mulholland nods. There is nothing to miss. Has a thought that maybe the rest of the investigation will mirror these last few minutes. Asking questions that have already been asked, receiving answers already given. A pointless round; an unbroken circle. At some stage he'll be kicked off the carousel and some other poor bastard put in charge. That is how these things go. Barney Thomson might well just have disappeared, never to be heard from again.

'And there was nothing different that morning? He didn't say anything, or pack a bag? Eat a little more than usual, wear different clothes? Anything?'

'Tell you he was going to Bermuda and that he'd never see you again?' adds Proudfoot. Draws a look from Mulholland.

Agnes shakes her head. They all ask the same things, in the same way. What is the point?

A thought occurs. She puts her fingers to her mouth, stares at the ceiling. A vague light comes to her eye. Maybe there was something after all.

'Ye know, Ah think Ah might remember somethin', now that yese ask. Ah remember he asked me if British folk needed a visa fur tae go tae the Seychelles. Ah mean, daft eejit. How am Ah supposed tae know? So that wis whit Ah says. Tae him, ye know whit Ah mean.'

Proudfoot and Mulholland lean forward. If they hadn't talked that morning, how did he manage to ask her a question about anything? Still, maybe this is it. Maybe Woods is as much of an idiot as everyone thinks.

'The Seychelles?' says Mulholland. 'Are you sure?'

Agnes shakes her head. Doesn't smile.

'Naw, Ah'm only pullin' yer leg, ya daft haddie. Yese no' think that if he'd said something like that Ah'd telt someone already?'

Mulholland keeps the expletive in check.

'This is a serious business, Mrs Thomson. Very serious. Your husband stands accused of . . .'

'Look, Ah know fine an' well whit he stands accused of, awright? The bloody eejit. But Ah don't know anythin' about it. Ah've already telt ye, an' Ah've already telt about a hunner folk before ye.'

The three of them sit and stare at one another. There are other questions to be asked, but Mulholland knows there is little point. And of all the people who have suffered through the previous two weeks of hysterical press speculation, Agnes Thomson will have suffered more than most. The husband disappears; the wife is left behind to face the music.

'Look, why dae yese no' jist accept it? Barney went oot o' the shop that mornin' fur tae buy himsel' a sangwich. When he got back tae the place, he saw polis a' o'er the shop, 'cause your lot hud charged in as if they were roundin' up a Mafia gang or somethin'. So, fur whatever reason, on seein' youse lot he does a runner. An', whatever yese're thinkin', Ah still doubt it was 'cause he murdered anyone. Ma Barney wis too stupit for that. Too bloody stupit.'

Mulholland sits back, staring at the floor. You are told so many lies in this job; along the way you develop the instinct for what's the truth and what isn't. How well the instinct develops leads to how good a copper you are. He likes to think he can always tell. Truth or lies.

Agnes Thomson is telling them the truth. They are wasting their time.

'So, you haven't heard from Barney since he disappeared?' he asks. Has to.

Agnes breathes deeply, shakes her head.

'Naw, Ah huvnae,' she says eventually. If they never spoke when they lived together, why should he make any effort to speak to her now that they don't?

'You'll let us know if you hear from him?'

She shrugs – the interview is over; stares at the blank television screen. Almost time to lose herself again. 'Might,' she says. 'Might no'.'

Mulholland and Proudfoot stand up. Mulholland nods. This is about as much as you can expect to get. Why should Agnes Thomson tell them anything?

37

She looks up at them. The eyes say it all, and the two police officers turn away and see themselves to the door. When they have gone, she sits alone, staring at the television. Her hand rests beside the remote control, but it is a long time before she presses a button.

✂

'What do you think?'

Mulholland shrugs. 'I think we were wasting our time. And from the absence of the press, I think that that lot obviously realised a lot quicker than we did – Agnes Thomson's got nothing to say for herself. Two weeks ago there were about eight million of them outside her door.'

They walk on down the stairs in silence. Holdall and MacPherson must have walked down these stairs, thinks Proudfoot. A shiver scuttles down her back, even in this broad light of day. She tries to think of something else but keeps seeing MacPherson's face. Can feel him.

'Inverness?' she says, to take her mind off it, as they emerge into a bleak Glasgow afternoon.

Mulholland shakes his head. 'Not now. Tomorrow morning. We can go to the barber's shop now and check it out. The Death Shop from Hell, or whatever it is they're calling it in the *Record*. Might as well speak to a few other folk who can sneer at us the minute we turn our backs.'

'The minute we turn our backs? You think they wait that long?' says Proudfoot.

Mulholland stares at her across the top of the car. Looks away up the street, along the line of cold, grey tenements. This is all there is in police work. Trawling around depressing streets, speaking to pointless, uninterested people with nothing to say and nothing to give you other than their disrespect.

'Brilliant,' he mutters under his breath as he gets into the car.

Chapter 4

That Whole Life Thing

'Forasmuch as it hath pleased Almighty God of his great mercy to take unto himself the soul of our dear brother here departed, we therefore commit his body to the ground; earth to earth, ashes to ashes, dust to dust; in sure and certain hope of the Resurrection to eternal life.'

Words hang in the cold air, then disappear in the mist which evaporates before the Abbot. The monks, slightly over thirty in number, watch the hard dirt bounce on the lid of Brother Saturday's coffin, then settle with a cold finality. Three deep around the grave they stand, heads bowed in solemn prayer and sorrow; all but one.

Edward; Ash; Matthew; Jerusalem; Joshua; Pondlife; Ezekial; Mince; Festus; and so on around the grave they stand. Lost in sadness, unaware that many more of them will die, and that Festus's gargoyle in the head will be but one death among a great legion of others.

It is nearly eleven years since they have lost one of their number to that fell sergeant, Death. Mammon, the evil succubus of fornication, and the lure of a comfortable life had taken their toll in that time; but not death.

Not since Brother Alexander fell from the escarpment around the third floor of the abbey.

The Abbot opens his eyes from one last silent prayer, then, head low, begins the short walk back down the hill to the shelter and slender warmth of the monastery. Two steps behind, an ecclesiastical refugee from the Secret Service, walks Brother Herman; brown hood drawn up around his head, sunken eyes watching the Abbot's back, long white face. Hooked nose, the beak of some deranged bird of prey; Brother Herman suspects everyone. Whoever it was who plunged the knife into the neck of Brother Saturday, who held it there while Saturday wriggled and squirmed away his painful final seconds, who watched the blood flow along the corridor and down the weeping steps, must not be allowed access to the Abbot.

None shall pass, thinks Brother Herman. None shall pass.

As their feet crunch into the frosted snow, the remainder of the assembly stare into the grave. Think their thoughts; death and murder and God and resurrection and everlasting life. A test of Faith; at a time like this, how many of them truly believe? The snow-covered hills rise around them, reaching to a blue sky, pale in the anaemic light of dawn. And over the hills, in the middle distance, the bitter sea washes upon a barren shore.

One by one they pay their last respects, and head off slowly back to the austere grey building which is their home. Breakfast awaits. Two remain behind, burdened with shovelling the hardened dirt over Saturday's coffin. Pale brown wood, soon to be home to God's final act of desecration upon the human body.

They stand with spades at the ready, waiting for the others to return to the monastery before beginning their task; the last kick of the ball in the football match of

Saturday's life. The younger man, his face unfolded, thoughts elsewhere. His lips betray a knowing smile; an acceptance of fate – what will be done is done. Tonsured head, hair a little long at the back. Could do with a cut, thinks the other man. Older. Face creased with worry, full head of hair, greying with years.

The last monk disappears from view. They glance at one another; it is time. The younger one digs his shovel into the waiting pile of dirt; the older man takes a look around him – the path leading from the graveyard to the monastery; the surrounding forest, trees white with snow; the low hills, which doom the monastery to the pit of the glen and the bitter wind which howls through; the distant edge of the freezing waters of Loch Hope – then bends his knee, thrusting his shovel into the dirt.

Already their hands are numb with cold, yet aching with an insistent pain. Brother Steven shovels the dirt without emotion, knowing not the burden of his work. He is content to do as he is bid even though, being neither the newest monk nor the youngest, he should not be called upon to perform the task of the gravedigger. For this he has his unquiet tongue to thank.

He glances at the older man, who is performing his task with grim determination. Not for Brother Steven to know that this man, the latest addition to their complement, has become used to death in all its iniquitous guises.

'So, what brings you here, Brother Jacob?' he says to the older man, continuing to shovel dirt slowly, monotonously.

Barney Thomson, barber, hesitates. A man on the run, a man with a dark past. Secrets to hide. He shovels. 'No' sure,' he says eventually. 'Just needed somethin' different, ye know.'

Brother Steven nods, tosses another pile of dirt into the

41

grave. The top of the coffin is now completely obscured. Brother Saturday is gone.

'Got you,' he says. 'It's that whole vicissitude thing. The basic need for something new. We all feel it. It's like Heraclitus says: "Everything flows and nothing stays . . . You can't step twice in the same river." It's why I'm here.'

Barney stares at him; Steven shovels. Knowing smile on cold, blue lips.

'Aye,' says Barney. 'Right.'

Barney has never heard of Heraclitus. Wonders if he played centre-forward for some Greek football team. Doubts it. Has to accept that he has come to a new world, after twenty comfortable years in the barber's shop. Not all conversations will be about football.

'So what are you running from, Brother Jacob?'

Steven rests on his shovel, looks through the mist which has formed from his words. Barney feels the beating of his heart, but realises Steven cannot possibly know his secrets. None of these monks can know. He tries to sound casual. 'Life,' he says.

Steven laughs and begins once again the slow and steady movement of his spade. Barney wonders if he's said something funny.

'Life, eh?' says Steven, shaking his head. 'Oh, yes. That thing we do.'

Barney feels uncomfortable. A hand on his shoulder. Before he begins to shovel he sees a bird of prey in the distance, hovering, searching the snow-covered ground for breakfast. The sparrowhawk fancies some bacon and lightly scrambled egg, but accepts that he will probably have to settle for a vole or a mouse. If he's lucky.

Could be an eagle, thinks Barney, for he does not know birds of prey.

'But the thing about life,' says Steven from behind his

shovel, 'is that no matter how far you run, my friend, there's no getting away from it.'

Brother Steven tosses dirt with methodical abandon. Barney Thomson stares into the grave.

Chapter 5

We Will All Lie in the Same Grave; a Farrago of Twisted Flesh, Broken Dreams and Half-conceived Ideas

Mulholland taps his fingers on the steering wheel, watching the rain fall against the windscreen. In the carpark at Stirling services. Waiting for Proudfoot; paying for petrol, buying magazines, chocolate, drinks, music and everything else they have on offer in motorway service stations. Expecting her to return to the car wearing a new outfit and carrying a flat-packed kitchen unit.

Preoccupied with thoughts of Mrs Mulholland. On hearing that he was away up north on police business and might not be back for a few days, she had issued the classic ultimatum: if you go, I might not be here when you get back. Considers herself a police widow. Sees the prospect of becoming a real widow if her husband has to come up against the evil monster Barney Thomson. Will take this opportunity to go and stay with her sister in Devon; and not just for a week or two. His tapping on the steering wheel becomes a tight grip as he considers what else besides her sister might keep Melanie in Devon. But he isn't sure how bothered he'll be if she never comes back. Confused. How is it possible to be jealous and uninterested at the same time?

The car door opens and Proudfoot climbs in, preceded by a cold blast of air and a gallon of rainwater. The plastic bag she carries is ruffled by the wind as she sits down, buckles up. The law-abiding police officer.

'What's the matter with your face?' she says.

Mulholland grunts, determines not to look as if he's thinking about his wife. 'Nothing. You took your time,' he says. Starts the engine.

'Just buying a few things,' she says. Starts unloading the bag as he pulls out of the service station. 'Everything we'll need for the journey to Inverness.'

'It's only a couple of hours, Sergeant.'

'Might get stuck in snow.'

'It's pishing down, for God's sake.'

'Not up north. It's a snowfest up there.'

'A snowfest?'

'Aye.'

'Bloody hell.'

He pulls out onto the roundabout and then heads back down to the motorway. Driving a blue Mondeo, heating on full, windscreen wipers frenetic. The M9 mobbed with trucks and lorries and people heading up north so that they can escape the winter and be somewhere even colder. He settles in the outside lane and his car disappears beneath the torrent of rain and the spray from the wheels of articulated lorries.

'What did you get, then, if we're going to be stuck in snow for the next three weeks? A couple of sleeping bags? A tent, thermal underwear, socks, a flask of tea and some flares?'

She opens the bag, starts lifting out items. He keeps his eyes on what little of the road he can see, so that they don't die before Barney Thomson has the chance to kill them.

'Got a bacon, egg and tomato.'

'A sandwich, eh? That'll keep us warm.'

'A turkey ham and lettuce.'

'Turkey ham? Is that like a piece of turkey and a piece of ham, or is it just the one bit of meat taken from some weird crossbreed?'

'I'm ignoring you.'

He passes the final monstrous juggernaut in his path and settles into the inside lane, his view now marginally less obscured than it had been. Doesn't realise, but has already stopped worrying about Mrs Mulholland.

'I also got a brie and black grape and an egg and spinach.'

'Bloody hell. Where do you think Inverness is, Sergeant? Iceland?'

'You don't have to eat any of them, do you? Got a couple of cans of Coke, an Irn Bru and a bottle of water.'

'If we run out we can always stop at the side of the road and melt some snow on the bonnet.'

'Four packets of crisps, three chocolate bars, this month's *Blitz!* and a Simply Red tape.'

He laughs, and momentarily dices with death by taking his hands off the steering wheel to hold up his fingers in a sign of the cross.

'Not in my car, missus,' he says. 'This is not an elevator.'

'Piss off!'

'Sergeant.'

Proudfoot grits her teeth, shuts up. Settles back in her seat, cracks open the brie and black grape and a can of Irn Bru and rests the Christmas edition of *Blitz!* on her knee. Stares at it for a few seconds, then glances out of the corner of her eye.

'Sandwich, then?'

'As long as you don't think it's a trade.'

She hands him the turkey ham and lettuce; they steam through the rain towards the Dunblane bypass. Think their thoughts; vague feelings of disquiet about the outside possibility that they might come up against the infamous Barber Surgeon. Each die a horrible death. Ferguson told Proudfoot that he wasn't sure he'd be able to identify her body if she was reduced to twenty packets of frozen meat. All charm.

The visit to Henderson's the barbers the previous day had been as unhelpful as their entire investigation threatened to be. Three barbers – James Henderson, Arnie Braithwaite and Chip Ripken – none of whom had any insight into the disappearance of Barney Thomson. They had plenty of opinions and handy hints on what to do to him if he was ever found – Henderson in particular had several innovative suggestions regarding Barney's scrotum – but nothing that might actually help the police in their search. They left after an hour, aware that there was nothing new to be found out about Thomson in Glasgow. It was Inverness or nothing; and more likely Inverness *and* nothing.

Mulholland had considered stopping off in Perth and speaking to Allan Thomson, the suspect's brother, suspected that might be another waste of time, so made a phone call instead. Suspicions confirmed. Allan and Barbara Thomson had changed their surname to the wife's maiden name, and it wasn't until Mulholland threatened to turn up on his doorstep with the full weight of CID that Allan even admitted knowing Barney. However, he would concede to little more than that, and after fifteen minutes' fruitless discussion the brother had retired to share a bottle of £4.95 Chilean Chardonnay – fruity with a hint of lighter

47

fluid – with his wife, and sit unhappily over dinner, as they had for nearly fifteen years. Mulholland decided that he might call in on the way back down if he hadn't got anywhere. Fair chance of that.

'So, what does *Blitz!* have to say for itself, then? Usual stuff about how to have an orgasm with a staple gun?'

Proudfoot licks some Irn Bru from her lips, turns back to the cover. He glances over at the photo of the pale Bic, wearing midnight-maroon lipstick.

'Not far off,' she says. 'We've got "Jet Ski Sex – 1,001 Great Positions". "Tantric Sex – Don't Think about It, Just Do It!" "Cindy Crawford on Learning to Live with a Big Spot on Your Face". "Ukrainian Catalogue Hunks – The Best Thirty Quid You'll Ever Spend".'

'You're making these up,' says Mulholland.

Proudfoot shakes her head. 'Sadly, no,' she says. 'Want to hear the rest?'

'Why not? Might learn something.'

'"Getting the Most From Your Dildo". "How to Spot a Multiple Orgasm". "Toothpaste Tube Masturbation – We Test All the Well-known Brands". "Johnny Depp's Armpits – Hairy, Horny and Yours for a Fiver". "Men and Sex – Why You Might Be Better Off with a Doughnut". That's just about it.'

'A doughnut?'

'Oh, I missed one. "Why I've Had It with Men – Gretchen Schumacher Tells All". She shakes her head. 'I don't know. What do you think of Gretchen Schumacher? She just looks like a stick of rhubarb with nipples to me.'

'A doughnut?'

'All these supermodels are the same these days. The older ones with the boobs are all right, but these new ones. A bunch of wee lassies. They're all about twelve. Horrible. Most of them look ill.'

She lets out a long sigh, opens up the mag and starts where she left off in the Johnny Depp article. Mulholland sits in the outside lane again, passing a stream of octogenarian Sunday drivers, defying convention by going out midweek.

'A doughnut?'

She shakes her head. Ignores him. They drive on in silence.

Time passes; rain falls; cars are passed, cars get in the way, cars speed by on the outside lane, miles above the speed limit, but they are not on this road to be concerned about that. And for all that he concentrates on the road or tries to think about his wife or the woman sitting next to him, Joel Mulholland cannot help but think about Barney Thomson.

What kind of man would commit the crimes that he committed? Could you call such a being a man? Was he not a beast? Or was the mother the beast, and Barney Thomson the unwilling abettor?

But whatever his part in it all, in the previous two weeks he has become more than he was. He is an icon, suddenly. A means to sell newspapers, a wondrous talking point, a hate figure, a pity figure, a monster, a victim, if you listen to some. If they catch him, Mulholland knows that Thomson will still have his apologists, still have the women queuing up to support him and ask him to marry them. It is all it takes to achieve celebrity in this day and age – grotesque murder.

And how many of those who talk endlessly of the man genuinely want him to be caught? He serves so many purposes on the run. Continues to sell the newspapers, a colossal build-up to his eventual capture; if he is never captured then they will have something to write about for another fifty years; he provides something on which everyone can concentrate their fears, an excuse for the terror that they might feel towards this modern age. Barney Thomson has become an Everyman, the manifestation of the population's individual fears. A generic terror, representing dread, panic, loathing, sympathy and, in a desperate few, hope.

He has to get his mind off it. Knows you can't think too much about these kinds of things, can't dwell on what you might face in the course of your duties, else you might never go to work.

'A doughnut?' he says again, some fifteen minutes after the last time. Ignores her heavy sigh. 'Why a doughnut? Why not a banana? Why not a tube of Italian sausage or a Toblerone or a black pudding? Why a doughnut?'

She looks up at him, dragging herself away from 'Twelve Great Reasons to Have Sex with Your Marriage Counsellor'.

'You want me to explain it to you?'

'Aye, please. That would be good. I'm just a simple man, after all.'

Simple indeed, she thinks.

'It's pretty straightforward. Can you think of anything more useless for a woman to have sex with than a doughnut?'

Shakes his head. 'That's my point,' he says.

'And yet they still manage to find fifty reasons why doughnuts are better than men.' She pauses for dramatic effect. 'Do you get *their* point?'

He looks at her, but not for long. The rain still cascades.

'So what are they saying? All those articles about eight million positions in the back seat of a Reliant Robin; what they mean is eight million positions with a doughnut in the back seat of a Reliant Robin?'

50

'No, of course not. They're all about men. You don't think that one article has to be consistent with another, do you? How many magazines do you read?'

A lesson learned. Mulholland drives on; Proudfoot returns to having sex with her marriage counsellor, wondering if you have to be married to get hold of one.

Banker

They sit before the manager of the Inverness branch of the Clydesdale Bank. An austere-looking woman; more hair than required, Alfred Hitchcock nose, skin the texture of mature cheddar. Narrow eyes, lips thinner. Voice like a slap on a bare arse. Both Proudfoot and Mulholland have the same thought; would you ask this woman for a loan? Wouldn't even ask her to tell me the time, thinks Proudfoot.

Their visit to the Chief Constable of the Highlands has been postponed until later in the afternoon, although this is something else from which they are expecting little.

'I really don't know how I can help you,' says the bank manager, to follow a few seconds' reticence.

'Humour us, if you would, Mrs Gregory,' says Mulholland. Has a quick vision of Mr Gregory. On the other side of the planet, if he has any sense. 'We can never cover old ground too many times. Our colleagues may have missed something.'

'I really don't think there is anything to miss, Chief Inspector. Mr Thomson withdrew two hundred pounds from one of our machines at six thirty in the evening, two weeks ago last Tuesday. None of my staff had any contact with him, and our records show that he has made no further attempt to complete any transactions with his accounts through this area. I really don't know what else there can be to say on the matter.'

'You're sure there's been nothing since then, Mrs Gregory?'

Mrs Gregory responds to this after the fashion of her face. 'Really, Chief Inspector. Just because the police have proved their own ineptitude in their inability to bring this notorious fugitive to justice does not mean that we are all incompetent in our chosen employment. I can attest, with the utmost assurance, that this man has not had any further dealings with our bank.'

Mulholland nods. Considers his next question. Doesn't really have any more. 'Can you tell us how much Barney Thomson has left in his account?'

She tuts loudly, exhales.

'Really, Chief Inspector. I don't know how many of your colleagues I've already told this to.'

'How much, Mrs Gregory?'

Shakes her head, answers. 'A little less than ten pounds.'

'And it's not possible to get five-pound notes from your machines?'

'That is correct.'

'So basically, he cleared his account as much as he could from the cash machine?'

'Yes, it would be true to say that.'

'And did he have an overdraft facility?'

She raises an eyebrow. Lips tighten, disappear altogether. 'I'm afraid you'll have to ask his own branch for that information.'

'Bollocks, Mrs Gregory,' says Proudfoot. 'You can tell us right now, and if you don't we can turn up here with a barrel-load of CID. Choice is yours.'

Mulholland looks out of the corner of his eye, but doesn't add anything.

'Really,' Mrs Gregory says, exasperated. Enjoying every minute of it, in a strange Calvinistic way. Will revel in telling her husband this evening. Verbal police brutality. Might even write to the *Press & Journal*. 'Well, as a matter of fact, I happen to know that he did not have an overdraft facility on his account. A very good account-holder, as it happens, Mr Thomson.'

Lets the words scissor out, hinting that Barney Thomson has, in some way, a much greater amount of moral fibre than either of the two police officers. Believes them to be the type to push their overdrafts to the limit.

'So, there will be no point in him going anywhere near another bank?'

'No, I shouldn't think there would.'

Mulholland nods. With admirable inspiration and only one day late at the races, Woods had alerted all banks to the possibility of Thomson using a cash machine. Not to disallow him from doing it, but to give them the chance to notify the police as it was happening, if that was possible. But the stable door was closed, and the horse already in a field on the other side of the mountains.

'Right, then, Mrs Gregory. I think that might be all. You'll let us know if Mr Thomson attempts any further transactions with your bank?'

'I'm sure I shall, Chief Inspector. And I am equally sure that you will not be hearing from me again. I think you might find that your Mr Thomson has disappeared.'

'You just leave that to us, Mrs Gregory. I'm sure we'll manage to find the truth in this matter, regardless of whether Barney Thomson visits another bank.'

He stands up to go; Proudfoot follows. They would both

love to do that police thing where you arrest someone for no reason other than that you don't like them. But it can get nasty if you do it off your own patch.

'Truth, Chief Inspector? Many from an inconsiderate zeal unto truth have too rashly charged the troops of error, and remain as trophies unto the enemies of truth.'

Mulholland nods. 'Aye, very good, Mrs Gregory. Watch you don't strain your tongue with talk like that, and see a doctor if your condition gets any worse.'

They take their leave and walk from the office. The door closes behind them, and Hermione Gregory is once again alone with her negligible empire.

'Wanker,' she says to the empty room. Goes about her business.

✂

Mulholland and Proudfoot stand outside the bank. Cold and damp, although the sleet which has been falling since they arrived in Inverness is taking a ten-minute break. Depressed. Another irrelevant line of questioning to another irrelevant non-witness in the Barney Thomson case.

'What now?' Proudfoot says.

'Bollocks, Mrs Gregory? I think that must contravene a police charter or two, don't you think? She wasn't a criminal, Sergeant.'

'Well, she was a pain in the backside. Bloody woman.'

Mulholland shrugs his shoulders. Can't be bothered arguing. And he himself had been on the point of arresting Hermione Gregory on suspicion of not changing her underwear every day.

'What now?' he says. 'Now we start trawling around every hotel and B&B in the Highlands, see if anyone recognises him. After we've spoken to the local Feds, of course. God knows what they'll be like. Wonder if they speak English.'

54

'Every hotel and B&B?'

'Aye, every hotel and B&B.'

'That's got to be thousands.'

'Very possibly.'

'But it's not as if these people won't have seen the pictures of Barney Thomson on the news. If anyone recognises him and they're prepared to tell us about it, they'll already have reported it.'

'Any other brilliant ideas about what we should do with our time?'

She stares at the sodden ground. Notices the first splash of a renewed shower of sleet. Has an idea, but decides it is best kept to herself.

'No,' she says.

'Right, that's settled, then. He didn't come all the way up here to head back down south. So, he's in Inverness or else he's moved on. Probably north-west. We check out every guest house, every B&B, every hotel, every room that he might have stayed in, between here, Wick, Durness and Fort William. And if we don't find him there, we start heading east towards Aberdeen.'

'Just you and me?'

'Aye.'

'You don't want to get help on this?'

'We're not getting any help, Sergeant. The press might be pishing in their pants; the public might be shitting buckets, but the Chief sodding Super wants instant results without spending any money on the case. You can't expect them to pay to put police on the ground when they've got managers and accountants to employ, and endless reports to produce. All the other officers involved in this bloody thing are doing something else, so we're going to do this. You happy?'

'Damp,' she says.

55

'Good. Right, you get to the tourist information board and get the addresses of as many of these places as you can.'

She shivers, pulls her coat around her as the sleet intensifies. 'And what are you going to do?'

'Go for a pint.'

'A pint?'

'Goodbye, Sergeant. Meet you back here in half an hour.'

'A pint?'

Mulholland turns and is gone, walking into the sleet. Proudfoot stands, the slush driving into her face, watching him go. Can already feel her coat giving in to the weather, and with it her mind giving in to misery and gloom. What is the point in all this trailing around? All those people, butchered and frozen and then casually disposed of. They're already dead, aren't they? The fact that the murders stopped when the mother died made it obvious; Barney Thomson was clearing up after her. There aren't going to be any more murders. The ones that are dead are dead, eventually everyone else will join them – but not by the hand of Barney Thomson – and we will all lie in the same grave, a farrago of twisted flesh, broken dreams and half-conceived ideas. Because that's all there ever is.

She watches as Mulholland disappears into the crowd, on his way to the pub.

'Wanker,' she says, then turns on her heels and mournfully heads towards tourist information.

Chapter 6

We Are All One Egg

The monks are at breakfast. A full and delicious meal. Four rashers of bacon, two sausages, a poached egg, mushrooms, black pudding, tomatoes, haggis and fried bread; mugs of steaming tea; all the toast and marmalade they can eat.

In their dreams.

The first bread of the day is usually broken by the light of dawn – well after eight o'clock this late in the year – but today it has been postponed until late into the morning, following the burial of Brother Saturday and all the prayers which need to be said for his departed soul. And so they are unusually hungry as they sit down to their meal of porridge, unleavened bread and tea; having waited in further prayer for Brothers Steven and Jacob to return from gravedigging detail.

Conversation is not encouraged at mealtimes. The Abbot gives thanks to the Lord and the monks dine in respectful silence, grateful for the gift of food. At least, that is how it is supposed to be.

It is but one day since the body of Brother Saturday

was discovered. Clothed in a long white tunic, turned bloody red; his feet bare and blue, sitting against a tree in the forest. Eyes open, face relaxed, at peace with the world; and with God. A knife had been thrust deep into his throat, so that the blade disappeared up to the hilt and protruded from the back of his neck. One of the old knives, kept at the monastery since the fourteenth century; a gift from a Knight Templar, of uncertain and mysterious provenance. A knife that might have seen action in the Crusades, but certainly never since. Until it pierced the throat and rendered the flesh of Brother Saturday.

He had been a popular member of the order, much loved by the other monks. He had answered the call thirty-seven years previously, on the back of a series of rejections at the hands of women, which tormented him throughout his teenage years. A wayward eye, unruly hair, lips that meant he could do naught but kiss like a sea anemone, skin like the surface of a Rice Krispie, and many times had his heart been broken. However, he had found his peace with God, believing him to be not judgmental; ignoring the evidence of the Old Testament, where God wins the Olympic gold for being judgmental for several consecutive centuries.

For nine years past he worked in the library, keeping meticulous care of the seven thousand volumes in his possession. Losing himself in books, the only way. He had come to the position of librarian at an early age. He should have been librarian's apprentice for many years. However, after but six months in the post, the librarian of the day, Brother Atwell, gave in to the lure of compliant womanhood, and fled the abbey on an evil, stormy night. Brother Saturday was given premature promotion; Brother Morgan became the librarian's apprentice. No one, however, particularly suspects Morgan of the heinous crime perpetrated upon Saturday.

There are many of the monks who would be grateful for the opportunity to work in the library, away from the cold of the fields. The chance of working among the warmth of the books could be a powerful motive; for an unbalanced mind. And there is no doubt that the killer came from within the walls of the monastery itself, the murder weapon having come from the vaults of the abbey.

No one suspects the Abbot, or indeed Brother Herman. That leaves thirty others under suspicion; everyone from the longest-serving – the aged Brother Frederick, who came to the monastery from the killing fields of Passchendaele – to the newest recruit, Brother Jacob. And there are few who doubt that many of their fellow brothers within those walls are hiding from dark secrets and dark pasts.

'Brother Jacob?'

Barney stops and turns. Breakfast is over, the company beginning to disassemble, the day's tasks ahead. Tending the livestock; fortifying the buildings and the land against the harsh winter to come; kitchen, cleaning and laundry duties. The mornings are for the work of the monastery, the afternoons for prayer and study with the Lord. Barney must clean the floors.

'Aye?' he says to Brother Herman. Feels nervous in his presence.

Brother Herman's eyes stare out from deep sockets, from a long, thin face. Long Face, they called him in school. Behind his back.

'The Abbot will see you in his study in five minutes.' Deep voice. Ominous.

Barney nods. The Abbot. Brother Copernicus. He has been awaiting the call. All new students of the order are called to the Abbot at the end of their first week. Barney has already been questioned by Brother Herman about the murder of Saturday; wonders now if this is why the Abbot will see him. Further questioning. Barney, a man under suspicion. Feels as if he cannot get away from murder.

Five minutes. His heart races.

✂

Barney sits before the Abbot in the spartan surroundings of his study. A simple desk, a wooden chair on either side. Bare stone floors and walls, a row of books along one. A long, slim cut in the wall behind the Abbot, the window open, so that the cold of the room is the cold of outside. The light of day is augmented by two oil lamps mounted on the walls, an unlit candle sits on the desk. The Abbot reads. Left hand turning the pages of the book, right hand tucked away inside his cloak.

Barney stews.

Forgive me, Father, for I have sinned, he can imagine himself saying, though he has never attended confession in his life. I have committed murder. Well, more manslaughter really. I didn't mean to do it. Chris and Wullie, the men I worked with. They were a pain in the arse – sorry, Father – but I didn't really want them dead.

Then my mother died and I discovered six bodies in her freezer. As you do. Forgive my mother as well, Father, she knew not what she did. I wronged, I know that. I should have confessed all, like Bart does in that episode of *The Simpsons* when he cuts the statue's head off. But I panicked. I disposed of all the bodies and made it look like Chris was the killer. There were four policemen on to me, but they all shot each other. That definitely wasn't my fault. So, I suppose I thought I'd . . .

'Brother Jacob.' The Abbot closes his book, looks up.

Barney's heart dances; he ends his silent confession. 'It's not too cold for you?'

Barney is freezing.

'Naw, naw, Ah'm fine,' he says. Shivers; hairs stand erect, goose bumps rampage across his body like German storm troopers.

The Abbot nods; knows he lies.

He takes his time, considers his words. The Abbot, Brother Copernicus. Renounced the pleasures of the world in his early twenties, has been at the monastery since the fifties. Hair has greyed; the paunch of youth has long ago given way to a sinewy body, engulfed by the cloak. Thin lips, a sharp nose, green eyes which see more than eyes are meant to see. Not, however, a man without humour – a smile sometimes comes to those cold, thin lips.

'I'm sorry that your first week has been blighted by such terrible circumstances, Jacob. A terrible business.'

Nae bother, thinks Barney. I'm thinking of opening a shop; Cadavers 'R' Us.

'I'm sorry too, Your Grace,' he says.

The thin lips stretch and smile. The eyes too. 'It's all right, Jacob, you don't need to call me "Your Grace". I'm not the Pope. Brother Copernicus will do.'

Barney smiles and nods. Relaxes a little. Feels more at ease.

'How are you settling in, Jacob?'

Barney thinks.

Bad points: no gas or electricity; no hot water; lamps out by eight o'clock, up at five thirty; a thin single bed, hard wood, two coarse blankets; no entertainment, no distractions but for the scriptures and other works of religious learning; day after day on his hands and knees cleaning the floors; praise be to God; God the Father,

61

God the Son, God the Holy Ghost; God all-seeing, God divine; God this, God that, God the next thing; God, God, God, God, God, God, God. Bloody God.

Good points: the food isn't too bad; a cup of wine with dinner every night; there is no contact with the outside world, so no one has ever heard of Barney Thomson. That's about it.

'No' bad, ye know.' Laughs a little self-consciously. 'Takes a bit o' gettin' used tae, but Ah'm awright.'

The Abbot nods his head. Drums the fingers of his left hand on the desk. Long, cold fingers. Barney can feel them at his throat; shivers, tries to clear his head of fears and sorrows.

'Our monks come here for all sorts of reasons, Jacob. It is not for me to question or examine those reasons. We, each of us, must be content in our hearts that we are where we belong. There are many who come here and realise after a time that this life is not for them. One such was Brother Camberene, who came to us for a few sad months last year. He'd been involved in a tragic accident, and blamed himself for the resulting fatality. He was racked by guilt, his life had become tortured by anguish. He stopped going to work, his dear wife walked out on him. And after a time, the river of fate, which winds its way through the lives of everyone, led him to us. But I am afraid that even we could not provide the answers for which he searched. He spent a few unhappy months and then moved on. A sad and desperate, restless soul. We all still say our prayers for Brother Camberene, but I am afraid that we might never hear of him again. However, wherever he might be, we know that God is with him.'

Barney swallows, stares at the desk. Sees himself in the story of Brother Camberene. 'What sort of accident was he in?'

The Abbot shakes his head. Sombre eyes.

'He ran over a six-year-old boy with a full trolley in Tesco's.'

Barney stares.

'That's a supermarket, apparently,' says the Abbot, 'although I presume you know that.'

Barney shakes his head. He wants to meet Brother Camberene. Sounds like his kind of man.

The Abbot scratches his chin, then looks up. Lets the weight of Brother Camberene lift from his shoulders.

'So, what I'm trying to say is this. If you do not find your answers among us, we shall not condemn. We're here to help you. If you find this life is not for you, we would wish you on your way with the love of God and the love of all our hearts. And should you find contentment here, you will have our love and understanding as you learn our ways, and the ways of the Lord.'

Speech over. Barney stares.

It is like being at Sunday school. He is reminded of Miss Trondheim. Tall, dark complexion; black hair, one growing out of a mole on her left cheek. And Mr Blackberry. Short; Stewart Granger hair, although he did once come in with a Robert Mitchum.

Barney knows he is supposed to say something, but no words come his way. He nods slightly, tries to look as if he is at one with God.

The Abbot is used to such reticence.

'However, Jacob, having said that, if there is something about your past which you wish to share with me, I am here to listen. If there is something from which you run, it is often best to face it, even if it is from within these walls.'

Giving the new brother his first chance to speak, the Abbot knows he will say nothing. They all turn up with their secrets and insecurities, and in time they will out. But not yet.

'Naw, naw, ye know,' says Barney. 'Ah thought Ah'd try something new. Ah'd grown a bit disillusioned, ye know. Wi' life an a' that.'

The Abbot nods, purses his lips.

'It is late in life for a change, Jacob. No man putteth a piece of new cloth unto an old garment, for that which is put in to fill it up taketh from the garment, and the rent is made worse. Neither do men put new wine into old bottles: else the bottles break, and the wine runneth out, and the bottles perish: but they put new wine into new bottles, and both are preserved.

'You should remember those words, Jacob.'

'What?' says Barney, surprised. 'Do youse make wine up here? This far north?'

The Abbot smiles. 'You have much to learn, Jacob. You should read your Bible.'

'Aye. Right.'

The Abbot looks into the heart of Barney Thomson. Wonders what lies therein. Knows that sooner or later it will emerge, but there is no hurry. Has no reason to suspect him of the murder of Brother Saturday. No more than any of the others, at any rate.

'One final point, Jacob, as you start out on this new road which lies ahead. As you can see, ours is a simple life. We have little contact with the outside world and we take care of most of our own needs. Might there be a skill from your past which you would be able to share with us?'

Barney thinks. Dare he tell them about barbery? Might it put them on to him? But they obviously have no idea what is going on. Would they knowingly accept a suspected serial killer into their fold?

64

'Ah've done a bit o' haircuttin' in ma time,' he says.
The Abbot raises an eyebrow.

'Oh. A barber?'

'Aye.'

'Well. It is indeed many years since we had a professional hirsutologist in our midst. A most noble trade.' His hand automatically strays to the back of his neck. 'Brother Adolphus does his best, but sadly his skills in this direction are somewhat lacking. Despite all our prayers.'

Barney feels a swelling of his heart. It has only been two weeks, during which time he has given the odd one-off haircut around the Highlands, but he has missed the click of the scissors, the bite of the razor into the back of the neck, and the pointless chatter. Wonders if St Johnstone are managing to hang on at the top of the league.

'Could do with a bit of a haircut myself,' says the Abbot.

'Oh, aye?' says Barney, feeling useful. 'Ah'm sure Ah could help ye out.'

'That would be good,' says the Abbot. 'Later on this afternoon perhaps. After prayers, before it gets dark. I wouldn't mind a Brother Cadfael.'

Barney smiles and nods. A Brother Cadfael, eh? Has done one of them a couple of years previously. Piece of cake. Wonders if he'll be able to give the monks anything other than a Brother Cadfael.

✂

The door closes behind Barney Thomson; the Abbot stares after him for a short while. A closed door. How many doors are closed within this monastery, and for what reasons hidden in the depths of a mysterious past?

He sighs, slowly lifts himself out of the chair. He turns

65

and stares out at the bright, white morning. Snow upon snow, stretching across the forest to the hills in the distance. And yet the full cold blast of winter has not arrived.

For a time he watches a buzzard circle above the forest. Silent brown against the pale blue sky.

Meanwhile, Barney Thomson walks along the corridors of the monastery, a whistle marginally beneath his lips. Light of heart for the first time in a fortnight, having completely failed to notice the exact meaning of some of the Abbot's words. That the monks have little contact with the outside world. Little, but not none, as he had thought.

As he takes to his bucket and mop for the first time that morning, 'The Girl from Ipanema' momentarily escapes his lips.

A Conspiracy of Shadows

The third floor of the monastery, at the north end, a room of bright light; the library. Brother Morgan leans over his desk, large hand gripping small quill pen, etching out the clear rounded figures. Translating the original Greek of a series of third-century letters, into English. He is one of only three of the monks who read Greek – for some of the others there is a painful learning process, and for the rest, ignorance.

The translation is a task he has been with for some weeks; begun when he was still Brother Saturday's assistant, content with his lot, with little thought for advancement. A monk is all Morgan has ever wanted to be. Librarian's apprentice was a bonus. Anything else is unasked for and unwanted. He will be happy for someone else to be made librarian and for him to go back to the role he has had for so many years. Trusts all of the brothers, but at the same time is worried that a similar fate might befall him as befell Saturday. Maybe Saturday died because of some lovers' tiff within the monastery walls – as has been the rumour among a certain section of the monks – or maybe he died because of his position. It is the latter possibility which worries Brother Morgan.

There is a noise across the room, from within the rows of shelves. Morgan lifts his head, stills his pen. Even in the bright light of the room, the shelves are in shadow. A conspiracy. He feels a shiver at the back of his neck. Insects crawling across his skin.

'Hello?'

A movement. A rat? There haven't been rats in the monastery for over a hundred years. That's what they say.

'Hello?' he says again, this time with a little more urgency. Annoyed. Doesn't like being disturbed at his work. Knows how easy it is to make mistakes when you lose concentration. One of the reasons he dropped out of life.

The annoyance masks his trepidation.

A figure appears from among the shelves. He relaxes.

'Oh, hello, Brother,' he says. Relief. Impatience too, as the monk emerges from the conspiracy of shadows. 'I didn't realise you were there.'

The monk holds up a small volume. Doesn't smile. Stares from the depths of plunging eye sockets.

'It is many years since I have studied the original Latin translation of the letters of Paul,' he says. 'I have been most remiss. You will record that I have removed the volume from the library?'

'Certainly, Brother,' says Morgan. Wonders why

people have to be so clandestine.

Brother Morgan watches as the monk slowly walks from the library and closes the door behind him. He shakes his head and lifts his pen. Back to work. Why do some of his brothers feel the need to be so mysterious? There is enough darkness in the monastery as it is.

As he begins the slow movement of the pen across the thick page, he feels a cold draught of air at his feet. Looks up. The door to the library swings open an inch or two.

And a cold wind blows.

Chapter 7

Is He Is, or Is He Ain't?

Mrs Mary Strachan bends her ear towards the television, trying to listen to the news above the sound of her husband rifling the *Scotsman*, at the same time as she struggles through a tricky interpretation of Quintus Horatius Flaccus's second book of epistles.

'For pity's sake, man, would ye haud yer wheest wi' yon paper. I cannae hear the television.'

James Strachan shakes his head, tuts loudly. Rustles the paper even more.

'Help m'boab, woman, whit are ye on about? Ye know fine well that ye cannae watch television and translate Horace fi' the original Latin at the same time. No' since ye lost yer eye in the sheep incident last March.'

'Ach, flech tae you, James Strachan, flech tae you. Ma mother always said ye were a manny o' little vision. I should have listened to her.'

'Ach, away and bile yer heid woman,' he says, settling on the inside sports pages. 'Rangers Fail in £45 million Bid for Six-Year-Old Italian'. 'Whit did yer mother know? The woman spent a' her days doin' wee jobbies at the bottom o' the garden. Didnae have a clue about anythin'.'

'Don't you be malignin' my mother, James Strachan. It wasn't my mother who was arrested for stealin' underwear off Mrs MacPherson's washing line.'

He looks over the paper for the first time. 'Jings tae crivvens, woman, I don't believe it. Dae ye have tae bring yon up every day? Can ye no' forget it? We read that we ought tae forgive our enemies; but we do not read that we ought tae forgive our friends. Think about that, woman.'

'Don't you go quotin' Cosimo de'Medici at me, James Strachan. Dae ye think I can show my face in the supermarket wi'oot people talkin' about it? Well, dae you? There's not a day I walk down the street that I don't hear the whispers. Not a day goes by.'

'For pity's sake, woman. It was seventy-three year ago.'

'That may be, James Strachan, that may be. But it might as well have been yesterday as far as this town's concerned.'

'Ach, get away wi' ye, Mary Strachan, away wi' ye, I say. There's nae a'body in this town whae wis alive seventy-three year ago, 'cept me and thee.'

'Ach, jings tae goodness, James Strachan, whit does that matter? Ye think anyone alive today wis around when the English sucked us intae the Act o' Union? Na', na', but we still a' hate them fur it.'

'Ach, help m'boab tae jings tae goodness, whit are ye on about, Mary Strachan? You an' yer Act o' Union. If it wisnae for the Act o' Union we'd still a' be livin' in peat bags and eatin' oats fur wur dinner.'

'Ach, there ye go, haverin' again, James Strachan. Haverin' again. Here, look at yon!'

She breaks off, pointing at the television. The lunch-time news.

'See, I telt ye, did I no'?'

James Strachan tuts loudly and shakes his head. Rustles the paper. 'Telt me whit? Whit are you talkin' about?'

'That picture on the television. That Barney Thomson. He was the one who stayed here just o'er a week ago. I telt ye it was.'

He glances at the television, then buries his head in the paper. 'Ach, away an' stick yer heid in a pan o' tatties. Whit would a serial killer be doin' stayin' in a place like Durness, away oot in the back o' beyond. Serial killers live in big hooses wi' a' the windaes boarded up. I've seen it in the films.'

She shakes her head, points at the television. 'Look at those eyes, I'd recognise them anywhere. That man's a serial killer if ever there was one, and he stayed right here in this house. Slept in the bed that yon German couple are sleeping in at the moment.'

James Strachan lowers the paper again. He stares at the television, then looks at his wife. 'And what if it was him? What of it? He's gone now, isn't he? Are you gonnae tell the police, or what?'

Mary Strachan bristles. Shoulders back, chin out. 'Well, I don't know about that. He looked a nice enough lad. Maybe they've got the wrong one, ye know.'

'Ye just said he looked like a serial killer!'

'Aye, but ye know, these things are hard tae tell. And it's no' as if you're one tae talk.'

'Ach, away and shite, wummin,' he says, from deep within the rugby reports. 'Scotland Select New Zealander Whose Granny Holidayed on Skye Once'.

Proudfoot climbs into the car beside Mulholland. Finds him reading her *Blitz!* and eating the last of the sandwiches. She doesn't mind, as she had everything she was going to get from the tourist information within ten minutes and stopped and had something to eat. Got talking.

'Surprised you're not listening to Simply Red,' she says. Shivers, takes her coat off and throws it onto the back seat. The sleet is softening, turning to snow.

'I'm sure you are. Just reading something here,' he says, tapping the magazine. 'Apparently, if you coat your breasts in dried alligator milk, it'll improve your orgasm strength. I'm assuming that it's aimed at women, but who knows?'

'Didn't do anything for me when I tried it,' she says.

He gives her a look; disappointed to see that she's joking. Closes the magazine.

'Right, then. What are we looking at? You get a list?'

'Yep. Everywhere that anyone could stay in Inverness; and a long list of places outside of town as far north as you can go, but she said that wasn't so comprehensive. There's a lot of them closed for the winter, so that should help.'

He looks at his watch.

'Right, just after two. Got to see Inspector Dumpty of Highland CID, get that over with, and then we can start. Split up and get on with it. Should be done with Inverness before it's too late. No reason why each one should take longer than a minute or two. Meet back here between six and seven. You get two lists?'

'I'm not an idiot. Of course.'

'Just checking. Ferguson wouldn't have thought of it.'

Proudfoot thinks of the woman she dealt with in the tourist information. Ferguson would still be there, trying to fix up a visit to her bed that evening.

'Right, let's get it sorted how we're going to split this. At the end of the day we find somewhere we can spend the night, then set off tomorrow and take each town as it comes.'

She nods her head. Can't think of anything else she'd less like to be doing; can't think of a single aspect of police work which now appeals to her.

'How was the pint?' she says.

Mulholland looks up from the list of guest houses. Smiles. 'Very informative,' he says. 'Too bad you weren't there.'

How do you mean, very informative? is on the tip of Proudfoot's tongue. Decides the better of it. If he wants to be cryptic, then so be it. Bastard.

And, as it happens, it meant nothing at all.

✂

As they might have supposed, they have to wait to see the Chief Constable, a man of whom they have heard tell. They find themselves in a small room, unsatisfactory mugs of tea having cooled on the table, the Moray Firth slate grey to match the skies, barely visible between the walls of wet buildings. Unsure of what to expect of their man, for what policeman likes outsiders coming into his patch?

In turn they sit at the desk, then pace the short floor space, then look out at the grey day. Wrestle, in their heads, with their own thoughts of depression and loneliness and unease. Proudfoot more comfortable with these thoughts than Mulholland.

Finally the door opens, shattering the atmosphere.

73

Relief swipes at Mulholland.

'The Chief Constable will see you now,' says the maroon cardigan, masquerading as the middle-aged woman beneath.

✂

The Chief Constable stands with his back to them, staring out over the cold estuary. Looking for dolphins, although he hasn't seen one in over three months. The door closes behind them and they wait, much as they have already been waiting.

They are in the midst of the opulence they have come to expect from chief constables: thick carpet, huge desk, comfy chair, photographs on the wall with the senior police officer in question shaking the hand of an even more senior officer or a low-budget member of the royal family – although, in this case, all Chief Constable Dr Reginald McKay has been able to manage is a picture of himself directing traffic outside Balmoral Castle.

'Dolphins,' he says.

Mulholland and Proudfoot glance at one another. Here we go.

'What about them?' asks Mulholland, reluctantly playing the game.

'Used tae be a cartload o' them out there. Used tae be able tae stand at this windae for hours on end and watch them in the distance. Where are they now, eh? Havenae seen one in months.'

The question disappears into the room. Dolphins? It's probably Barney Thomson's fault, thinks Proudfoot.

Reginald McKay leaves them standing for another minute before turning round, nodding at his visitors and sinking into the green depths of his comfy chair. He stares absent-mindedly at some papers on his desk while ushering them into two less salubrious chairs. Finally engages their eyes, looking from one to the other. 'I'm greatly troubled, I must admit,' he says.

'Aye,' says Mulholland, wrongly assuming they're about to embark on a discussion of Barney Thomson.

'I've spoken to all sorts of groups, but no one seems to have any idea what's happened to them.'

'Them?'

'The dolphins. Ach, I know it's cold out there, but they're fish.'

'No they're not.'

'Whatever. They don't mind the cold. But I havenae seen one in months. Did I say that already? Hard to believe that something really terrible hasn't happened. Some terrible tragedy. Effie thinks it's the Russians, but I wouldnae be surprised if the Norwegians didnae have something tae be doing with it. Bunch o' idiots the lot o' them.'

'Barney Thomson?' says Mulholland.

'Thomson?' says McKay. 'Norwegian, is he? Not surprised.'

'No, he's not Norwegian. We just need to talk about him. That's why we're here.'

The Chief Constable nods. A man of infinite years, hair greyed, face lined, eyes dimmed. 'Of course, laddie. You big shots fi' Glasgow, I suppose you'll be wanting tae be getting on wi' things.'

'Aye,' says Mulholland, 'we wouldn't mind. Got a bit of work to do up here.'

'So I understand. You'll be intending to traipse all over the Highlands, will you?'

'For as long as it takes?'

'Well, good luck tae ye, laddie. I'm sure you'll find some traces o' the bloke, but I can't promise you'll find the man himself.'

'You've heard tell of him, then?'

'Ach, aye, we've been getting reports fi' a' over, ye know.'

They lean forward; Mulholland's eyes narrow.

'Now, laddie, don't go peeing yer pants wi' excitement. There's nothing definite, ye know. It's all conjecture and vague noises. Whisperings, you might say. Rumours in the wind.'

Mulholland leans back in his seat. Eyes remain narrowed, staring at the old man.

'What kind of rumours?'

Dr McKay taps a single finger on the desk, looks from one to the other. Doesn't like outsiders; they never understand. Not like dolphins; they always know. Know everything.

'We're getting reports. Vague things wi'oot any real meaning, ye know, nothing you could put your finger on. We think he might be working to get some money. We've been hearing of whole communities where the men have all suddenly been given the most wondrous haircuts. Hair of the gods, so they're saying. While some say he's more of a loose cannon, bouncing all over the place, giving out haircuts with fickle irregularity. You'll have heard of the Brahan Seer?'

Mulholland shrugs his shoulders; Proudfoot nods her head, so McKay turns his attention towards her.

'They say that he wrote of such a man. Prophesied his coming.'

'What?' Mulholland.

'He told of a man who would come into the community and wield a pair of scissors as if his hands were guided by magic. A man who could call the gods his ancestors. A man who would cut the hair of all the warriors in the kingdom so that the strength of many kings would be in the hands of each of them. A man who would come out of tragedy and leave one morning in the mists before anyone had risen, never to be heard of again. A god, may be, or a messenger of the gods. But whatever, his time would be short, his coming a portent of dark times ahead, and yet his passing would be greatly mourned. A messiah, in a way, although perhaps that might be too strong a word to be using. Anyway, they are saying that maybe Barney Thomson might be that man.'

'You're taking the piss, right?' says Mulholland.

The lined and furrowed brow creases a little more, the old grey head shakes.

'I'm only telling you what is being said, Chief Inspector, but these are deeply superstitious people you will encounter up here. Once you head into Sutherland and Caithness they're not like you Lowlanders with your English ways and your Channel Five reception. Oh, no. You must respect them, for only then will they respect you. However, I think if you find anyone who has had contact with this man, they will be reluctant to talk. He is seen by many in these parts to be wronged.'

'Wronged? He and his mother murdered eight people. How exactly is he being wronged?'

'We've all read the papers up here and, for myself, I have read the reports, such as you have deemed to send my way. Clearly the mother was the main culprit, and if he only acted to cover up the actions of his sick parent, then should a man be a criminal just because he would protect his family?'

They stare at him. Proudfoot sees his point. Mulholland is speechless. This is a police officer he's talking to, not some brain-dead hippie or civil rights activist.

'And how is he hounded by your press,' says McKay,

going on. '"Barney Thomson Ate My Goat". "Barney Thomson Slaughters Virgin in Sacrifice Blunder". "The Congo – It's Thomson's Fault". It's absurd, you must see that. All of it.'

Mulholland rests farther back in his chair, shaking his head. It may be absurd, the media may be totally bollock-brained and desperate bedfellows of sensationalism, but it doesn't mean that Barney Thomson should be excused his crimes, no matter how much was his mother's doing.

Having said his piece, McKay looks uncomfortable as he shuffles some unnecessary papers on his desk; drums his fingers, scratches an imaginary itch at the back of his left ear. Breathes deeply enough through his nose that it almost becomes a snort.

'Anyway, I thought I might assign someone to you to ease your way around.'

'What?'

'Help you out, you know. Show you what's what.'

Mulholland leans forward in his chair. Knuckles go white. The Chief Constable stares at a report on his desk. 'Dolphins – Talk Show Hosts or Talk Show Guests?'

'For God's sake! It's not like we've come to some bloody alien country. Their accents might be a bit weird up here, but no weirder than Glasgow, and it's the same language when it comes to it. We're not children, we don't need any bloody help.'

McKay lifts his eyes, not used to being spoken to in such a way by junior officers.

'Chief Inspector, you will remember your place,' he says quietly.

Their eyes clash and fight some pointless testosterone-laden battle, destined to go nowhere, before Mulholland inches backwards and gives way. Fuming, he is. Proudfoot watches him out of the corner of her narrowed eye, while McKay puts his finger to the intercom.

'Could you send in Sergeant MacPherson please, Mrs Staples,' he says.

Ah! thinks Proudfoot. Another Sergeant MacPherson on the Barney Thomson case, just as before. Must be something in that. Must be. No such thing as a coincidence in policing. Or any other aspect of life, as a matter of fact.

The door opens; in he comes. Tall, broad-shouldered, kind face. They look round; Proudfoot likes what she sees, Mulholland thinks he recognises him.

'This is Detective Sergeant MacPherson, who'll be working with you. I'm sure he'll be of great assistance.'

He nods and the two of them return it; Mulholland grudgingly.

'My name's Gordon,' says MacPherson, Highland accent broader than the Firth, 'but everyone calls me Sheep Dip.'

'Sheep Dip?' says Proudfoot.

'Aye,' he says. 'Sheep Dip.'

I'm not going to ask, thinks Mulholland. Turns back to the sound of the Chief Constable pushing his chair away from the desk.

'Right then, Chief Inspector, if there's anything else you're needing you can let me know. Keep me posted, and if you have any activities to undertake in and around the towns you visit, perhaps you'd be kind enough to notify the local constabulary. Sergeant MacPherson will help you out there, I'm sure.'

'Aye, nae bother,' says Sheep Dip.

Fucking brilliant, thinks Mulholland. Wonder if I have to tell them every time I check into a B&B, or put petrol in the car, or take a piss.

They step outside the office, past Mrs Staples, and then

out into the open-plan where the heart of Highland crime detection snoozes the afternoon away. A lost dog in Buckie. A child stuck up a tree outside Drumnadrochit. A teenager baring his bum in Forres, that second can of McEwan's proving his undoing. An accident involving a tractor and a low-flying Tornado on the road between Aviemore and Granton. Heroin with a street value of £23 million seized on a Russian trawler in the Moray Firth.

A normal day.

Chapter 8

The Barber Surgeon's Hairshirt

Barney feels at home. A pair of scissors in his right hand, a comb in his left, a cut-throat razor at his side. No other tools with which to work. Barbery at its most coarse, unfettered by electric razors or blow-driers or artificial lights. No cape around the victim to squeeze the neck and protect the virgin body from epidermal contamination. Barbery as it must have been practised in olden days, when men were men and the earth was flat. Raw, Stone Age barbery, where every snip of the scissors is done by instinct; where every cut is a potential disaster, every clip a walk along a tightrope of calamity, every hew a cleave into the kernel of the collective human id. Barbery without a safety net. Barbery to put fear into the breast of the bravest knight, to quail the heart of the stoutest king. A duel with the Satan of pre-modernism, where strength becomes artistry and genius the episcopacy of fate. Total barbery; naked, bloody, stripped of artifice.

'Apparently Jesus wis a shortarse,' says Barney, care-free around the left ear. Forgetting where he is, to whom he is talking. Brother Ezekial raises an eyebrow.

Barney is revelling in the primitive conditions. In one afternoon he has reeled off a Sean Connery (*Name of the Rose*), a Christian Slater (*Name of the Rose*), an F. Murray Abraham (*Name of the Rose*), and a Ron Perlman (*Name of the Rose*); as well as the Abbot's Brother Cadfael. No cash, no tips, just quiet words of praise and heartfelt thanks for doing the Lord's work. Barney has never before thought of himself as doing the work of the Lord.

'Four foot six, they say. Wi' a hunchback.'

Brother Ezekial coughs portentously into the back of his hand.

'You're forgetting where you are, Brother Jacob.'

Barney stops, scissors poised. Thinks. Says, 'Oh, shit, aye. Ah forgot.'

Brother Ezekial closes his eyes in silent prayer for the errant monk. Disparaging the Lord, swearing – you can always tell a new recruit.

Barney lapses into silence. He runs the comb through the hair, clicks the scissors. The light from outside is beginning to fade and he is glad of the three candles which flicker on the small shelf beside which he works. He is supposed to be keeping his head down and his mouth shut. His language isn't too bad – not by Glasgow standards – but it is still unnecessarily unsavoury for within the walls of a monastery.

He had been doing fine. Head down, speak when you're spoken to. Like any new recruit to any walk of life. Don't make a noise until you've got your feet under the table. However, a couple of hours of barbery has undone him. He'd been all right during the Sean Connery and the Abbot's Brother Cadfael. Finding his feet, getting back into the groove, reacquainting himself with his scissor fingers. However, ten minutes into the Christian

Slater, Brother Sledge had made an innocent remark about the weather and Barney was off, his mouth running ahead of him like a leopard on amphetamines.

And so, he's covered all the great topics of the day: the profligacy of this year's December snow; the situation in Ngorno Karabakh; apparently Tolkien wrote *The Lord of the Rings* in a fortnight; fifteen reasons why Beethoven wasn't as deaf as he made out; six kings of Scotland who were circumcised at the age of fifty; how Sid James nearly beat out Giscard d'Estaing to the French presidency in 1974; why Kennedy only won the US presidency because he kept J. Edgar Hoover supplied with edible underwear; Errol Flynn was a woman; apparently Jesus was a shortarse. Barney has been full of it; total, inexorable, ineffable bollocks. He's been at the peak of his form, talking the sort of crap of which most guys with fifteen pints in them can only dream.

The monks have sat and listened; smiling occasionally, nodding sagely at the appropriate moments, which has been mostly at moments at which Barney did not expect them to nod. For they have seen it all before. The new monk, unfamiliar with the conventions and truths of monastic life, whose tongue will not be still. Every now and again one of these types survives the unfamiliar rigours of this austere existence, but usually they will last no longer than a snowman in the Sahara – on a particularly hot day.

Few within the walls are prepared to put their money on Brother Jacob lasting longer than a few weeks; even if any of the monks possessed money and if the Abbot had not closed down the tote operated by Brother Steven.

Now, however, after the admonishment from Brother Ezekial, Barney snips quietly. He keeps his mouth shut, his thoughts to himself. Tries to think of everything else he has said this afternoon, wondering if he strayed beyond the boundaries of discretion; words which were allowed to pass but which did not go unnoticed. He cannot remember; thinks of goldfish.

Brother Ezekial stares at the wall; no mirrors here. His thoughts, like those of many of his colleagues, are still consumed by the unfortunate demise of Brother Saturday, and by futile speculation on who might have perpetrated the crime. Ezekial is among those who believe that the Abbot should call in the outside agencies of the law, but the word of the Abbot must be respected. If he has faith in the ability of Brother Herman to get to the bottom of this murky river of truth, then so should the rest of the monks. But what if Brother Herman is not as above suspicion as everyone thinks? Ezekial's brow furrows; he makes a mental note not to voice that doubt to anyone else. And certainly not to Brother Jacob.

The door swings open behind them, the cold air rushes in. Barney shivers and turns round. Remembers to stop cutting as he does so. How many times in the old days before his renaissance of the previous March had he forgotten that fundamental law and inadvertently swiped off an ear?

'Time for one more?' says Brother Steven, closing the door behind him. 'I hear you're only doing this barber gig twice a week.'

Barney looks down at the tonsured head of Brother Ezekial. Dome shaved to perfection, back of the head cut with Germanic precipitousness. In fact, the haircut is finished. Realises that the only reason he is still cutting is because he doesn't want the haircut to end. When he's done cutting hair, he will be required to spend an hour or two in religious contemplation; to commune with God.

'Aye, aye, fine,' he says. 'Come on in. Ah'm done, in fact.'

He lifts the towel from around Ezekial's neck, shakes the detritus of the cut onto the floor, steps back, allows Ezekial to stand up from the chair. Ezekial runs his fingers behind his cloak along the back of his neck. Is impressed with the lack of hair having worked its way down to irritate and annoy.

'Thank you very much, Brother,' he says to Barney. Just in time, Barney stops himself sticking out his hand to receive a tip. 'A good haircut, I believe,' says Ezekial, although he cannot possibly know. 'Your hands must have been guided by God.'

Barney smiles, nods. Thinks, Bugger off, God had nothing to do with it, mate. But he knows that he should not be having such thoughts.

'Goodbye, Brother,' he says instead, as Ezekial takes his leave. He goes in search of a mirror, knowing of at least two of the monks who keep one hidden beneath a pillow.

Brother Steven takes his seat; he turns, giving Barney an encouraging look.

'Heard you're doing some good work, Brother,' he says. Barney says nothing but feels pleased. 'They're saying in the kitchens that if Marlon Brando had cut Martin Sheen's hair in *Apocalypse Now*, this is how he would have done it. Cutting hair like a god-king.'

Barney shrugs, places the towel around Steven's shoulders.

'Ach, ye know, it's nothin' an' a' that. Just ma job, ye know.'

Steven nods. Knows exactly from where Barney is coming.

'What'll it be, then?' asks Barney. Presumes it's going to be another *Name of the Rose* job, although wonders how any of these monks got to see *Name of the Rose*. Or

Brother Cadfael for that matter.

Steven runs his hand across his chin. Contemplates.

'Think I'll go for a Mike McShane *Robin Hood, Prince of Thieves*). What do you think? Think that'll suit me?'

Barney stares at the top of Steven's head. Has never heard of Mike McShane. Presumes that it can't be much different from any other haircut he's given any of these people. Presumes correctly.

'Aye, aye, it'll suit ye just fine.'

'Great. Go for it, then.'

Steven settles back, that look of satisfied contentment on his face. The look of someone who knows that life is a bowl of curried lamb keich, but is quite content with the fact. At one with his own foibles and with the foibles of others.

Barney lifts his comb and scissors and sets about his business. A contented customer and a contented barber; the perfect customer/barber combo. He is about to launch into a discussion of the casuistic fundamentals of Morton's Fork when he remembers his earlier edict to keep his thoughts to himself. So he sticks to his barbery as the light fades and the candles flicker.

Brother Steven's tongue can never be so still, however.

'Incensed with indignation Satan stood unterrified, and like a comet burned that fires the length of Ophiuchus huge in the Arctic sky, and from his horrid hair shakes pestilence and war,' says Brother Steven. Lets the words mingle with the flickering shadows and the dim orange light.

'Aye, right,' says Barney. Pauses. No reason for not talking now; he is being invited to talk. 'Whit wis a' that, exactly?'

'Milton,' says Brother Steven. 'I always dug that line about hair. You know, shaking out pestilence and war.

Must have seen some hair like that in your time, eh?'

Barney nods, wondering what to say. As out of his depth as he used to be talking about football.

'Aye,' he says. 'Ah've seen some amount o' shite come out o' hair, right enough. Oh, shit, sorry, Ah didnae mean to swear. Ach, bugger, Ah did it again. Ach . . .'

'No problem, Jacob, I know where you're coming from. It isn't easy coming here. I've got the same problems myself. You think the Abbot wants to hear his monks quoting Milton? Uh-uh, not a chance. It's swearing in its own way, too. You've just got to try to come to terms with the new way of life. But don't sweat it, my friend, we've all been there. I shall sleep, and move with the moving ships, Change as the winds change, veer in the tide. That's what I always say.'

'Aye, very good,' says Barney. 'Ah'll dae that 'n all, then.' Is not quite sure to what Brother Steven is alluding. Wonders if the abbey possesses any ships. Decides to get the conversation back on his own terms.

'It's funny whit ye were sayin' about findin' things in people's hair, ye know. Pestilence, that kind of thing. 'Cause ye find the strangest things sometimes, ye widnae credit it.'

Brother Steven attempts to look round without turning his head and endangering his life.

'Oh, aye, sounds good, Jacob. What kinds of things are we talking about here? Treasure? Some weird-limbed bug, which nevertheless is from the same primordial gloop as ourselves? Or a strange pink fungus, maybe, like a bad special effect on *Star Trek*? All that stuff must be pretty cool.'

Barney snips quietly away at the back of Brother Steven's head. Hasn't found anything like that in anyone's hair. In fact, when he thinks about it, the

87

strangest discovery he can remember making was the end of a cotton bud, left over from a fearsome ear excavation. He decides maybe he should keep it all to himself.

'Aye, well, ye know. Stuff like that. Aye.' He lapses into silence. Considers that sometimes silence is best. Brother Steven is a talker, however.

'So, you know what you're doing with all the hair clippings, Jacob?'

Barney doesn't. Shrugs.

'Puttin' them out, Ah suppose.'

Steven shakes his head; Barney narrowly avoids penetrating deep into the flesh of his neck with the icy steel of the scissors. 'Barber Accidentally Murders New Best Friend – God Unimpressed,' thinks Barney. He knows that any headline he sees himself in will not be anything like as overwrought as the one or two he saw from the real press before he dropped out of life. 'Barber Surgeon Ate My Cat, Claims Housewife'; 'Killer Barber on Run, Eats Human Flesh'; 'Depraved Sex Secrets of Barber-Pervert.'

'Oh, aye,' says Barney. 'Whit is it Ah dae wi' them, then?'

'This is a poor place, Brother, as you'll have seen. We have to use everything we can get our hands on. There's very little that's not recycled. The hair that's cut from our heads will go into the making of pillows and cushions, you know. The whole comfort bag. It's that "what goes around comes around" kind of thing. I know some of them think it's a bit out there, but I like it. I mean, the traditionalists, Brother Herman and all that lot, well, they're peeing in their cloaks about it. You can't worship God without suffering, all that kind of rubbish. But, you know, I always think that God must enjoy his little comforts too. There's got to be some nights when the Big

Man just kicks off his Air Jordans, sticks the feet on a stool, downs a couple of cold ones, switches on the TV and gets a few angel babes to snuggle up to his beard. What do you think?'

Barney continues snipping quietly at the back of Brother Steven's neck. This just isn't the same as discussing theology with his friend Bill Taylor over a couple of pints in the pub.

'Ye mean, that's the kind of thing that goes on here?'

Brother Steven smiles. 'You're kidding me, Barney? Of course not. We're talking about pillows here, not fifty channels of satellite TV and a six-pack of Bud Lite. But the Abbot knows how to do it. Just the odd bit of comfort here and there to keep the natives happy. That's all it takes. 'Course, there's a lot more he could do, but you can't go too far, can you? We're monks after all.'

'Aye, fair enough.'

'But then, of course, there's the yin-yang business. The whole enigma of good-bad, dark-light, positive-negative, all of that. The Abbot allows us the comfort of pillows and cushions, but at the same time you've got to keep the product of your hirsutery so Brother Herman can use it for making hairshirts. Equal and opposites, that whole bag. Pain-pleasure, you know.'

'Hairshirts?'

Barney stops; the scissors hover over Brother Steven's head.

'Hairshirts. It's a medieval thing, yet still relevant in today's monastery. It's what your modern penitent monk likes to wear.'

'Aye, right,' says Barney. He is totally lost.

'You know, when you've committed a sin. You get a shirt made so that all the hairs are prickly on the inside. Really jaggedy-arsed. It's a pain in the backside. Brother

Herman loves the damn things. Well, he loves getting the other monks into them the minute he has an opportunity. Just wait till you see him with the scent of blood in that long, thin nose of his. So, on how bad the sin depends how long you get to wear the shirt. Do your penance.'

Barney's eyes are opened. He has never heard of the hairshirt before. Might think it's a good idea, except that if the Abbot finds out about his past he's going to have to wear his hairshirt for the next three or four centuries.

'So who makes them?' he asks, getting his mind off his own guilt, to which it has begun to stray.

'Brother Herman himself. Mad as they come, that's what I think. Wouldn't be surprised to find he sticks razor blades in there sometimes.'

'You're jokin'? You ever had to wear one?'

Brother Steven smiles. 'My friend, he makes them specifically so they'll fit me. I'm his best customer.'

'Oh.'

Barney snips away, doing a fine job around the back of the neck. Distracted, yet nevertheless performing with consummate ease and control. Brother Steven's neck has never been in safer hands. But Barney can already feel the hairshirt around him. Not the worst punishment on the planet surely, but if it was to be worn day after day for a long time – and his sins most definitely merit a long time – then it would indeed be hell. Begins to wonder if he should leave before Brother Herman gets the chance to indict him for something.

'Well, you know, I can live with it. Learned to. Anyway, he hasn't got me for a couple of months. Not since he caught me taking a quick suck on a smoke out in the forest one day. I swear he's got cameras out there. Watching.'

Barney stands back. The scissor work is finished; now

for the more delicate razor operations. His hand is steady. Thinks, Concentrate.

'That's it, Jacob. He's got to have cameras out there. I'd bet on it.' He smiles and relaxes. Doesn't care if Brother Herman does have cameras out in the forest. 'If they hadn't closed down my operation, that is.'

Much Later ...

The forest is still. Late evening, darkness long since descended. A clear sky, no moon, so that the number of stars is beyond counting. A panorama of brilliant white dots against the fathomless black background. The air is freezing, the night bright with the stars and the snow. Nothing stirs; the forest sleeps.

And in among the white farrago of Christmas trees, beside a burn where a slender stream of water trickles through the ice, sits Brother Morgan. Back resting uncomfortably against a young Douglas fir, hands and face blue with the cold, lips purple, yet a smile on those lips and in the eyes. At peace with the Lord. The front of the thin white tunic in which he is clothed is soaked through with blood, which has dried to a dark red, now frosted white.

And inserted deep into Brother Morgan's neck, the instrument of his death – a pair of scissors. Long, thin, cold steel; scissors which, a few hours earlier, had been used to cut the hair of Brother Steven after the fashion of Mike McShane in *Robin Hood, Prince of Thieves*.

Chapter 9

Where Are You, Barney Thomson, Barney Thomson?

A few phone calls made; breakfast eaten; the day ahead planned out. They set off. No conversation over their food, no conversation in the car. They pick up Sheep Dip, insert him into the back, and head off across the Kessock bridge for the Black Isle and then Dingwall. Endless hours down labyrinthine country roads in search of elusive bed and breakfasts. Knowing there's little chance of success; an awkwardness in the car, born of discomfort and attraction, the strange intruder in the back, and a knowledge that they might well be wasting their time.

Phone calls for Mulholland the night before. One to Chief Superintendent McMenemy. Nothing to report, and duly he'd had his verbal punishment. What was he supposed to have achieved after one day? More than he had achieved, and that was all he was to know. The country expects. Felt the whiplash of his tongue down the line; felt two feet tall.

Three calls to Melanie; three messages left on their answerphone. Had begun to assume that she had already gone to Devon when she phoned their guest house late at night. Had heard on the police grapevine that he was up north with Detective Sergeant Proudfoot. Knows Proudfoot from station nights out. Jealous. Thinks Proudfoot is more attractive than she herself, and isn't wrong.

So it became a fifty-minute phone call which was even more uncomfortable than talking to the Chief Super. On the defensive right from the off. No one up front, eight at the back, and only a couple of guys in the midfield, hopelessly trying to wrest control of the game. No chance.

Came off the phone unsure if he'd ever speak to her again; unsure if he ever wanted to speak to her again. Confused as always. He doesn't want to think about it; can't help it.

Proudfoot. Unhappy. In her work, in her personal life. Nothing to be done about it. The ever-present fear of the unknown; except now she can put a name to that fear. Barney Thomson. Not for her to know that Barney Thomson is a harmless unfortunate. A man for whom bad luck is as much a way of life as bad judgement. Sees him dressing in human skin and stalking his prey; might never know him for the man that he is. Fluffy.

What could she do other than police work? That's what she thinks as she sits silently in the car. What does the police train you for other than for the police? Security guard? Not a chance. Minder to someone with more money than humility? A mega-celeb perhaps? Trailing around the world in private jets and limousines; getting sucked into all-night sex with Hollywood stars; having Brad Pitt cover you in chocolate sauce then lick it off; meeting presidents and attending premières; going to the States and getting to shoot lunatics with impunity. She could do that, but wonders how you find out about such jobs. Never heard of anyone from Partick getting one. It would be all down to luck, and that is something which she never gets. Except now she's getting to drive around with Joel Mulholland for a few days; stay in the same place every night. Away from his wife, and from the station. Another world. Wonders if something might happen, but there's no way she's making a move. So she doesn't much think about it. Not seventeen any more; no point in being foolish. And now he's got competition, of course, so she might as well make the most of it. Maybe she is seventeen after all.

Sheep Dip stares at the cold, snow-covered hills as they go by and wonders.

They pass from village to village to town. Stop at every B&B, every hotel, every guest house. Blank looks; no one with anything to tell. A flicker of recognition every now and again, but only because of the television. Nothing to be gained. The snow flurries on and off, the hills come and go in the low cloud. Hardly a word is spoken between them. The tension ebbs and flows, wanes and grows. Comments are made, replies given or not. Both unhappy, Sheep Dip oblivious.

Early afternoon, two things happen. Lunch has passed with a hurried sandwich, without a word. Two things; they start speaking, and they encounter someone who has met Barney Thomson. Approaching Tain, heading up the east coast; Proudfoot tires of the atmosphere.

'Not saying much today,' she says. 'You all right?'

He glances at her to check that she's talking to him; not for too long. The weather is gradually deteriorating as they go; he needs to concentrate on the road. He lets out a long sigh. He needs to talk, and would but for the inhibiting presence behind.

'Hacked off, Sergeant, that's all. You look pretty much the same.'

A quiet laugh escapes her. Mulholland feels it at the back of his throat.

'I suppose,' she says.

'Right, then,' he says. 'You first.'

She glances over, but he is not looking at her. The snow falls; headlights glare towards them.

She takes her time. How much do you tell your boss, even if he's only temporarily your boss? Can't go saying the works, but knows what she's like. Once she gets going.

'Barney Thomson?' Mulholland volunteers on her behalf.

Shrugs her shoulders. Doesn't know.

'Maybe. Can't get rid of the image of him wielding a meat cleaver and salivating. Haven't woken up in the middle of the night in a cold sweat, or anything like that, but I expect it'll come to that. It's weird, though. You just can't see it in the pictures. God knows what he's like, but from the photos he just looks like some middle-aged sad bastard.'

'Aye, I know. John Thaw without the effervescent personality.'

Sheep Dip smiles in the back. A man with his own opinions on Barney Thomson, but he decides to keep them to himself. Let the Lowlanders get on with it.

'Aye. Something like that,' she says. Lets go. 'Anyway, it's not just that, 'cause let's face it, we're not going to find him. If the guy's got any sense whatsoever, he'll have disappeared off the face of the earth, and no matter how many hotels we show up at, he isn't going to have stayed at any of them.'

'Unless he's a total idiot.'

'Suppose. I've still got him down as a mad, calculating bastard, though.'

95

'Maybe. But then again. You always fear the unknown, but maybe he's running 'cause he's scared. Maybe he didn't mean to kill those two he worked with. Maybe he had nothing to do with his mother's homicidal rampage, just had to clean up after her. Maybe it was the mother who killed his two as well. Impossible to say. He might just be a sad wee bloke who's made a hell of a lot of bad judgement calls. The entire country's quaking in their boots about him, but it could be he's quaking in his boots about everyone else.'

She considers this. Feels a cold quiver, despite the warmth of the car.

'Then again,' says Mulholland, continuing, 'maybe he's a weirdo psycho headcase. Sleeps with a chainsaw under his pillow. Eats babies. Wears a human finger pendant. Who knows? Hopefully we'll find out, but we might just end up being on holiday for a few days.'

'Now there's something I really need, but not in the sodding Arctic. We'll be seeing penguins at this rate.'

'You don't get penguins in the Arctic,' volunteers Sheep Dip from the back.

'Whatever.'

'It's not just Barney Thomson, then?'

What the hell, she thinks. Might as well out with it. What difference does it make anyway?

'No. I've just had enough at the moment. Too much paperwork, too much crap. Don't even enjoy the good stuff. Don't even get a buzz from sticking the light on the top of the car and dashing home just so I can get my fish supper back before it gets cold.'

He laughs; says, 'Never done that. Did put it on a couple of times because I was dying to go to the toilet, mind.'

Sheep Dip raises an eyebrow, but having several times

a few years past used his blue light to facilitate relationships with three women at once, he is not going to be judgemental.

'Done that as well,' she says, 'but nothing does it for me any more. Interviewing, catching people out, investigating, all the good stuff. Just don't care, you know. So when the good stuff doesn't matter, you know the bad stuff, which is most of the sodding job, is going to be a total arse.'

He nods, keeps staring ahead into the driving snow. He could probably be having this conversation with most of the people on the force. They all faced it at some time, if not all the time, and they mostly carried on because there was sod all else they could do.

'Difficult tae get out, though, isn't it?' says Sheep Dip. 'I don't know what it's like down where you are, but there's nothing up here. A bit o' farming, the holiday trade during the summer, then there's the low-budget porn flics they're making these days in Scrabster and Wick, but that's about it.'

'Right,' says Proudfoot, turning a little to include him in the conversation. Mulholland's teeth grind. 'What else is there? Go and be some night guard at a factory, where sooner or later you're going to get a brick in the back of the napper and spend the rest of your life in a home getting Brussels sprouts spooned into your gob by a fifty-year-old spinster with a beard. No thanks.'

'You could do one of those personal bodyguard things,' says Mulholland, trying to reclaim the conversation for himself. Feels ridiculously in competition.

'And have Brad Pitt smother me in chocolate?'

He takes his eyes momentarily off the road. Looks at her. Turns back before he smashes into an advancing tractor.

'That wasn't quite what I was thinking.'

'Oh. Anyway, I doubt it. Don't see myself trailing after some pompous prick who think he's so important he needs personal protection.'

'Fair point.'

The signpost heralding Tain whistles past in the snow, and they turn off the main road and down into the village. Another drive through small-town northern Scotland in search of places to stay.

'Your turn,' says Proudfoot. 'What's getting at you?'

Mulholland doesn't answer. Doesn't want to talk about Melanie. Doesn't, now that it comes to it, want to talk about anything. And certainly not with the inhibiting presence in the back. Retreating inside his shell.

'Later,' he says, as they approach the first B&B, Vacancy-sign swinging in the snow outside.

Blatant retreat, thinks Proudfoot. Wonders about him and how close she'll get. Switches off; readies herself for the tedium of another pointless interrogation.

He parks the car outside the house, leads the way up the garden path. Bitter cold, hands like ice; Proudfoot, jacket pulled tight around her, follows. Head bowed. Sheep Dip traipses behind. Mulholland rings the bell; they stand and shiver. Think that there should be constables out on this kind of duty.

An enormous wait in the snow and cold. An eternity. Feels like they're freezing to death where they stand. They're about to abort when the door creaks open and an old woman appears. Wrinkled face; extravagant hair, savage and feral, which has seen battle with many a pink rinse.

'Chief Inspector Mulholland, Sergeant Proudfoot, Sergeant Dip,' says Mulholland, presenting his card. Proudfoot smiles; Sheep Dip doesn't mind.

The woman looks them up and down, hands folded across her chest, keeping her cardigan close around her.

'The police?' she says. Soft Highland accent, belying wild exterior.

'Aye,' says Mulholland. 'The police. I won't keep you long.' Produces the photo of Barney Thomson, holds it out. 'Do you recognise this man, Mrs . . .?'

'McDonald, Nellie McDonald, that's me. And aye, I do recognise him. It's that Barney Thomson character they're aye on about in the papers.'

'Aye, that's right.' Keeps the photo held out where she can see it. Proudfoot shivers, stares at the snow on the ground. 'He's known to have visited this area in the past couple of weeks. Now, there's no need to be alarmed, but is there any possibility that he might have stayed here with you? Maybe worn some kind of disguise and used a false name, or anyth . . .'

'Oh aye, he was here. Stayed for a couple of nights, you know. A week or two back.'

Mulholland does not immediately reply. He stares. The snow falls, although he does not feel it.

'Excuse me?' he says.

She tuts loudly, looking behind them at the snow.

'It's right cold tae be standing out in the snow, is it no'? Why don't you come inside? You must be frozen.'

'Thanks,' says Mulholland, and they follow the landlady as she retreats into the warmth of her house. Huge bum waddles down the hall. Sheep Dip closes the door behind him, and they walk into the front room. A small fire burns in the hearth; lamps are on giving the room a warm glow. Two tables are already set for the following day's breakfast. No television; a silent record player loiters by the window.

'Sit yourselves down,' she says. 'Now, you'll be wanting a cup of tea?'

99

'Och, aye, that'll be brilliant,' says Sheep Dip.

'No, really,' says Mulholland, giving him a sideways glance, 'if we could just ask you some questions.'

'Ach, for goodness' sake, you look frozen. Ah'll just get you a wee cuppy, and some biscuits. I'll no' be a minute.'

'That'll be lovely, thank you, Mrs McDonald,' says Proudfoot.

'Aye, you take care of that man of yours, lassie – he looks like he could do with a bit of fattening up.'

Mrs McDonald bustles from the room.

'Bloody hell,' says Mulholland, voice lowered, once she's gone. 'We could be about to have our first contact with the ghost of Barney Thomson, and you two eejits encourage her to mince off and start making tea.'

'She'll tell us anyway, and even if he was here, it's not as if he's still lurking in the basement. And besides, you need fattening up,' says Proudfoot.

'Piss off, Sergeant.'

The fire crackles, coals snap. Mulholland gets up and stands in front of it, looking down into the flames. Proudfoot stares at the floor, glances up at him occasionally. Tries not to let him catch her looking, but he doesn't turn. Lost in the flames. Sheep Dip wonders if it'll be Tetley, Nambarrie, or some less popular brand.

'Right, then, you three, here you go.'

Nellie McDonald charges into the room, places an overladen tray onto the coffee table. Besides the pot of tea and three cups, milk and sugar, there is a whole chocolate cake, three slices of some other lemony-looking cake, four slices of buttered fruitcake, a box of mince pies, a round of crumpets with strawberry jam, a couple of scones, some toast, six chocolate biscuits, a packet of ginger creams, ten pieces of shortbread, fourteen Jaffa

Cakes, sixty or seventy digestives, and at least eight hundred butter creams.

'Now then, here's a wee something for you to be getting on with until you can get your dinner. I expect you've been having a long day.'

'Can we talk about Barney Thomson, Mrs McDonald?' says Mulholland.

'Now there'll be plenty of time for that. You just have a couple of pieces of cake and a nice cup of tea. Do you take milk or sugar?'

'Milk, no sugar, thanks,' he says. Proudfoot smiles.

'And what about you, lassie?'

'Milk, two sugars, please,' she says.

'That's grand. Now you help yourself to some cakes as well, 'cause you're looking a bit thin around the jowls.'

'Yes, ma'am.'

'And you, laddie?'

Sheep Dip leans forward. 'A wee bitty milk and seven sugars,' he says.

Nellie McDonald smiles, says, 'A man after my own heart.'

They move over to the table, start helping themselves to food from the platter. Feel like children at their gran's house on a Sunday afternoon. Expect to get offered sweets when they've finished. And fifty pence for being good.

'You said that Barney Thomson stayed here, Mrs McDonald,' says Mulholland eventually; piece of chocolate cake stuck to the side of his face. Proudfoot does her best not to laugh.

'Och, aye, he did,' she says. 'A couple of weeks ago, or so, you know. Only for two nights.'

'Were you not aware at the time of the crimes of which this man has been accused?'

101

'Ach, I didnae believe any of that rubbish. He seemed like a lovely chap. Very quiet. No trouble at all. Paid in cash. I'd have him back any time.'

Mulholland and Proudfoot exchange looks. Serious business, but Proudfoot is having trouble not bursting into a fit of giggles.

'But there's a nationwide manhunt for this man at the moment. You didn't think of reporting his presence here to the police?'

'Ach, I didnae want tae be bothering anyone wi' this. And I'm not sure he's guilty anyway, you know. Are you sure you've got the right man? He was a lovely lad. Paid his bill in cash, you know.'

'That may be the case, Mrs McDonald, but really, you ought to have reported his presence here to the local police.'

She smiles back at him. Nothing to say. You don't go reporting your guests to the police. Against the B&B code.

'Can you tell us anything about him?' he says to her. Lets the sigh escape.

'You'll be having another piece of cake, lassie,' she says to Proudfoot. 'You'll no' get by on that little you've eaten there.'

'Certainly,' says Proudfoot. Smile on her face. Moves forward and swipes a piece of chocolate cake and a biscuit.

'Mrs McDonald?' says Mulholland.

'All right, all right,' she says. 'I suppose there was something a wee bitty strange about him.'

'And what was that?'

'Well, it was most unusual. On the first morning he wanted a full fried breakfast, but here, if it wasn't just the thing, he only wanted a boiled egg on his second morning. Very strange. And no cornflakes either.'

The sound of Proudfoot trying to stop herself laughing draws a look from Mulholland. He charges on.

'Apart from that? What can you tell us about his stay here?'

'Och, well, not a lot, you know. I didn't realise who he was at first, 'cause the laddie gave a false name.'

'Oh aye? What was that?'

'Barnabus Thompson, he said his name was. That was Thompson with a "p". So I was a wee bitty confused, you know, even though I thought I recognised him. But I worked it out. When was it? Maybe on the second day I realised that he'd just stuck that "p" in there to confuse me. I'm no' as stupid as I look.'

'Right. Anything else? What was he wearing? Did he look like he does in the photograph? When did he leave? Where did he say he was going? Anything like that?'

'Help m'boab, what a lot o' questions. Will you no' be havin' another wee bitty o' cake, dear? You're lookin' awfy thin.'

'No, really, Mrs McDonald. Could you just answer my questions please.'

'You'll no' hang on tae your woman here if you dinnae eat properly. Is that no' right, lassie?'

Proudfoot nods. Mouth full of cake. Trying not to laugh and spit it out over the floor.

'Right, I suppose you'll be wanting your questions answering, then. The laddie got here late one night. A Tuesday I think, but I'm no' sure. Said he'd got the bus up from Inverness. Wanted a room for a couple of days, you know. Paid up for two nights right at the start. I mean, I told him no' to bother, but he insisted. Very courteous. I thought I recognised him fi' the news that night, you know, but I wisnae sure. What wi' his name being different and a' that, you know. I mean, I said to Margaret in the grocer's the following morning about him, and she said aye, right enough, he might well be up here. Anyway, I think he went out briefly the day after he arrived and bought himself some clothes. I'm no' daft, you know. It was then I realised that he was on the run, you know. It's no' as if a'body comes to Tain to buy their clothes, you know. He got a couple o' nice shirts and some underwear. But he was just wearing the same jacket. You know, the one they described on the news.'

'So, why didn't you phone the police when you realised who it was?'

'Ach, well, he seemed like an awfy nice laddie. Judge not, that ye be not judged. You know what they say. Who am I to say this man is guilty o' murder?'

'No one is asking that. He hasn't been convicted yet. It'll be up to the court to decide if he's guilty.'

'Ach, away, you cannae persuade me o' that. The puir laddie's already been convicted by the press. O judgement! thou art fled to brutish beasts, and men have lost their reason.'

Mulholland stares at her; looks at Proudfoot. Proudfoot shrugs. Still smiling. Sheep Dip demolishes cake.

'And when did he leave, Mrs McDonald?'

'Oh, let me think now.' Purses her lips, stares at the carpet. 'About ten in the morning, two days after he arrived. And as I said, he didn't even have a full breakfast inside him, the daft laddie. Don't know what was the matter with him.'

'And did he say where he was going?'

'Oh, now let me see. We got talking, but you know how it is. My memory's no' the best.' You can remember what he sodding had for breakfast, thinks Mulholland. 'Here now, I think he said something about going some-

104

where where no one would ever have heard of him. When I think about it now, there might have been a wee bitty something in the paper that morning which upset him, you know. Here, you don't think that was why he didnae have his full breakfast, do you?'

Mulholland stares at her. You just don't get people like this in Glasgow. When people are obstructive in Glasgow they do it intentionally, and enjoy every minute of it. Ignores the question.

'That was all? Nothing about a specific destination?'

'No, no, I don't think so. He went away and got the bus, you know, and that was that. Have seen not hide nor tail o' him since. Now, you'll be wanting another cuppy o' tea.'

'No, really, thanks, Mrs McDonald, but I've another couple of questions, then we ought to be going.'

'Ach, don't be silly. You're not going anywhere until you've cleared the tray. Now you three just sit there while I make a fresh potty. I might even join you myself in having a wee cuppy. And you, you big lummox, you're no' saying much for yerself. Cat got your tongue?'

Sheep Dip smiles, but doesn't reply. A mouth full of cake. Enjoying every minute.

Receiving no answer, Mrs McDonald disappears from the room, clutching the enormous teapot in her right hand. Proudfoot and Mulholland stare at each other. Proudfoot on the point of laughter. Mulholland raises his finger.

'Don't, Sergeant. Don't even think about it. Bloody woman.'

Proudfoot smiles, says, 'Maybe she'd have taken you more seriously if you hadn't had that big bit of chocolate cake attached to your cheek.'

She glances at Sheep Dip. Eyes say it all, and maybe a little more. Mulholland runs his hand across his face and once again feels five years old.

Chapter 10

Blank Looks from a One-Eyed Pig

Barney sits and waits. Like a prisoner before the execution. The deed is done, the verdict given, the firing squad stand outside, cleaning gun barrels, checking rifle sights, chatting idly about last night's Premiership action. All in a day's work for them; the final act for Barney. Can feel the bullets zinging into him, can feel his body rock with the shock. Seen it in the movies. His chest riddled with gunshots. And what if he doesn't die? That's what he keeps thinking. What if he doesn't die? If the seven or eight bullet wounds aren't enough. Can see himself falling to the ground, can feel the pain. Presumes bullet wounds hurt; has never had one. Was told about it once by a customer in the shop; but he couldn't have been more than mid-twenties, and he'd said he'd picked up his injuries in Vietnam. Wullie had said the guy had probably been listening to too many Springsteen songs, and if Barney had known about whom he was talking, he would have agreed.

Barney's mind rambles all over the place. His crimes of the past; bad haircuts he has known; lives he has ruined, either by inadvertent murder or by giving one of his infamous *Poseidon Adventure* cut-and-blow-dries; the life he has left behind, the life he has come to; the milk-soaking-up time of cornflakes as opposed to Frosties.

But most of all, Barney wonders what he is doing there. Sitting in a cold, damp corridor, waiting to be seen by the Abbot, or Brother Herman. Or both. He has not the faintest idea what he has done to warrant the attention. Presumes it is because he's given the Abbot a bad haircut; though he'd thought at the time that, as Brother Cadfaels go, it'd been all right.

Trouble is, you just never can tell. How many times in the past has he given a haircut of which only kings can dream and the gods deliver, only to be rebuked by some ignorant cretin with no eye for a cut of wondrous beauty and construction. Like his famous Billy Connolly '81, which he had given to a young chap, on request, a few years previously; a haircut from God's own factory, a haircut from Satan's nightmares, a haircut of erudition and infinite jest; yet a haircut which was scorned by the customer, resulting in no tip and a near bar-room brawl when they'd bumped into each other in the pub three days later. Some people just do not appreciate talent.

Barney is an artist, and like all of his kind, misunderstood in his lifetime.

He cannot imagine that the Abbot is such a man; he'd seemed happy enough after the cut. Perhaps, Barney ponders, he has a secret mirror somewhere, and checked the cut after it was given. Barney's imagination races. Maybe the Abbot has a lot more than a hidden mirror. Suddenly sees the Abbot inside his secret hideout, a massive operations cell underneath the monastery. Something from a Bond film – huge maps on the walls with lights displaying the locations of all the Abbot's nuclear warheads. Sees the Abbot sitting in a large white leather chair, stroking a cat. SPECTRE: Special Executive for Corruption, Terrorism, Revenge and Ecumenicalism. A worldwide network of monasteries, ostensibly there to lead a Christian life straight out of the Dark Ages, but in actuality a front for an organisation of religious terrorism.

Barney begins to wonder what world events, seemingly innocent, have in fact been the work of these heinous men. What earthquakes and volcano eruptions and fires and plane crashes have been caused by this fevered band of zealots. He wonders if beneath the monastery there is a tropical pool of piranha fish, kept starving for weeks, waiting for food; waiting for Barney, and all because he gave the Abbot a bad haircut.

Barney clenches his fists, palms sweaty; closes his eyes, swallows. He is aware of the faint rumour of his heart, becoming stronger. After all he has been through, is this to be the end?

With a violent click of ominous quiet, the door to the Abbot's study opens. Barney swallows; Brother Herman summons him into the Demon's Lair.

✄

The Monks sleep two to a room, so under normal circumstances, when Brother Morgan had not returned to his room by eight o'clock in the evening, it would have been noticed. However, since the death of Brother Saturday, Morgan has had the luxury of a room to himself; a luxury he could not enjoy for long.

Morgan's agitation over dinner had not gone unnoticed. Conversation, while not encouraged, was still commonplace, and those attempting to speak to the librarian's apprentice were greeted with edginess or no reply whatsoever. The food was left untouched on his plate; when supper was over, Morgan left quickly before any of the others. They assumed that he had gone to the privacy of his own room, to commune with God over whatever it was that ailed his spirits. It occurred to some that what troubled Brother Morgan was fear; fear that the dark forces which had seen the end of Brother Saturday's life would also be the end of his. However, he had seemed so phlegmatic in the immediate aftermath of that awful crime; perhaps he was facing some other terror. One or two of the monks determined that they would try to get to the bottom of it, should Brother Morgan still be in such a frame of mind the following morning. Not to know that that would be much too late.

When he didn't appear for breakfast, they knew. They all instinctively knew. Brother Morgan was dead, and by the same hand as that which killed Brother Saturday. And so they went out, the monks, into the forest in twos and threes to look for the body; and it was found, and Brother Herman was called, and the monks went about their business as if nothing had happened. Except that they now all had fear in their hearts. No longer could they think that Saturday had been killed as the result of some lovers' argument. There was more to it than that, and none of them knew upon whose shoulder the black hand of murder would next rest.

✄

Barney sits before the Abbot; Brother Herman stands at the Abbot's shoulder, the hired hand. The Abbot looks troubled.

'You know why you are here, Brother Jacob?' asks the Abbot.

Barney swallows. Eyes shift between Abbot and bodyguard. His heart has kicked into low gear for rapid acceleration; feels like it is about to come crashing out

109

through his chest to throb on the desk in front of him. Wonders if the Abbot has a switch under his desk; a trap-door. One press, an instant, and Barney would be food for the fishes. Shark breakfast. Raw Barney; plenty of meat on him. The sharks will love it. All because of a bad haircut. It had been bound to happen one day.

'Aye, Brother Blofeld, Ah dae,' he says. Mouth dry.

'Blofeld?' the Abbot squints, as if looking directly into the sun.

'Abbot, sorry. Brother Abbot,' says Barney. Tries to get his concentration under control. His imagination is leaping so far ahead of him it is in a different time zone; a different dimension, slightly out of sync with his own. 'It's about your haircut. Ah'm sorry. Really. Ah did the best Ah could. Honestly, Ah thought Ah'd done a good job. Ask any o' the others, they'll tell ye. Ah'm sure they're a' happy wi' the cuts they got. Maybe Ah could dae ye a Sean Connery or an F. Murray Abraham. You'd suit one o' them, nae doubt. Whit dae yese think? Eh?'

The Abbot shakes his head; recognises Barney's babbling for what it is. Normally he would have smiled, but today is not for smiling. He has lost another of his monks; there is nothing about which to smile. He raises his hand. His left hand.

'Brother, dear Brother. The haircut was fine. I couldn't be happier about the cut. In fact, the whole monastery is talking about the great breadth of your God-given talent. You are a barber apart. A hirsutologist of the highest order. The wings of angels must flutter in your presence when you take to the scissors. If only Eve could have resisted eating apples like you cut hair, then there would be a lot less misery in the world.'

Barney relaxes. Almost smiles. Wings of angels, eh? he thinks. That's me, no mistake. Nice to be appreciated.

Brother Herman frowns. A haircut is a haircut is a haircut. Doesn't know what all the fuss is about. Thinks that all the junior monks should have their heads shaved and be forced to wear a crown of thorns. A jaggedy-arsed crown of thorns at that, just in case there's such a thing as a crown of thorns which isn't jaggedy-arsed. Is about to contemplate whether it's possible for a crown of thorns not to be jaggedy-arsed, but decides he'd be better off scrutinising the reaction of Brother Jacob to the information he is just about to be given. Knows that the Abbot's approach will be too soft.

'And talking of scissors, Brother Jacob, it is scissors which have led me to bring you here today. The very scissors, I believe, with which you showed your mastery of hirsutery yesterday afternoon.'

Christ! thinks Brother Herman. Would you stop going on about how good a sodding barber he is! Reproaches himself immediately for taking the Lord's name in vain.

'You will be aware that Brother Morgan was missing from breakfast this morning, and that the search for our dear Brother was called off after no more than twenty minutes.'

Barney nods. Brother Morgan. Thinks, Bugger. About to be accused of murder! Of course that's what it will be. And he's known it all along. He never truly believed that he would be roasted for giving a bad haircut; that had merely been an exercise in denial. When the search for Morgan had been called off so quickly, it was obvious something had happened to him.

'The minute they called it off,' Brother Steven had said, 'and Morgan hadn't hoved into view with a couple of Uberbabes under his arms, reeking of weed and breathing alcohol fumes all over the Abbot as he told him what he could do with his monastery, it was obvious the guy had been stiffed.'

'I'm afraid our dear brother was found dead.' Barney nods. Naturally. 'And it further ails me to tell you that he had been murdered.' Barney continues to nod. Almost goes without saying. Did anyone die without being murdered any more? Still hasn't spotted the connection with the mention of scissors. 'And it pains me greatly to tell you that Brother Morgan was stabbed. Stabbed with a pair of scissors.' Barney nods again. The penny still refuses to drop. Considers that scissors are indeed a good instrument of death, having used them himself; even if he hadn't meant to at the time. 'The scissors with which you cut the hair of six monks yesterday afternoon.' Barney nods. Haircutting scissors. Long, thin, sharp. Excellent for the job. Kill someone every time.

The penny drops. So does Barney's chin. Suddenly words are rushing to get out of his mouth, like troops over the top of a World War I trench. To the same effect.

'Ah didnae dae it. Yese don't think Ah'd dae somethin' like that, dae ye? Why wid Ah want tae kill Brother Morgan? Ah hudnae even spoken tae the guy. In fact, Brother Morgan? Morgan, yese say? Ah thought the librarian's name wis Florgan. Brother Florgan, Ah thought. Ye see? That's how much Ah couldnae huv killed the guy. Ah didnae even know whit his name wis. See? See? Ah couldnae have done it. Brother Florgan, Ah thought it wis. Or maybe even Gorgan or Jorgan. But certainly no' Morgan. Brother Morgan? Is that whit his name wis? Shocker, who'd have thought it, eh? Brother Morgan. Never heard o' him.'

The Abbot lifts his hand once more; indeed, has had his hand raised almost since Barney started talking.

'Jacob, Jacob. Be still your tongue. No one is here to accuse you of killing Brother Morgan.' There is an

112

almost imperceptible twitch in Herman's eye. 'No one suspects you, dear friend. At least, no more than they suspect anyone else, for we must all be under suspicion at this grave time. It is the Lord who will be our judge.'

'Aye, aye,' says Barney. 'It'll be the Lord, right enough.' Thinks, as he says it, that if he is to be judged by the Lord, he's in serious trouble. He doesn't know who he would like to be judged by. Himself, maybe. Not sure if that's allowed.

'I have called you in so that Brother Herman can ask you certain questions about the scissors. When you last saw them, what you did with them when you were finished, and so on. Just because you were known to have had them last does not make you any more of a potential killer than the rest. Any one of us could have taken the scissors. Be not afraid, Brother. Answer Brother Herman's questions truthfully, and God will be on your side.'

God. Right. Good old God. You can always count on the Big Guy.

Barney shifts uncomfortably in his seat, nods at the Abbot; looks to Brother Herman. Herman speaks, his lips hardly moving. His voice the low, threatening monotone that Barney has grown to dread.

'Brother Jacob,' says Herman. Says the name Jacob as if it might be Judas. 'Can you tell us the names of all the monks to whom you administered barbery yesterday afternoon?'

An easy enough opening to the inquisition. Reminds him of his police questioning from the past. And that always developed into something much more sinister and difficult to negotiate.

'Well, there wis the Abbot. That was a Brother Cadfael, as yese know. Then there wis a Sean Connery

113

for Brother Brunswick.' From deep within the folds of his cloak, Brother Herman produces a notebook and begins to write down the names. Momentarily he throws Barney from his stride, but he takes up again after a glance from those sunken eyes. 'A Christian Slater for Brother Jerusalem, an F. Murray Abraham for Brother Martin, and a Ron Perlman for Brother Ezekial. Oh, aye, then Ah finished aff wi' a Mike McShane for Brother Steven. Have tae be honest, Ah wisnae sure whit a Mike McShane looked like, ye know, but he seemed ha . . .'

'Enough commentary, thank you, Brother,' says Herman. Barney quails before the voice. 'At what time did you finish cutting Brother Steven's hair?'

Barney stares at the floor; thinks. The questions seem easy enough, but you can never be sure. Having difficulty getting it into his head that this time he hasn't actually done anything wrong.

'Oh, aye, Ah'm nae sure, ye know. It wis definitely dark, mind, right enough. So, maybe about five, something like that.'

'Five,' says Herman in a low voice, writing it down. 'And what did you do with your equipment after that?'

Barney bites his lip. Wonders how guilty he is looking. Herman makes him nervous. Notices that the Abbot also bites his lip, wonders if Herman makes him nervous too. He wouldn't be surprised.

'Ye know, Ah just kind of left it there beside that wee sink, ye know. Ah thought it just stayed there, ye know, that wis whit Brother Adolphus says tae us.'

Herman scribbles something else in the notebook; Barney waits. Wonders what he can find to be writing about. *Scissors left beside sink*. Big deal. How long can it take to write that?

'And of the monks whose hair you cut yesterday afternoon, was there anything suspicious about any of them? Any of them take any undue interest in the scissors, or any other instrument at your disposal?'

Barney stares once more at the floor. Thinks hard. Did any of the brothers enquire about the scissors? Why should they have? Is about to dismiss the question when he remembers Brother Martin; the F. Murray Abraham. He'd mentioned it. He'd asked about the scissors. What was it he'd said? Something about them being extremely sharp. Can't remember exactly.

Looks up at Brother Herman. Martin's words come back to him as he lifts his head. *Sharp scissors, Brother*, he had said. *You could kill someone with them*. That was it. Damning words, but surely just a chance remark. There is no doubt in Barney's mind, however, that Martin would be damned by Brother Herman.

'Naw, naw, nothin'. Nothin' that Ah can think of, ye know.'

Herman notices the hesitation; the doubt. Files it away. Every little bit will be useful.

'Your last cut was Brother Steven?'

'Aye, aye, that's right.'

'And he was with you when you left?'

This is a dawdle, thinks Barney.

'Naw, naw, he'd already gone, ye know. Ah stayed behind just tae clear up. Make sure Ah kept a' the hair clippin's, ye know. For the hairshirts 'n a' that.'

'Hairshirts?' says the Abbot.

Brother Herman gives Barney a *Reservoir Dogs* look and Barney doesn't answer the Abbot.

'And what did you do once you'd finished clearing up, Brother Jacob?'

Barney has a good answer to this one; takes his time.

'Went and prayed, ye know. Tae God,' he adds as an

afterthought, just in case anyone was going to have any doubts.

Herman scribbles something else in his book. The Abbot seems distracted. His mind elsewhere. He finds it all disturbing. Would confide this to no one, but the murder of two of his monks has begun to make him question his faith. And if he has doubts, how many of his number will feel the same way?

Brother Herman scribbles on. Barney wonders what he's doing. Cannot imagine that he's given him so much to write about.

Finally Herman raises his eyes. 'Thank you, Brother. That will be all for the moment.'

'Oh. Right. Stoatir.' Barney feels relief wash over him, like a sponge soaked in honey.

'Stoatir, Brother Jacob?' says the Abbot. 'These are dark times for us, my brother. You would do well to spend much of it in prayer.'

Barney nods. 'Aye, of course, Your Grace. Brother, Ah mean. Aye.' Looks at Herman, is further reduced in size. Decides it is time he took his leave. Opens his mouth, but there is nothing else to say. Walks backwards slowly towards the door, then turns and is gone.

As he walks down the corridor, relief continuing to wash over him like a towel submerged in champagne, he wonders why it is that when he has nothing to fear and nothing about which to feel guilty, he still feels only one step ahead of the inquisition.

Chapter 11

Life, Death, and Socks

Once again, Brothers Steven and Jacob are on grave-digging detail; so soon after the first time. A hole for Brother Morgan; late, lamented. An afternoon's work, for the burial the following morning. Accompanied by Brother Edward; a telegraph-pole youth, face like white wine. Three to dig the hole – an arduous task in this frozen, crusted earth – two to fill it in again after the funeral. Barney thought that he might escape the work, now that he is the official monastery barber. His hands need protecting. Had been on the point of taking out an insurance policy on them before he'd had to disappear. Got the idea from something he'd read about Betty Grable. A million dollars on her legs. Or was it her ears? He doesn't actually know who Betty Grable was, anyway. Thought that maybe he'd escape the heavy work, now that they all realised what a precious commodity are his hands. Yet, no; no such good fortune. Realises he has a long apprenticeship to work before he will be offered the small gifts which pass for favours in this murderous place.

It is the same day as the body is discovered. Mid-afternoon. Brother Herman has examined the corpse, discovered everything he needs to know. Not much doubt over the cause of death, every other avenue examined, no intensive post-mortem required. A cold day. The clear blue skies have clouded over, replaced by low, grey cloud. But still bright. It'll snow again later, some of the monks are saying. Reckon that this might be a winter like the winter of '47. Snow around the abbey from November until June. That's the prediction.

The mere mention of June has had Barney thinking. Could he possibly still be here then? Still hiding? Might not the world have forgotten Barney Thomson in six months' time? Moved on to some other huge macabre story. What he needs is for some other serial killer to strike; preferably in Glasgow. Take the country's mind off him. Of course, the minute anyone else is killed in Scotland, until Barney is caught, the murder will be blamed on him. That is how it goes, on the tail of fevered press speculation.

Barney is not to know the headline in that morning's *Record*: 'Barber Surgeon in Sheep Slaughter Mystery; Farmers Outraged'. He is right, however, in thinking that every crime that has ever been committed is being placed at his doorstep. A robbery in Dundee; a rape in Arbroath; shoplifting in Paisley; an unsolved murder in Edinburgh from 1981; Bucks Fizz winning the Eurovision Song Contest in 1981; Don Masson's penalty miss against Peru in Argentina; the murder of Riccio. There isn't a crime against humanity that isn't being laid at his door by an hysterical press and public whose imagination is being whipped to a frothy cream. Barney Thomson is the ultimate demon figure, to such an extent that within two weeks the Barney Thomson of the newspapers is unrecog-

118

nisable from the Barney Thomson of reality. Only the police have maintained a sense of proportion, having a not unreasonable number of officers on the case, now headed by DCI Mulholland; while telling the press that they have every available man and woman in Scotland on it. And all the while, the monks are unaware of the evil within their midst. As yet, unaware.

The earth is hard; rock-like. Brothers Steven and Edward hack away with pick-axes, Barney shovels out the broken earth. A slow business, and although it is yet two hours until nightfall, they know that they will do well to have the hole dug by then. They are cold and hungry. Steven, accepting of his fate, cold and hungry; Edward, happy that he is doing penance for his perceived crimes of the past, cold and hungry; and Barney, miserable, fed up, shaking, wishing he had run off to the Caribbean, cold and hungry. Keeps letting out heavy sighs, waits for one of the others to take him up on the offer he is making to complain. He waits in vain. Feels like his ears are about to drop off. And his nose. 'Killer Revealed as Man with No Nose or Ears; Fingers Also Gone'. Barney shivers.

'It's a bit cold, in't it no'?' says Barney, to break the monotony. Needs to complain.

Brother Edward continues to swing the blunt pick-axe into the frozen ground. Enjoying the cold and hardship. Sometimes it pays to suffer. He doesn't care if Barney is cold.

Steven straightens up; looks at Barney, then surveys the surrounding countryside. Breathes deeply the cold air, feels it sting the inside of his nostrils. Smiles and looks back at Barney.

'Come on, Jacob. It makes you feel alive, man. Breathe it in. Enjoy it. Just think how you'd be feeling if

119

you were having to do work like this in some sweltering hot place, with the sweat dripping off you and bugs chewing at your face. Bend your back, get stuck in, my friend. This is life as it is. Look forward to dinner and a cup of the Lord's finest wine.'

Barney shakes his head. 'It's bloody freezin'. Ah doubt Ah'll survive tae huv ma dinner. Ah'm knackered, so Ah am.'

Steven smiles. White teeth show bright under grey cloud.

'All went lame; all blind; Drunk with fatigue; deaf even to the hoots of tired, outstripped Five-Nines that dropped behind. Tiredness, my friend. You haven't known it until you've known it in war. That's what they say.'

'Experience of that, huv ye?' says Barney.

Steven smiles again and once more bends his back.

''Fraid not, my friend. But Brother Frederick, he'll tell you all about it. He may be old, but there's not a shell or a rainfall or a bath of mud that he can't remember. You could learn a lot. As for me, the wars of the soul and the mind are the only ones I've fought. Though who knows? Perhaps they may be the bloodiest wars of all. What say ye, Edward?'

Brother Edward stares into the hole which is slowly taking shape beneath their swinging axes. Carries on working as he thinks about his answer. Has always considered the war with the opposite sex to be the bloodiest of all. Won a few battles there; now suffers the guilt of the victorious.

'Might that have been First World War poetry you were quoting there, Brother?' says Edward. Doesn't want to talk about his own private battles. Three years in God's house have not healed the scars.

'You recognised it?'

120

'Aye, aye, I did.'

First World War poetry? thinks Barney. What a load of keich. He wishes they could talk about football. Doesn't know the irony.

'There's something always bugged me about the First World War,' says Edward.

As they talk, they begin to swing their axes in time, one striking into the solid earth rhythmically after the other. Barney shovels.

'What was that, Brother?'

'Gas.'

'Gas?'

'The poison gas issue, I mean,' Edward says, unconsciously speaking in time with the striking of the axes. 'They say that when the Germans first started using gas, and before the Brits had been given masks, they used to pish into a sock and hold it over their mouths. Breathe through it, you know.'

Brother Steven has heard this. Strikes robotically, his pick-axe a dull scimitar of the Lord's will.

'What I want to know,' says Brother Edward, 'is this. Who was the first guy to do it? I mean, I'm sure the chemistry's all right, and all that.'

'Something to do with ammonia, probably,' says Steven.

'Aye, no doubt. Anything about pish is to do with ammonia. But here's the thing. Who was the guy who first thought of it? Who, when the gas came over and all the troops were running around bricking their pants, panicking and turning yellow, was the first guy to stand there like James Bond, be really cool, and say, "Don't know about you lot, but I'm pishing in my sock"?'

Steven strikes mightily into the ground; the earth yields to his strength.

'See what you mean. The guy must have been out there. On the edge. A visionary.'

'Exactly,' says Edward. His axe strikes mightily the earth. 'The guy was a visionary. So how come none of us have ever heard about him? I mean, there's all sorts of famous blokes from the First World War. Owen and Sassoon and all the rest of that lot; Haig; Kitchener; the Red Baron; Blackadder. So, how come this bloke's not famous? He must have saved thousands of lives.'

'They probably shot him,' says Steven, axe cleaving its way through sundered earth.

'Shot him?'

'Sure. Think about it. Picture the scene,' says Steven. Barney, despite himself, is picturing the scene. He's in the trenches. In fact, he's digging a trench, steadfastly shovelling dirt; his spade claws into hard, lumpy earth. 'Early on in the war. Everyone already realises it's a bum rap and they're going to be there for years. A few shots are getting fired every now and again. The men are sitting around, smoking a few joints, reading letters from home, hanging out. You know the score. Suddenly, a few shells come over and next thing they know, the air smells of some cheap French toilet water. Within seconds everyone starts choking and turning yellow.' Pauses. 'Can you see it?'

Edward nods. 'I'm there.'

'So, our hero, we'll call him Corporal Jones, is a bit of a chemist. Realises the only way to survive is to breathe through pish. So in the middle of the mayhem and panic and tumult, he sits down on a bench, cool as a pint of cider, takes off a sock, and whips out his wanger and pishes into it. Then he sticks it over his gob. Easy. The rest of the men are looking at him as if he's an alien. Pointing and saying to each other, "Check out Jonesy.

The bastard's pishing into his sock." So they all stand around and gawp, and despite Jonesy's best efforts to get them to follow his example, within minutes they're all dead.

'So, a bit of wind picks up, blows all the gas away. Some lieutenant-colonel or other charges up to the front to check it out, once the danger's past, of course, and there's Jonesy safe as houses and everyone one else dead to the world. "What went on here?" asks the officer. "Well, sir," says Jonesy, "the Germans gassed us and I was the only one to pish in my sock." Think about it. Our hero was going to have a bit of a credibility problem. Next thing he knows he's been court-martialled and shot, because that's what they did in those days. Two minutes late for work and you got a gun in the back of the head.'

Edward heaves his axe into the hard ground with mighty abandon.

'Could be right. But if he got shot and all the others died, how did it catch on?'

'They probably tested it out to see if he was telling the truth; but not until after they'd killed him, of course. Probably sent Mrs Jones an apology along with the telegram telling her he was dead. That's the kind of thing they did. So days after Jonesy died for his trouble, pishing in your sock was all the rage. In fact, there were probably blokes who pished in their socks even when they didn't have to. Sock sniffers. Expect there were a few of them shot as well.'

'Aye, I suppose you're right, Brother. Too bad the guy has never been recognised.'

Steven nods. Plunges the axe verily unto the frozen soil.

'Aye. I can see the statue,' he says, and laughs. Brother Edward laughs along with him. Barney laughs too, to cover the feeling of exclusion. But soon the laughter dies among the three men, because this day is no day for laughter, and this is not just any digging work they are undertaking. This is work to bury one of their own – the second in a few days.

They lapse into silence, the sound of their digging travelling clear up the snow-covered glen, through the thin, cold air. Monks at work, and despite the laughter and the idle conversation, weighed down by sadness and fear.

A Brave Man

'How many more monks will die here?' says the Abbot.

Brother Herman stares out of the window of the Abbot's study, across the forest and hills of snow. A bright afternoon despite the cloud, but snow will come later, he thinks. His arms are folded across his chest; his face is long; eagle eyes stare out from deep sockets. His arms move under the swelling of his chest, but faintly so that it appears he is hardly breathing.

'We cannot allow the police in here, Brother Abbot, you know that. Any time the outside world has been allowed to breathe its fetid breath upon the abbey in the past, it has spelt disaster. There is nothing to suggest it would be any different this time. There can be no outside influences. They would contaminate, they would insinuate themselves into the very fabric of our lives, like a cancer, until we are destroyed utterly. That is how it will be, Brother Abbot.'

The Abbot sits at his desk, head bowed; the two men with their backs to one another.

'But I say again, Brother Herman. How many more monks will die here? How long must this go on? Until we are all dead? Until only one survives, whoever it is who has committed these foul deeds? It cannot be allowed to continue.'

'And neither shall it, Brother Abbot,' says Herman. He turns and faces back into the study; the Abbot turns to engage his eye. 'Give me a few days, that is all I'll need.'

'You have some clue as to the perpetrator?'

Herman hesitates. Eyes narrow. 'Not as yet, Brother, but I will. It is clear after this second crime that these deeds are related in some way to the library. I will go there; I will leave no monk unturned until I have discovered the truth. I am confident that I can uncover the meaning behind these deaths.'

The Abbot looks away. He stares at the floor, heart heavy. The tragedy of life.

'I must appoint a new librarian, but who would I give that post to now? Who would take it?'

Herman's eyes narrow even farther. They burrow into the back of the Abbot's head. Fingers twitch. 'Me, Brother. Let me be the next librarian.'

The Abbot swivels. Looks into the narrow slits of Herman's eyes.

'Brother? But you are not a learned man.'

'Only until I discover the identity of Brother Saturday's and Brother Morgan's killer. And if they should come after me, well, then indeed shall they be found out and brought to justice.'

The Abbot breathes deeply and looks away. Two librarians dead. Anyone expressing an interest in the library now might possibly be the one who wanted rid of the previous incumbents. Maybe it is wise to have Brother Herman on hand to deal with all enquiries to the library. But then, what if the brother becomes the next victim? What if Herman is not as safe from the black hand of Death as he believes? Can he sacrifice Brother Herman to his desire to bring this killer to justice?

'I am not sure, Brother. I am not sure that I can ask any of my brethren to put their lives at risk at this time.'

Herman nods; a long, slow movement. He knows well how to play the Abbot.

'Give me two days, Brother Abbot, that is all I need. If I have not found the killer by then, I will go along with your desire to bring in the police from outside.' He lets the words hang in the cold air. Says 'Two days' again, for emphasis.

The Abbot stares at the floor. He wonders if he will find God there, for in these last couple of days he has lost sight of his Lord. These are his darkest hours.

Eventually he speaks. He feels as if it is not him who is doing the talking. His voice sounds strange. Alienated from his body. Apart.

'Very well, Brother,' he says. 'Two days you shall have. But then, I am afraid, I must prevail upon you to bring in the outside agencies of the law. And who knows then what troubles we shall be in, for burying our dear departed brothers.'

Herman stares from deep eye sockets; pupils shine. He knows he can always get his way with the Abbot. That's what they are like, abbots; all of them. There to be manipulated. And, of course, on this occasion the Abbot is right to give in to his request.

'Thank you, Brother. I shall not fail you.'

The Abbot looks past furrowed brow, up into the black eyes.

'May the Lord be with you, Brother,' he says, then looks away. He thinks that the Lord has forsaken this place; and that the Lord will not be with any of them for a very long time.

Brother Herman bows his head; the hood of his cloak moves forward and his face falls into shadow. Slowly, his feet noiseless on the stone floor, he walks from the room.

✂

The hole is almost complete. Regulation. Four feet wide, seven feet long, six feet deep. Awaiting Brother Morgan.

The work of Steven and Edward is over, the earth chopped and hacked into shovel-friendly dirt. They stand at the edge of the grave looking down into the pit, watching Brother Jacob heave the soil up and over the top. Nearly finished. No longer cold now, Barney; sweating with the effort. Hands raw.

'Feels kind of weird,' says Steven. The expression on his face never changes.

'How do you mean?' asks Edward.

'The scissors thing,' says Steven. 'The same scissors that were used to cut my hair a few hours later are used to murder poor Brother Morgan. There's got to be some weird karma thing going on, don't you think?'

Barney hesitates before his next shovel. Not sure if Steven is addressing him or Edward. Too busy thinking about the words of Brother Martin. 'You could kill someone with those.' What had that been about? Would they really be the words of someone who intended to use the scissors as a murder weapon?

He decides to ignore Steven. Nothing to do with karma, he thinks. It's God. God continuing to shit on him everywhere he goes; surrounding him with death and murder. He thinks that if he were the only person left on the planet, God would still find someone to die in his proximity.

'See what you mean,' says Edward. 'Definitely something going on, no mistake. The interconnectedness of it. Got to be some Jungian thing happening. You must be geeked.'

127

Steven shrugs. 'Don't know about geeked, Brother. I mean, I'm sure God's cool about it. Same with Jacob here. Just trying to do his job, and the next thing he knows his work implement has been embedded in Brother Morgan's neck. Could just as easily have been your pick-axe, Brother Brunswick's trowel, or Brother Raphael's soup ladle. I suppose we've all got to be geeked, but that's just life.'

'You're right there, Brother. It's no different out there. You know, in the real world. Lachlan, the young lad who makes the meat deliveries from Durness once a month, he was in this morning. Mentioned something that's been happening in Glasgow. Some serial killer's on the loose, apparently. He was about to tell me all about it, but I asked him not to. Don't want to know about all that stuff; particularly not at the moment. I wasn't going to mention it to anyone. Anyway, I expect Brother David will find out all about it when he goes into Durness next week.'

Edward shrugs his shoulders and raises his eyebrows. Sadly, it seems, life in the monastery is more a mirror of contemporary life than any of them would wish.

'Are you all right there, Brother Jacob?' says Brother Steven, staring down into the grave. 'You're looking a little faint.'

Chapter 12

Uma Thurman Serves Barney a Beer. Naked.

Late at night in the monastery; the monks lie awake with their fears, listening to the storm. Trees are tossed, shutters rattle, doors and floorboards creak. They imagine that every noise is the sound of a killer on the move; wonder if they will be the next victim, the next on the slab of death. Each one can feel the sharpness of cold steel, piercing their neck. They expect it at any second. Know that if they fall asleep they might never wake up.

The Library Murders; that is what they are calling them, even though there is no evidence that that was where the murders were committed. There is perhaps some comfort to them in that so far it is the librarians who have died; these men, brave with their faith in God, would all have refused the position of librarian had it been offered to them. Delighted that Herman has taken it on; doubt that any killer will be so bold as to tackle Herman. There would be a brave man indeed; and foolish.

And so much for those rumours which suggested that a liaison between Morgan and Saturday had soured, leading

129

to the murder of the latter by the former. There must be more to it than that, but the gossip of the monastery can furnish no clues. Something hidden among the books, they presume – and they are wrong – but no one has any real idea. How long since that great collection was added to by anything other than one of the brothers' own hands?

Must be Brother Jacob; that's what some of them are thinking, although none will say it. Unchristian to think so ill of someone, just because he is unfamiliar. But it all ties up. A new monk arrives, some of the regular monks start getting murdered. Jacob must have brought something with him; some evil intent or malign spirit.

Through no fault of his own, Barney is as mistrusted within the monastery as he is on the outside.

And he lies awake also, this evil Barney Thomson. Cold. Listens to the sound of the wind, knowing that a blizzard blows without. He can feel it as if the snow were falling directly on top of him. His mind is a tangle, a swirling array of unfinished thoughts and ideas. Remorse, regrets, doubts. Dwelling upon his past crimes, constantly replaying them. How would it be now it he'd done things differently?

When he had killed Wullie; an accident, undoubtedly. If he had called the police immediately, what then? Would he have gone to prison, or could he have got some hot-shot lawyer to get him off. Guilty of manslaughter, no doubt, but a three-year suspended sentence. Then he would never have had to kill Chris; as long as he hadn't been in police custody when his mother died, he could cheerfully have got rid of the body parts of all her victims at some future date, and no one need have thought of any connection between those murders and himself. He might have had to leave the shop, but if you play these things correctly you can become a bit of a celebrity. Write a book; appear on one of those chat shows, Kilroy or Jerry Springer – 'I'm a Killer, But Really I'm a Decent Enough Chap'. He'd have been an ideal guest.

Public sympathy would have flowed. He could have sold the film rights to the book, then taken the cash and set up his own shop up north somewhere. He remembers the cold. Bugger it. He could have gone to the Caribbean and set up a shop. Or managed to swing a job haircutting on a cruise ship. Left Scotland behind for ever, to cut the hair of the stars. Sees himself giving Sean Connery a Sean Connery, and getting an enormous tip. He could have forgotten all about Agnes – which he has done anyway – and had his pick of women. Maybe even Barbara, the sister-in-law from the gods, would have come and joined him. He would have had one over on his brother – his sodding brother – for the first time in his life. He could have stolen his wife.

Barney smiles in the dark. A beach-side shop; the waves lapping gently on the shore; a calypso band playing near by; Barney cutting Robert Redford's hair, at a charge of several hundred pounds; while Barbara serves them both cocktails, topless. And all that if only he had called the police after he'd killed Wullie, instead of bundling the body up and sticking it in the back of his car. What a fool he'd been.

Instead, it is the depths of winter, and Barney is renowned for all the wrong reasons. He is this month's pet hate figure, centrefold in the Christmas edition of *Serial Killer Monthly*, hounded from his home, hounded to the farthest ends of the country, to feel his feet and testicles freeze up under a slender blanket in the bleakest inhabited building in Scotland.

The door to his room creaks slowly open; his senses awaken. But he does not move. Strangely he does not live

131

in fear of the killer, as the rest of the monks do. Too close to death for too long, he doesn't care any more, perhaps. He does not fear death – just detection. Assumes it is Brother Steven, with whom he shares a room. Is aware that the brother left not five minutes previously. A visit to the Lord's toilet, he assumed.

He feels a presence standing over him, but still does not open his eyes.

'Brother? Brother Jacob?' comes the strained whisper. Not the voice of Steven.

Barney's heart flickers; he opens his eyes. In the dark, he can make out the figure of Brother Martin, hood drawn back from his face. His heart does more than flicker. Brother Martin! A man well aware of the lethal properties of a pair of scissors. Maybe Barney fears death after all.

'Brother Jacob, we must talk.'

Barney sits up, looks through the gloom; is aware of the noise of the wind; can feel the cold even more bitterly as the blanket slides from him, his nightshirt thin protection.

'Brother Martin?' he says.

'Brother, you must promise me. What I said yesterday, while you cut my hair. You know it was nothing, don't you? The sharpness of scissors. It was just a remark, you know that. You haven't mentioned it to Brother Herman, I hope. Have you been called to see Brother Herman?'

Brother Martin stands breathlessly over Barney. Barney wonders if within the folds of his cloak he holds a dagger, or some other weapon. Something which he could drive into the breast of Barney should the need arise. Are these not the actions of a guilty man? he thinks.

'Ye've got nothin' fur tae worry about, Brother.'

He is aware that Martin takes a step back.

'That is indeed good news, Brother. For you know that it was but a chance remark.'

'Aye, Brother Martin, nae bother. An' Ah've seen Brother Herman right enough.'

'Indeed?'

'But Ah didnae say nothin', ye know. Ah, mean, Ah had tae tell him that Ah'd cut yer hair, 'n a' but Ah didnae finger you in partic'lar, ye know.'

Barney can see the head nod in the dark.

'That was very wise, Brother. Very wise indeed. And you will also be discreet about this visit, I am sure.'

Discreet. Barney has to think about that. He perceives a threat, unsure if there is one intended. If in doubt, he remembers someone saying at the height of the Glasgow serial killer panic, assume that your every interlocutor is a killer. Especially when they call on you in the middle of the night.

'Aye, aye,' he says eventually. 'Nae bother, Brother Martin. Discreet as fuck, me. I mean, sorry, Brother. Sorry. About the language, an' a' that, ye know.'

He is aware of Brother Martin retreating through the room. He swings the door open, and the creaking of it merely blends in with the roaring creaks of the monastery in the storm. Barney can see the dark figure as he stops at the door. Wonders; decides to ask.

'How come ye knew Brother Steven widnae be here, an' a' that?' he says.

There comes no immediate answer. In among the groans of the old building, Barney is aware of Martin's breathing. Heavy; ominous; deliberate. The hairs on the back of Barney's neck begin to stand to attention, zombies from the grave. He can feel them crawl across his neck, bumping into each other.

'Some things are easily taken care of,' comes the cold reply across the darkness of the room. Martin lets the words hang there, freezing the room already slumped into arctic winter, then slowly leaves, closing the door behind him.

Barney shivers; cold and fear. Lies back down on the bed, pulls the blanket up to his neck. Goose bumps career across his body with wild abandon; shivers rack every inch.

What had been meant by that? Some things are easily taken care of? He wonders if Brother Steven sits out somewhere in the forest, a knife embedded in his neck, the smile of the dead on his face. But he'd only left a few minutes before Brother Martin had arrived. Hardly time for Martin to strike; especially with the storm. Except, perhaps, that Martin has taken care of Steven elsewhere, and only now will drag his body out into the cold. A young, fit man, Brother Martin. Can't be any more than twenty-five. More than capable of killing one of the brothers then dragging the body out into the snow.

Yet, Brother Martin? It doesn't make sense. Why, if you are going to use something as an implement of murder, mention it to someone before you do it? A double bluff, perhaps? To rule himself out by saying something which he obviously wouldn't have said if he was going to commit murder. Perhaps he thinks that by telling Barney to keep his mouth shut in as suspicious a manner as possible, Barney will mention it to Brother Herman. By the mere fact of looking so obviously suspicious, Martin might distance himself from the crime.

So, Martin must be the killer, thinks Barney. Or else, he's definitely not the killer.

He feels pleased that he's narrowed it down to one of two possibilities. He could have been a policeman. Better than some of the clowns he's come across in the past year.

I will not yield, thinks Barney. If Martin's plan, by coming here this evening, is to force me to talk to Brother Herman, I won't do it. And if he doesn't want me to talk to him because he's innocent, then that's fine. And if he doesn't want me to talk to him because he's guilty and he's not devious . . . Barney's mind implodes in a tangle of labyrinthine confusion.

He closes his eyes, and in this renewed claustrophobic darkness, he feels the pain of regret. If only he had confessed to killing Wullie Henderson he could now be lying on a beach in Antigua, with Sharon Stone stroking his forehead and Uma Thurman serving him pints of heavy. Naked.

Barney wonders many things as he gives in once more to the bitter cold. Do they serve heavy in Antigua; will he ever see Brother Steven again?

Chapter 13

Breakfast - Just About the Only Meal to Have in the Morning

Mulholland and Proudfoot. Breakfast. The full business. Sitting at the window of a small guest house just outside Helmsdale; as far as they got the previous evening. Looking across fields of snow; a bright morning. Blue skies, and a better mood. Mulholland helped by not being able to speak to Melanie the night before and, although he doesn't realise it, the temporary absence of Sheep Dip. He assumes his wife has gone; feels the release. A problem put off to another day is a problem solved. Wonders if this is it; marriage over. He is in such confusion about it that he has fallen back on fragile good humour. Taken Proudfoot with him.

They eat well, the hunger of the relaxed. Feel like they might be getting somewhere, having picked up the scent of Barney Thomson. Enjoying the renewal of enthusiasm; not thinking about what might happen if they ever find their man. Engrossed in food and serious debate.

Bacon, link sausage, Lorne sausage, fried egg, haggis, potato scone, black pudding, tomatoes, mushrooms, toast, marmalade, tea. All the main food groups.

'It was Velma,' says Proudfoot.

Mulholland shakes his head. 'Definitely Thelma,' he replies.

Proudfoot deals with a piece of toast, smothers it with marmalade. Pops the remnants of a sausage into her mouth, then some of the toast. Detective Sergeant Dip eats in much the same way, but he is spending the night with friends. Something he is able to do in virtually every town in the Highlands.

'Definitely, definitely, definitely Velma. No question,' she says.

Mulholland clinks his knife and fork down on a cleared plate, turns his attention to the toast. Wonders whether to request jam; decides against.

'What are you talking about? Velma? What kind of name is that? Velma's not even a real name. It's not a word, it's not a food substance or a brand name, it's not a place, it's not a disease. "What's the matter wi' you, mate?" "Touch o' velma, Big Man." No chance. It's nothing. Not a name, not a disease, nothing. No one's called Velma. Do you know anyone called Velma?'

'No, but then I'm from Glasgow. People don't get called Velma in Glasgow. I don't even know anyone called Thelma, but it doesn't mean I'm disputing its existence as a name. It was definitely Velma.'

'Get out of my face. Velma! The reason people don't get called Velma in Glasgow is because it's not a name. No one gets called Velma anywhere. What kind of idiot would call their daughter Velma?'

Proudfoot finishes off the last of her bacon, then lays the cutlery quietly down on the plate. Downs some tea, lifts the pot to pour some more.

'Doesn't have to be any kind of idiot. She's a cartoon

character. She doesn't actually have parents. Scooby Doo isn't real.'

'Get out of my face.'

'Right, bet you,' she says.

Mulholland shrugs. 'You're on. How much?'

'A million pounds.'

He smiles, says, 'Right, it's a deal. I can start thinking how I'll spend the money, and you can start thinking how you're going to raise it.'

'Won't have to. It's Velma.'

'Bloody no way,' says Mulholland. 'Anyway, that wasn't the main issue. The real question was, were Fred and Daphne shagging?'

Proudfoot laughs. the woman of the house appears beside their table. They look up and wonder if they're about to be told off for having an inappropriate conversation at the breakfast table.

'There's a call for you, Chief Inspector,' she says, sounding suspicious. At the mention of the job title, nervous glances are cast from the two other occupied tables. If they'd only known there was a policeman in their midst, then perhaps they would not have been so loose with their tongues; assuming that all police are constantly on the lookout for people to arrest.

'Thanks,' says Mulholland. Glances at Proudfoot, rises from the table. 'Probably being called back to Glasgow because we haven't found him yet.'

'Watch your testicles,' she says.

'Thanks.'

Mulholland walks from the small dining room. Proudfoot looks out of the window at the snow-covered fields stretching away to low hills. The other five people in the room look warily at her. Wonder. Might she also be the police, or is she some policeman's moll? A bit on the side he carries

138

around with him; or maybe a one-nighter he picked up in one of the seedy strip joints in Helmsdale or Brora. An uncomfortable silence dominates the room. The clink of knives, cups on saucers, toast crunching between teeth. The silent sounds of suspicion. Proudfoot feels it, is too bored with the police to enjoy it any more. Stares out of the window at the early snow, mind rambling. Wonders if they're in for a long winter of it. Doesn't think about Barney Thomson; can't help thinking about Joel Mulholland. It never does any harm to think.

He returns, walks quickly into the room. Good humour gone. Businesslike.

'Come on, Sergeant,' he says. Knew it, think the other five in the room. Polis. 'We've got a sighting of our man. Sergeant Dip's come up with something. Some hotel Thomson's stayed at near Wick. We'd better get a move on before Sheep careers off across the Highlands on some wild-goose chase.'

A Good Place for a Serial Killer

A small hotel on the sea-battered east coast. They can already hear the sound of the waves crashing onto the rocks, a great tumult of noise. The hotel looks not unlike the Bates house, high on a promontory. Gothic. Good sea views. Gives the hotel its name. *The Sea View.* They both think the same thing as they get out of the car, hugging their jackets around them to fend off the biting wind, whistling in off a bitter North Sea; wonder how long it took some genius to think that up?

A couple of other cars in the car park. No other buildings in sight. A desolate, dreary spot. Difficult to imagine there being any life in this place, even on the brightest of days.

139

A good place for a serial killer.

Mulholland pushes open the door and marches into reception. Hit by a wonderful warmth, and Proudfoot quickly closes the door behind them. Had expected the inside to be as bleak as the exterior, but instead, thick carpets, heating up full. No evidence of Gothic darkness. This could be any of a hundred hotels in Scotland. Red carpet, pictures of stags on walls, warm, smoky smell of an open fire. Mulholland thinks of his honeymoon; long nights and long mornings, lazy afternoons; a time when the rest of his life had been set. He banishes the memory, consigns it to the appropriate bin.

A young woman appears. Canadian; although, as with all Canadians, this does not outwardly manifest itself.

'Hi, what can I do for you? Would you like a room?'

'No thanks,' says Mulholland. 'Chief Inspector Mulholland and Sergeant Proudfoot. Here to speak to Mr Stewart.'

'Oh, right, yeah. The police. About that serial killer guy. I'll just get him for you. Wait up.'

She disappears from reception, leaving faint traces of soap and hotel shampoo in the air. Mulholland rests his elbows on the counter; looks at nothing. Proudfoot wanders; she studies paintings of open moor and stags on the hoof. She has never stayed in a hotel like this. Already wants to stay here this evening, but knows there's a long day ahead of them. They might end up far from Wick.

A woman bustles into reception. Late sixties perhaps; grey hair and breasts you could use on a major engineering project. A man follows behind. Dungarees and dirty hands. Face like the underside of a football boot.

Mulholland holds out his card.

'Mulholland and Proudfoot,' he says, 'Partick CID.'

'Partick?' says the woman. 'By jings, but you got here quickly. We only phoned this morning.'

'We were in the area. I presume Sergeant MacPherson's here already?'

'There's nae MacPherson here, laddie, and there hasnae been since Big Jock MacPherson stayed here yon night he thought he could get away wi' shagging Wee Sammy Matheson's daughter. But Ah'll tell ye, Wee Sammy wis having none o' it.'

'Right,' says Mulholland.

'Partick, ye say,' she says, displaying a firm grasp. 'Have they no local police they could send? I thought we'd be seeing Alec. Had a nice cup o' tea all ready for him as well.'

The man shakes his head; looks at his wife in the usual way. 'Ach, away with you, woman, this is much too big for Alec. If you want someone tae tell you the quickest way tae get tae Golspie he's fine, but he's bloody useless at solving crimes and all of that. Still hasn't worked out who robbed the post office last March even though Wee Jamie Drummond's been driving around in a brand-new Skoda ever since.' Nods at the two officers. 'No, these are the big boys up from Glasgow we've got here. Come on in and sit yourselves down. You get us some tea, Agnes.'

Agnes Stewart looks at the visitors. 'You'll be wanting a wee biscuit or two,' she says, and disappears before she can get a negative reply.

Donald Stewart beckons them on, and they follow him into the hotel lounge. Another warm room, large fire crackling. Smells like Christmas, thinks Proudfoot. A couple of sofas, seven or eight comfortable armchairs. Coffee tables with two-year-old *People's Friend*s on the shelves underneath.

141

'Now, now, then, sit yourselves down, won't you. I expect you'll be having a few wee questions for me. Is that not right?'

Mulholland and Proudfoot sit next to one another on the sofa beside the fire. Donald Stewart sits across from them. Leans forward, the better to face the inquisition. Knows what it will be like. Here is a man who watches *The Bill*.

'I understand from what my colleague told me that you thought Barney Thomson had been staying here. Is that right?'

Stewart nods enthusiastically. 'Oh aye, nae doubt about it, nae doubt about it at all. A week past on Thursday, and then the next night as well. I checked my records before you came.'

A week past on Thursday. Mulholland lowers his head. Thinks, God, what is the matter with these people? He had thought as they drove here that they were getting closer. This isn't much more use. A bit further up the coast and this would have been his next port of call after Tain. But even if he'd been here for a couple of days, it still leaves them a week and a half behind.

'So he left here when?' asks Mulholland. Keeps the annoyance from his voice.

'The Saturday. So that would be about twelve days ago, ye know.'

'Twelve days.'

Mulholland stares at him. Knows that the bloke doesn't see anything wrong. Casts a glance at Proudfoot, who returns it. Isn't laughing this time.

'Mr Stewart. If Barney Thomson was here twelve days ago, and you knew that the police were looking for him, why did it take you so long to get in touch with us?'

Donald Stewart laughs. 'Well, ye know what Matthew

Arnold said. Thou waitest for the spark from heaven! and we, light half-believers in our casual creeds . . . Who hesitate and falter life away, and lose tomorrow the ground won today – and, do not we, Wanderer, await it too?'

Mulholland stares at him; the smile on the football-boot face. The headache which has been lingering since he awoke threatens to burst through.

'What the fuck was that all about?' he says. Shakes his head again, holds up his hand. Mumbles, 'Sorry.'

'Well, I'm no' so sure,' says Donald Stewart, 'but I thought it might apply. I do like my poetry. I think what I'm trying to say is this. He seemed like a nice enough lad, you know. Paid his bill in cash, so he did. Would have him back any day. Just couldn't see him as a serial killer, you know; and the way the press are going on, I hardly thought that the boy would get a fair trial.'

Mulholland buries his head in his hands. Rubs his forehead, comes up for air. Trying not to lose his temper. 'So, why did you decide to contact the police now, Mr Stewart?'

'Ach, well, I was just thinking that maybe I might have been wrong about the lad.' His wife bustles into the room with a food-laden try. 'I mean, on the telly last night they were saying it might have been his fault that Billy Bremner missed yon sitter against Brazil in Germany in 1974. I mean, if that's true, then the lad belongs in prison. It's a shame, but there you are.'

Mulholland stares at him, mouth dropping open a little. Proudfoot smiles and looks into the fire. Prefers to leave these ones to the boss. There is never anywhere to go with them when they start coming up with this kind of thing.

'Now then, how many sugars would that be in your tea?'

143

Mulholland looks at Agnes Stewart; for the first time at the tray she has laid down. A fruit loaf, twelve Danish pastries, six almond slices, one large apple pie, seven custard pies, a selection of chocolate-covered digestives, a packet of finger biscuits, fourteen iced buns, twenty or thirty jammy dodgers, and several hundredweight of cherry bakewells. He doesn't answer; looks back at Donald Stewart.

'Two for me and none for him,' says Proudfoot.

'Right, then, dear, that'll be lovely.'

The velvet sound of pouring tea fills the room.

'Aye,' says Donald Stewart. 'Looks like a fine cuppy o' tea you're having. Think I might have a wee cuppy myself.'

'Mr Stewart,' says Mulholland, 'on the planet you're from, is it normal to think that only one person is guilty of every bad thing that's ever happened?'

'Aye, well, you know, it's just what they're saying in the press, like. I'm no' so sure about it myself.'

'How could Barney Thomson possibly be to blame for Billy Bremner's miss against Brazil? He was two feet out from goal with no one to beat. How could it possibly be anyone's fault but Billy Bremner's?'

Donald Stewart lifts an almond slice and bites contemplatively into it. Points the remainder of it at Mulholland.

'Aye, well, manny, you might have a point. But there is a point o' view which states that all things are connected, like, you know? You stick a ball in the net at Hampden and someone falls off their motorbike in Thurso. You've heard that? So, I think it's very close-minded to rule anything out.'

'What is it Adam Smith says?' says Agnes Stewart, still filling the room with the warm sounds of pouring tea. 'Something about philosophy being the science which pretends to lay open the concealed connections that unite the various appearances of nature. Is that no' what we're talking about?'

'Well, Agnes, I don't know if that was quite what Mr Smith was getting at. There's more to this than philosophical ramblings.'

'Ramblings, you say? There was much more to Adam Smith than ramblings, Donald Stewart.'

'Aye, well, that might be right enough. But I don't know how much he has to contribute to a discussion on Billy Bremner missing a sitter against Brazil, the elegiac nature of it notwithstanding.'

'Look!'

Mr and Mrs Stewart raise their heads. Ignore Mulholland. Donald Stewart polishes off the almond slice and starts making a move on a large piece of apple pie.

'There's your tea, now, you two. Help yourself to a little bitty of cake.'

Proudfoot has given in to it. Wants to burst out laughing again. Reaches forward; takes her tea, loads a plate with cakes and biscuits. Is resigned to putting on several kilos before they get back to Glasgow.

'Really, Mr Stewart. This has nothing to do with Billy Bremner. However, the crimes of which Barney Thomson stands accused are very real and very serious. We believe him to be a dangerous man.'

'Ach, that laddie? I hardly think so. He seemed nice enough.' Puts his hand to the back of his neck. 'Even gave me a quick trim. An Andy Stewart; and he only charged me three-fifty.'

Mulholland stares at him. Wonders who in their right mind would let Barney Thomson anywhere near them with a pair of scissors. Gives in. Leans forward, lifts his tea, and places a Danish pastry, a custard pie and two

145

iced buns on his plate. Resigned to putting on several kilos by the time he gets back to Glasgow; and Melanie won't be there to complain about it.

There comes the sound of heavy footfalls in the corridor outside, and then the sight of Sheep Dip marching the lounge. He stops short of the crowd and looks down at the table.

'You're late, Sergeant Dip,' says Mulholland. 'Where've you been?'

'Ach,' he says, 'just got a wee bitty distracted. Met a couple of farmers who'd had their hair cut by your Thomson fellow, but it was last week, so I don't suppose it helps you.'

'What? Where?'

'Down by Helmsdale way, you know, but I think it's too late tae be worrying about it,' says Sheep Dip. 'Now, that looks like a fine platter you have there, m'am. Would you mind if I helped myself to a wee cakey or two?'

'Not at all, son, you go right ahead. And here you, I thought you said the lad's name was MacPherson?'

Mulholland stares from one to the other. Proudfoot feels a hint of pity for the man. That among the other emotions. She decided to have a go at interrogation, perhaps not wanting to be sucked into the contempt that Mulholland is going to feel for everyone else in the room.

'Did he say where he was going when he left you, Mr Stewart?' she asks.

Donald Stewart strokes his chin, bites ruminatively into his slice of apple pie. Nods his head. Says, 'You know, I think this might have been better heated, Agnes.'

Chapter 14

Elohim, The Big Guy

Brother Herman sits at the desk in the library, pouring over records. Books brought in; books taken out by monks; books yet to be returned. Unfortunately, no record of how many times each individual monk has visited the library. This instead: the record of monks who made transactions on each of the last days of Brothers Saturday and Morgan.

Only two names appear both times. The first need not be thought about, or shown to the Abbot. No need to point suspicion at a quarter where it is not wanted. The other is Brother Babel, a name that keeps cropping up. Returning a book on the day that Saturday died, removing another, returning that book the day Morgan died, removing a further volume. Firstly, *The Elohistic Chronicles*, by the Marquis François d'Orleans, a fourteenth-century French treatise on the Old Testament; followed by *The Path of Right*, an obscure twelfth-century work by an anonymous English monk. Comedic, some called it. Babel has not yet paid a visit to Brother Jacob's new hair emporium, but that hardly means that he will be unaware

147

of the location of the scissors.

Herman decides he will talk to Brother Babel. One of the younger monks, and a man who will be easily cracked. It is time to apply some pressure.

A few other names on the library lists, but Babel's is the one which stands out. Nevertheless, he must speak to each one in turn. One more day to go, and the Abbot will be calling in outside agencies of the law; Brother Herman cannot afford for that to happen. He must have a suspect before then.

He closes the returns book and settles back in the hard chair. Looks into the heart of the library shelves, the thousands of ancient volumes, and sees the faces of all his monks there. He had studied them all at Brother Morgan's graveside that morning, but there was nothing there but grief. Grief and fear. He knows he is dealing with subtle and dark forces, and that he cannot act too boldly. He must bide his time. It will be like a game of cat-and-mouse. Without the cat.

Or the mouse.

The Penitent Men Kneel Before God

There is a certain macabre beauty in cutting a customer's hair with a pair of scissors which has been used as an instrument of murder. So thinks Barney Thomson, barber, as he snips quietly away at the head of Brother Edward. A requested, and slightly racy, (Tonsured) Roger Moore; a revolutionary haircut, never before executed. Barney is at the cutting edge of style; he knows he is out on a limb.

Back behind the seat two days earlier than planned, thanks to public demand. Only one pair of scissors capable of the job, so Brother Herman has had to release them for Barney's use; but is unimpressed. Barney is aware that, at the current rate, he will have everyone's hair cut in a couple of weeks, then it'll be back to full-time cleaning floors. He has wondered if maybe he could request to expand; cut the hair of people in nearby villages. Knows the answer. And he is trapped here, in any case. No less of a prison than he would end up in if caught; and maybe not as comfortable. Consequently, he has begun to allow his mind to run along those lines. If captured, he would be considered a highly dangerous prisoner – and aren't all those guys given three-room suites instead of cells? TV and video, bathroom, double bed, and the right to invite women in at weekends? Maybe he'd be better off in prison, and he might still get to cut hair in there. Give everyone a Tim Robbins (*Shawshank Redemption*).

Bored with his own thoughts, he decides to talk.

'So, whit are ye in for, Brother Edward?'

Edward raises an eyebrow. 'In for?'

Barney snips quickly away around the back of the neck.

'Oh aye, right. But ye know whit Ah mean. Why are ye here, 'n a' that?'

Edward stares into the dark, blank wall in front of him. How many times in the past did he stare at the mirror as some new dream haircut unfolded before him, another killer look which he would use to devastating effect, out on the Friday night sexquest. Ed the Bed, that's what they'd called him. Lure a woman from fifty yards without a word. A different woman every night of the week, if he'd wanted; and how many of them had he sent to the grave of abandoned desire? He has never talked about it; but there's something about being in the barber's chair.

'Women,' he says to Barney, surprised by his own candour.

'Oh aye,' says Barney, nodding, 'God's second blunder.'

'Brother?'

'Oh, Nietzsche. Said that wimmin were God's second blunder,' says Barney.

'German philosophy, eh? And what did he consider God's first blunder?'

'Allowing McAllister to take the penalty against England,' Barney says. Laughs as he says it, so that Edward knows it's a joke. Not that he thought of it himself; heard someone say it in the pub once, when they'd had a European philosophers evening. Not much good at jokes, Barney Thomson.

'Right, very good, Brother. I wouldn't let Brother Herman hear you talk like that, or he'll have your testicles on toast.'

Barney swallows, hesitates, continues clipping. A vivid image.

Suddenly, Brother Edward feels released. It is time to get it off his chest. The years of loathing and self-flagellation, the agonies he's caused; the women cast aside and lives ruined.

'I was a heartbreaker, Brother,' says Edward. 'I used women like you'd use razor blades. Swept them up with the great Hoover of my personality and good looks. Then, when I was done with them, I reversed the suck to blow and spat them out like so much dust in the wind.'

Barney snips away. He sneaks a glance at Brother Edward's face. Looks about fifteen. No oil painting either. Wonder if he's delusional.

'Loved 'em and left 'em, that was me. I used to keep a book, you know. A catalogue of success. Page after page

150

of women who had succumbed to my charm and outrageous good looks. It read like a *Who's Who* of
Edinburgh babe society. I broke up marriages, I drove
girls to suicide, I led them down the path of carnal degra-
dation. But I changed, Brother Jacob, I changed. It'd
make me sick to look at that book now.'

'Oh aye. Where is it?'

'Hidden away,' says Edward, 'where neither man nor
beast will ever set eyes upon it again.'

'Why'd ye no' just burn it?' says Barney.

He feels Edward's shoulders shrug. 'Not sure. Suppose
I thought that if things didn't work out here, there might
be a few new chapters to write.'

'Oh.'

Another penitent man kneeling before God.

Barney has worked in a barber's shop long enough to
recognise it; had thought that in this place he would not
encounter such a person. The top-division, highly paid,
agented, professional bullshitter. Always a mistake to get
them started, but Barney has realised it too late. He has
opened the box.

'But even after I got here, Brother Jacob, I questioned
myself for a long while. Had I given up women for the
right reason, or had I merely tired of them? You see,
there are two types of women.'

'Oh aye?' says Barney. Had thought there was only
one type, and has enough trouble understanding that.

'Aye. There's your Sharon Stones, and then there's
your Madonnas.'

Barney is almost finished. Wishes his next customer
would arrive, as he is sure Brother Edward will not be so
talkative in company.

'It's the difference between *Basic Instinct* and *Body of
Evidence*, Brother. In *Basic Instinct*, you know the scene

151

where they're in bed, Sharon Stone's lying there, and Michael Douglas darts down and gets stuck in. Giving her oral pleasure, you know?'

'Aye,' says Barney. He had got to watch some of it once when Agnes had incorrectly set the video when attempting to tape the bumper final episode of the seventh season of *Destiny Drive*, successful offshoot of the failed Patrick Duffy vehicle *Only the Good Have Big Hair*. He hadn't really known what they were doing.

'Well, you're watching that and you're thinking, Is he really doing that to her, or is he in fact nowhere near her and it's all done by camera angles? Does he really have his face buried between her legs, or are they fake legs? Is that real pubic hair sticking up his nose, or is it a wig? You're just not sure. So, you see, that's one kind of woman. The kind you're just not sure about. Then there's *Body of Evidence*. You'll remember the scene with Madonna standing on top of the car?'

'Aye,' says Barney; hasn't the faintest idea.

'Willem Dafoe buries his face between her legs. But he's up there, man, there's no denying it. There's no artifice; there's no elaborate camera angles; there's no sophistry; there's no question that it's Madonna. It's her all right, not some stunt duff. So it's all there for you to see. And you know what you're thinking, Brother Jacob?'

'Ah hope she's had a shower?'

'You're thinking, that's it. It's all there, out in the open. So what's left? There's no mystery. Everything there is to see you've seen. And when there's no mystery, what is there? You see my problem, Brother?'

Barney has no idea what he's talking about. He runs a comb down the back of his head. Haircut finished. Hoping that he'll be able to send Brother Edward on his way.

152

'Either you don't get it all, in which case you get annoyed because you wonder what they're hiding. Or you see everything and you get fed up because there's no mystery. You can't win. So that's my predicament. Did I run from womanhood because of my guilt, or because I was fed up with the continuing contradictions?'

Barney has no answer, believing him to be talking absolute rubbish. A good moment for the door to open, which it does – a prayer answered – and in walks Brother Adolphus and Brother Steven. Greetings are exchanged.

'I'm just finished,' says Barney, removing the towel from around Edward's neck, and mightily relieved with it. 'Would you like to step up, Brother Adolphus?'

Brother Adolphus comes forward. Steven sits in one of the three seats behind the barber's chair, where Edward joins him after brushing off his shoulders.

'What can Ah dae for ye, Brother?' says Barney, fixing the towel around Adolphus's neck.

'I hear you do a wonderful Sean Connery (*Name of the Rose*), Brother,' he says.

'Aye, that'll be nae bother.' Barney taps the scissors against the comb, turns and quickly looks at Steven before he starts. 'Unhappy wi' yer cut fi' the other day, Brother?' he says.

Steven smiles. 'No, no, Brother, not at all. I'd finished my work for the day, and thought I'd come along and watch a master craftsman ply his trade. One of God's own artisans. You have the Gift, Brother. Angels must weep in ecstasy when they hear the euphonic clip of your scissors, and trumpets sound in Heaven to herald the triumph of corporeal entity over the fantasy of imagination. The mighty swords of the warriors of Gog and Magog could not have been wielded with such eloquence and pulchritude. The demons of impotence and repugnance must flee to their pungent burrows when faced with the edifying totality of your finesse. I see you have realised a (tonsured) Roger Moore upon Brother Edward here. Wonderful work, Brother, wonderful work.'

Barney smiles.

'Aye, right,' he says. His head might swell, he thinks, if it wasn't for the fact that he's as good as everyone says he is.

'Indeed,' says Brother Edward. 'I thought I'd stop a little longer myself.'

Steven nods, and the two men settle back to watch the master craftsman. Barney settles down to the subtle differences between a Sean Connery and an F. Murray Abraham.

Scissors click, but the silence will not last long. The Pandora's box of Edward's confession cannot yet be contained.

'We were just talking about women,' says Brother Edward. Knows that he shouldn't be having this discussion in the monastery, but that Steven will be a willing interlocutor. He ignores Adolphus, one of the quiet ones. A mistake, maybe.

Brother Steven smiles. 'Ah, women,' he says. 'This is a good life we have here, but sometimes you have to miss 'em. O Woman! in our hours of ease, Uncertain, coy, and hard to please, And variable as the shade, By the light quivering aspen made; When pain and anguish wring the brow, A ministering angel thou!'

'Walter Scott,' says Brother Adolphus from the chair, to everyone's surprise. 'Wonderful. How about Eternal Woman draws us upward.'

Steven nods his head. 'Faust. Very impressive. Better not let Brother Herman hear you quote Goethe, however, although who knows how many of us monks are here

154

because of some calamitous Faustian pact?'

He receives no answer to that, for how many in that very room are there for dark and devilish reasons? The scissors of Barney Thomson click.

'Woman's at best a contradiction,' says Steven, to take the curse from the conversation.

'Pope!' says Adolphus. 'A woman's preaching is like a dog's walking on his hind legs. It is not done well; but you are surprised to find it done at all.'

'Excellent, Brother,' says Steven. 'Samuel Johnson. Let us have wine and women, mirth and laughter, sermons and soda-water the day after.'

'Ah, the Lord Byron,' says Adolphus. 'Those days are gone for us, Brother.'

'Indeed.'

A pause. Edward, feeling left out, makes his move.

'A bird in the hand is worth two in the bush,' he says.

Neither Steven nor Adolphus have an immediate riposte. A brake has been put on the momentum of the conversation. Edward seems quite pleased with himself, but perhaps realises that further revelations about his past might be inappropriate. Barney takes his chance.

'Hell hath no fury like a woman's scone,' he says.

Scissors click; hair falls gently to the ground; the dark grey walls of the monastery keep their secrets.

'Looks like we're in for a long winter,' says Brother Steven after a while.

Chapter 15

Snow, Sex, Thurso, Etc.

'What crap are you reading now?'

Proudfoot looks up as Mulholland arrives at the table with lunch. Soup, sandwiches, warm drinks. A small restaurant in Thurso, first-floor, looking down on the snow and the few cars out battling against the blizzard. Cricket highlights from Australia incongruously playing on the television.

'The January issue of *Blitz!*' she says.

'Isn't it still November?'

'Aye, but you know how it is with these things. The Christmas one's been on sale since the middle of August.'

'So how come you only bought it two days ago?'

''Cause it's a load of mince,' she says.

'Ah.'

Mulholland sits down, passes her lunch across the table. Three o'clock in the afternoon. A few hours spent in Caithness, persuading themselves that Barney Thomson had not remained in this area. The man has headed west.

They have come as far as Thurso, where the snow has driven them off the road. So, lunch. They seem to be spending all their time eating.

'So what have we got this time?' says Mulholland through a mouthful of sandwich. Turkey, brie, tomato and cranberry sauce.

'It's a special sex issue,' she says.

'*This* one's a special sex issue?'

'Aye. Just the usual stuff, you know, but more so.'

'Sex?' says Sheep Dip, joining them, his plate brimming with food.

Proudfoot smiles at him, enjoying the belief that Mulholland will be jealous. She swallows a spoonful of soup, feels the warmth slide down inside her like a satin glove; if you were to eat a satin glove. She lets the magazine close and Mulholland takes it off her and spins it around on the table. Reads the cover headlines, printed over the picture of an anorexic foetus with eyeshadow.

'Mel Gibson or Bruce Willis – Who's Got the Bigger Cock', 'Collagen Implants – Why They're Not All They're Blown Up to Be', 'Why I've Had It with Breasts – Meryl Streep Tells All', 'Extra-Large Mars Bar v. Cucumber – You Decide', 'Alien Sex – Not All It's Cracked Up to Be', 'Why Isabelle Adjani Is Through with Sex', 'Ninety Great Ways to the Five-Second Orgasm', 'Gretchen Schumacher on Why She's Shagged Her Last Horse', 'Lose Weight through Instant Sex', 'Why You Might Not Be Getting All the Sex You Should', 'Forty-Eight Great New Ways to Have Sex', 'Cybersex – Coming to a Computer Near You'; 'Why Male Models Have Huge Cocks', 'Trapped between the Thighs of a Cosmic Prostitute.' And much, much more.

Mulholland shakes his head, pushes the magazine away

157

from him, turning it over so as not to look at the cover. Back page: a wafer-thin wee lassie, in the pouring rain, naked but for wellies. A tampon advert, the subject of which looks as though she won't start menstruating for another three to four years.

'We need to talk,' he says, getting stuck into the soup.

'Why?' says Proudfoot. 'I'll read what I want.'

'Not about that, you numpty,' he says. 'I'm ignoring that. About Barney Thomson.'

'Oh.'

'We need to get inside the man. Try and work out what his next move might have been. We're on the right road and closing on the guy, but he's still a week and a half in front of us.'

'We're not going on any road in this weather,' says Sheep Dip, nodding at the blizzard which blows outside. It is unrelenting, sweeping in from the west. No sign of a let-up. 'It's biblical out there, so it is. Biblical,' he adds again, displaying local knowledge to its fullest.

'Aye, well, if it doesn't look like easing today, we find somewhere to stay tonight. Hope it's eased by tomorrow. We might go along to the local plods and see if we can commandeer a decent vehicle for the weather. They might have a Land Rover they'll let us have.'

'And back on Planet Earth,' says Proudfoot.

'All right, they might have a Land Rover that we can take after a few calls have been made. Whatever. We head west, but it would help if we had some idea what he was doing. So we have to think about everything we've got, come to some sort of conclusion. See if we can get somewhere that Thomson might have visited in the past few days, not a week and a half ago. And hopefully somewhere where there's not some bloody woman who thinks he's a lovely lad and insists on filling us up with

158

the entire contents of Safeway's cake shelves.'

Proudfoot mixes soup and sandwich, begins to feel life return to the freezing extremities of her body.

'It does seem strange, though, doesn't it?' she says. 'Everyone we've spoken to who's had anything to do with him, they all think he's a nice enough man. There's none of the usual stuff that comes with serial loopos. I just can't equate the Barney Thomson that we're supposed to be looking for, and the Barney Thomson that everyone who's met him describes.'

'She's got a point,' says Sheep Dip. 'They've been talking about him up here for a couple of weeks now. The lad's nae killer. Unless he's one of these, what dae ye call them, schizohaulics, or whatever.'

Mulholland shrugs. 'Who knows. Nothing he does displays the slightest cunning or criminal intuition. He decides to run, but waits until he gets to where he's going before he takes money out of the bank. If he'd done it in Glasgow we'd have no idea where he'd gone. He quite openly stays in B&Bs. Calls himself Barnabus Thompson, and thinks he'll pull the wool over someone's eyes.'

'He did,' says the Dip.

'All right, but somewhere out there, there's got to be a landlady who can see past a man's capacity to eat breakfast.'

'Don't count on it. How many phone calls have we had?' says Proudfoot.

Mulholland shakes his head. If only they didn't have to deal with the public. If it was just them and the criminals with no one else in the way, it would be so much easier. He takes a huge bite from his sandwich and mushes it up with soup. How can it be so difficult to catch a man who's such an idiot?

'There is an alternative,' says Proudfoot. Mulholland

raises his eyebrows, speech being lost to him at the moment. 'He could be taking the piss. Intentionally leaving the trail, so we'll know where to find him. Either wants to get caught, or else he's confident he'll stay one step ahead of us. Pishing himself laughing at our expense.'

Mulholland swallows. 'Could be. If that's the case, I'm going to kick the shit out of him,' he says.

'Me too.'

'Barney Thomson?' says Sheep Dip. 'Ach, away wi' ye. The lad's taking the pish out o' nae one.'

'Anyway,' says Mulholland. 'Ignoring his motives. Let's say by the time he buys his one-way ticket to Inverness he's not got much cash left. Lifts two hundred pounds when he gets there, so that's all he's got in the world. So far we've got him down for four nights' B&B. How much?'

'Fifteen a night in the first place, twenty-two in the second. So that's . . . seventy-four,' says Proudfoot.

'Right. And we know he bought some clothes in Tain. He must have had to get the bus or the train around. Eaten something for lunch and dinner. Must have spent well over a hundred. Maybe a hundred and fifty almost. And that was twelve days ago. The man has got to be running out of cash.'

'Remember he's been working,' says Sheep Dip.

Mulholland shakes his head. 'Of course, I keep forgetting. There's this huge queue of Highland eejits waiting for the most notorious psycho in Scottish history to start probing around their heads with a pair of scissors. Still, by the sound of it he's not making that much cash doing it. Can't have cut too much hair, for goodness' sake. Not everyone up here can think the guy's all right, surely?'

Sheep Dip shovels food remorselessly into his mouth.

160

'That I wouldn't count on. The lad's nae mair of a hard man than Wullie Miller, and he used tae get a' sorts o' folk speaking tae him.'

'Could be he's robbing banks or something like that,' says Proudfoot, not believing it for a second. Is instantly annoyed at herself for this pathetic sucking up; trying to persuade herself that that's not what she's doing.

'Think we'd have heard,' says Mulholland. 'All the crimes that have been reported to us as possible Barney Thomson vehicles, they're just a load of shite. You know that. We obviously don't know much about the guy, but he's just not a petty criminal. He did his crimes eight months ago, he thought he'd got away with it, and now he's having to do a runner. That's it.'

'Could be desperate,' she says.

'No, I don't think so. He doesn't have the brains for it, or the guts, or the inclination. No, there's something that first woman said. The one in Tain.'

'What?'

Sheep Dip pipes up from behind his cottage pie. 'She said that Thomson had told her he was going somewhere that nae one would have heard of him.'

Proudfoot tries to remember her saying that, but she'd been too busy trying not to laugh. Now it is her who suddenly feels in competition with Sheep Dip; a ridiculous notion. She rhythmically spoons her soup, blowing over the top of the spoon, lips round and full and moist; she swallows. Mulholland tries not to stare, but feels he has a certain leeway. Hopes he's not going to get carried away, ignore Sergeant Dip, and say something cheesy like 'I really love the way you eat your soup.'

'Abroad?' says Proudfoot, looking up and catching him.

He nods. 'All right, abroad fits the bill. But why come

to Sutherland and Caithness? It may be out of the way, but it isn't abroad. They still get the BBC and the *Daily Record*.'

'Iceland?'

He shrugs. 'Same again. You don't travel to Iceland from here. He might go to Orkney or Shetland, but they're still going to know who he is. There must be somewhere up here that he thought would have no outside contact.'

'A remote village, then,' she says. He watches her lips. Shakes his head. 'Suppose you're right,' she goes on. 'It's not like it's the Amazon or something.'

'Exactly,' says Mulholland. 'There's back-of-beyond places, but everywhere still gets the morning paper, even if it isn't until three in the afternoon. There might be places that are a little behind, but not weeks behind like he'd need. Has to be something cut off from the world. A commune, maybe.'

'Do you still get them?'

He shrugs again. Wonders if she's staring at his lips the way he's staring at hers.

'Sergeant Dip? Is there some tribe of hippies out there like those Japs that came out of the jungle forty years after the war? They're still smoking dope and doing all that Krishna stuff, think the Vietnam War's still on and Wilson's Prime Minister. Think it's cool to like Petula Clark.'

Sheep Dip chews ruminatively on some springy mince. Proudfoot laughs. Mulholland thinks, I could shag that laugh; then wonders what's getting into him. Keep talking about Barney Thomson, that's what he has to do. And try not to say something stupid like 'I love the way your nose does that little thing when you smile.'

'I dinnae think so,' says Sheep Dip. 'There are still

communes and the like, monasteries 'n a', a' that kind of thingy, but for all their shite, these people are even mair up wi' the modern world than the rest o' us, ye know? They've a' got their ane websites an a' that. There's nae one backward any mair, nae in this day and age.'

'Suppose you're right,' says Mulholland. 'The minute you get above Inverness, you still tend to think of them all as a bunch of retro sheep shaggers. But it just isn't like that any more.'

'Oh,' says Sheep Dip, shovelling bread and potatoes into his mouth, 'they still shag plenty o' sheep.'

'Right.' And Mulholland wonders for the first time about the exact origins of Sergeant MacPherson's nickname. 'Right. We can ask the local plods when we go along and take one of their cars off their hands,' he says. 'See what's in the vicinity that might make a good hideout for the most famous person in Britain. Might be a commune or a monastery after all. Who knows?'

'You still get them? Monasteries?'

Mulholland shrugs again. 'Don't know. They're not like normal people up here, are they, Sergeant Dip? Who knows what we'll encounter?'

'Life, but not as we know it,' says Proudfoot.

'Aye. Better set your phaser on stun, and be prepared to recalibrate your anophasic quantum confinement capacitor.'

'Only if you remember to bring your protoplasmic photon iridium deflector array.'

Sheep Dip munches slowly on his third slice of bread. 'You don't half get some fancy-sounding equipment down in Glasgow,' he says.

'Chief Inspector Mulholland, you say? From Glasgow?'

'Aye. This is Detective Sergeant Proudfoot.'

Sheep Dip has disappeared again; more friends or relatives to visit, Mulholland is assuming, making enquiries, he has said.

The large policeman behind the desk in the Thurso station smiles. Extends his hand across the counter.

'Sergeant Gordon. Always nice to have some colleagues up from Glasgow. We usually just see the boys from Inverness, ye know. Come on round the back and we'll get you a cup of tea. You must be frozen if you've come all that way.'

They follow him round the other side of the counter and through the door into the small back-room office. Have visions of being presented with another tray full of pastries and biscuits.

'No, it's all right, thanks. We haven't just driven from Glasgow today, and we've just had lunch.'

'Och, aye, of course,' says Sergeant Gordon. 'I've been hearing all about you. On a great odyssey across the Highlands in search of the wanted man. Thrilling stuff. But you must have a cup of tea and a biscuit. I'll just put the kettle on.'

He doesn't have to leave the office; the kettle is on another desk, surrounded by opened packets of biscuits.

'I thought the Dipper was with you?' he says.

Mulholland smiles. The Dipper . . . 'The Dipper's off making other enquiries.'

'Aye, aye, right enough, he will be. A good lad, Sheep Dip, a good lad. Now, what is it I can do for you?'

Mulholland hesitates. He has never liked interfering on

other people's patches. It is guaranteed to cause argument and upset, and nothing helps the opposition more than when the police are fighting among themselves.

'We're not setting off again tonight,' he begins.

'Good Lord, no, of course not. It's awful out there.'

'We're hoping to get on tomorrow, if it's a bit clearer. But we'll need a better vehicle for the snow. A four-wheel drive. I hate to pull rank, and I don't want to have t . . .'

'Don't be daft, lad, we've got a Land Rover you can have. As long as you bring it back in one piece, it's all yours. None o' that fancy Starsky and Hutch stuff that some o' the Glasgow lads seem tae like.'

The kettle begins to grumble. Sergeant Gordon starts placing biscuits on plates, teabags in the pot. Things are usually quiet in Thurso, but even quieter when it snows. Glad to have visitors.

'You're sure?' says Mulholland.

'Ach, nae bother, son. We've got the old one out back if we need it for emergencies. There's no point in your chief phoning up my chief and all the keich flying. Just take it and try tae bring it back in a reasonable condition.'

'Thanks a lot. Appreciate it.' He looks at Proudfoot and raises his eyebrows. At last. Help.

'Nae bother,' says Sergeant Gordon, 'nae bother at a'.'

'Now, we think Barney Thomson might have passed through this way. We're not sure. Have there been any sightings of the man, any hints of his being around here? Maybe a crime that's a little out of the norm?'

'Ye mean have we found a collection of body parts in a freezer? 'Cause we've had none of that, not for a couple o' year at any rate. Not since Big Hamish threw himsel' aff the pier at Scrabster.'

165

'No, no, we're not expecting that. Anything really. Anything unusual.'

Sergeant Gordon holds the handle of the kettle while it shudders to the boil. He smiles as he starts pouring the water into the teapot.

'Oh, aye, there was something. Old Betty down at Tongue. You know, Betty McAllister, with the enormous bosoms. She's got that auld B&B place. Seagull's Nest, or something like that, it's called. She phoned us a week or two back. Said she thought she might have this Thomson bloke of yours staying at her place. Said he seemed like a nice enough laddie, and she definitely wasn't happy about phoning, bless her.'

'What happened?' asked Mulholland. Voice dead, staring at the floor. A week or two ago. Not even beginning to get excited about this. Why is it, he thinks, that everybody on the planet is a complete and utter moron?

'Well, ye know, I was a bit busy that afternoon. It was a Sunday, I think, and ye know, what wi' lunch and a' that, and me having tae take Mother back tae the hospital in the evening. It was the following day before I got around to calling her back, and it seems like I just missed him. Barney Thomson, that is.'

Sergeant Gordon turns round, two cups of tea in hand. Notices that Mulholland is turning red. Smiles. 'Keep yer knickers on, laddie, I'm only joking,' he says. 'I've heard not a word about the man. And, as everyone knows, Betty McAllister's got pancakes for tits. Now, would you be wanting sugar?'

✁

They hurry down the path from the police station, back into the car. Out of the cold and the blizzard. Twenty-five minutes later. Cup of tea and three biscuits; nothing to be learned. Ended up chatting about Sergeant Gordon's

166

children. Have been directed to the Caithness Hotel to spend the night, where they can sit and fester and hope the blizzard passes. Pick up the Land Rover in the morning. Questions asked about any communes or similar venues where Barney Thomson might be able to hide away without fear of recognition, but the sergeant had been unable to help them. Nowhere thereabouts, as far as he could remember.

As Mulholland skids into second, slithering through the snow, Sergeant Gordon puts the kettle on again. Have a cup himself, he thinks. There are only two mugs so couldn't have one with his guests.

As he removes a couple of chocolate digestives from the packet, he remembers about the old abbey halfway between Durness and Tongue. The name escapes him, but as far as he knows it's still active. The monks keep pretty much to themselves, so he believes. Wonders if he should call the hotel and mention it to Mulholland, but midway through his first chocolate digestive, he decides not to bother. A serial killer like Barney Thomson wouldn't be wanting anything with monks, nor they with him. No point in bothering them.

By the time he bites into his second biscuit, he's already considering more important matters. Will all this snow dissuade the widow Harrison from coming over for dinner tonight?

167

Chapter 16

Mouthing Off

The depths of the night. The blizzard dives and fizzles; the dead can hear it engulf the ancient walls. White noise; wind howling through cracks and spoors and holes. A noise of giants; to fear. Life flickers in its midst, struggles against the cold. There is much will give in to its bludgeoning force this evening; and so the monks wonder as they lie awake. Will any from their number be found this coming morning, propped against a tree in the forest? A covering of snow, begun to drift? A knife or scissors or some other pointed implement embedded in the neck? The smile of the contented upon the face? Tunic soaked with blood . . .

All but one. Only one of the monks knows that there will be no body found in the forest; only one knows that tonight is not a night for murder. A night for dark deeds; a night for discovery; but not a night for death. As the blizzard rapes the Highlands, and ice descends, Death is busy elsewhere.

The monk sits in a corner of the library, book in his hand, small candle burning at his side. While all that does not worry sleeps.

This man has worked the shelves and knows this library well. All the secrets and lies of these books. All but the information that he seeks. He has almost come to the end of his search, with nowhere else to look; but nowhere can he find an account of Two Tree Hill. He had felt sure it would be written, for how could so fateful a day not be recorded? He must accept that if he cannot find the account for which he searches then his plans must change. In recent weeks his search has become ever more feverish as he has neared the end of his quest; a fever which led to his discovery, and the necessary, if unfortunate, elimination of the Brothers' librarian. Although, of course, Saturday had had it coming anyway.

Slowly he turns the pages of a book of records, but it is one he has seen before. This is the double check, and he knows that he will not find what he is looking for here.

A sliver of sound.

Almost nothing, but he turns his head sharply. Eyes wide, pupils huge, used to the black of night despite the candle. Holds still, not even his breath, but there is nothing. Senses are sharp, but this is one man who does not have a reason to fear.

A gentle blow from his lips and the candle is extinguished. Not much difference it makes its light had been so insignificant. The vestige of light, of snow and low white clouds, is smuggled into the library, but once there is engulfed by the dark. The monk waits.

Was the noise that of someone going out or coming in? Has he been spotted again, but this time by someone with the good sense not to make himself known? The monk stands, silent. Every sense concentrated on his awareness of the library; and yet he is annoyed at the interruption. There is work to be done, decisions to be made.

169

He hears another sound, a definite footstep, and so knows that he is not alone. Yet he is not afraid. He fingers the comb within the folds of his tunic. Has another cold plan for murder, although he had not thought to use it so soon; another device to shift suspicion onto their newest recruit, the hapless Brother Jacob.

He becomes aware of a figure in front of him, can sense him as much as see him in the gloom.

'Why do you not step out of the darkness, Brother?' he says.

He hears the breathing for the first time, is aware that his visitor takes another couple of steps towards him.

'There is no light into which to step, Brother,' comes the reply.

'Ah, it is you,' says the brother. 'I should have known. So good of you to join me at this early hour in the library. While the blizzard rages outside. You could not sleep, then?' One of the monks on his incomplete list; an opportune visit.

'There are many within these walls who cannot sleep, Brother. And I, equally, am not surprised to discover that it is you who are here, lurking among these books. Might I enquire for what it is that you search?'

'Truth, Brother, nothing but the truth.'

'Then you are not alone among us.'

'But not religious truth, Brother. We all know religion is nothing but a glue that binds us together. There is no truth in religion, no truth to be found in God. It is a stabilising force, it gives humanity some purpose, some sense of perspective, but there is no truth to it. Nothing to be gained.'

The visitor monk does not immediately answer, and in the dark the two men gradually become more aware of the physical presence of the other. A few yards apart; and yet, they could not be farther away.

'God will surely find you out, Brother. And you will suffer his wrath for all eternity.'

The Brother laughs, and the other shivers at the sound in the midst of such darkness.

'There is no God, Brother. If there was, he has forsaken us. He has forsaken you. But you know, everyone here knows, deep in their black, pathetic hearts, that there never was a God. There was but a Church, run by the best spin doctors of the first few centuries, and out of it has come all of this. The modern world the way it is. There is no God, no faith, no belief. There are no rules. It's every man for himself, Brother, every man for himself.'

The visitor laughs quietly, but the nervousness of it betrays him. 'I thought I recognised you when you first arrived. Something in the eyes, or maybe the nose. Yours was a face from the past. But I cannot believe that this is all because of what happened at Two Tree Hill. That was an inconsequence.'

The words hang in the cold air, are engulfed by the darkness and the cruelty of cold, the creaking of the monastery under the weight of the storm.

'An inconsequence? On the contrary, my friend. It had very many consequences, and they will continue for some time to come.'

It is time. They both know that something must be done. Nothing left to be said. A murderer, and now someone who has stumbled across him. Thought must become deed.

Brother Babel walks slowly through the darkness.

They've sat up later than intended, neither wishing to let the other go, neither willing to make the big move. His wife may have left, but it has not given Mulholland an immediate guilt-free shag voucher, to be cashed in at the first available motorway service station serving all-day sex. He is still a married man. Proudfoot might wonder about Mulholland's marriage, and yet does not care, but this is still the boss and you have to be careful. Perhaps if she was given some signs, but she's bad at reading signs. Generally needs a man to remove his clothes and drag her to the bedroom by the hair to feel sure she's got the go-ahead to get stuck in.

'Seaman Stains and Master Bates and all that lot,' he says.

'Load of pish,' she says.

'What do you mean?'

'All that stuff about Pugwash getting taken off the air because of pathetic double-meaning names is a load of nonsense. There weren't characters with those names at all.'

'There bloody were!'

'Oh, aye. Can you remember them?'

He hesitates, shrugs his shoulders. 'No, but it's what everyone says. Everyone knows it. It's well known, so it is.'

'It may be,' says Proudfoot, 'but it's still nonsense. It's just one of those things that gets popularised and becomes fact, when it just isn't true. Like when Norman Mailer invented the fact that Bobby Kennedy slept with Marilyn Monroe; now it's a fact. That Disney film about lemmings throwing themselves off cliffs, which everyone now believes, but it's mince. Captain Kirk saying 'Beam me up, Scotty' and Humphrey Bogart saying 'Play it again, Sam'. They're all untrue. Mere manifestations of the gullibility and willingness of humankind to believe any rumour they like the sound of.'

He drains his final glass of wine. Bottle finished; determined not to have any more.

'If that's true, then why was Pugwash taken off the telly for so long? Eh? Answer me that one.'

''Cause it was shite.'

'Oh.' He stares into the bottom of his glass. 'Aye, well, maybe you're right.'

They smile at each other. Drinks finished. Well after twelve o'clock. Wind howling outside; not sure if the snow still drifts against the walls.

'Should be getting to bed,' says Mulholland.

'Aye.'

Neither of them makes a move. Both would go to the other's bed if given the opportunity.

'Who knows,' he says, 'what horrors we might encounter tomorrow? Any amount of landladies armed with nuclear amounts of cake and biscuits.'

He stands up as he says it; Proudfoot follows. They walk to the stairs and the slow march to the first floor. Proudfoot behind, staring at him. Thinking. They walk along the short stretch of corridor. Creaking floorboards, thick red carpet. Fly-fishermen on the walls, low lights. The smell of wood fires, warm and damp and rich.

Her room first. He stops, turns, waits the brief second. She puts the key in the lock, opens the door, then stops and stares.

Want to come in for the night? That's what she thinks, but her tongue is silent when it comes to say it. Both eyes cry out, but there's nothing there. Not from either of them; and so they take the silence from the other as rejection.

She smiles weakly. 'I've had a nice evening. Thanks,' she says. I don't want it to end yet is left unsaid.

'Aye,' he says. 'Me too.'

A few more painful seconds, then goodnight. She walks into the room, closes the door. Stands on the other side, lets out the long sigh.

Joel Mulholland stares at the closed door. Mutters, 'Fuck it.'

Retreats. He begins the slow walk to his bedroom, only not turning back downstairs to the bar because he knows the barman has already closed up for the night. Perhaps he might find some relief in sleep; perhaps he will lie awake until four in the morning, staring at a red ceiling.

And in a B&B near by, Sheep Dip eats a late supper.

Hudibrastic Head Boiling

'Jings tae goodness, would ye no' put that light out, Mary Strachan? Whit time might it be, anyway?'

Mary Strachan glances at the bedside clock, then looks down at the prostrate bulk of her husband, wrestling as usual with most of the covers.

'It's almost four,' she says.

James Strachan opens his eyes and looks up at her.

'Four o'clock! Help m'boab, woman, whit are you doin' awake at four o'clock in the morning? Can ye no' just get some sleep for a wee whiley?'

'Ach, would ye listen tae yon storm. I cannae sleep, can I, what wi' yon racket and you snoring.'

'Away and stick yer heid in a bucket o' kippers. If I snore, I don't know whit it is that ye'd call whit you do.

174

Can ye no' put the blinking light out?'

'I'm reading, so I am. Can you no' see that?'

'Jings tae goodness, whit is it now? Ye're no' reading mair o' that Dostoevsky nonsense, are ye? I've telt ye before, it's a' a load o' keich.'

'I'm reading Molière, if ye must know.'

'Jings. That French pish? Whit are ye reading yon for? Have ye got nothing better tae dae wi' yer time? *On ne meurt qu'une fois, et c'est pour si longtemps*, eh? Absolute shite, so it is. Absolute shite.'

'It is not, so it's not. If you must know, I just happen to like the sub-Hudibrastic lineage of the prose. So much better than his Scottish or English contemporaries.'

James Strachan finally sits up in bed. Wide awake. Aware of the wind piling the snow against the side of the house; he ignores it.

'Hudibrastic? Ye mean his writing employs a burlesque cacophonous octosyllabic couplet with extravagant rhymes?'

'Aye.'

'Away an' stick yer heid in a bucket o' sludge, Mary Strachan. Molière did no such thing.'

'He did so!'

'Ye know fine well he didnae. You just wanted tae say "Hudibrastic".'

'I did not.'

James Strachan snorts, then lowers himself back into the bed. He grumbles a few times, pulling the covers another inch away from his wife and up around his neck, then closes his eyes. Shivers noisily with the cold.

'If you wouldn't mind just hudibrastically putting the light off when you're finished, Mother.'

Mary Strachan gives him a glance; ignores him.

'I'm just going to try and get some sleep,' he continues. 'As long as the hudibrasticity of the weather doesnae keep me awake.'

'You're not funny, James Strachan.'

'Aye, I cannae believe how hudibrasticomatic the wind's being. If we're lucky by the morning it'll have hudibrastised and the hudibrastocity of the snow will have given way tae weather of a much more hudibrastrous nature.'

'No one's laughing, James Strachan. Least of all me.'

He grumbles, but doesn't reply.

Mary Strachan decides to give in to the night. She closes the book and places it on the bedside table. She removes her glasses and places them on top of the book. She sighs, moves down under the covers before she turns off the light. She does her best to retrieve as many of the blankets from her husband as she can; thinks of something as she reaches for the light and switches it off. Her head settles back on the pillow.

'That Barney Thomson was on the news again tonight. After you'd come to bed, ye know.'

James Strachan grumbles in reply.

'Seems he's suspected in an armed robbery in Dumfries. I'm no' so sure, but I suppose he could've gone down there after he was here. But he did say he was going to yon monastery for a wee whiley, did he no'? Maybe I should say something tae the police, what dae ye think? We don't want him being accused of things he didnae do.'

James Strachan grumbles again. Finds the words. 'I think ye're havering, Mary Strachan. Now would ye try and get some sleep?'

She ignores him. 'Oh, aye, and another thing. Apparently they're saying it was his fault that Stevie Nicol missed yon sitter against Uruguay in Mexico in 1986.'

James Strachan grumbles some more. 'Aye, nae doubt. That sounds reasonably hudibrastoplastic tae me.'

The old couple settle into their bed, as the wind blows and the snow piles against their house. And some twenty miles away, while Barney Thomson sleeps and the blizzard howls up the glen, the third murder in five days is committed at the monastery of the Holy Order of the Monks of St John.

'Away and stick yer heid in a sheep's stomach, James Strachan.'

Chapter 17

'The tree o' liberty must be refreshed fi' time tae time wi' the blood o' patriots and tyrants. It is its natural manure.'

'Oh, aye, Mary Strachan, that's a' very well. But just whit has that eejit Thomas Jefferson got tae dae wi' the fact that they're sayin' it was Barney Thomson's fault that Jim Leighton sold the goal against Brazil in Italy in 1990?'

Woke Up This Morning, With Nothing To Lose Soon Turns Out, I got the Busted Gearbox Blues

Clear blue skies; thick snow on the ground, white and fresh. A gentle breeze blowing off the land, out to sea. The blizzard and high winds gone in the night. Freezing temperatures, but the kind of cold a good coat can combat; faces shine, noses run, ears go red.

They sit in the Land Rover, heating on full, slithering out of Thurso and heading west. Sheep Dip in the back, eating the third of five rolls 'n' bacon. The snowploughs have already been along the road; snow piled high at the sides, great hedgerows. Blocking out the view; like driving through Devon. Along the top of Scotland, no particular destination in mind. The plan is as before, to stop at every hotel and B&B, but they know that that is not where their destination lies. Barney Thomson will not be holed up somewhere where he has to pay his way. He could not automatically trust to all his keepers' innocence. He must have found some other refuge, or else gone on. He could easily have gone to the north islands, and it might be that they come back this way. They will have to anyway, for the exchange of cars. For the moment, they must leave Thurso behind.

Sergeant Gordon had had it in mind to tell them about the Sutherland monastery when they came to pick up the Land Rover, but somehow it slipped his attention. He will remember some time in the afternoon, and smile wryly to himself, then he will make another cup of tea. Serial killers do not haunt monasteries. They go for places like underground caverns and houses in the woods. He's seen the movies.

Past Melvich and Strathy, on towards Bettyhill. Slow going, stopping intermittently; occasional forays along small roads, down which the snowplough has not bothered to venture. Skidding and slipping and sliding. Glad of the four-wheel drive, although Mulholland has not much experience. Proudfoot has some, but keeps her mouth shut. Not sure if Mulholland's ego could handle a woman telling him what to do. She decides only to open her mouth if they get stuck. Sheep Dip has been used to four-wheel drive since he was seven, but does not feel it is for him to say anything. He enjoys the ride, laughs quietly to himself, and munches his way through a couple of movie bags of Doritos.

A succession of rejections and blank looks. A few

179

possibles, slipping away to nothing. Most places this far north closed for the winter. A few hotels, a few forlorn B&Bs. Sometimes they come to houses; the sign's up, but the building is along some inaccessible road. So they have to struggle on foot, which only Sheep Dip is dressed for. Feet and trousers soaking after the first couple, so they end up sending Sheep Dip on his own.

A couple of tortuous hours into their day, not long after twelve, Mulholland first notices the problem with the car. Trouble getting into third, all the other gears still available. Slowly, as they go, gears vanish, until he is driving solely in second. Waiting for it to disappear at any time. They struggle into a small garage in Tongue. Just before he pulls in off the road, he notices that it has not been cleared ahead. He parks in the garage next to the snowplough.

Feet cold and soaking, no amount of heat directed their way having any noticeable effect. Fed up. Getting nowhere. The ups and downs of humour. Proudfoot no different.

He takes the car out of gear. For the last time. Switches off the engine, looks at Proudfoot. Has forgotten about Sheep Dip.

'Fuck it,' he says.

'How long do you think it'll take to fix?' she says.

He shakes his head. Getting annoyed at her, because he wants her and he's too racked with pusillanimity to say anything.

'I don't know, do I, Sergeant? If I was a mechanic I'd have fixed the bloody thing by now.'

He gets out of the car and slams the door. He stops and stares at the snow at his feet. What is he doing? There's no point in losing his temper at her; some pseudo-Freudian knee-jerk reaction just because he's too much of

180

a jessie to try to sleep with her.

'He fancies you,' says Sheep Dip from the back, before taking a bite out of a spectacularly green apple.

'He does not,' says Proudfoot. She gets out of the car, and looks at him. There is nothing there as he returns the look. He can apologise later, he thinks. Shrugs his shoulders.

A mechanic, yellow-overalled, appears from behind the snowplough, rubbing his hands on a dirty rag. Why do they always do that? thinks Proudfoot.

'Good afternoon,' he says, looking suspiciously at the police vehicle. 'It's a bitty of a day tae be out, is it no'?'

'Duty calls,' says Mulholland. Not in the mood for conversation.

'Not from around here, then,' says the mechanic. 'Still, I see you're driving Lachlan Gordon's car. You must be the folks up from the Big Smoke looking for this serial killer fellow, is that no' right?'

'Brilliant, Holmes, how do you do it?' says Mulholland.

'Ach, it's nae difficult. A'body knows yer up here, drivin' around in yer fancy motors and stayin' in a' the best hotels.'

'Is that right?'

'Aye, aye. So are youse two lovebirds sleeping together yet, or whit?'

'Sorry?'

'Ach well, it doesnae matter, doesnae matter at a'. What can I be doin' for ye?'

Proudfoot looks at the ground. Mulholland tries not to lose his temper. He has stopped analysing his feelings of hostility. Given in to them and determined to enjoy it. He is about to speak when the door of the Land Rover opens and Sheep Dip crunches into the snow.

'Hey, hey, hey,' says the mechanic. 'If it isn't the auld Dipmeister himself. How are ye doing, Sergeant? It's been a wee whiley since you've been up in these parts, is it no'?'

'Aye, well, ye know, after what happened wi' Big Mary and the combine . . .'

'Oh, aye, aye, right enough. Some things are better left alone, especially now wi' Donald back fi' the Falklands.'

'Hello!' says Mulholland. 'Can we get on? I've got a problem with the gearbox.'

'No!' says the mechanic.

'Aye,' says Mulholland.

'Ach, that blasted thing. There's nae a mechanic in Caithness or Sutherland who hasnae had a go at Lachlan's gearbox. And tae be honest wi' ye, we're a' fair scunnert by it.'

'This happens a lot?'

'Aye, aye. A' the time, laddie, didn't he tell you? Ach, no, no, I suppose he didnae.'

'So you'll know how to fix it?'

The mechanic puts his hands on his hips and shakes his head. Looks at the Land Rover like he'd look at a horse with a broken leg.

'Oh, it's no' easy as a' that, I'm afraid, laddie. It's a big job, and a' that, ye know, and what wi' me havin' tae fix Big Davie's snowplough. That's got tae come first, ye know. Have tae have the roads through tae Durness cleared by this evening.'

'Listen, this is police business. I need that car to be fixed as soon as possible.'

'Don't you go spouting yer fancy police business talk at me, sonny. And just where dae ye think ye're going to be going wi' nae snowplough on the roads? Tell me that, laddie? He sows hurry and reaps indigestion. Robert

182

Louis Stevenson. Mark those words, laddie.'

'I'm not going to get indigestion if you get a move on fixing the sodding Land Rover.'

'Oh, but you will if you have some lunch at Agnes's wee shop up the road while you wait.'

Hand to forehead, rubs his brow. Other hand on hip. Aware that a vein throbs in his head. Not at one with the northern people, Joel Mulholland. He is not coping well with the stress of marital difficulties, combined with the hunt for a serial killer, unfettered testosterone, and a melancholy gearbox. He doesn't know what to say next. He has visions of getting a helicopter up to fly the three of them around, but imagines McMenemy would not be too keen on that.

'How long will it take, Mr . . .?' says Proudfoot.

'Oh, Alexander Montgomerie. You can call me Sandy.'

'How long,' says Mulholland, looking up, voice steady, that monotone clipped wordage of the excessively angry, 'will it take to fix the snowplough?'

Sandy Montgomerie turns and looks at the large yellow truck. Rubs his hand across his chin. Thinking, probably.

'Oh, I should say another couple of hours at the most. Ye know, it's a problem with the carburettor and the . . .'

'And how long after you've done that to fix the Land Rover?'

He turns back and stares at the Land Rover. Scratches his chin again then narrows his eyes and purses his lips in scrutiny.

'Ach, it's hard tae say, ye know. It's a big job, mind, a right big job. Doubt I'll get it finished the night.'

'Aw, bloody fuck,' says Mulholland. He turns away, staring at the white hills behind.

'Now, laddie, there's nae need for that. I'll work as fast as I can.'

Mulholland doesn't turn back. Becomes aware of his freezing feet, the damp working its way up his legs. Feels like screaming.

'Is there any other way to get along this road today?' asks Proudfoot.

'Ye mean like a bus or a car hire company, or something like that?' says Montgomerie.

'Aye.'

'No, no, there's nothing like that up here. Nae bus'll be going along on a day like the day.'

'Brilliant,' says Mulholland from behind.

'So what is there along here? Bed and breakfasts and hotels and the like. Anything?' says Proudfoot.

Sandy Montgomerie stares at the blue sky. Watches a couple of gulls joust in the cold air. Mournful cry, sharp in the cold. Sheep Dip bites into his apple.

'How many dawns, chill fi' his ripplin' rest, the seagull's wings dip and pivot him, Sheddin' white rings o' tumu . . .'

'For God's sake, would you shut up with all this bloody literature! I've had enough of bloody Stevenson!'

'That was Hart Crane, laddie, no' Stevenson.'

'I don't give a shite who it was, would you just answer the questions?'

'Aye, aye, nae bother. Keep yer heid on, laddie.' Looks at Proudfoot. 'I think ye're gonnae have tae shag him, lassie, the way he's carryin' on.'

'Right,' she says. Stares at the ground.

'Now as far as I know, there'll be nothing open between here and Durness this time o' year. Once you get there, there's a couple o' hotels and the like, but there's probably only one B&B open. That'll be Mrs Strachan. You might like to check that.'

'And do you think we could get a lift in the snow-

184

plough?' she asks.

'Aye, I don't see why no'. Big Davie's a lovely big lad, I'm sure he'd be delighted tae gie yese a lift.'

'Big Davie?'

'Aye, Big Davie Cranachan. Drives the snowplough, just like his father before him and his father before him, and so on. A' the way back tae the days o' the Clearances. Ah remember ma old father tellin' me so . . .'

'Where can we find him?' says Mulholland, turning round.

Sandy Montgomerie looks up the road. Thinks. Points.

'He'll be havin' a spot o' lunch at Agnes's place. One o' her chicken pies, if I'm nae mistaken. Could dae wi' one o' them myself at the moment, but I should be gettin' on.'

'Thanks,' says Proudfoot. 'We'll go and speak to him.'

'Aye, fine, I'm sure he'll be obligin'.'

Proudfoot starts trudging off in the direction of Agnes's place. Mulholland looks to Sandy Montgomerie, nods, trails after his sergeant. Foul mood intact. Sheep Dip stops to chat.

'What's the matter with you?' she says, as he catches up with her.

'Leave it, Sergeant,' he replies. 'Just leave it.'

'Aye, fair enough,' she says. 'But don't think I'm shagging you in that mood.'

Mair Shite

'Away an' stick yer heid in a bucket o' puddin', Mary Strachan, ye're haverin' again.'

'Ach, I'm nae haverin', James Strachan. If there's

either of us haverin', it's you. Look at yon ugly mug,' she says, pointing at the television. 'That's him, I'm tellin' you. He stayed right here in this house. Sure as Wee Fiona Menzies went saft in the heid after Hamish left her for yon stripper fi' Inverness.'

James Strachan shookles his paper and once more disappears behind the sports pages of the *Scotsman*. 'Gers Grab Dutch Embryo in £80 Million Swoop' – 'If It's a Girl, She Plays on the Wing,' Says Unconcerned Boss.'

'That's how much you know, wummin. She wisnae a stripper, she was a cheese-o-gram. Now would ye hawd yer wheesht aboot yon Barney Thomson? I'm tryin' tae read ma paper.' 'Scotland to Field Nine Defenders in Friendly against Andorra – 'Their right wing back plays Spanish 8th division football, and he worries me,' admits Brown.'

'Ach, away you and roast yer feet in the oven, James Strachan. As soon as this snow clears, I'll be goin' to see the FBI, so I will. Nae mistake.'

'The FBI! The FBI! Whit are ye bletherin' about, Mary Strachan? I keep tellin' ye, ye watch too much shite on that television. That's why ye think we've had a serial killer staying in Durness. But I'm telling ye, missus, the only serial killer we've had wis yon bloke who ate a' the Weetabix.'

'Ach, away and stick yer heid in a roaring fire, James Strachan.'

'Aye, well, you away and stick your heid in a blazin' furnace, Mary Strachan. If Barney Thomson was goin' tae the monastery, why did he no' just go there straight fi' Tongue? It's the same distance and it would have saved him the bother o' comin' a' the way up here.'

'Whit? Look, Ah'm nae sayin' he's no' an eejit, but the man was definitely here, so you away and stick your heid inside an active volcano, James Strachan.'

'An active volcano? It's like that, is it? Well, away you and stick your heid inside an exploding star, Mary Strachan.'

The discussion continues, but the sharp edge of intellectual debate has been lost, and so the argument degenerates into petty name-calling and insults.

Chapter 18

The Sort of Turning Point You Just Don't Want to Know About

It is Brother Frederick who discovers the latest body; the latest murdered monk. The corpse resting against a tree in the wood, covered in snow from the blizzard which still rages. He shouldn't be out at his age, that's what some of the monks think, but Frederick is still active. He has no intention of going quietly in his bed; a man who will die on his feet, that's what he's always thought. And he wonders now if he'll die at the hands of a killer, like the rest of the monks at the monastery, now that some new evil has been visited upon them.

Frederick is the only one who knows about the murders of 1927, when fourteen of the monks were poisoned in little more than a month. There had been many more of their number in those days, but fourteen still cut into the very heart of them. And yet the police had not been called; the monks had rooted out the killer on their own, dealt with him summarily. God's judgement. but he is now reminded of those terrible days.

When the latest victim did not immediately appear at breakfast, there was no particular notice paid. This monk was frequently kept away at mealtimes, such were his duties, and the more so now. One or two might have suspected there was something wrong, but only Frederick felt it. Felt evil as there had been seventy years before.

He went out into the cold after breakfast to search. The snow howled around in the wind, small flakes in a hyper-tensioned frenzy. Knew that he could not stay out in it for long, but reckoned that the killer would not have done so either. Did not have far to search for the body.

And now he stands. One hundred and four years old, Brother Frederick, having found the latest victim of the monastery killer in the usual position. Sitting upright, legs splayed, but this time no blood. No knife or pair of scissors in the neck. No weather for an old man to be carrying out a post-mortem, but he takes a quick look. The eyes smiling in death, as with the brothers librarian, but not the mouth this time. The lips are opened and slightly distorted by something inside the mouth. He tentatively takes an old frail hand from within his cloak and pushes the top lip slightly higher. Inside the mouth a comb, lodged against the top of the mouth and back against the tongue, forcing the tongue down the throat so that the victim must have choked on it.

Death by comb; a bitter smile comes to the face of the old man. He has seen many things in his time, many horrible deaths, but never this.

He lets the lip go, and it stays in the position into which it was pushed. Takes one last look at the corpse, then begins his retreat through the snow back to the monastery. He does not fear that one of the men who waits inside is a killer. Prescient death awaits Brother Frederick, this he knows. He worries for his brothers, but saw so much death in those early days that eighty years with the Lord have not done anything for his

189

ambivalence to it. Death, good or bad but inevitable.

The wind in his face, cheeks frozen, lips drawn tight and purple across bared teeth, Brother Frederick struggles back to the partial warmth of the monastery. How many of those murders of '27 had it been his painful duty to report?

✂

Barney Thomson undertakes what he now sees as most definitely the secondary of his two tasks. Cleaning the floors. On his hands and knees, scrubbing the stone. Must polish next. Good upkeep is the only thing that has kept these buildings together, that's what he was told early on.

He has already worked the corridors of the third floor and now finds himself in the library. In between the shelves. Hidden from the rest of the room, but there is no one else there. He wonders why Brother Herman is not on duty. Presumes he is out bending someone's thumbs backwards or putting their testicles through a clothes press in order to discover some incontrovertible truth.

Wonders at what stage the investigation into his own disappearance is at, whether the police have discovered any of the places he stayed at on his short journey across the Highlands. How soon will it be safe for him to venture back out from the monastery? He is aware of the fads of modern life; how something can dominate the news for a few weeks and then be gone as if it never existed. Could that happen to the myth of the cold serial killer, Barney Thomson? He is not to know the headline in that morning's *Daily Record*: 'Barber Surgeon Blamed for Stock Exchange Débâcle.' Occasionally he thinks about Agnes, and assumes she is comfortably at home with her hideous soap operas. He wonders how Allan is coping with the stigma of having a brother wanted by the police. Rightly assumes that he will have changed his name.

But where could he go if he fled from this cold prison? What could he do for money? What can life possibly offer him now?

He knows he has no option. He must wait it out at the monastery of death, and hope he is not farther sucked into the macabre happenings. Something might come along, or maybe time will make him less visible in the outside world. By next summer, perhaps, there will be a new hate figure. He must keep his head down, and hope that the monks do not hear news of him from the outside world. This blizzard will help that, and maybe by the time the next contact has been made, some other poor bastard will be dominating the front pages.

Head down, mouth shut, on with his work, and try not to get on the wrong side of Brother Herman. Barney Thomson scrubs the floor a little bit harder.

A minute, then he hears footsteps, voices. Stops scrubbing; holds his breath. Not sure if the library is out of bounds. Had only ventured in because Herman was not here to ask. He crouches against a bookcase, recognising the voices as those of the Abbot and Brother Adolphus. Quick steps, stopping as they get into the centre of the room.

'Brother Herman!' the Abbot calls out. Nothing. Barney hears the footsteps, agitatedly around the back of the desk. Wonders if he should make himself known, but something stays him. Either a sixth sense, or that quality which allows him to make the wrong decision in nearly every difficult circumstance.

'Goodness,' says the Abbot, 'where can the good brother be?'

'If you would tell me the reason for your agitation, Brother Abbot, perhaps I would be of some comfort to you. You appear most distressed.'

You appear most distressed, repeats Barney to himself.

191

Creep. He has not taken to Brother Adolphus. A pause, then comes the Abbot's reply. Barney's heart beats a little faster.

'There has been another murder, Brother!'

A strangled gasp from Adolphus, then, 'In the Lord's name, who is it this time?'

No immediate reply. Barney stares at the cold, dark ceiling. Another death among them. He tries to think who was not at breakfast, but there were a few. Always some who chose to go without.

'It is dear Brother Babel. Brother Frederick found his body at the edge of the forest, not ten minutes ago.'

'Brother Babel!'

Brother Babel. Fifty-three, surprisingly corpulent of build, balding and warm-hearted. Friend to them all, enemy to none. A pure and honest man, one of the few at the monastery with genuine motive. Used to be a fine left-back. In the wrong place at the wrong time.

There is nothing else immediately said, while the Abbot wrings his hands and Brother Adolphus digests the news. That is, if he didn't already know it, thinks Barney Thomson, for one of these monks must be the killer, and the possibilities are getting fewer each time. Three dead already, and it certainly wasn't he himself.

'I need to find Brother Herman. It is his investigation. There's little chance of the police managing to find a way up here, or of us getting out to them in the first place. Not with this blizzard. We are trapped in our own prison, Brother Adolphus, with a killer on the loose. I should not have allowed myself to be guided by Herman. I should have had the police in here five days ago. This is a terrible business. Terrible.'

Brother Babel. Barney continues to stare at the ceiling. He hadn't spoken to the man. A Brother Cadfael haircut, albeit one administered by the wayward hand of Adolphus; obviously ate a little too much food. What else? Nothing, nothing at all. Just another man he has hardly known, and who is now dead.

How did he manage to be so foolish as to come to this place? But then, how was he to know? He had read an article about the monks and their solitary existence cut off from the world in the *Herald* the previous spring. It had seemed such a natural place to hide when the whole of the Western world was looking for him. But as soon as he arrived . . .

Could he have brought some evil with him? Some malign spirit?

'How did he die, Brother Abbot?' says Adolphus. He has not been part of the previous investigations, but has heard the rumours of stabbing, as have all the others.

'With a comb,' says the Abbot.

Barney hears the gasp of Adolphus. Only just manages to contain his own gasp.

'He was combed to death?' says Adolphus, having never heard of such a thing.

'The comb had been rammed into his mouth, forcing his tongue back down his throat, so that he choked on it. That is what dear Brother Frederick seems to think.'

'Good heavens, Brother! A comb. But there would be only one brother in our midst with a comb.'

'Exactly. Brother Jacob. Oh dear, oh dear. I really shouldn't have insisted that Herman be so easy on him after the murder of Brother Morgan with his scissors. It appears that it all ties up. These deaths did not start until Jacob came among us, and within a few short days of his being here, three of our number have been killed. Now a second with an implement under Jacob's control. We must find the wretched brother, and we must find Brother

Herman. God help us if anything should have happened to him.'

'This is indeed a most wretched business, Brother. Is there no way we could get a message to the outside?'

'Listen,' says the Abbot. And Brother Adolphus listens to the wind of the blizzard batter against the side of the monastery. 'We are trapped, Brother, only ourselves and our Lord to protect us. I shall put it around the monks, see if there is one of the younger ones brave enough to go out into the storm, but it is hardly something I can ask.' Because it would appear that we cannot rely on our Lord, he thinks, but does not voice. Wonders why they have been deserted, and why this evil has come to them. 'Come, Brother Adolphus, we must find Brother Herman and tell him this most grievous news. Then we must apprehend Jacob. And the body of dear Babel, he must be brought in from the cold. By God, this is a most heinous day.'

The footsteps recede quickly from the library, the heavy door closes and the sound vanishes behind the heavy oak.

Silence.

Barney Thomson still stares at the ceiling. In a trance. Suspected of murders which he hasn't committed. And yet? he wonders. Is he a schizophrenic? Does he lose himself sometimes in his sleep? All these murders have been at night. And for all his trouble drifting off, once he has gone off he sleeps soundly. Not even dreams. Perhaps he sleepwalks; sleep-murders. Disposes of the bodies, then slips back into his bed. Murder committed and none the wiser. He has heard of it happening.

And if not that, could someone be trying to frame him, because he is the newest monk and an obvious suspect? Brother Martin perhaps? Or even Brother Herman himself? There's a possibility, he thinks, but there is nothing he can do about it. He has no defence, and he is the outsider. There is no reason why he should get a fair trial from these people. He knows how dangerous religious fanaticism can be. He has read books, discussed it over a pint with Bill Taylor.

But there is no getting out; no escaping the monastery at this time. He would be a fool to head off into the hills in this weather; as certain a suicide as putting a gun to his head. He must find some hiding place in the monastery, then wait out the storm. Go on the run when the weather has broken, before they can get in the outside agencies of the law. Once the police have been called, he is done.

Barney Thomson drops his eyes from the ceiling to the floor. There are no answers to be found, but he has to move quickly. No decisions this time. His temporary respite has gone; he is once again a fugitive. Perhaps he should make himself known to the Abbot, defend himself. By running he will be implicated beyond any doubt in their eyes. But he cannot believe that he will be judged fairly. He has heard the Abbot's own words, and they sound like those of a man whose mind is already made up. So, just like he did when he accidentally killed Wullie Henderson eight and a half months previously, he will once again avoid confrontation with the authorities for as long as he can.

He stands, but leans against the shelving. He feels weak, but knows he must hide quickly. As he considers what he knows about the monastery buildings and whether he can find somewhere to hide where he won't die of cold, he wonders if outside there might be some part of these islands where the name Barney Thomson is not considered evil, where someone called Barney Thomson might walk a free man.

He is not to know the headline in that morning's *Scotsman*. '"Bring Me the Head of Barney Thomson", Slams First Minister.'

195

Chapter 19

Bullshit

'Aye, aye, it's a long time since we had one o' you lot up fi' Glasgae, an' a' that, ye know,' says Big Davie. The snowplough grinds horribly slowly towards Durness. Mulholland, Sheep Dip and Proudfoot are squeezed into the cab, thighs pressed against thighs. Sheep Dip takes large bites from a small chocolate bar, and Mulholland can feel himself resenting every mouthful, as if it reduces his space by some infinitesimal amount. A doppelgänger for his annoyance at not getting to press his legs against Proudfoot's.

'You're from Glasgow yourself, then?' says Proudfoot. Recognise that accent anywhere.

'Oh, aye. Ma mother an' faither split up when Ah wis a wean, an a' that. Ma mother took us back tae Cam'slang, ye know. Load o' shite. Came back up here as soon as Ah could get away wi'oot her phonin' the *Daily Record*. Huvnae seen her in aboot six year. Daft cow.'

Mulholland stares at the snow on the road ahead. Mind numbed. Attempting to switch off, but not achieving completion.

Big Davie looks across Mulholland and Sheep Dip, who for his purposes might not be there, at the alluring Proudfoot.

'So, you're a wummin, then?' he says.

Proudfoot doesn't look round. She stares at the snow on the road and doesn't really have an answer for that. Hasn't thought about it in a while.

'Check the big brain on Davie,' says Mulholland, muttering.

'Aye,' says Big Davie, 'Ah notice these things, so Ah dae. No' often ye get a wummin polis around here, ye know. No' that ye look like a polis, or anythin' like that.'

'Oh. So what do I look like?' she says.

Big Davie gives Mulholland a quick glance. Wonders how much he can try it on with the Bad Cop sitting beside him. Bugger it, he thinks; in for a penny, and a' that.

'One o' they supermodels or a film star or somethin'.'

Crap line; but it's worked in the seedy bars of Bettyhill and Scrabster. Wee Alison McVitie; Big Janice McLeod; Esther 'The Bedtester' Comrie; Phyllis 'Froglegs' Duncan; Big Effie MacFarlane. The list is long.

Mulholland laughs. Proudfoot switches from cynicism to annoyance. Sheep Dip cracks open a bag of Maltesers and pops six of them into his mouth. He's had the same thoughts about Proudfoot himself, but he knows what Mrs Dip would have to say about it. The Big Mary incident was just about the last straw.

'Piss off, you,' says Proudfoot, addressing Mulholland.

'Aye,' says Big Davie, seeing his opportunity, 'could see you on wan o' they magazine covers, ye know. *Cosmopolitan*, or somethin'.'

'Aye,' says Mulholland. 'Erin Proudfoot on why she's shagged her last beefburger.'

'Would you shut your face?' she says.

'Aye,' says Big Davie, 'ye get a lot o' they polis wimmin who are absolute stankmonsters, ye know. Look like they could crush a cannonball between their thighs, and a' that. A bit o' rough. You'll know whit Ah mean,' he says to Mulholland. Nudges him in the ribs.

'Aye,' he says. Already beginning to wonder if he should commandeer the snowplough. Toss Big Davie into a snowdrift. He glances at him. Big Davie is well named. Not unlike Big Effie MacFarlane.

'The only time ye usually get a good-lookin' bit o' pig crumpet is on the telly, ye know. Like yon *Charlie's Angels*, or something like that. See yon Farrah Fawcett. She's got a face like a bag o' spanners the now, ye know, but see when she wis younger, Ah'd've dragged ma ba's three mile o'er broken glass just tae wank in her shadow. A' tits and arse and nae brains in her heid. Ye cannae beat that in a bird.'

Why is it, thinks Mulholland, that wherever you go in life, you'll find a Glasgwegian talking pish?

'So how long ye been in the polis, then, hen?' says Big Davie. Turning on the charm.

'Ten years,' Proudfoot says. Can't be bothered with him, but she's spent all her life talking to idiots like this, so she can do it and switch off at the same time. And it's annoying Mulholland.

'Ten year, eh? Stoatir. Ye must have caught a few criminals in that time, eh?'

'Aye, one or two,' she says.

'Brilliant. Ah mean, bein' a wummin, an' a' that, ye know. 'Cause wimmin jist arnae like us, ye know. In't that right, Chief,' he says. Nudges Mulholland in the ribs.

'Brilliant deduction. Ever thought of being a policeman yourself?' says Mulholland.

The snowplough grinds on; slower than a slow Sunday when it's raining outside, the BBC are showing a forty-year-old Doris Day movie, and Sky have plumped for Motherwell versus Dundee.

'The one that always gets me,' says Big Davie, 'is the toilet thing.'

For a second he concentrates on a tight bend in the road, leaving them in suspense. When he resumes on a short straighter section, he says nothing. Knows how to hook an audience, does Big Davie. Well aware of the nation's scatological fascination. Does not have to wait long.

'Go on, then,' says Proudfoot. 'You're going to explain that at some point, so you might as well get it over with.'

Sheep Dip tilts back his head and pours the remaining Maltesers down his throat.

'Think about it,' says Big Davie, lifting a finger. 'You'll know whit Ah'm gettin' at, Big Man. How many times have ye been sittin' in the boozer, in a crowd, ye know; a few blokes, a few birds, and then one o' the wimmin'll say, "Ah'm away fur a pish".. The next thing ye know there's some other bird sayin', "Aye, nae bother, hen, Ah need wan masel'; Ah'll come 'n a'." An' aff they go, hand in hand, tae the shiter. How many times ye seen that?'

'Lost count,' says Mulholland.

'Hundreds,' says Sheep Dip, chocolate in his teeth.

'Exactly. So whit Ah want tae know is whit dae they do when they get there? Ah mean, nae one's sayin' they're screamin' lesbians, or anythin' like that, ye know. So whit is it they dae? Ah mean, if you're sittin' there an' some bloke says tae ye, "Ah'm goin' fur a pish, want tae come?", what are ye gonnae think? Ye think, This guy's a bloody poof an' Ah'm gonnae kick his heid in. There's jist no way on this earth that two guys are gonnae go tae the bog the gither unless their flamin', know whit Ah mean. But wi' wimmin it's different. They quite happily swan aff tae the bog, arm in arm, tae squeeze intae the same cubicle the gither an' compare knickers.'

They leave him to it. Proudfoot tries to remember the last time she went to the toilet accompanied, and has to admit it wasn't so long ago. Mulholland drums a mental finger.

''Course,' says Big Davie, 'if Ah wis a wummin Ah expect Ah'd need some help goin' for a pish. Ah mean, it's no' as if they've got anythin' tae hang on tae. Who knows, eh?'

Doesn't get an answer. The snowplough is another fifty yards nearer Durness. Big Davie is not finished.

'Oh, aye, that wis another good-lookin' polis bird. Whit wis her name? The wan in *Cagney an' Lacy*. The blonde bit. Good-lookin' bit o' stuff. Shite programme, o' course, but she wis awright, ye know. Ah mean, back then. She's nothin' tae look at now, mind, but see ten year ago, Ah'd've smeared my ba's in raw meat an' swum through shark-infested waters jist tae get a whiff o' her duff.'

'Often thought that myself,' says Mulholland. Wonders if he can arrest Big Davie. Talking mince in adverse weather conditions.

'Ah think that might jist about be it, though. Whit dae ye think, Big Man?'

Mulholland doesn't answer. Wonders, How about driving a snowplough under the influence of stupidity?

'See, that's ma point, hen,' Big Davie says, once more directing his attention to Proudfoot. 'Usually good-lookin' wimmin don't join the polis. But here you are, pure in there, 'n a' that. A dream thing in uniform. A babe in blue. A bit o' snatch wi' some authority. Ye

200

cannae beat it. So, whit's the score?'

One of the great laws of physics, she thinks. Proudfoot number eight hundred and thirty-five. If you're in a snowplough with two guys (she ignores Sheep Dip; Sheep Dip is like having a dog along for the ride), one of whom you want to smother in ice cream, and one of whom you wouldn't touch with a stick the length of the diameter of the universe, you can guarantee that it'll be the pre-humanoid who'll make the move.

'Not sure, you smooth-talking bastard,' she says. Which is the truth. 'Enjoyed it on TV, I suppose. Always wanted to be in the police.'

'Right,' says Big Davie. 'Nae bother, hen. Sometimes it jist seems like life leads ye wan way or the other an' there's nothin' ye can dae about it. Yese'r jist driftin' doon the river wi'oot a paddle, the trees o' the forest passin' ye by, like shite aff a stick.'

'Aye,' she says. 'Something like that.'

'Very existentialist,' says Mulholland. He has had enough.

'Existentialist, Big Man?' says Big Davie.

'Whatever.'

'Did you just say existentialist?'

'Aye, aye, whatever.'

'Existentialist?'

'Aye,' says Mulholland. 'So what?'

'Dae ye actually know whit existentialist means?'

Mulholland doesn't answer.

'Are you sayin' that livin' a life where you drift fi' wan course o' action tae another wi'oot rhyme nor reason, wi' nae control o'er any eventuality, is an existentialist existence? Clearly, ye've nae idea whit ye're talkin' aboot. The existentialist ideal covers a shit-load o' doctrines denyin' objective universal values, holdin' that

201

a bloke's got tae create they values fur himsel' through action, an' by livin' each moment tae the full. *Carpe diem*, an' a' that. Whit's that got tae dae wi' driftin' aimlessly through life takin' whit comes, like ye're gorgeous sidekick here?'

'My life's not aimless,' says Proudfoot.

'Now that ye've met me?' he says.

Mulholland raises his eyes. Wants to be anywhere else on the planet. Back policing Partick Thistle home games. Anything.

'Lookin' for a date tonight, Davie?' she says.

'Ye askin'?' says Big Davie.

'Davie, if the choice was between a night out with you and three hours with a headache and a nine-tonne earth remover wedged up my nose, I'd reach for the Nurofen and take my chances with the JCB.'

'Oh,' he says. Sweeps powerfully round a tight corner. 'So sex is out o' the question, then?'

'Aye.'

'Fair enough,' he says. Rejection is no problem. Big Davie's Law of Acquisition: if you proposition a hundred women a week and ninety-nine refuse, you're still getting a shag.

Time to move on. Or back, as it might be.

'Oh aye,' he says, remembering, 'Ah forgot aboot yon whitshername on that cop show. Whit dae ye call her? Stoatin' bit o' stuff, an' a' that. Bit o' stank now, right enough, but see when she wis younger, Ah'd've skinned ma nuts an' dragged them through five miles o' salt jist tae drool on her pubes.'

✂

The snowplough chugs noisily on up the road, heading for Rhiconich and on to Laxford Bridge, where it will meet up with the plough from Ullapool. Proudfoot,

202

Mulholland and Sheep Dip watch it go for a few seconds, glad to be released; they walk up the drive of Mr and Mrs Strachan's bed and breakfast.

This one to check, then two hotels. Take it from there. They are not sure where the next hotels are going to be down the road; not sure how they're going to get there. Each of them thinking privately that they might be coming to the end of the road. For all the obvious signs and myriad clues, it could be that Barney Thomson has just disappeared into the ether. They can spend a point-less night in Durness and then what? Turn back, head down to Glasgow, give it another few days before the Chief Super kicks them both off the case and lines up some other sacrificial dope to take the drop. The future.

And so they walk up the garden path of the last bed and breakfast at which Barney Thomson was to stay before he retired to the monastery. Unaware that their immediate destiny depends on whether it is Mary or James Strachan who opens the door. Cold. Each with a small bag draped over their shoulder.

Mulholland rings the bell and waits.

'You all right?' says Proudfoot. Annoyed for feeling concern.

Mulholland grunts.

'Feel like I've just had my balls dragged over broken glass for three miles,' he says.

'Oh aye. And whose shadow are you going to wank in?'

Voice edge suddenly. Mulholland looks round. Feels a dryness in the throat. Door opens. Sheep Dip stares away at not-so-distant hills, watching the storm coming slowly towards them.

'Bit o' a cold day tae be oot, is it no'?' says James Strachan.

The moment has passed. They look at him. Mulholland holds out his ID card.

'Good afternoon, sir. Chief Inspector Mulholland, Sergeants Proudfoot and Dipmeister. Just doing a few rounds in the area. We were wondering if you've had this man staying at your house in the last couple of weeks.' Shows him the picture.

James Strachan tuts loudly, and shakes his head.

'That'll be yon eejit who caused Alan Hansen and Wullie Miller to collide against Russia in Spain in '82?'

'Don't believe everything you read in the papers,' says Mulholland.

'Aye, well, ye shouldnae just dismiss everything either.'

'Anyway, that's not really our concern. Have you had him as a guest here, or have you heard of him staying in any other establishment in the town?'

James Strachan tuts loudly once more. 'Ach, away and bile yer heid, son, we're in Durness, an' this is a respectable establishment. Yon serial killers stay in hooses wi' the windows boarded up an' a' that kind o' thing.'

'Bit of a sweeping assumption, Mr . . .?'

'Strachan, James Strachan, that's me.'

'Well, Mr Strachan, you can't be too sure. You're positive that no one remotely resembling this has stayed at your house? Maybe under a different name, or with a slightly different appearance?'

James Strachan hesitates. He wonders if he should express his wife's suspicions. Thinks, Ach, whit does she know, the daft old puddin'.

'Ach, no, son, no one like that. Why don't ye try some dodgy area o' Glasgow, or one o' these places?'

'We know him to have been in this area.'

'Oh, is that right, now?'

'Aye.'

'Well, well. Still, we've no' had him here. Why don't ye try the Cape Wrath Hotel down the road? Big place, yon. Would have space for a serial killer or two in the basement, nae doubt.'

'Aye, fine,' says Mulholland.

James Strachan stares at them for a few more seconds. Shrugs. Feels the cold.

'Thanks for your help,' says Mulholland, as another door closes.

Pointless, he thinks. Proudfoot thinks the same, though neither speaks. A mirror of virtually every place they go. The majority haven't seen Barney Thomson; the minority have seen him, but still are no help whatsoever.

From nowhere, the long fingers of the coming storm slowly reach out, and snow begins to fall, in sparse, swirling, white fluffy flakes. They turn and start to walk down the road. Freezing, dispirited, unhappy, the mood and general pointlessness of their current occupation even infiltrating Sheep Dip. They are feeling useless; and unaware that the Cape Wrath Hotel is another mile and a half away.

Chapter 20

Along Came a Spider

'Psst!'

Darkness. No sound but the muffled howl of the wind outside. Late at night or early in the morning, Barney Thomson does not know. He has lost all sense of time, except that it has been dark for many hours, the monks long since in their beds. A day hidden in the attic above the library; after removing his brush and bucket, so they would have nothing raising suspicions as to his location.

Cold up there. Dark, damp; lonely. Spiders for company; creatures unseen that brush past his face. Scuttling noises from near by, but the darkness is impenetrable, no amount of time allowing his eyes to grow accustomed. No fear of any of that, Barney Thomson; no phobias. A simple man. But knows he cannot live for ever in the cold, damp attic of the monastery. Some warmth reaches there from the floors below, but not much. He will eventually die of hypothermia. He realised after a time that once the monks were all in bed he could safely come back down below. Lurk in the shadows; plunder the kitchen. Has had his fill of bread and cold meat; more stashed away inside his cloak for later, for tomorrow, as he can see nothing but another day hidden away.

Hours alone in the darkness allow you time to think. Barney Thomson has done a lot of thinking. Regrets. Mistakes he has made. What the future holds.

He is like a fish out of water in this place; like a priest at Ibrox, as Wullie used to say. And it is of Wullie that he continues to think. Which he finds funny. He has hardly given him a second's thought in all these months. Between March and November, once the initial danger had passed. Wullie was gone, and that was that, and he would never have given him another thought had not the body of Chris Porter been discovered.

So now, are his regrets over his actions in March merely as a result of this discovery? If Porter's body had never been discovered, if Barney Thomson had not suddenly been vilified by an entire nation, would he ever have regretted his actions after killing Wullie Henderson?

Not a chance.

'Psst!'

And is he the worse for it now, this regret? Regrets about his actions *after* killing Wullie, not about the death itself. Accident it might have been, but he still killed a man. That was what had started it all off. He considered, as he sat frozen in his miserable hideout, that this was his penance; his hairshirt. So much for avoiding detection, when he has to hide away in conditions that are worse than he would experience in prison. The blizzard will not last for ever, but it might last long enough for him to get caught. He has spent some of his day in the dark wondering if there might be some higher force at work. A God after all; vengeance to be taken.

'Psst!'

At the third attempt there is a stirring in front of him. The body shifts under the sheets. A low grumble, a hand moves, mutters something about not using enough cream, Sarah.

Sarah? All the brothers have secrets. Barney Thomson has realised that much.

'Psst! Brother Steven!' A forced whisper. He has been in the room for a couple of minutes and has already lifted a blanket from his own bed, and what clothes came easily to hand.

Finally the brother's head moves, and he raises himself from the pillow. He squints into the apocalyptic darkness.

'Who's there?' he says. Plucked from the depths of sleep. Still hasn't got around to remembering where he is. Could be in any one of a hundred beds he's woken up in.

'Brother Steven! It's me. Jacob. Brother Jacob,' he adds, to avoid confusion. Glad that Brother Steven has not succumbed to the killer's rampage as he had once suspected.

A small gasp, sheets are moved back; Barney sees Steven sit up. Shakes his head, runs his hands across his face.

'Brother Jacob? Everyone's looking for you, man. Where've you been? We thought you'd run off into the blizzard.'

'Hiding,' he says. 'Look, Brother, Ah know whit everyone thinks, but it wisnae me. Ah didnae have anythin' tae dae wi' they murders.'

'You didn't?'

'Naw, Ah didnae. Ah'm no' that sort o' bloke.'

'Well, why did you run, then Brother? Everyone thinks you're guilty. Maybe they wouldn't have, because we're not judgemental here, but after you disappeared . . .'

'Ah had tae. Ah knew whit everyone wis think'. What wi' the murders just startin' after Ah arrived, and my barber's tools gettin' used fur tae commit them. Ah'm nae mug.'

'So where've you been, Brother?'

Barney hesitates. He has decided to trust Brother Steven to find out exactly what's going on, but will not trust him all the way.

'It disnae matter. Just hidin'. Ah just need tae know a few things, ye know? Are there no other suspects? Is that bastard Herman just after me, 'cause if ye ask me, that bastard's got somethin' tae dae wi' it. And a' they other suspicious-lookin' ones, like Martin and Goodfellow and Ash and Brunswick. They're a' dodgy.'

No immediate reply. He can see Brother Steven move forward slightly in the bed.

'Do you mean what you just said, Brother?'

'Aye. Why, whit dae ye mean?'

Another pause. Barney feels the eyes of Brother Steven upon him, even in this sepulchral darkness.

'Brother Ash is also dead.'

'Whit?'

'They found his body in the forest not far from the body of Brother Babel. Head bashed in.'

'Blinkin' fuck!'

'Yes, Brother, indeed,' says Steven. 'No more the subtlety of a knife in the throat from our killer friend. Changed his whole bag. What goes around comes around, and all that. I remember old Ash saying he was going to live for ever. Forgetting that old Horace thing: *Pallida Mors aequo pulsat pede pauperum tabernas regumque turres*. Yep, you can't argue with that.'

'Aye, right,' says Barney, then adds, 'Blinkin' fuck. And Ah'm gettin' the blame for all four o' these murders now?'

'I'm afraid so, Brother. The Abbot's already sent Brother David out on a mission to get to Durness and contact the police. To be honest, I don't know if you have to worry about that, because the guy's a dead man. Not a chance he'll make it in this weather. The poor Abbot must be really desperate. I don't think Herman was too happy, but that's his authority hang-up.'

'Aw, shite, that's a' Ah need. The blinkin' polis turning up here.'

'Indeed, Brother. Are you in trouble with the police as it is?'

Barney Thomson. Cool in a crisis. 'Me? Wanted by the polis? Ye kiddin'? Whit would Ah be wanted by the polis fur? Ah mean, me? The polis? Whit dae ye think, that Ah look like the kind o' bloke who'd kill the people he worked wi'? The polis? Nae chance.'

'All right, Brother. Then if you didn't kill our brothers, you have nothing to fear.'

'But they a' think Ah did it. Ye've got tae know human nature, Brother. Ah've got nae defence, nae a leg tae stand on.'

He can see Brother Steven nodding in the dark.

'Got you, Brother. It's that whole guilt-innocence trip. It's like what Bacon said: "For what a man would like to be true, that he more readily believes." I suppose it's just more comfortable for us all to believe that it's the newcomer who's guilty, rather than someone among us who we've grown to love over the years.'

'So you think Ah'm guilty 'n a'?'

'Guilt, innocence, that whole bag; you know, Jacob, I haven't a clue, man. I've not known you too long, but we get along all right, don't we? It's not like I had you pegged for a killer or anything, but then I've no idea who I might suspect. I don't think any of the brothers really have the genocidal edge in their eye. If I say it's definitely not you, then I have to accuse someone else. I just don't know, man. I'm trying to be in the zone on this one, but it's a tough call.'

Barney hesitates, then asks the burning question. 'Ye willnae turn me in, Brother, will ye? Ah need tae wait until they've found the real killer.'

'Don't worry, I'm not turning anyone in. It's every man for himself out there. But they're not looking for anyone else, Brother, and if someone else dies, they're going to assume it's you who did it, because they don't know where you are. You have a long road ahead of you, my friend.'

They stare at one another, each man barely able to make out the other in this biblical darkness. This is what counts for friendship in this bloodied place, thinks Brother Steven. But what does Barney Thomson know about friends? They nod, a gesture which penetrates the night, and then Barney is gone, out into the Gothic black of the long hallway outside. And so, once more, he begins to wander the corridors of doom, a fugitive from someone else's reality.

Brother Steven settles back down under the coarse blanket. Eyes open, staring at the ceiling. He thinks of Brother Jacob, running from something which brought him to the monastery, now running from something within. A tortured soul. It's like Catullus said, he thinks. *Now he goes along the darksome road, thither whence they say no one returns*. That was about it for Brother Jacob.

He closes his eyes, feeling the tiredness come over him, and soon he is once again slipping into the arms of Sarah Connolly on a warm summer's afternoon.

✂

Barney Thomson huddles in his corner in the attic. Extra clothes retrieved, food in his stomach. Fortified for the rest of the long night, and another bitter day ahead, when he will have to stay out of sight of the rest of the monks. Glad that he did not tell Brother Steven his whereabouts, but also pleased that he has been to see him. He feels he has at least one friend in the world.

And so, Brother Ash is also dead. Four down, twenty-eight to go. He wonders if the killer will aim to do away with the full complement of monks, one by one, until there are only two of them left, with both denying everything.

But Brother Steven is right. Any further deaths will be blamed upon him. The only thing for him now, if the weather is to prevent his escape from this place, is to find the murderer himself. Only then will it be possible for him to have his reprieve. Only then might he be able to prevent the police from turning up here in their hundreds. Barney Thomson – a man with a mission. He does not know the full weight of accusation against him, only knows that he must do everything to clear his name. He is not guilty of any of the monastery murders, so he must prove himself innocent; something he can only do by turning in the real killer, and that is what he must discover. Then he can hand him over to the Abbot and the police, and at the same time turn himself in – that is his latest decision after another while in the black of night. Then he can stand trial for the crimes of the past, for another hour of lonely reflection in the darkened attic has given him hope. He has persuaded himself; been a spin doctor to his doubts on behalf of his earlier deeds.

He can hand himself into the police and get a good lawyer. What exactly has he been guilty of? Murder certainly, but accidental murder. No more than manslaughter, and not by any dangerous or foolish act of his own. Wullie slipped into a pair of scissors he was holding; Chris fell and cracked his head during the course of a minor stramash of which he had been the instigator. Disposing of the bodies instead of informing the police had obviously been a mistake, but perhaps it could be forgiven? As for disposing of the bodies of his mother's victims, surely any jury would understand that act. Could anyone stand to see their own mother vilified as a serial human butcher? Virtually all his actions were those of a desperate and panicked man. Horrible, perhaps, but also forgivable.

This is what he has persuaded himself. So he has a plan. Find the monastery murderer and turn him into the Abbot, so that when the police arrive he can hand himself over to them with at least a decent reference from the man of God. There is nothing he believes he can't prove himself innocent of.

Of course, he hasn't seen the following morning's selection of newspaper headlines. The *Sun*: 'Thomson Rapes Ninety-Eight Women in Terror Week'; *The Times*: 'Sadat Assassination – Thomson Accused'; the *Star*: 'Barber Surgeon on Kidnap Spree'; the *Guardian*: 'Barney Thomson Quits Tories'; the *Daily Record*: 'How Barber Surgeon Made Goram Let in Five against Portugal in '93'; the *Scotsman*: 'Uproar as Boffins Set to Clone Barber Surgeon'; the *Herald*: 'Wave of Naked Bank Robberies Pinned on Thomson'; the *Express*: 'Thomson Kills Seventeen More'; the *Mirror*: 'Cool' Killer in Downing Street Invite Mystery'; the *Mail*: 'Barney Thomson Wore My Daughter's Skin, Claims Upset Mum'; the *Aberdeen Press and Journal*: 'North-East Man Goes to Dentist.'

He will have to be quick, and he will have to be

discreet; he will have to use the sum of all his investigative powers and intuition. He must cut a swathe through the confusion, the deceit and the treachery. He will have to become all that he has run from; the prey become the predator. He must be a leopard, ready to pounce upon the wounded wildebeest of the truth; a lion, poised to plunge his jaws of revelation into the warm flesh of veracity; a panther, suspended on the doorstep of betrayal, the slashed and gouged hyena abject prey to the incisors of integrity; a behemoth, hovering at the graveyard of inevitability, the cruel fangs of rectitude and probity a brutal witch-smeller pursuivant to the calumnious obloquy of injustice; a wolf, slavering at the tombstone of fealty, vengeful vitriolic teeth plunging brutally into the blackened wasted heart of the Little Red Riding Hood of vituperative denigration. He will have to be savage, cunning, astute and shrewd. He must mix the deviousness of Machiavelli with the guile of Sherlock Holmes; the vigour of Samson with the finesse of Ronaldo. He must scale the peaks of intellect, while at the same time abrade the depths of artifice. This must be Barney Thomson's finest hour.

'I'm buggered,' he mutters to himself.

He closes his eyes and lets his head fall onto his chest in an almost comfortable position; and soon sleep comes to take him away to a world which is even darker and colder, a world inhabited solely by killers and their victims.

Chapter 21

Pissed

The tide is in on the Kyle of Durness, the long stretch of beach covered by a wash of deep, choppy sea. Low cloud, so that the water is dull and cold grey. Mulholland looks over the sea to the dark shapes of the hills beyond, from his room in the Cape Wrath Hotel. Another pointless day gone by, his foul mood given way to resignation and acknowledgement of probable defeat. It was always hoping to chance to come all this way across Sutherland expecting to meet the infamous Barber Surgeon face to face. And so he is thinking of abandoning the search. There is no point in going towards Aberdeen now, since he obviously headed north. Maybe Shetland and Orkney, but he is not sure and is too dispirited to make a decision. He can decide in the morning when he has a clearer head; his mind fudged by a bottle and a half of wine.

The door to the bathroom behind opens and Proudfoot emerges. He doesn't turn and continues to stare out at the dark, black night. She joins him at the window; stands next to him but does not touch. A mellow evening, away from arguments and endless discussion on the motives and mind of Barney Thomson – deranged criminal mastermind or unfortunate idiot? A three-hour meander through aimless conversation on life and all its iniquitous injustices. Mulholland's marriage; Proudfoot's loves and mores; Rangers, Celtic and the Great Divide that pollutes the city; a list of twenty-seven good reasons for not being in the police, as opposed to a list of two for remaining there; plain chocolate versus milk; Stallone versus Schwarzenegger; the Beatles versus the Stones; and, as the wine took over, Meryl Streep versus the Wombles; why sugar is a poor alternative to paint; how Scotland could have beaten Holland by three goals in Argentina if Alan Rough hadn't had a perm and Graeme Souness had broken John Cruyff's knee-caps with a baseball bat in the first minute; the effectiveness of Mollweide's projection as representative of a globe. Three bottles of Australian Sauvignon blanc; brie in breadcrumbs, chicken in honey and white wine, raspberry crumble with ice cream, a large and varied cheeseboard; coffee.

They watch the sea. Listen to the sound of waves crashing on the rocky shore a hundred yards away. White spray breaking into the night, disappearing. Can see the cold outside, feel the warmth of the hotel and the evening. Their shoulders touch. Mulholland relaxed at last, weighed down finally by his melancholy.

They know the time is right at last. No advances need to be made, no rejections to be risked. Inevitable. They will have each other, and they can consider the consequences the following day. Sex after food; a glorious pleasure.

'So,' she says. Leaves the word hanging in the air; with the spray and the snow and the few seagulls still haunting the freezing night.

He turns and looks at her. Eyes that dance. Feels it all over his body, but he hesitates. Savouring the moment. How long since he'd had anyone other than Melanie? Can't

216

think about her now. Proudfoot; no make-up, soft lips, a body to be tied up and smothered in something sweet.

'So,' she says again, 'you going to fuck me or what?'

He smiles. Neck stretches a little. Lips hover.

There comes a knock at the door.

They continue to hover, their lips a fraction apart, not wanting to give into the reality. Could be nothing, but is it ever nothing in a policeman's life? The knock comes again; the moment snapped like a brittle bone. He pulls away. There'll be other moments. In about ten seconds' time.

'You order another bottle of wine?' he asks.

She laughs. 'I was about to ask you the same thing.'

She looks out of the window again as Mulholland goes to the door. White. Pine. Opens it, looks at the old woman waiting outwith. Curlers in her hair, an old cardigan pulled tightly round her bountiful chest. They stare at each other.

'Can I help you?' he says.

'Maybe, laddie,' she says, 'but I think mair like that I'll be able tae be helping you, if you get my drift.'

'Why? Are you selling condoms or something?'

The cardigan is pulled a little more tightly around her chest.

'Why, I'll be doing no such thing. Will you be wanting my help or not?'

Mulholland relaxes against the door frame. This may be a pointless interruption, but at least it's not Sheep Dip with some breaking news on which he'd be forced to act. Be thankful for small mercies, etc . . .

'Sorry, ma'm,' he says. 'Just what sort of help do you think you can give me?'

'You'll be the young policeman fellow from Glasgow that everyone's been talking about, will you?' she says.

'That I am.'

'Well, I don't mean tae be interrupting you, or anything of the sort. I expect you've got that young lady in there with you. Have you slept with her yet, by the way, because Mrs Donnelly from over the road was just wondering?'

'How was it you could help me again?' says Mulholland. 'Handy tips on the seven erogenous zones?'

'Seven? Help m'boab, there were twice that number in my day. 'Course, we knew what tae dae wi' the cheeks o' the arse and a three-week-old kipper back then.'

'Thanks, I really don't want to know.'

'So you won't be wanting my help, then?'

'It depends,' he says. This is stupid. Why is life always stupid when you're about to enjoy yourself? 'Is your help going to be about kippers, or is it going to pertain to the Barney Thomson investigation?'

'Jings tae goodness, laddie, your an awfy sarcastic one, are ye no'? It's about this Barney Thomson character, of course. Stayed in my B&B, if you will.'

Here we go. Passed fleetingly by about four weeks ago, only stopping to have tea and shortbread.

'Did he? And what did he have for breakfast?'

'Breakfast? Why would you be wanting to know that, now? Are you compiling one of those profile thingies that they talk about on the TV? Is it that a man who has sausage is mair likely to commit murder than a man who has bacon?'

Mulholland shakes his head. This is taking so long Proudfoot will be asleep by the time he gets back into the room.

'Look, missus, I don't know who you are, but will you stop talking mince. We're going to do this really quickly and then you can go home and to your bed, which I'm sure you should have done a long time ago. So, when did Barney Thomson stay with you?'

She gives another yank to the cardigan, ignores it straining against her shoulders.

'About a week and a half ago,' she says.

Mulholland shakes his head. Of course it was a week and a half ago. When else? It is the standard reaction time up here. A week and a half to go to the police; and he wonders if it takes them a week and a half to go to the grocer's when they run out of milk, or a week and a half to go to the toilet when they're desperate.

'And you're sure it was Barney Thomson?'

'Oh, aye, aye, nae doubt about it. Mr Strachan, now he thought it wisnae, ye know, but I says all along. Nae question, nae question at all. It was him. I mean the wee manny's been on the TV so much. Is it true, by the way, that it was his fault that yon Tommy Boyd shouldered the ball into his own net against Brazil in Paris?'

'Aye, that was definitely his fault; that and the three goals we let in against Morocco. So why didn't you go to the police at the time?'

'Ach, well, ye know how it is. Mr Strachan thought he wisnae the laddie, ye know, an' so I procrastinated, I must admit. I know what ye must be thinking, laddie, I know what you're thinking. Procrastination is the thief of time, aye, isn't that the truth. But nevertheless, all that being said and done, here I am now tae tell you what it is I've got tae tell you.'

Mulholland's shoulder leans a little more heavily against the door frame.

'Have you a bet with Mr Strachan that you can keep me talking until the middle of next week?'

'Well, if you don't want tae know where Barney Thomson was going after he left me, that's your business.'

This certainly makes a change, he thinks. A forwarding

address. Thomson must have been slipping, or else he was getting even keener on taking the piss.

'All right, Mrs Strachan. I presume you're Mrs Strachan. Where was Barney Thomson going after he left you?'

'Well . . .' she says, but gets no further. Her attention is arrested by the pounding footsteps of a large man thumping along the creaking wooden corridor towards them. Sheep Dip.

'Chief Inspector?' he says, voice loud, giving no due attention to the lateness of the hour.

'Sergeant Dip,' says Mulholland. 'Just in time.'

'I think you should come downstairs, sir. There's someone you should talk to.'

Mulholland stares at the sergeant, then at Mrs Strachan. Finally, irrevocably, with the damning impact of a fifty-tonne bomb on a brothel, the evening's fun is over. Time to sober up. Time to start taking everything seriously. Time to descend once more into the sodden, miserable, plagued mood which has burdened him for the last few days.

'Barney Thomson, by any chance, come to give himself up?'

'No, sir, it's a monk.'

Mulholland lets out a long sigh. 'Why, for one second, would you think that I'd want to speak to a monk?' he says. Then, looking at his watch, adds, 'At half past one in the morning?'

'There's murder, sir. Serious murder. Murder tae make the Barney Thomson business look like Hiroshima.'

'I think that came out wrong, Sergeant. Can't the local plods deal with it?'

'In this weather, sir? There's probably no' another policeman for fifty mile.'

220

Mulholland closes his eyes. That's life for you, isn't it? No matter how bad it is; no matter what troughs of depression and despair it has dragged you through; no matter what fetid sewer it has dumped you into naked; no matter how shitey, miserable, pish, crap, fucking rubbish, shabby, squalid, abject, lamentable and pitiable it gets; no matter how much putrid mince it vomits onto your plate; no matter how much manure is heaped onto your bed before you've even got up in the morning . . . it can always get worse.

With his eyes closed, the wine starts to take hold. A bottle and a half? Hadn't he used to be able to take about three bottles of the stuff and do everything the way it's meant to be done? Now he feels himself falling down down some black tunnel, speed increasing, stomach beginning to churn. Loses himself in it for a while, then suddenly opens his eyes and looks up. No idea how long he was away. Sheep Dip stares at him. Proudfoot has appeared at his shoulder. Mary Strachan is gone.

Mulholland stares down the corridor, waves an unsteady hand.

'Where is she?' he says.

Sheep Dip shrugs. 'Said something about how if you had more important matters than Barney Thomson, then she'd be getting tae her bed, ye know. I told her just tae go.'

Mulholland stares at him for a while, then turns and gives Proudfoot a glance. He's pissed. Completely pissed. On a bottle and a half of wine. Just how much of an idiot is he?

Slowly, elegantly, balletically, he leans back against the wall, his knees fold, and he slides down onto the floor.

Chapter 22

Cold Meat Pie

'God, I feel like we're in *The Lord of the Rings* or some shite like that. Setting out on some great bloody journey into the heart of darkness.'

The wilderness of snow stretches before them. Brother David strides ahead into the clawing cold of early morning, Sheep Dip at his side. Mulholland and Proudfoot mince along a few yards behind. The skies are grey, but bright, the wind bitter, the snow fresh. No other sign of life. No deer, no birds, no sheep, no cattle. Every other creature is hidden away from the worst ravages of winter, yet unaware of the long wait for spring which lies ahead. There has been more snow in the night, so that the roads are once again blocked and they must go the whole way on foot.

'Oh, aye, see yourself as Aragon, do you? Or one of those wee pasty blokes with hairy feet?'

Mulholland sniffs, and feels the damp to the bones of his feet, and every chill blast of wind cut through him. 'Don't think so. I'm the guy whose wife just left, he's screwed up, wants to give someone a doing, and the last

222

thing he needs is a bunch of prepubescent, psychopathic monks who can't look after themselves.'

'Oh,' says Proudfoot. They walk on. 'I don't remember that character,' she says after a while.

They trudge on through the snow, and on and on into the white of morning. Gradually Mulholland and Proudfoot drop farther behind, gradually they lose their bearings, so that they appear to be in the middle of some great white mass; the hills and troughs become indistinct shapes, the horizon merges with the sky. The two figures up ahead get farther and farther away; Proudfoot puts her foot through a thin pocket of snow into a knee-deep river, then Mulholland does the same, not long after.

Relief – temporary relief – comes at lunch-time. They see the two distant figures ahead come to a halt and begin to clear snow from some rocks. And so the next twenty minutes only takes them ten, as the thought alone of warm soup and cups of coffee gives them added energy. But they are cold, cold like cold beer, when they catch the others.

Sheep Dip sits on a rock, a plastic sheet spread out beneath him, a sandwich drifting between hand and mouth. Brother David stands a few yards away, ear to the hills, surveying the weather. Perhaps expecting a lost tribe of Apache to appear along a hilltop. Mulholland and Proudfoot struggle soggily up to them, then settle against the rocks. Breathing hard, breaths in unison, the sound of a car exhaust rasping on a cold morning. Proudfoot is thinking of a bath, sinking slowly into the warm water, letting it inch up her skin and slowly take away the cold. Mulholland is thinking of Melanie, presuming she is somewhere warm, presuming she is much happier than he; and so he pictures himself bursting into the bedroom, finding her with another man, lifting the baseball bat he always carries with him in violent fantasies, then crashing it down repeatedly onto the head of the cuckolder. Hot blood sailing through the air in strange parabolas. That's the warmth he feels.

'We shouldn't spend too long in this place,' says Brother David, eye to the sky, as if in receipt of some divine guidance. 'The storm is returning. It'll be snowing again before it gets dark.'

'Zippity-fucking-doodah,' says Mulholland. 'We could do with some more snow. I was worried that this lot was going to melt.'

'Oh no,' says Brother David, 'we'll be lucky if these snows melt before the spring. Brother Malcolm says it reminds him of the winter of '38.'

Mulholland accepts a sandwich from Sheep Dip. 'Oh, aye,' he says, 'remind me. What happened in the winter of '38?'

David looks at Mulholland in the way he always used to look at policemen before he was captured by the monastery. 'It snowed a lot,' he says. 'What did you think? That this reminded Malcolm of '38 because Dundee are struggling against relegation?'

Sheep Dip barks out a laugh, then devours the rest of his fifth sandwich. Feeling pleased with himself for getting the hotel to double the number of packed lunches which Mulholland had ordered for the day.

He sees the chief inspector as the classical Lowlands nihilist, hell-bent on introspection and the denial of substance; so self-involved as to be disappearing up his own backside and, as a consequence, having absolutely no appetite – for food, for crime, or for life. He likes him nevertheless, although he's yet to establish why. Perhaps the man's inner angst appeals to some submerged anguish of his own. Either that or he just feels sorry for him.

'Apparently it was a winter like no other,' says Brother David. 'The ways deep, the weather sharp, the days short, the sun farthest off *in solstitio brumali*, the very dead of Winter.'

'Enough, already!' says Mulholland. Sounding like a schmuck. David continues regardless.

'Many of the monks were to die that year,' he says.

'Not unlike this year, then,' says Mulholland, and immediately regrets it. Foul mood, and he ought to keep his mouth shut.

'What'd they die of?' asks Proudfoot, trying to extinguish the last remark. The endless sensitivity of the Glasgow polis.

'Cold,' says David. 'Cold and starvation. The monastery was cut off for over six months. The winter went on and on and on. They say,' he says, then looks nervously around him, 'that in order to survive, the monks who were left had to feast upon the flesh of the deceased.' The wind whips snow from the top of a rock, so that it looks like sand blowing in the desert. 'I shouldn't really be telling you that,' he adds as an afterthought.

'They ate them?' says Mulholland, pausing before he takes another bite of his gammon sandwich. He stares at the meat, then lets his hand drop away. 'You're making that up, right?'

David takes another nervous glance over his shoulder, but this is too good an opportunity to miss. It's not often they get the chance to talk to people from without the monastery walls. And virtually never a woman. Proudfoot, thinks Brother David, would be worth breaking your vows for. So he lowers his voice, and it seems to mix with the low drone of the wind and the silence of

225

the snow, and the others have to stretch forward to hear him.

'It was a terrible winter, indeed. For months and months the blizzard blew, and the monastery had no contact with the outside world. Ten monks set out for help at various times during that long dark night of winter, set out to bring relief to the monastery, but none of them ever returned. When spring finally arrived and the animals and birds returned, and the snow melted and the flowers came, they found nine bodies, all within five miles of the monastery walls. Their features had been preserved by the cold, the terror and torture of death still etched on their faces.'

'What about the tenth?' asks Sheep Dip, biting into an apple. He loves this kind of thing.

'Oh,' says David, 'that'll have been Brother Dorian. He made it to safety, all right. It was just that he fell into bad ways in Durness, and by the time he'd sobered up and was able to tell anyone what was going on, it was the middle of summer.'

'Ah.'

'So the rest of the monks were stranded,' says David, continuing the narrative, the unfortunate case of Brother Dorian having been dealt with. 'As the weeks went by they gradually worked their way through the provisions of food and firewood. Too quickly at first, but soon they realised that this was to be a winter like no other; a winter where men would become kings, kings would become gods, and gods would become the frozen umbilical cords of unfettered life-blood . . .'

'Stop talking rubbish and get on with the story,' says Mulholland. 'I want to know whether or not I can finish this sandwich.'

'It was on Christmas Day, that Day of Days, that grand

testament to man's great fortune and the wonders of God, that the first of the monks was to die in the monastery. Thereafter, it is told, they died at regular intervals. By the beginning of March, including those who had gone in search of help, half the complement of the monastery were dead. There was barely enough food for one man to survive there a week, there was no heat, there was nothing. And so those who remained were faced with a difficult choice.'

'Go to that great refrigerator in the sky,' says Sheep Dip, 'or make chops out of their colleagues.'

'Exactly,' says David, with unexpected relish. The furtive glances over his shoulder have given way to eager excitement. 'They were in a quandary, for these were men of God, don't forget. The arguments raged day and night. Men with strength for little else found themselves in calamitous debate into the small hours of the morning. This was more than life or death; this was everything about the nature of existence, the eulogy of actuality against the precipice of faith and, above it all, the great question of flesh as the body of Christ.'

'Of course,' says Proudfoot. 'Communion and all that. The eating Christ's flesh thing.'

'Exactly – just the argument the Cannibalists used. Debate was furious, and soon internecine war had erupted. The monastery was in chaos. The factions split apart, with the Humanists guarding the bodies of the dead, while the Cannibalists made daring raids in the middle of the night to try and retrieve some frozen flesh. It was a bitter and bloody struggle. Even within the factions themselves there was bitter fighting. A brother was stabbed over an argument about which was the best way to cook the arms. It was awful.'

'Bloody hell,' says Proudfoot. 'What happened?'

227

David pauses, staring into the snow. A shudder trips through his body at the thought of it. 'I think they decided they were better grilled than boiled,' he says eventually. 'But then what isn't?' he adds.

'Not the arms, you idiot,' says Mulholland, who has given up waiting for a conclusion and is chewing his gammon sandwich.

David turns and looks wistfully across the barren snowfields, white upon white, stretching for many, many miles.

'No one knows. All things must pass, after all, and eventually the blizzard went. Most of the Humanists were dead, from cold and starvation; most of the Cannibalists survived. It could have been a triumph of will over providence, or it could have been that they tucked into a few of the dear departed brothers. That part of the story was never recorded.'

'I suppose sixty years is a bit too long for any of these characters to still be about?' says Mulholland.

'Oh no,' says David, unthinking. 'There are three. Brother Frederick, Brother Malcolm and Brother Mince.'

'Brother Mince?' says Proudfoot.

'Yes. I believe it's a nickname dating from around that time. No one knows how he came by it, however.'

'Right, then,' says Mulholland, as the snow begins to fall with greater ferocity, the edge of a new blizzard beginning to encroach. 'Even if we can't find your killer, we might just arrest those three.'

David's eyes go big and wide, his cheeks a little paler. The phrase *help m'boab* forces itself into his head. What has he done?

'Oh dear,' he says. 'Oh dear. I didn't mean that. I mean . . .'

'Come on,' says Sheep Dip. 'This snow's closing in

228

again. We should be going. Still got a few miles, have we no'?'

Mulholland looks at the rest of his first sandwich. Proudfoot stares at the barely touched cup of tea. The snow cascades around them and the wind once again begins to bite into their skin through their meagre clothing. And the phrase *help m'boab* also forces its way into their heads.

Scottish Inquisition

The Abbot awaits them, Brother Herman at his side. A bleak day is this in the annals of the abbey. The outside forces of the law come to investigate murder. And now that they are here, there can be little doubt that the story will spread around the country; appear in newspapers, be discussed on talk shows, become part of a promotional campaign on the back of cereal packets. The floodgates will open. The press will arrive, across mountain and glen, and the peace of the monastery will be lost for ever. This day could be the end of the monastery as they know it. Already dark, already well into evening; perhaps the sun will never shine upon them again.

What can save them now but the Will of God? And God's Will has not been in their favour these last few days. If the snow keeps up for long enough, the press will be unable to get near, and maybe they will have become bored with this story by the time the weather has cleared. But that thought makes the Abbot think of the winter of '38, and that depresses him even more. Perish the thought that the police ever find out about that.

Mulholland, Proudfoot and Sheep Dip are ushered in before them. Warmed by soup, drunk on the heady wine

229

of the relief of journey's end, the safety of indoors and the comparative warmth within those great stone walls.

'Welcome,' says the Abbot, the voice that of the classical man of sorrows.

Mulholland steps ahead of the others. 'Chief Inspector Mulholland, Sergeants Proudfoot and MacPherson.'

The Abbot shakes his head. 'I never realised you would arrive in such numbers.'

'Numbers?' says Mulholland. 'With what's been happening here, if it hadn't been for the weather, there would have been a hundred of us. As there will be when the snow clears.'

The Abbot shakes his head again, staring mournfully at the desk behind which his authority languishes. 'Perhaps then we should be thankful for the gift of bad weather,' he says. 'I trust your journey was not too harrowing.'

'Could've walked another twenty miles,' says Mulholland.

'It's absolutely bollock out there,' says the Dip. 'Biblical, so it is.' And indeed they can hear the storm continuing outside, intensifying with every hour. 'If it hadnae been for Brother David, we'd never have made it.'

If it hadn't been for Brother David, thinks Mulholland, we would never have had to come here in the first place.

'A fine man,' says the Abbot, but his voice trails away. So what if he is a fine man? Can he be that much longer immune to the assassin's knife, or scissors, or comb? Is he not destined to go the same way as the rest of them?

Time for business. Mulholland would like to get it over with as quickly as possible, but the thought of walking back through the storm he has just endured fills him with the sort of anticipation he gets from visiting Olivier & Sons, dentistry with a smile, for all your cavity needs. He

230

is here until a Land Rover or helicopter can get through.

'There have been three murders?' he says.

Murder, bloody murder, everywhere he goes. He can remember a time when he went nearly four years without investigating a murder. A long time ago. In a galaxy far, far away.

'Five,' says the Abbot without raising his head.

'Five?'

'Yes. We found the body of Brother Ash this morning. He'd been stabbed seventeen times in the throat. And Brother Festus we found in the abbey, impaled through the top of the head with the nose of a gargoyle.'

'God!' says Proudfoot at the back.

The Abbot stares at the floor, not even bothering to raise the eyebrow which that exclamation would normally deserve. God indeed.

'So why didn't you contact us before?'

The Abbot looks up quickly. An awkward question. What can he say to that? The monastery, and everyone in it, is already in enough trouble. How can he say that they wanted to treat it as just a little local difficulty?

'The weather,' says Herman from his shoulder. 'It is always worse in this glen than the surrounding area. The murderer has picked his moment, knowing that we wouldn't be able to get out to get help.'

Mulholland can smell the lies. Lets it pass for a moment. 'And you've no idea who it is?' he asks.

The Abbot looks to Brother Herman again. Perhaps he should let him take over. This is too much for him and, although he has nothing to hide, he is liable to say something incriminating.

'We know exactly who the killer is,' says Herman. 'It is Brother Jacob. The man is the spawn of Satan himself. He was born of the Devil, and he has brought the ways of the Devil and the Devil's deeds among us. This is a house of God and he has turned it into a house of Darkness. He has breathed the fetid breath of evil upon us. Have you ever encountered true evil, Chief Inspector?'

Mulholland shivers, feels the cold, the draught from the insubstantial shutter placed against the storm on the window behind the Abbot. Evil? Does he ever encounter evil in his endless boring days? Probably not. Stupidity and thuggery account for most of what he has to deal with; but not evil. Barney Thomson, maybe, but somehow that is looking less and less likely. Barney Thomson is just a stupid wee numpty. They'd set out on the trail of a serial killer and have come to realise along the way that he is a casual innocent in the world of crime. However, what has he led them to?

'Where is he now?' he asks.

'We do not know,' says Herman. 'This man came among us a little more than a week ago. A lost soul, we thought, someone who could come to us and learn the ways of God, and one day be rid of the demons which haunted him. The first murder, that of Brother Saturday, came but five days later.'

'Coincidence?'

'Might have been,' says Herman. Coincidence nothing, he thinks. 'But we have reason to link Brother Jacob with at least two of the murder weapons, and once our suspicions had been aroused, the brother disappeared.'

'How do you know he has not been murdered himself?'

Brother Herman hesitates. The eyes narrow, then click back to normal setting. 'He was seen lurking in the shadows by one of the brothers. This is an old building, Chief Inspector. It was built for a much greater complement of monks than we have here now, even before Brother Jacob began his evil task. There are many unused rooms where a man might hide; secret passageways too.

And there are few monks here who have the stomach for hounding this man.'

'Prefer to sit and wait to get slaughtered?' says Mulholland.

'We are men of God, Chief Inspector!' says the Abbot sharply, raising his head. 'We are not equipped to go chasing lunatic killers.'

Mulholland nods his acceptance of that. Has his own demons to contend with; the demons which condemn him to treat everyone else with contempt. These are clearly desperate men he has come among, and their problems are far greater than his are ever going to be. Picked off one by one. Although, now that he is here and trapped by the weather, his problems have become the same as theirs. Most assuredly he should not be contemptuous of them. And he feels worry for the safety of Proudfoot; followed by worry that Detective Sergeant Dip might be a better protector of her than he himself.

'What can you tell us about the victims, then? Any connection between them? Any pointer to other potential victims?'

'We thought at first it was something to do with the library,' says Herman. 'The first victim, Brother Saturday, was the librarian; the next, Brother Morgan, his assistant. But the last three, they have had no connection with that seat of learning.'

'What were their jobs?' says Proudfoot. Sheep Dip stands silent, attempting to work some bread from between his teeth.

'Brother Babel was one of the gardeners; Brother Festus worked in the kitchen; Brother Ash . . .' Herman hesitates. 'Brother Ash was the gatekeeper. No connection at all, and they were not together in any other way within the monastery.'

'How long'd they been here?' asks Proudfoot.

'A long time,' says the Abbot, head dropping again. 'A very long time.'

'How long exactly?' says Mulholland. 'Did they all arrive together? Might there have been something between them before they got here?'

The Abbot shakes his head. The eyes are vacant. Here is a man whose faith is being tested to the limits; beyond the limit. The Abbot has always said that you can see, in every man's eye, a little of God's light. And here he sits, disproving the theory. Or being the exception to the rule.

'I can't believe that, Chief Inspector. It was so long ago.'

'You can never tell.'

'That may be the case, but sadly they are not here for us to ask them. Certainly, I can tell you that they did not all arrive at the same time. They've all been here for very many years; indeed, over thirty-five in the case of Brother Ash.'

Christ, thinks Mulholland. Thirty-five years in this place. This Godforsaken place, then wonders if you can use that word about a monastery. Maybe this one you can.

'A long time,' he says. 'Strange that they've all been here such a long time.'

'Not really,' says Herman. 'Most of our monks have been with us for a considerable number of years. It has always been a happy place.' Not in the winter of '38 it wasn't, thinks Mulholland, but he can leave that one for later. Doesn't know yet that he will never get around to it, for it will become an irrelevance.

'And how many of you are there exactly?' he asks, mind thumping headlong into a wall of incredulity. What kind of man would come to a place like this? Cold, barren, remote, desolate. And it isn't as if you escape life and get away from it, because you still have to spend your time with the rest of the unfortunates. Who knows the reasons that would bring a man to a place like this? What secrets they hide, what dark skeletons hang in every cupboard.

'There were thirty-two,' says Herman. 'Twenty-seven remain. That is not counting Brother Jacob, of course. We cannot call him one of us.'

Thirty-two. Bloody hell. Thirty-two. Thirty-two sad bastards stuck away in the remotest part of Scotland, where even the Dutch tourists don't go.

'And Brother Jacob?' says Sheep Dip from the back, finally joining in the investigation. 'What can you tell us of him?'

'The man's a total bastard,' says Herman.

'Brother!'

Herman bristles will ill-concealed hatred and loathing; has suspected Brother Jacob from the first, even before a murder had been committed. Has long said there should be greater screening of the sad cases who request to join them. At this moment there is nothing. Anyone who comes among them is greeted with open arms. They could be anybody with any motive. They should have introduced a vetting procedure, such is the nature of these troubled times, and now they have been caught out.

'The man was obviously here for some dubious reason. It was quite apparent. He was not a man of God, and there was nothing about him to suggest that he was willing to learn the teachings of Jesus.'

Don't blame him, thinks Mulholland, but says instead, 'Had he made any friends in his time here? Anyone who might know where he's hiding, anyone who might know his reasons for murder, if that's what he's done?'

'Oh, there's no question but that this man is a killer, Chief Inspector. And you might want to talk to Brother Steven. It is obvious that there is some connection there, although I concede that it might only be because they shared a room.'

Mulholland nods. Brother this; Brother that. Insane; the whole thing is insane.

'Have any of you lot ever thought of getting a life?' he asks. Almost. Stops himself and says instead, 'Where might we find Brother Steven now?'

'He should be at prayers,' says the Abbot. 'As we all should be.'

'I don't know that prayers are going to do you any good, Brother,' says Mulholland.

The Abbot smiles for the first time. The eyes crinkle, his face looks gentle and old and wonderful; and then the look is gone. 'They brought you to us, Chief Inspector,' he says.

Mulholland laughs and shakes his head. Weirdest-fuck gift from God you're ever going to get, he thinks. Feels the weight of the responsibility and automatically says, 'Aah, Brother, I think you might be in for a disappointment there.'

'I'm sure you won't let us down.'

Proudfoot catches the eye of Brother Herman, and the look of spite dies at that moment. The eyes relax, the tension forcibly ebbs from the face; he welcomes the glance of Proudfoot.

'We should get on,' says Mulholland. 'I know you've got a big monastery here, but there are three of us, and Brother Jacob can't have gone very far. Not in this weather. Now, if there's anything else you can tell us about him it'll be helpful.'

The Abbot shakes his head. 'I'm afraid he appeared a

236

very private man. I had him in here a couple of times, but he gave nothing away about what brought him to this place. He was obviously running from something, but then aren't we all?'

'I wouldn't know,' says Mulholland. Running from something. His brain kicks in at last. He has the same thought that Sheep Dip had had the night before when Brother David had first appeared at the hotel, and that Proudfoot had had twenty minutes earlier. Could it be Barney Thomson? Could he be a killer after all? They'd begun to think he had merely been caught up in his mother's business before. He was no killer himself. A man of comforts, Barney Thomson; even someone on the run wouldn't come to this place.

'Well,' says the Abbot, 'perhaps Brother Steven will be able to shed a little more illumination on the man for you. We have our problems with Steven as well; nevertheless, he is a man of some insight and erudition. He sees things to which others are blind.'

Mulholland nods. Turns his head and raises his eyebrows at Proudfoot and Sheep Dip.

'Right,' he says. 'We should get cracking.'

'Brother Herman will show you around,' says the Abbot. 'Oh yes, there is one more thing which might be of interest to you.' He subconsciously feels the back of his neck. Those scissors, that razor; they had been so close to his own cold skin. 'He is the most wonderful barber, Brother Jacob.'

'A barber?'

'Indeed. The man could cut the hair of the Lord.'

Chapter 23

The Monk who came in from the Cold

Somewhere between death and dawn; somewhere between hell and heaven; somewhere between pain and the bitter-sweet gratification of pleasure; somewhere between the cold, clammy hand of denial and the exuberant exploding can of Guinness that is freedom; somewhere between fourteen years at a drive-in movie theatre showing *Ishtar* on continuous loop and an eternity of chocolate-enrobed naked women playing blow football with your testicles; somewhere between a glutinous mountain of charred bodies collapsing on your table during breakfast and the exiguous indulgence of four rounds of toast and marmalade; somewhere between bad and good, wrong and right, yang and yin, Queen of the South and Juventus; somewhere between them all, between the great effervescence of miasma that colludes with the protozoa of fate, and the munificence of time and space, the very enemies of delirium; somewhere between them all, there lies a man. And that man is Barney Thomson.

And he's freezing.

His teeth chatter, tapping out some strange, almost

Caribbean, rhythm. Involuntary shivers rack his body. Goose bumps and upstanding hairs career across his body like some deranged Mongolian horde sweeping across the Asian plains, doing their best to combat the cold, but to no avail. All the body's natural defence systems are at work and failing miserably.

The storm rages outside, and at every conceivable weakness in the structure of the building the cold seems to creep in. Barney has spent the day on the move, constantly in search of warmth. But every time he became settled or seemed on the point of finding what he was looking for, another monk would come along and he was forced, once again, to skulk off into the shadows. He has heard through the walls faint rumours of the winter of '38 and the need to preserve as many provisions as possible. And so the fuel is saved to heat the bare minimum of rooms and Barney can find nowhere to banish the chill in his bones.

His movement around the monastery, his lurking in the shadows, has told him many things; he has learned some of those dark secrets which all the monks keep so close to their chests. Not the identity of the killer; but he now knows why Brother Sincerity and Brother Goodfellow are so friendly, and why Adolphus spends so much time in the library. He also knows that the police have arrived, and that they will be searching for him. He is not sure whether they are searching for Brother Jacob or for Barney Thomson, or whether they will already have worked out that they are one and the same.

However, he is being forced in from the cold, and all the determined bravado which he had about finding the killer and handing him in to the authorities has vanished through a day of unremitting freezing temperatures. It could take him days or even weeks to establish the killer's identity when, he has realised, he probably has only a couple of nights before this frozen hell gets the better of him.

So much for Barney Thomson, the Great Detective. He is going to have to be Barney Thomson, the Great Guy Who Gives Himself Up So That He Doesn't Freeze His Arse Off.

However, he has decided to test the water first of all. A tentative toe, before he goes leaping into the loch of confession. A couple of hours previously, from one of his hideouts above the toilet, he shoved a note through a small hole, inviting Sheep Dip to a meeting. Having decided he could more easily trust the Highland polis than the two Glasgow ones. He has learned not to trust Glasgow polis.

In the note he requested Sheep Dip to come alone; threatened that he wouldn't show himself and that many more monks would die if the Dipmeister were accompanied. Not that Barney Thomson is going to kill anyone, and maybe the note was injudicious, should his case ever come to trial, but he's not a man known for his fast or accurate thinking.

And so Barney Thomson sits and freezes, still an hour short of the time appointed for his meeting with the police, and he wonders, as his teeth clatter noisily together, what lies ahead.

They huddle around the fire in the corner of a large dark room. Shadows cavort randomly behind them, and every so often they feel compelled to stare over their shoulders, expecting to see the ghost in the darkness, the very real ghost that is murdering these monks.

Mulholland and Proudfoot sit beneath great swathes of blanket, grasping warm mugs of tea between trembling fingers. Given a pen and a piece of paper, they could both make lists of some three or four hundred million other places they'd rather be, and they run through some of those places as they shiver and shake and their enthusiasm wanes and dies.

'Firhill.' 'The Bahamas.' 'Ibrox.' 'The Seychelles.' 'Parkhead.' 'Must be bad. The Maldives.' 'Where are the Maldives?' 'A kick in the backside across the Indian Ocean from the Seychelles.' 'Oh aye, right. Heard of them right enough. Iran beat them seventeen–nil or something like that in a World Cup qualifier. Rugby Park.' 'The top floor of the Paris Hilton, watching the snow fall around the Eiffel Tower, drinking expensive champagne and eating stinky cheese.' 'At least mine are realistic. At least I'm still bollock-freezing in all of mine.' 'We're dreaming, for God's sake. You can have anywhere you want.' 'Aye, right enough. The Maracana.'

And so they go on, and all the while Sheep Dip sits slightly detached, well wrapped against the cold, keeping the fire going, an entirely different set of dreams playing in his head. Every now and again he fingers the note in his jacket pocket, the note which dropped into his lap as he sat on the cold toilet. The note from Barney Thomson. He knows he should tell Mulholland, but he convinces himself that he's doing the right thing. Doesn't want any more of these monks getting murdered. But really it is all because he sees his chance of glory; his name in lights. The chance to get on the front page of the *Press & Journal*. Have his pick of all the two-bit fisher chicks in the seedy underground dope joints in Peterhead and Fraserburgh. A bit of celebrity, and he'll be eating dinner off a different woman's stomach every night for a decade. Add to that the promotion that will inevitably follow the capture of Barney Thomson, a bit of extra cash – maybe some TV work and the odd modelling assignment – and he'll be made.

Pinch a kilo or two of coke from the lock-up in

Inverness, and he could dash off to Bermuda and lie on some sun-drenched beach surrounded by hundreds of women, all paying close attention to his naked body.

'Bermuda,' he says, and Mulholland and Proudfoot pause in their conversation and consider that Bermuda would be a good choice.

Of course, thinks the rambling mind of Detective Sergeant MacPherson, the fact that Barney Thomson probably isn't killing all these monks might be a bit of a problem. But obviously all the monks think he is, and it looks as though Mulholland thinks he is, and if that's the case, then he might as well go along with it. There's just no way that Thomson could have killed anyone; far too much of a big jessie for that. But there's more celebrity beckoning for his capture than for the capture of a killer of a bunch of monks. *'Monk Killer Caught.'* Who would care? Other monks, maybe, but that would be it. *'Monk Murderer Snared as Dons Lose One-Goal Thriller to Motherwell.'* That would be about the extent of it.

Still, if Thomson isn't a killer, even better, then, to catch them both. Maybe Thomson is going to give him some information regarding the real killer, in order to get himself out of trouble.

He looks at his watch. Almost time. He throws another couple of small logs onto the fire, then stands up and stretches. Late at night, and a perfect time to be going for final ablutions.

'Just off to the bog for a shite,' he says, pulling his jacket close.

'Thanks, Sergeant. A little more than we needed to know.'

'Well, ye know, I'll be a wee whiley, so don't go getting your Glasgow knickers in a twist if I'm no' back in thirty seconds.'

242

'I'll try not to,' says Mulholland, and Sheep Dip makes for the door.

'Jersey,' he hears Proudfoot say, before he closes the door behind him. 'Snogging Bergerac.'

'You're kidding me?'

✄

They all have their secrets, these monks. Dark and sombre; black and blue; the Devil's secrets. Brother Ash – the man had never forgiven himself for sleeping with his brother's wife, and now he need feel that regret no more. Brother Goodfellow – homosexuality and drugs; he has flirtations with Brother Sincerity to indulge the first of those, and he can never forget the second, so that not a single night goes by when he does not feel the needle piercing the soft flesh; the first gentle resistance of the skin, followed by the easy glide of steel. Brother Sledge – a complex web of deceit on a salmon farm in the early seventies, leaving a suicide and a broken marriage. Brother Pondlife – a series of broken homes and a lingerie shop laid waste. And Brother Satan – a man with no end of secrets.

But of them all, only Brother Herman had come to the monastery truly on the run from the police. A murderer on the loose. That is why he so confidently recognised it in Brother Jacob, because he can always tell one of his own kind. Someone like him. He can see it in the eyes.

But then, he can always tell all their secrets. Give him a few days, and he'll know why any of the brothers has come to them. And obvious, he had thought it, when Brother Jacob had honed into view, bleeding heart and bloodied hands laid bare for all to see. Or, at least, for him to see. Because he knows what it's like, Brother Herman. Knows what it's like to feel rage and hurt and anger and embarrassment and humiliation. Knows what

243

it's like to determine you're going to kill someone; to go after them with a knife; to stalk them, hunt them down, corner them; to enjoy their fright, breathe in their terror, swim in the soup of their fear, knows what it's like to plunge the knife in to the hilt, and feel the warm flow of blood on your hands.

It has been a long time for Brother Herman, but you never forget. And so . . .

He is surprised when he encounters the murderer. Shocked even, although he would have thought himself too hard to feel shock.

It happens in the depths of night, as Brother Herman knew it would. There is an inevitability about it. He has, for five days now, envisaged this meeting. Played it through his mind, knowing what he is going to say, knowing how he is going to fend off his attacker, extract a confession, and then do whatever else is going to have to be done. And he has no fear. God will be his judge and his protector. And should something go wrong, it will be because God wills it. Although, on this occasion, he will not give God's Will too much of a say in the matter.

The oldest trick in the book. One of them anyway. A pillow beneath the harsh sheets on the bed to make it look as if he sleeps. For Brother Herman knows his attacker will come, and on this third night of his vigil, it begins.

At the slow creak of the door, Herman's head bolts up, although he had not been in the deep throes of sleep. There is a sliver of light from outwith, the dark figure etched against it, then the door is closed, the room is engulfed in darkness again, and the only sound is the soft pad of bare footfalls across the stone floor. A brief hesitation and then the sudden and frantic thrash of the knife into the padded bed. A burst of furious anger, then it is over, and the killer fumbles in the dark for the object of his vengeance. Emits a low curse when realisation dawns.

Were Brother Herman to strike now, were he to approach the killer from the back and bring the knife down into his neck, were he to strike the mighty blow from behind, unannounced and unexpected, then victory might be his, and Herman might live for many more years. But this has never been his intention; deceit is not his way. And especially not now, now that he has seen, in the obscure light of the doorway, who the killer is. There are too many questions to be asked. This man cannot die, taking his secrets with him.

'Brother?' says Herman, at the same time as he flicks a match and puts light to the small candle on the table beside him.

The killer turns. 'Herman,' he says. 'You were expecting me?'

Herman stands, so that the two tall men face each other in the dancing gloom. 'Not you, I must confess, but someone.'

The killer takes a step towards him and stops. He still holds the knife in his hands, a light and comfortable grip. Herman keeps his weapon concealed within his cloak.

'Why, Brother?' says Herman. 'Before we finish this, you must tell me why.'

The killer stares through the dark, their eyes engaged. Sweat beads on furrowed brow, tongues flick at narrowed lips. Many a half-hour sequence in a spaghetti western has been built around such an encounter.

'Two Tree Hill,' he says eventually.

Herman stares quizzically back. Two Tree Hill? He knows of the place, not many miles from the abbey. There was a time when the monks used to frequent it, but those days are long since gone.

'What do you mean?' asks Herman. 'It is years since we've been there. Not since . . .' And his voice trails away at the bitter memory which belongs to Two Tree Hill. 'But that was long before you came to us, Brother,' he says.

'My father was there,' says the killer, and the voice is dead.

'Your father? But how could that be?' Herman is on the back foot. He hates being on the back foot, but he is too confused, too intrigued to do anything about it.

The killer hesitates. What do these idiots know? Why is he even bothering to waste time explaining himself? It's not as if he's some two-bit villain in a Bond movie, who wants everyone to know his motives. He just wants these men to pay for their crimes and, if there is a hell, they will have eternity to feel remorse.

'Brother Cafferty,' says the killer. 'My father was Brother Cafferty.'

Herman gasps. Cafferty! There's a name he has not heard in many years, and his mind quickly fizzes through the events of that fateful day on Two Tree Hill. Cafferty had been at the centre of it all. In a way, Cafferty had been the casualty, but it was nothing.

'You're joking?' he says, aghast.

The killer takes another step forward, the knife nestling snugly in his clenched fist.

'You're taking revenge?' says Herman. 'You're taking the lives of all these fine men of God because of what happened that day? Why, it's absurd!'

'Are you forgetting my father was kicked out of the abbey?' says the killer, the voice spitting venom; years of hate boiling over, like some goofily overfilled pan of rice. 'He was never the same man again, to which my very existence testifies.'

246

Herman stands amazed. His mouth opens, his eyes widen, and, in the dim light of the candle, the killer can see the saliva glinting on the tip of his tongue, behind which the inside of his mouth becomes a black hole.

'But Two Tree Hill?' says Herman. 'It was nothing! Brother Cafferty could have gone to another abbey. We wouldn't have said anything. That meagre stain would never have followed him.'

'He didn't want to go to another abbey, though, did he? You ruined him. Meagre stain, indeed, you bastard! You tarnished him for life. You painted him with the brush of odium, dipped in a paint pot of ignominy and humiliation. He turned to drink and drugs and gambling. The man I grew to know as my father was a broken man. He'd been decent and honest once, until you killed him. You,' he says, dragging it out again, 'killed him.'

Herman's mouth closes; the hardness returns. This is, by some way, the most ridiculous thing he's ever heard. Even more ridiculous than Brother Adolphus's explanation on why he'd had a lingerie catalogue under his bed. It would be laughable, if it weren't so serious.

'This is absurd, Brother,' he says, and this time it is he who takes a step forward, the knife clutched firmly in his right hand, hidden by the dark and the great swathes of cloak. 'You cannot possibly be commiting these murders because of what happened at Two Tree Hill. That really would be the most stupid thing anyone's ever heard in their entire life.'

The killer is offended; furrowed brow and narrowed eyes. 'What do you mean?' he says.

'This,' says Herman, and his left hand gestures through the air, indicating all the murders that have gone before. 'Who in their right mind would commit these atrocities over this? It would be the most futile gesture which could possibly be conceived of. Two Tree Hill was nothing. It was an inconsequential event, on an inconsequential day. Good heavens, it must be almost thirty years ago now.'

'Twenty-seven,' says the killer. 'Twenty-seven.'

'Hah!' barks Herman. Going for it. Provoke his man into anger is his thought, and then take him when he is consumed by his wrath, his effectiveness duly diminished.

'You sad little cretin, Brother,' says Herman. 'You think that anyone still remembers that day? You think anyone cares? What use is revenge, Brother, when no one knows why you're doing it? What use is revenge, when the reason is so mediocre as to be completely insignificant?'

'Mediocre? Is that what you're saying?'

'Aye, Brother,' says Herman, 'it is.'

'Mediocrity be damned!' says the killer, the voice beginning to strain, a quality of pleading to it.

'All this, and it's for nothing! You pathetic little man!'

One last taunt. It happens, and Brother Herman is proved wrong. The killer's effectiveness has not been diminished by wrath. He is a younger man, he is stronger, he is faster; and while he is being all these things, Herman's knife becomes entangled in the luxurious and sweeping fabric of his cloak.

The knife pierces mightily the throat of Brother Herman, and he staggers back, his fingers clutching at the warm explosion of blood. He falls heavily against the wall, the eyes stare wildly at his murderer, and then, as he begins the slow slide to the floor, his hand finally escapes the prison of his cloak, only for the knife to drop uselessly to the ground.

Herman sits on the floor, eyes staring up at the man who two minutes before he'd thought he could easily take in a fight. On the back foot, that'd been the problem. And deserted by God, and maybe he's had that coming.

248

And also this: you just never know when you're getting old. That is his one last thought.

Their eyes meet in one final wrestling match which, even now, Herman manages to win. His mouth opens as the killer's eyes drop, and Herman utters his final words on God's earth.

'He lied to you, son. Your father must have lied.'

✂

He can still feel the blood pumping through the veins. A mad, liquid rush – he can feel the pain of it squeezing through confined spaces. Heart racing, chest thumping, head aching, mouth dry, hair standing on end, frantic points of pain jagging his body – the biggest rush he has had yet from murder. Brother Herman. One of the ring-leader bastards who had condemned his father to a life of ruin. Brother Herman, the biggest bastard in this place of bastards. Deserved everything he got. The other monks would probably throw a feet-up party when they heard he was dead.

On a high of murderous delirium, the killer almost stumbles into Barney Thomson. Would have done so, has not Barney heard his irregular footfalls coming towards him and hidden behind a pillar at the last minute.

However, the killer senses something as he comes into the small hall, the interconnection of four corridors. The place where Barney Thomson has chosen to make a rendezvous with Detective Sergeant Dip. A curious place for a secret assignation, but Barney Thomson is no conspirator.

The monk stops, slows down; he fingers the knife, now thrust into the folds of his cloak, but still red with warm blood. Blood that he can taste; and he can smell the presence of another human being. His nose twitches. Someone is watching him, he can feel it; someone lurking in the shadows. He hasn't been followed, he's quite sure of that, so whoever it is will not know the sad fate of Brother Herman.

'Hello?' he says to the empty chamber. 'Who's there?'

No reply, and he begins slowly to circle the room. Almost completely dark, but for the bare light of a smouldering fire, itself only minutes away from death.

Barney Thomson hides behind a pillar and waits. He watches the man before him, on the cusp of showing himself. Some of the monks he can trust; some of them he can't. Already has the two lists drawn up in his mind. This man is on the A-list. This man he thinks would not betray him.

Yet something stays his hand as, all the while, his heart ba-booms inside his chest, the sweat beads on his face and he forces his teeth together to stop them chattering. He's had too much of this in the past year, and this won't be the last time, he thinks. Or, then again, it might.

'Hello?' says the killer, and his eyes sweep past the pillar behind which Barney hides, and Barney can feel his bowels uncramp once more. But the predator keeps circling, and all the while Barney grows more uneasy. There's something in the way he moves; and the monk is quickly removed from the A-list. Could this be the killer? he wonders. Who else, apart from himself, would be wandering the corridors at this hour? This is not a part of the monastery where any of the monks need go at night; that is why he's chosen it.

The monk circles; Barney twitches.

'Hello?'

'Hello,' comes the reply.

Barney twitches so hard his head bangs silently off the stone pillar. He manages to keep his mouth shut as his hand goes to the instant bump. He risks a glance round the corner of the pillar. The polis. Of course.

The killer stares through the gloom, himself surprised. Sheep Dip has appeared as if from the shadows, and instantly the killer assumes that here is the man who has been watching him for the past few minutes.

'Good evening,' he says, cool regained, fingers once again clutching the sticky hilt of the knife.

'You're not Barney Thomson,' says Sheep Dip, and is immediately annoyed at himself for mentioning the name.

'Barney Thomson?' says the monk. 'Never heard of him. Not one of the brothers,' he adds warily.

'No,' says Sheep Dip. Has to move the conversation on. 'Late to be abroad, is it not, Brother?'

The monk shrugs. 'I couldn't sleep, Sergeant. Too many things going on, you know.'

His mind racing. Going through all the options. His hand clutches the knife, and that remains his favourite option of all; especially since his blood still fizzes with the rush of the last murder. There are pros and cons to be considered, however. This man before him is no Brother Herman, stupid and slow. This is a sensible policeman, a big man who'll be faster than he looks.

'And dae ye think it's wise tae be walking corridors when there's some lunatic on the loose?'

The monk's eyes narrow. Barney Thomson? Brother Jacob. It makes sense. This must be some criminal who's on the run, and they've tracked him to the monastery. They think that he's the killer, and he only just manages to keep the smile from his face.

'I have God to protect me,' says the monk.

They can't be that stupid, can they? he thinks. The only thing Brother Jacob can kill is conversation.

'God hasn't made a very good job of protecting your brothers,' says Sheep Dip, staring through the gloom at the monk. Something is missing and he doesn't know it.

251

His instinct has gone; he stands before a killer covered in blood, and he doesn't see it. Sheep Dip has always had instinct. Now repressed by this house of God.

'This Barney Thomson,' says the monk. 'You think that he's the one who's been doing these terrible things?'

'Barney Thomson?' says Sheep Dip. 'Naw, not him. He's just a feckless idiot. I doubt the man can tie his own shoelaces. Folk like Barney Thomson are what God had left o'er when he'd finished making snot.'

Barney Thomson bristles; and in any other situation he'd seriously think about almost doing something.

'So whom do you suspect, then, Sergeant?' says the monk.

The tone of voice, and instantly it hits Sheep Dip. The killer stands before him. Sure as eggs is eggs and the day will die, this is the man they are looking for. What is wrong with his radar that it's taken him two minutes to realise?

The monk sees it in his face. The dawning recognition. Sheep Dip is too surprised to hide it; and instantly the knife in the killer's hand has been freed and is lunging towards Sheep Dip.

Sheep Dip dives to the side, stumbling. Brain in confused overload. Fumbling for the gun tucked in his back. Kicking himself. He avoids the first lunge and regains his footing. Hand on the butt of the gun, he sweeps it forward. The killer knows what's coming. Knows he has to make one last effort before the gun is upon him.

His knife sweeps wildly through the air; the blade, dulled by blood, black-red in the emaciated light of the wretched fire; the killer-monk gasping with effort, his head exploding with the outrageous pleasure of the fight.

Chapter 24

At least once in his life, every Policeman is going to have to search a men's toilet

'I know guys are weird, 'n all, but surely it doesn't take half an hour to go to the toilet?'

The listing of dream alternatives has long since expired – too painful to think about – and they have been sitting in silence. Mulholland stares into the fire, which has gradually burned lower. Contemplating the thought that he will have to add more fuel, coming along with the realisation that Sheep Dip has been gone a long time; realisation which he has been doing his best to ignore.

'It takes all kinds of lengths of times,' he says. 'Surely you've read that in a *Blitz!* article? *"Why Men Take Ages to Shit." Or "Tell the Length of a Man's Cock from How Long He Spends on the Toilet." Or "Men and Shit – What Really Goes On."'*

'Very funny. You don't think something might have happened to him?'

'Sheep Dip? The Sheepmeister? Mr Dippidy Fucking Idiot-Face? I doubt it,' Mulholland says, presuming already that Sheep Dip lies dead, throat slashed, blood

253

everywhere. Feeling guilty about being so callous. 'The amount that guy eats, it might well take him half an hour.'

'We should go and look for him,' Proudfoot says, ignoring the ill-humour which she has quite got used to.

'How do you mean that, exactly?'

'How do you think I mean it? We should go and look for him. Something might have happened.'

'Look, it's freezing out there, down those corridors. It's warm in here. He's probably just gone in search of some more food, and if he hasn't, and he's already dead, it's not as if we're going to be able to do anything for him now, is it? You a doctor?'

'Chief Inspector?'

Mulholland rubs his hand across his face. Looks with yearning once more into the fire.

'God, all right, then, I suppose you're right. But if we find him sitting on the bog reading a fuck mag, I'm going to be pissed off.'

✁

Mulholland appears from the toilet, clutching a candle in his right hand, the jumping shadows mixing with those from the candle of Proudfoot. Proudfoot shivers.

'Well?' she says.

'Now I know how George Michael feels,' he says. 'Anyway, the cupboard is empty. Not a bare arse to be seen, Sheep Dip's or otherwise.'

'So what do you think, then?'

'I think he was lying when he said he was going to the toilet. I think he had other things to do. Some lead he wanted to follow up and not tell us about; some other business with one of the inmates; who knows?'

'So, do we look for him?'

Mulholland stares through the gloom. Proudfoot is an

254

attractive woman; in this light she is glorious. Ravenous, sexy, seductive; all of those things. His ill-humour, his impatience, his rampant apathy, combine to make him want her even more. Right now, in a cold, dark, damp corridor, in a freezing monastery, with a killer on the loose, in the middle of nowhere.

'Do we fuck,' he says. No matter what you're feeling, you can't mask ill-humour this ill.

'We've got to look for him. It doesn't matter what his motives were. If he'd intended to be long about it, he would have given some other excuse. Something must have happened to him.'

'I don't care, Erin,' says Mulholland, and he almost spits the name out, and the use of it sends a shiver down her spine, makes her take a step back. 'If he wants to be such a bloody idiot as to go poncing around the sodding Monastery of Death in the middle of the night, on his own, well, sod him. He deserves to die.'

Mulholland, candle blazing its way in front, begins to move off down the corridor. Proudfoot stands her ground. 'Don't be such a selfish arsehole,' she says after him.

And he stops. His shoulders are hunched against the cold. The candle dully illuminates holes and nooks in the walls where spiders live and small insects come to die. And the thrown shadows move with him as he slowly turns around.

'What did you just say, Sergeant?' he says. Voice on the edge, but she has had enough of it, and is not cowed.

'I said you're being an arsehole. You're not the only one stuck in this bloody awful place, you know. You're not the first person who's split up with his wife, you're not the first person who hates his job, you're not the first person to spend a freezing night in a place they could not

255

want to be in less. Get a fucking grip of yourself. And cut the "Sergeant" crap 'n all, because I'm not letting you get away with this. There's a fellow officer somewhere in this building and he very likely needs our help. Now, come on!'

Proudfoot marches off in the opposite direction, further into the bowels of the monastery. Towards the chamber where Sheep Dip lies prostrate on the floor; cold stone, warmed by policeman's blood.

Mulholland breathes deeply. Maybe she's right, but the thought doesn't even begin to formulate itself. Nevertheless, with the chill bitter and clutching his coat close around him, he begins to walk after her, several paces behind and making no effort to catch up.

'If we get back to the room and that big bastard is sitting there, you're dead, Sergeant,' he mutters to the darkness between them. And if she hears him, she doesn't let on.

✂

Barney Thomson shakes. He has moved on from shivering, and now his whole body vibrates wildly with cold and fear. He has seen so much death, more than in a gaggle of Bond movies, and yet this is worse than all of it.

He has seen the killer at work, from no more than five yards away. He has seen him strike repeatedly with a knife, carried away in a crazed frenzy of diabolical delight. He has seen him drink from the cup of evil, and eat the meat from the calf of villainy. This was a man who enjoyed his work, who was carried away with a brutal felicity. And this is a man whom he knows, whose hair he has cut, whose skin he has pressed his scissors against.

If only he had let those scissors penetrate that skin.

256

What now? Barney thinks as he shakes. The killer-monk had fled the scene, leaving Barney alone with the corpse of Detective Sergeant Sheep Dip MacPherson. Stabbed at least nine or ten times, when once would have sufficed. Blood sprayed around, although invisible in this non-light. Barney had fled, footfalls silent in the dark, in the opposite direction.

All the way back to his hiding place, however, he imagined he was being followed; every time he stopped he thought he could hear the sound of movement behind him. A breath, a softly laden shoe, a cloak brushing against a wall; a laugh. So that now, as he sits in the attic, who knows what creatures for company, he is frightened for the first time since he came to this place. For the first time in many, many years.

And he sits against a cold wall, and not a single coherent thought can he get into his head. He can turn himself in in the morning – should he survive that long – and at the same time tell the police who the real killer is. But who is going to believe him now? Now that the sergeant lies dead, with a note on his person, welcoming him to a meeting with Barney – and threatening death to others if he came accompanied?

Only two corridors closer to the sanctuary of the loft had Barney thought to return and check Sheep Dip's clothes for the note, but nothing he could think would allow his body to turn around and head back towards the scene of death and towards the demons which trailed his every move.

And now he sits and shakes, wondering if he should hand himself over to the police. But the storm continues to rage outside, so he still won't get out of this place. He'll be kept prisoner in some small room, and then he will be sitting prey for the killer. Or will the police and the monks just take revenge upon him immediately – a kangaroo court – on the assumption that he is the guilty man?

Barney shakes; and goes on shaking.

✂

They find Sheep Dip's body nearly an hour later. An hour's search, interrupted by a brief return to their room to make sure Sheep Dip wasn't sitting eating chocolate fudge bars, drinking beer and reading the February edition of *Blitz!*

Down endless corridors, the storm always evident outside, no matter how deep within the bowels of the monastery they go. When it happens, they become aware that something is wrong before they see it. As they close on the chamber, Mulholland now in front – irascibility having given way to unease – they slow down, extend their candles a little father in front and stare more intently into the gloom. They are about to encounter death; they can feel it. Goose bumps goose-step across their bodies, from one to the other.

'You still back there?' asks Mulholland, needing to hear noise shatter this awful silence.

'I was going to stop for coffee, but I changed my mind,' says Proudfoot.

'We can get it later. That and some . . .'

The joke drifts off into silence as he gets his first sight of the body; his slow pace becomes even slower. Proudfoot emits an inaudible gasp as she sees the corpse. Big, ugly, crumpled and, as they get nearer, the bloody swirl around it.

Detective Sergeant Gordon MacPherson. Sheep Dip. The Dip. The Dipmeister. Diporama. The Big Dipper. The Dipsmeller Pursuivant. General Dipenhower. The Dipster.

Dead.

'Shit,' says Mulholland, as they come alongside the body and stand over it. Proudfoot's hand reaches up to her mouth; she swallows. Mulholland bends down and he touches the blood on the floor, then on Sheep Dip's mutilated body.

'Cold,' he says. 'Mind you, of course it's cold in this place, so I can't say how long he's been dead. Could be ten minutes, could be an hour.'

He stands up and they stare at one another, the shadows jumping a little more vigorously from Proudfoot's trembling hand. Mulholland forgets his anger of an hour earlier; Proudfoot forgets that she was going to be angry with him if something had happened to Sheep Dip.

'Stabbed?' she asks.

'Aye. Quite a few times, by the looks of things.'

'Barney Thomson?'

Mulholland shakes his head and looks off into the shadows. Strange that they should stand over this mutilated body and not fear for their lives; not fear that the killer might still lurk near by. A sixth sense of some sort; a knowledge that this is not their time.

'It just doesn't seem right. This is a guy who's been swanning around the Highlands cutting hair on the cheap. We didn't hear one bad thing about him. And the only bad stuff they had to say back home was that he was boring. Doesn't make him a raving nutter.'

'You want to search him?' says Proudfoot, and Mulholland looks down at the bloody mess.

'Aye, I should. We'll have to tell the Abbot, but no doubt the minute they find out about this they'll want to whisk the body off to be with God, or something like that.'

'He's not one of them. We can stop them.'

Mulholland bends down and starts to wade through the cold blood. 'We can try, Sergeant. But we're stuck here for God knows how long. There's no back-up; there's thirty-odd of them and two of us. They can do pretty much what they like at the moment.'

Proudfoot turns away and looks around the small chamber where Sheep Dip drew his final breath. Her skin crawls again as shadows trip in some terpsichorean nightmare; and she sees things in corners and movement in holes in the wall; and maybe, after all, she is afraid. Death might be closer than their instincts will allow them to believe.

Mulholland comes up with pieces of paper from the pockets of Sheep Dip's shredded clothes, and carefully he dries them of blood and holds them to the light of the candle.

A list of women's phone numbers – mostly strippers from Thurso, although Mulholland is not to know that; a Visa bill for £161.89 from a lingerie shop in Inverness; a recipe for bread-and-butter pudding; a notebook with general notes about the case, which Mulholland slips into his pocket; a photograph of a sheep, with the words 'Mabeline, Spring '96' written on the back; a £21.62 itemised bill from a grocer's in Huntly. All that and this – a note from Barney Thomson offering to meet Sheep Dip in the chamber in which he now lies dead, at midnight, come alone, or others will die.

Mulholland stands, still looking at it; letting the other pieces of paper fall to the floor. He holds his candle close and lets Proudfoot read the note.

They both breathe deeply, then stare around the dark chamber which surrounds them. Feel the chill, and not just the chill of night.

'Right,' says Mulholland eventually. 'From now on you and I stick together. Not even one second, Sergeant, all right?'

Proudfoot lets a silent nod drop into the night.

'We should go and find the Abbot. And Herman 'n all – he's just about the only guy around here who knows what's going on.'

Mulholland places Barney Thomson's note in his pocket and then, leading the way, picks a corridor and, having no idea if it is in the right direction, sets off in search of the Abbot's bedchamber. And as they leave Sheep Dip's mutilated body, they don't notice that his gun is missing, because they never knew he had one in the first place.

Chapter 25

A Hard Snow Falls

They arrive in twos and threes, but none of them on their own. The rumours have spread through the monastery like an infectious disease; a syphilis of the mind. There have been more murders in the night, of that all these monks are certain; and anyone who wasn't at breakfast is assumed to have been a victim. They each have their theories; on who might be dead, who might be next, and on who is carrying out these crimes against God.

Brother Mince had missed breakfast on the back of a thumping headache/extravagant bottom combo, and there were those who assumed the worst. Brother Malcolm had also been missing and again presumptions were made – but only by those who forgot that Malcolm always missed breakfast. Strangely, however, despite the absence of Herman, no one thought the worst of that. No one imagined for a minute that something could have happened to Herman. A bastard, maybe, but also the rock on which the integrity and strength of the monastery were built. Nothing could happen to Herman because, if it did, then what did that say of the chances for the rest of them?

Something they prefer not to think about.

And so they gather in the dining room, two fires blazing to keep the cold at bay. What would once have been a gathering of thirty-two, now reduced to twenty-six. Muted conversations, muted humour; they assume they are to be addressed by Herman or the Abbot. A few eyebrows raised when Herman is not at the Abbot's side, but still they do not suspect. Assume that Herman is off doing that Sherlock Holmes/Spanish Inquisition amalgam at which he is so proficient.

An exhaled breath of surprise when the legendary Brother Mince arrives, as the rumour of his demise had quickly spread; a few heads nodded in self-reproach at the arrival of Brother Malcolm.

They are all present and seated on benches at the required time, with the Abbot and two of the three police officers standing at the head of the room. It is not the Abbot who speaks, however; he simply passes the authority for the abbey and this situation to Mulholland with a slight nod of the head, then joins the other monks on the benches.

A low murmur. Has the Abbot relinquished control?

Mulholland surveys the worried, anticipatory faces. What is it they expect him to say? He swallows, he lowers his eyes, he shuts out the sound of the wind and the storm; the blizzard as furious as it has been for days. A hard snow falls.

'Gentlemen, there's a lot to be said, and the Abbot thought it best that I speak to you.'

A few eyes narrow, and he knows they're wondering if he gave the Abbot no choice. Everywhere is the same; the basis of any organisation can be religion, it can be sport, it can be drinking, gambling, sex or backgammon, but when it comes down to it, it's all about politics and people looking after themselves and trying to dictate to others.

'As some of you might have heard, there have been another two murders in the night.' Silence. Two? And a few eyes are thrown shiftily around the room. 'I'm afraid that one of the victims was Brother Herman.' Silence again, stunned this time, for a few seconds, and then the differing reactions around the room. The usual thing, including tears from Brother Sincerity. Mulholland gives them a while, knowing that the next reported victim will not elicit the same reaction. 'And the other was one of my men, Sergeant MacPherson.'

'The Dipmeister!' comes an anguished cry from the back.

Mulholland nods. 'Aye, I'm afraid so,' he says. 'Both killed by the same knife as far as we can tell.'

He lets the news settle in, unaware that many of the monks are even more affected by the news of Sheep Dip's death. For if even the police aren't safe . . .

'Gentlemen, Sergeant Proudfoot and I are obviously Glasgow polis, but we didn't set out up here to investigate these crimes. We knew nothing of them until Saturday evening. We were in Durness on the trail of a man who is wanted in Glasgow in connection with several deaths last winter and spring. We now have little doubt that by some strange coincidence . . .' No such thing as coincidence in police work, thinks Proudfoot; no such thing as coincidence in religion, thinks the Abbot; I wonder if I can get Herman's thirteenth-century Italian lithograph collection, thinks Adolphus. '. . . the man we sought was hiding here at this abbey under the name of Brother Jacob.'

Definite gasps this time, coupled with a few cries of 'I knew yon bastard was a serial killer'.

264

'His name is Barney Thomson and, although we had our doubts that he was the killer even when we discovered he was here, it now looks as though there is little doubt that he is the man we seek. As far as we know there have been no sightings of him in the last thirty-six hours, but clearly he is still at large somewhere within the monastery.' Brother Steven stares at the floor and wonders whether or not to keep his own council. 'With the weather the way it is, he's not going to be going anywhere. Therefore, we all need to be extremely vigilant. Already six of your number and one of ours have died, and we have to do everything in our power to make sure those numbers do not rise.'

He pauses and looks around the small pond of worried faces. Poor bastards, he thinks, then the thought is gone. If you're going to be so stupid as to live in a place like this, shit is going to happen. But then, the shit that is happening here is a product of the outside world.

That's what he believes.

'So, from now on, gentlemen, we go everywhere in twos. You pair off before you leave this room and, after that, you never let your partner out of your sight until this weather clears and we get some relief. And I don't care if there are some things which you'd prefer to do in private. You don't let your partner out of your sight until we have been evacuated from this place and the threat of Barney Thomson has been removed.'

He looks around the room again, from face to face. Trying to convince them. Not even sure that twos will be enough. Maybe they should stick together in twenty-sixes.

'Hey, it's that whole murder thing,' says Brother Steven from within the midst of the monks. '*The Cat and the Canary*; *And Then There Were None*; all that jazz.

265

Picked off one by one. Kinda freaky, but exciting in a strange way. But you know, about all this stick-together stuff. What are we supposed to do once darkness comes, and sleep takes us, Chief Inspector? Methought I heard a voice cry, "Sleep no more! Macbeth does murder sleep", the innocent sleep, sleep that knits up the ravelled sleeve of care, the death of each day's life, sore labour's bath, blame of hurt minds, great nature's second course.'

'Aye, what he said,' says Brother Edward, nodding vigorously.

Mulholland takes a deep breath. Fixes Brother Steven with his best 'shut up and stop talking pish' look. 'Very good, Brother, keep talking like that and you might bore the guy out of hiding.'

Steven smiles ruefully, then retreats behind the cloak.

'I reiterate,' says Mulholland, wondering if anyone in the Highlands has words of their own, 'we do nothing alone. Not pray, not eat, not shit, not change clothes, not jerk off, if that's what you lot do to relieve tension. None of that stuff alone. Limpets, gentlemen, be limpets to each other. And if we can cut down the number of rooms we visit and places we go in the monastery, we do it. Those of you who sleep in rooms at the other end from this hall, when we're done, go and get your things and move them to a room within the vicinity. We don't stray, gentlemen – it's very important that you all obey this rule. Furthermore, if any of you have had any contact with Barney Thomson or Brother Jacob or whatever you want to call him, then please come forward. No matter how trivial, no matter any of it, if you've got something to say, please say it. Co-operation is the only way we're going to protect ourselves and hopefully catch the bloke in a place like this.'

He stops and casts his eyes around the room once

more. He wonders as he does so how many more of them will die before this blizzard relents. Does not doubt that he will survive himself, however. A life this miserable is bound to continue for a long time.

'That's it. You can go now, but not too far. I don't want to order everyone to spend most of the day in here, but that might be for the best. So, can I suggest that if there's something you want, go and get it now and then spend the rest of the day here. Now, are there any questions?'

'Why is he doing it?' comes an edged voice from the front. Brother Martin. A man who has had words with Brother Jacob, but has not seen him in two days.

'To be honest, we don't know,' says Mulholland. 'And frankly, I don't know that it matters. There doesn't appear to be any pattern to his victims, and so we can only surmise that he's after everyone. No one is safe. No one can afford to be complacent. I know that's no an answer, but until we've done some more investigation, that's all there is. We'll be speaking to all of you during the day, just in case there's something that one of you might know which you don't realise is relevant. Anything else?'

They all have questions, but none of them ask. Maybe it is God whom they should be asking questions of at this time. It is He who appears to have deserted them all.

Mulholland removes himself from the firing line and sits at a lone table, where he is joined by Proudfoot. Slowly a murmur grows among the thrall, and quickly rises to its low zenith; and so the monks begin the jealous practice of pairing themselves off and deciding how best to spend their time until the blizzard clears or Barney Thomson is caught or they become his next victim. And many of them search their souls and wonder if they will

267

ever be able to sleep safe here again, even if the monster is caught; and whether they will ever be able to trust in God again, and whether this will be the end of the abbey as they know it.

And in the midst of them all, one man knows all the answers. And he has made many decisions in the night; and he knows that none will walk free from this place, and that this house of God will be left as a graveyard of hell. A necropolis to his revenge; a mausoleum to the injustices of the righteous against the honour of a simple man; a cemetery to all that is bad in this House of Good, and the perfidious nature of this band of Judas men.

Chapter 26

Frankenstein

Mulholland and Proudfoot stand at a first-floor window and look out across the glen, as far as they can see. About twenty yards. The snow has temporarily given in to the day, but the air is still thick with low cloud and the promise of more. The landscape is white, the shapes of trees evident but lazy, and the sky merges with the ground and nothing is defined against anything else. The wind screams past the walls of the abbey, but in the direction they're facing, so that all that comes in through the open shutters is the cold of day and not the wailing gale.

'Maybe one of us should have made a break for it this morning,' says Proudfoot. 'Taken Brother David and tried to get to Durness.'

Mulholland considers the wind and the snow, the landscape before them. Not a chance. He has already given it much thought, but they had barely made it to the abbey in the first place; even Sheep Dip, for all the Northern hardman stuff, had been suffering at the end. There are now several feet more snow on the ground, the winds are

269

heavier, the blizzard more violent, and if this temporary respite is to become more than that, how are they to know?

'No point. And what if one of us had made it to Durness? It's hard to imagine that the roads west or south are open.'

'We could have come back from Durness with some of the townsfolk.'

'What, you mean like in a Frankenstein movie? An angry horde of weird-whiskered villagers charging towards the castle, torches in hand and anger in their hearts?'

'Something like that.'

Mulholland shakes his head. 'The torches would have blown out in this weather,' he says, and Proudfoot smiles.

The sound of the wind dies for a second and they see their first movement for ten minutes as a snowflake dances down past them. The herald of much to come; and though they don't know it, and although it makes little difference, the snowstorm which now beckons is worse than the one which has moved on across Sutherland to Caithness.

'It's beautiful,' says Proudfoot, into the hush. 'I've seen pictures of snow like this, but not in real life. It's wonderful. If you take away the seven murders and the demonic serial killer, this could almost be romantic.'

'Seen pictures? So you read something other than *Blitz!*, then? *National Geographic* or a *Thomson's Winter Sun* catalogue?'

Proudfoot laughs. 'Right the first time, actually. "How to Stop Your Man's Cock Shrinking in the Snow", I think the article was called.'

'Right. I think I read that one. Load of mince. There

were much better snow scenes in "Why Gretchen Schumacher Loves to Do It with Strudel in a Ski Lift".'

Proudfoot laughs again. Beginning to forget where she is and what is going on. This is indeed romantic, looking at this obscured landscape, the latest object of her affections beside her and in a good humour for the first time since they got drunk in Durness.

'You think? I preferred the one where she was demonstrating how to achieve fifty orgasms a second with a choc-ice on your nipples in Lake Tahoe in January.'

'You see, I don't know if you're joking now.'

'Well, I am, but so are they. They're just taking the piss.'

'Oh.'

Leaning on the window, out into the cold, their arms touch; although neither of them gives in to it or leans farther towards the other.

They have had a long day of pointless questioning. Wherever Barney Thomson is hiding within the old building, he is doing it well. Not one of the twenty-six had anything to say that could help them. Plenty of them had suggestions about places he could be hiding, but there are so many of them that they are hardly worth knowing about. Another idea – to launch a search party, to spread out through the monastery in groups of four until they flush him out – has been rejected by Mulholland. These are not twenty-six policemen he's got here, they are twenty-six frightened monks, and for all that he has thought Barney Thomson weak and insipid, the way he's been going through this angelic horde Mulholland would put his money on Thomson against four of the monks any day. The two of them have had a look around the monastery, but it is so large, the halls and corridors so labyrinthine, that there is hardly a chance of stumbling across him. It needs more than the two of them, but a search party is not an option. Sending a messenger out into the cold is not an option. Calling in the army is not an option. He has a mobile phone with him, but it couldn't reach from one side of the kitchen to the other in this weather. They are stranded, there's no way they can get help, they are sitting ducks to the most notorious killer in Scottish history; they can do nothing but wait.

These thoughts once more intrude upon him, and the moment is snapped. That first flake of snow is belatedly joined by another, and then they start to come with greater frequency. The noise of the wind returns, and Proudfoot feels the chill and becomes aware of Mulholland's distance once more. The walls going up, as they ever do with the man.

'Come on,' he says, 'we should get back downstairs. Find out how many more of them he's got in the last half-hour.'

'So what, we just sit and wait?' says Proudfoot.

He shrugs, leading the way to the door. 'I know it's crap, but if you've got a better idea I'll take it. If we stick together as much as possible, I think we should be all right. I don't doubt the guy could take out more than one of these guys at once, but so far he hasn't. I'm hoping he'll stick to that, in which case we're sorted. No one goes alone. They should all be safe. And hopefully, this weather will clear in the next day or so and we can head west. Get back to some sort of civilisation.'

'And what if it doesn't clear?' she says, as they head back down a cold, dark corridor towards the main hall. 'What then?'

Mulholland walks in front, the candle lit and aimed ahead. We're done for, he thinks, and Barney Thomson will find a way to pick us off one by one.

272

'It'll clear, Sergeant,' is all he says. 'That's what weather does.'

✂

The evil Barney Thomson sits in the attic. He has ventured out briefly this day, pilfered a few more blankets, so that he is now almost warm for the first time since he effected his disappearance. Was aware at one point of someone coming up into the attic, looking for him presumably, but he knows where to hide up here now. Knows that unless ten men with searchlights come up, he can easily avoid detection. Two of them, it sounded like, with nothing but candles. The police probably. His heart had raced, but he has been in these situations before has Barney Thomson. Getting to be an old hand.

And so he has sat quite comfortably most of the day, nothing to think about except his hunger and how he can turn in the monk-killer while at the same time exonerating himself. Has realised the mistake he made with the threat to Sheep Dip. It had seemed a good idea at the time, but he had expected to be able to convince Sheep Dip of his innocence. He hadn't thought that the big guy was going to get murdered, leaving the note to be found; which he presumes it has.

And so, through his own stupidity, there is now evidence linking him with the murders. If he was vilified before, thinks Barney, it's nothing to what will happen now.

As usual, Barney is wrong, but he is not to know of that morning's newspaper headlines. The *Sun* – 'Barber Surgeon Innocent, Claims Blair', the *Guardian* – 'Thomson "Boring" But No Killer, Says Clinton'; *The Times* – 'Barney Thomson, the Alibis Stack Up'; the *Independent* – 'Thomson "Asleep" While Murders Took

273

Place'; the *Express* – 'Thomson Framed by Porn King in Camilla Scandal'; the *Daily Record* – 'It Was the English!'; the *Mirror* – 'That Guy Couldn't Lace My Boots, Says Saddam'; the *Press & Journal* – 'Dons In 0–0 Thriller with Forfar: "We Need Thomson on the Wing," Says Boss.'

The eddies and currents of public opinion; as dictated by a fevered press ever on the lookout for a new angle.

Barney knows nothing of this and, indeed, it matters not at all. The outside world might be twenty yards away through a thick stone wall; the nearest town might be only twenty miles across a snowfield; Glasgow might only be three hundred miles as the crow flies; but none of it matters. He is trapped in a monastery with twenty-seven monks and two police officers who think him guilty of seven murders; and one other monk who himself is guilty of those murders, and who will presumably be more than willing to take care of Barney if the opportunity arises.

He listens to the angry noises from his stomach and thinks of his fate. It is impossible to imagine an outcome from this that he would welcome. Already he has accepted much. He will never again see Agnes; he will never again see his brother Allan and his delicious wife Barbara; he will never again work in a Glasgow barber's shop, cutting hair and talking nonsense; he will never again mix with his own folk and simply be one of the crowd.

But what else? Will he ever again walk free from this prison? Will he survive to see another summer and feel warmth on his back? Will he ever again sit in a quiet pub over a game of dominoes and drink a freshly pulled pint of lager?

If he is to do any of that, if he is to taste anything

good, from beer to freedom, he will have to be as determined as he had determined he would be only two nights earlier. And here he sits, hungry, scared and broken. The man Mulholland believes could take on four monks and win.

How many more murders will there be here? Thinks Barney, as he drifts towards an uncomfortable sleep. How many more crimes will he be falsely accused of, how many more crimes will he have to prove himself innocent of?

And so he slides unhappily into a world of dreams, and when he awakes he will discover the answer to those questions.

Many more. Many, many more . . .

Chapter 27

A Big Bunch of Stones

As far as you knew you had eleven people to take care of. Forget the euphemism. You had eleven people to kill. Eleven monks. And so far you've taken out four of them. The four whose identity you were sure of before you started. Which leaves seven more. The only problem being that you don't know who they are. There are twenty-six monks remaining in the monastery, of whom fifteen could have been at Two Tree Hill twenty-seven years ago. But there are no records of that day in the library, as you had assumed there would be. You know that, because you've checked – and had to kill two librarians because of it. One of them was on your list anyway.

So, quick quiz question. What do you do?

Answer: You take them all out.

That modus operandi which had been working so well has already been thrown out of the window, carried away as you are by the euphoria of murder. Anyway, you have to grow and adapt to situations if you're going to be a serial killer in the modern world. Can't live in the past. It would take an age to gradually work your way round the monastery, knifing all these monks in the throat; and the chances are that eventually your work is going to get the better of you, and you're going to come up against a monk who is not so easily overcome. Or a policeman. It had been a close-run thing the night before with Sergeant Dip. Someone might fight back; and you, the hunter, become the hunted. All that stuff.

So, it is time to adopt a long-distance scatter policy; yet something prevents you from putting poison in that evening's dinner, and potentially wiping out the entire complement in one go. A need to feel more blood on your hands. So you opt instead for poison in a single carafe of wine; something which you know will be passed around maybe four or five of the brothers. A fair little cache of victims, almost doubling your tally. You can sit it out at the side, take note of who will die in the night from the slow-acting poison, and then deal with the others as you see fit. You might not get to watch the poisoned actually die, but it gives you a thrill just to think about it.

Curciceam perdicium – a strange-shaped insect of the Bornean rainforest, the blood of which decays into a deadly, slow-acting toxin. Seven to eight hours after ingestion, there begins the hideous seven-stage conse-quence[*] of the body's reaction. a) The victim breaks into a cold sweat. Nothing too hideous or worrying, but uncomfortable. b) From this gentle opening, the body leaps into convulsions and erratic spasms, lasting for nearly three minutes. c) There follows a period of intense pain, likened to that endured during childbirth, but concentrated in one small area just above the kidneys. d) Then there is the shortness of breath, manifesting itself in a dryness of the lungs and an intense craving to swim

[*]Scrabster's *Really Cool Poisons and the Gross Things that They Do*, Dr I. F. McKinley-McKinley, 1880.

277

naked underwater. e) As the body temperature rises, the mind is besieged by hallucinations of the 'large insects and spiders crawling over your face while your hands are tied' variety. f) The victim has an unstoppable desire to break into the second verse of 'Fernando', as strange liquids begin to ooze from the head. g) Then finally, as the body convulses, pain shoots through every cell, the victim froths at the mouth and the demons of hell are unleashed with venomous panache on every sensory perception in his possession, he will see strange visions in the darkness, there will come a dramatic easing of the pain so that in a moment of epiphany he might imagine that he has found salvation, before he dies and is deposited in his own private Gehenna.

Or worse . . .

You are not sure how many you can dispose of in one glorious night of hell-bent revenge, but the first will have to be your idiotic partner, then after that as many as possible so that the police, if you don't manage to take care of them, don't become suspicious about your partner being dead.

It will all start slowly at dinner, as they come in their twos for evening repast, and you can have the fun of seeing who drinks the poisoned wine. Those monks will die slowly, and as they lie in tortuous agony, you will do the rounds of the monastery and take care of as many of the rest as you can.

A simple plan, but why not? All the best plans are simple.

✂

'It's a big bunch of stones.'

'Stones? It's more than that, Brother.'

'Get out of my face. All these stone circles are the same. They may have been built without the aid of heavy

278

engineering equipment, they may be precisely aligned with the sun, they may be a conduit to some mystical higher force, they may indeed be the Westminster Abbey or Parkhead of their day, but when push comes to shove, they're just a big bunch of stones.'

'And I suppose you think the pyramids are just a big bunch of rocks on a polygonal base, and that the Amazon rainforest is just a big bunch of flowers? You are wrong, Brother, terribly wrong. Perhaps Stonehenge was built to some pagan god with whom we have no business, or perhaps not. Either way, there is no denying the beauty and the complexity of those stones. They are a wonder of invention; a glimpse at the grand delirium of the dreams of prehistoric priests; a portentous apocalypse of maniacal conglomeration; a majestic colossus of ethereal inspiration, glorying in the reverie of divine light and the eternal battle with the incubus of destiny; they transcend the thoughts of men, they exalt in the gemmiferous presumption of the whims of fate; they grasp the effulgence of assiduity, yet mould it with the miasmatic corruption of opprobrious indolence.'

Brother Pondlife walks slowly down the final flight of stairs towards the dining hall; Brother Jerusalem comes close behind, head shaking.

'You don't half talk some amount of shite sometimes, Brother,' he says. 'They're just a big bunch of stones. And you know the incredible thing? They charge a fiver, or something to get in. You go by that place and there's all these people standing there pointing at them, having paid their fiver, don't forget, and saying things like, "There's a big stone." "Aye, right enough, there's another one." Load of shite.'

Brothers Pondlife and Jerusalem walk into the dining room and fatally take their seats at the table with Brothers

Sledge, Brunswick and Columbane; the latter two of whom have already tasted the wine, and declared it exceptional.

The killer is fascinated, even though he knows that nothing is going to happen as he sits and watches. He is going to miss the good part, but he has other fish to fry. And as Brothers Jerusalem and Pondlife take their first sip of the wine that will kill them, the serial monk drinks water and thinks of the night to come. For it has begun . . .

Night of the Long Knives

Brother Joseph first. The killer's partner. Simply and easily strangled where he lies sleeping. The killer takes much pleasure in it, for he has never liked Joseph; has always found it tedious the way he brings every conversation around to the subject of why televisions don't have wheels. An old man screaming towards senility with blundering haste, and someone whom he feels certain must have been at Two Tree Hill.

And so he prolongs the death; allows him to wake, allows him to know his killer, allows him to breathe desperately through the strangulation, for an extended five minutes, his arms wafting ineffectually at his side. And then, cruelly, he finishes him off with ten seconds of biting hatred, the rope cutting Joseph's frail old neck, and his whimpers become a croak, and he dies with no knowledge of why. Discovers that in heaven televisions can have wheels if you want them to.

Brother Solomon and Brother Ezekial. Prone to nipping down to the cellars after dinner and sharing another bottle or two of the monastery wine between them. They know fine well that they shouldn't tonight, not with the notorious Barney Thomson on the loose – 'Thomson Innocent of Everything except Boyd Own Goal', says that day's *Evening Times* – but they like their wine and there's a good red down there that Brother Luke just never seems to bring to dinner. Either they are fatalistic, thinking that they will die anyway so they might as well die drunk, or they are thinking that it won't happen to them.

The great door to the cellar closes over them, and on a night such as this it locks them into their doom. The door is closed, the walls are thick; no one can hear their screams. In this intense cold that is all that it takes and, notwithstanding their attempts at shared bodily warmth, they will not see the break of day.

Brother Mince and Brother Joshua. Walking with trepidation down a long, dark stairwell; wall on one side, vertiginous drop on the other. Constantly in fear of an encounter with Barney Thomson, cloven hoofs and jaggedy-arsed tail and all. And so, when the real killer approaches them, they do not recognise him for who he is. They bid a pleasant evening greeting and, for their pains, are both sent tumbling to their deaths. Despite the efforts of his flailing arms, Mince's head smacks into the stone floor. Brother Joshua lands on top of Mince, and his fall is broken. Along with his neck.

The library is set on fire, the door is locked, and again the natural soundproofing of the rooms will mask the screams of Brothers Adolphus, David and James. Men who will die believing they are being punished by God, as shortly before their deaths they will be gathered around the library's illicit collection of nineteenth-century Vatican retro-porn; the pages of which are well fingered and, indeed, stained in one particular case, the result of an embarrassing incident involving Brother Edward after a particularly hard day of repentance and three carafes of wine.

281

For Brothers Luke, Malcolm and Narcissus, he adopts a slightly different approach. In fact he is carried away with the essence of what he is doing. He stumbles across them while they are in the midst of panic, Brother Sledge dying painfully in front of them from the slow-acting poison. They ask the Demon Brother for help, and for a brief second or two the killer plays the part. Then, suddenly, he is caught up in the hedonistic pleasure of seeing the poison at work; his nostrils flare, his cheeks balloon; and then, it is as if some higher force takes over and he loses control. The knife is in his hands, his body buzzes, and he swishes and swings through the air, this way and that, slashing wildly at the three desperate monks around him, until all lie dead. It is like walking on air; a dance in the clouds. A rush that no amount of drugs can mimic . . .

Brothers Sincerity and Goodfellow are caught in a certain position. Fear and cold have brought them together to share solace and warmth. They lie in bed, their naked bodies pressed against one another; at first trembling with nerves and trepidation and cold, but finally relaxing into one another so that at last, after years of undisclosed yearning, they have their first kiss. Long and warm and moist.

Fatally, they both think the other has locked the door.

It does not open silently, but the quiet movement of heavy wood is swallowed up by the roar of the storm; in any case they are oblivious, lost in the ecstasy of love.

The killer is pleasantly surprised. Two at once. Something suitable. Something good enough to match the heinous crime they are committing as he watches. Something simple.

He carries thick masking tape, a prerequisite to the travel kit of every serial killer. He had intended to use it on these two individually, and hadn't thought he would be so lucky as to find them in such a clinch. Has to be quick. Quietly extends the tape then, with the swift movement that led to his sobriquet of Cheetah at school, he passes the tape under the neck of Brother Sincerity – on the bottom, playing the submissive partner – then up around the neck of Brother Goodfellow, so that by the time they panic, they are already bound at the neck.

The next few seconds are a frantic thrash of arms and legs and various other appendages, but Sincerity and Goodfellow have been surprised and are instantly confused; they are naked; they have erections. No man is in a fit state to fight when he has an erection. Soon they are bound; bound but not gagged.

If they want to kiss, they can kiss, he thinks. They watch him as he goes about his business of binding their frantic limbs. They know who he is, and this he doesn't mind. For they will not live to tell.

Tape around their nostrils, so they must breathe through their frenzied mouths, raging against the inevitable. Then he forces their heads together, mouth against mouth, and binds them tightly with tape. If ever they were to get the chance it would be a bugger to pull that tape from their hair. They won't.

He satisfies himself that virtually the only breaths they can take are from the empty sacs of the other's lungs, then he politely excuses himself, and goes about his business. There might be a gap there, enough to let in a fraction of air they need, enough to extend their lives by an extra minute or two, and he smiles at that gently extended torture as he closes the door behind him, staring wildly up the corridor, wondering with whom he should next deal.

Before they depart, before they squeeze their final,

283

inadequate breaths. Brother Sincerity manages to croak his dying words from the recesses of his throat, and from the very well of his being.

'I love you, Goodfellow,' he tries to say; and Goodfellow senses and feels the words, rather than hears them. And so he himself summons one last monumental effort to produce his own stated memorial, the words dragged from some pit of desperation.

'Bugger that,' he tries to say. 'Can you not undo this sodding tape?'

And Brother Sincerity feels and senses the words, rather than hears them, and no more fevered breaths does he attempt to take, and soon his lungs are filled with used air, then he slips into unconsciousness, then he dies. And he will join the rest of his Colleagues of the Damned in their eternity of hell for all his unforgiven sins.

Goodfellow has more fight, but he cannot break free, cannot get enough air; and soon he too is dead and plummeting into the abyss of purgatorial infinity.

The night has worn away. The killer is in a fever, his blood rushing, the heady ecstasy of genocide causing his heart to pound. But he is tired also, and maybe he should leave the others until morning. He's bound to enjoy it more if he's awake. He can spend a leisurely couple of hours pottering around the monastery, picking off monks as he goes. They'll hardly notice, until they are all dead.

It's like eating a box of chocolates, however, and he can't immediately put them down. Another couple, that is what he thinks, and then he can put the knife and the masking tape and the matches which have been his weapons away for the time being. A few hours to recuperate, and then he can start his work again in the morning. It's not as if he'll forget to finish them off.

Brother Frederick and Brother Satan share a room. An

odd combination, but they seem to get on well. He knows that neither was involved in Two Tree Hill. Satan wouldn't have been here then, and Frederick was already too old for that kind of business. A studious man, a learned man of books, and always has been – that's what everyone says.

However, both must die on this night. He tries to push the door open, but it is locked. At least these two have a little more sense than those idiots Goodfellow and Sincerity, he thinks. He knocks lightly on the door, and waits in vain for a reply. Too quiet, or are they awake inside and quivering in fear? He knocks a little harder.

'Who is it?' comes the strained voice from within. Brother Satan. Now if ever someone did not live up to his name, thinks the killer. (Not to know, or care, of the dark secrets which Satan holds. A dark past – many lives are on his hands, such misery has he caused. This is not just any Brother Satan.)

'It is I,' says the killer.

'Oh, Brother, is there a problem?' asks Satan.

Just open the door, you pathetic numpty heid-the ba'd eejit, thinks the killer.

'I am afraid, Brother. Brother Joseph has disappeared. I awoke from a troubled sleep and he was gone.'

A hesitation on the other side, then the killer smiles as he hears the bolt drawn back, and then the great door is slowly opened. A head pokes round.

'Come in. Quickly, Brother, one never knows who is without.'

The killer walks into the bedroom shared by Frederick and Satan. A small candle flickers, almost burned out, on Frederick's bedside table. The old man looks at the killer and nods. It is obvious that neither of these men has slept.

'You say Brother Joseph has disappeared?' says Satan.

'Indeed,' says the killer, and he looks Satan in the eye.

In times gone past Satan would have been able to read the killer like a religious pamphlet. Piece of cake. One look at the guy and he would have picked him for a murdering scumbag, then he would have recruited him for his own bedevilled flock. But the years of repentance and honest living have ruined the man's instinct. It will only be too late that he realises his fate.

The killer wonders. He has charged in here without any aforethought. How to take care of Satan and Frederick? Obviously it must be Satan first, for even if Frederick watches, there will be nothing he can do about it.

'We agreed that we would only leave the room to answer the Lord's call, and then we would wake the other to accompany us. But I awoke more than an hour ago and Joseph was not there. I have awaited his return since then, but he has not appeared.'

And as he is speaking, the killer edges a little closer, so that he is well within striking distance. He is tired, and has had enough of exotic elaboration. He will strike with his knife and be done with Brother Satan; then he can murder Frederick as he struggles from his bed and makes his pathetic attempt at a getaway.

And then it suddenly hits Brother Satan. Joseph's room is nowhere near. Why come all this way down the corridor when there are nearer rooms? And all the old evil comes malevolently back to him, and he knows. These evil deeds within the monastery are not the work of Brother Jacob – the desperate Barney Thomson – they are the work of this man before him. And he knows instantly that it was not he who killed Brother Festus, and he knows instantly why he is doing it and, of all of them, he is the only one who understands.

286

And the knife strikes Brother Satan at this moment of Awakening and pierces the Adam's apple, and plunges through the neck, and comes ripping out, so that Satan collapses to the ground, body in spasm, arms waving futilely in the air, as he desperately strains for a final breath and tries to claw back the powers he forewent. And fails.

Satan lies dead. The killer turns to Brother Frederick. Frederick has not moved.

'Why?' asks the old voice, for he knows it is time to die, and since he expected to be killed eighty-three years earlier in the trenches of Passchendaele, this is no great trauma. He has had much more than many of his friends.

'Two Tree Hill,' says the killer, walking slowly forward.

Frederick raises his head and looks curiously at the man. And even in this pale light, his last candle beginning to fade and die, he can see it. The resemblance in the eyes.

'You must be Cafferty's son,' he says.

'Yes,' says the killer, standing over him.

'And all of this is to wreak revenge for what happened that day?'

'Yes.' The knife is raised high, ready to sweep down into the soft flesh of one more victim.

Frederick shakes his head. 'That has got to be the most stupid thing I've ever heard in my entire life,' he says.

And the knife plunges from on high into Frederick's forehead, and cleaves the skull, and scythes through human brain . . .

Like cutting into an apple crumble which has been left in the oven so long the top goes hard and crusty.

287

Chapter 28

Good Day Sunshine...

Some sort of daylight begins to penetrate the room; a shaft of it falls across Mulholland's face. He is deep in a dream, two victims to his assassin's knife lying at his feet, a third refusing to die, so that he is repeatedly stabbing at the head, and is finally reduced to sawing through the neck; and only then, as the eyes of his victim stop rolling, does he begin to stir to the stream of white light.

He opens his eyes, has that immediate feeling of relief that the dream is just that. But the ugly feeling will stay with him, until it is overwhelmed and surpassed by the much uglier feelings to come.

A few seconds adjusting to the day – where he is, why he's here, what has gone before – then he is up on his elbows and looking around the room. Still in darkness, still asleep, Proudfoot lies on the other side. He watches her a while, makes sure he can see her breathing, then lays his head back on the pillow. Looks at his watch; they have been asleep for eight hours. At least they have woken from it, and the fact that no one has come knocking in the night to tell of some new victim is another bonus. That is what he thinks, for he is not to know that there is virtually no one left to call. Perhaps, says his mind, wandering off into realms of fantasy, Barney Thomson has decided to take his chances with the snow and has fled the abbey.

The thought of anyone going out into the storm makes him listen for the wind, and for the first time he realises there is silence. No wind, no storm blowing, no creaks and groans from the old building. All is quiet.

He braces himself for the cold, then eases out of bed and away from the protective warmth of a hundred blankets. Stands at the window, undoes the catch and pushes the shutters open. Has the same thought for the twentieth time about why they are so insane as not to have glass in the monastery when they've got the stained stuff in the abbey church, but nothing up here makes any sense.

The shutters swing back, creaking to a halt before they bang against the walls, and the early morning lies before him. Blue, blue skies and snow stretching to a blue horizon. No wind; the day crisp and cold and clear and blue, the sort of day that makes winter worthwhile.

He feels it to his feet. Relief, pleasure, some prehistoric feeling within still generating excitement at such a day. Maybe they'll be able to get out, he thinks. Troop across the snow, like some gigantic, brio-laden von Trapp family, until they get to Durness, where the snowploughs will have cleared a road to the south and he can get the rest of the monks to safety.

He wonders how long the storm has been over, whether Barney Thomson has indeed made his break for safety. He looks over the fields of snow and considers that even he would be able to track someone across this.

His mind turns to freedom. They have only been at the monastery two nights, but already it feels like a month.

Entrapment will do that to you. Minutes like hours, hours like days, and so on. Now they have the chance to escape and they should take it before the blizzard returns. The snow might be thick on the ground, but Brother David, or one of the other inmates, must be confident of the way back. He can taste the steak in his mouth at the Cape Wrath Hotel; ignores the fact that there will be a million years of work to be done, and that he will be castigated to hell for what has already happened – the death of Sheep Dip.

No time to stand around – they must grab this opportunity while they have it.

'Hey, Proudfoot,' he says, turning round, and there is a moan and mild stirring from the bed. 'Proudfoot, wake up!'

There is the Standard Morning Delay of about ten seconds, and then her head is lifted from the pillow and she squints into the sunlight, which has worked its way around to where she lies.

'Come on,' he says. 'The weather's cleared. We should get going.'

'What?' is all she can manage.

'The weather. It's cleared. We should be getting a move on.'

She turns over, drops her forehead to the pillow; shakes her head to try to clear the gunge. Woken from some elaborate dream of Freudian construction, involving shoes, cornflakes, Mulholland and her mother.

'Right,' she says eventually. 'Right. Can I wash first?'

'Good idea. You look like the Borg Queen.'

'Thanks.'

He turns and looks back out of the window. Breathes in the air, like drinking ice, and feels his nightmare attacked and the torture of the last few days taken from him.

Everything is clean and white and fresh. A new start. A blank page on which to write a new, and maybe final, chapter in the search for Barney Thomson; and maybe a new chapter in this bloodied life of his.

He begins to think abstractly about snow; the good and the bad of it. Terrible while you are closed in and you never know when it will stop; glorious when the worst is over. Nowhere in the world looks bad with a covering of snow.

Proudfoot stands at his side and looks over the white-out scene. They are transfixed for several minutes, while their bodies edge closer together. Snow and silence. The long summer of a cold winter's day.

'We shouldn't stand here too long,' says Mulholland eventually, making no effort to move.

'Aye,' she says.

'Got to get these guys out of here and back to Durness or Tongue. We can sort the mess out from there. How many are there again?'

'About twenty-six or so. Twenty-seven if we count Barney Thomson.'

'Oh aye, right. We'll just see him safely back to civilisation, then give him, say, ten minutes' start, then we can chase him again.'

'Aye, that's what I was thinking. Maybe give him a car as well.'

'A car? I thought a helicopter.'

The aimless conversation drifts into silence, and they are once more consumed by the landscape. Proudfoot is not long consumed, however.

'Do you think they'll continue here? Come back after all this is over and go on as if nothing has happened?'

Mulholland feels the cold again; this time the stiff blast of reality. The snow-covered landscape is just an illusion, and soon it will be obscured by another blizzard or removed altogether by some minute rising of the temperature. Nothing perfect ever lasts. Not in this life. And he thinks of Sheep Dip and wonders what kind of family the man has left behind.

'Who knows? I wouldn't think so, but twenty-six of the sorry band is probably enough if they wanted to carry on. And the amount of publicity they're going to get when all this gets out, they'll probably have a queue of strange no-lifes waiting to join up.'

A frantic rapping at the door; a desperate man outside, that much they can tell from the knock alone. They both feel it immediately; this is what they had been thankful not to have had when they'd woken to find it already morning. Now it has arrived, like a shot bolt in the chest; and they are each bludgeoned by dread.

'Fuck,' is all Mulholland says, and he walks to the door. Almost doesn't want to open it, to unleash the demons which wait behind; although his imagination could not begin to conjure up the things he is about to discover. Not a bit of them.

The door opens. Brother Steven stands in the hall. Unshaven, hand red from knocking, but otherwise in the manner of a monk.

'Brother?' says Mulholland.

'There's some bad stuff going down,' says Brother Steven. 'Really, really bad stuff.'

There is a pause. Mulholland raises an eyebrow.

'That's it? Not some bad stuff like Aristotle talked about?'

'Come with me,' says Steven. 'Aristotle didn't know anything about bad stuff compared to this.'

✂

Try to describe the feeling and you can't. Like getting

your guts ripped out, that is as close as you can get. But that doesn't really cover it. Getting your guts ripped out is just going to be bloody sore and then you'll die. This is something else.

They have left the bodies where they are; everyone now accounted for. Took a while to find Brother Solomon and Brother Ezekial, but all the others were where they should have been. Not too far from the dining room. Not too far from the dining room, but still dead. The monks in the library had been a bugger to identify, but they had got there by a process of elimination.

Somewhere along the line of their monastery tour of murder and death, Proudfoot had been sick. The charred, tortured library bodies had been grotesque, but it wasn't that in particular. It was the overall effect; the realisation of what had happened. Murder upon murder. One bloody death after another, so that every corner they went round and every door they opened heralded a new corpse. All this death, while they had slept. The police. Supposedly protectors of these people. The Abbot had been delighted when they had arrived; had called them as if from God. And what had they done while this was taking place? That is what she thinks, and as a result the whole becomes even worse than the sum of the parts, bad enough though that is.

Mulholland gagged in the library, felt everything he had eaten the previous day display an interest in coming back to the surface, but none of it appeared. As if his stomach had nothing to offer in reply to this genocide.

They had found the odd live monk along the way, cowering in rooms. Alone, afraid, wondering what had happened to their partners. The men who were supposed to stay by their sides until the cavalry arrived.

There are five left. The Abbot, Brother Steven,

Brother Edward, Brother Martin and Brother Raphael. One of them had defied orders and slept alone; three of them had woken to find their partners in terrible pain, victims-to-be of the poisoned carafe; and one of them had had Brother Joseph as his room-mate.

They are all men who had received regulation Brother Cadfael, *Name of the Rose* or *Robin Hood* haircuts from Barney Thomson. All men who still feel the cold steel of those scissors at their neck, who wonder why they have been spared, who look into the pit of hell which undoubtedly awaits them, and face the desperate fact that their time is fast approaching. All except one. One who knows that Barney Thomson is no man to be feared.

Edward and Steven are busy packing provisions. Food from the kitchen randomly placed into rucksacks, to be carried on the journey to safety; for there is no option now but to make the break across the desert of snow. Any food will do, and they give it little thought. Bread, cheese, ham, Doritos, liquorice, Beluga caviar, smoked venison, three bags of Brother Mince's revolutionary chocolate cheese waffles.

Mulholland stares from the window of the hall, some three hours now since he first looked out. It is almost eleven o'clock and they will have to leave soon. Already it is too late for them to reach civilisation by nightfall. Not a chance at this time of year, and in this weather. So they will take equipment for sleeping out, and hope the blizzard does not return in the night.

And, of course, they can expect to be trailed all the way, and picked off one by one if they are not careful. For surely Barney Thomson will not rest where he is. He must keep going until everyone is dead, and only then will he escape blame.

If Barney Thomson is the man behind the deeds.

'This is stupid,' Mulholland says to Proudfoot.

'What?'

'This. Running from Barney Thomson.'

'So, what's the alternative? We stay here and wait to die?'

He shakes his head, watches some of the snow fall from the branches of a tree. Wonders if already there is a thaw, or if some animal lurks within. Or maybe that's where he is. Up there, in the trees.

'It's just Barney Thomson, for God's sake. Barney bloody Thomson. I could have sworn before we got here that the bloke had nothing to do with it. I still can't believe that it's him. Mild-mannered and boring, and that's about it.'

'Mild-mannered and boring and he killed at least one of his work colleagues, possibly two, and either chopped up six other bodies or at the very least happily disposed of them. Mild-mannered, maybe, but weird as fuck all the same. Even if he was normal before all that, and he was covering up for his mother, it's got to do something to his head.'

'Aye, but why come here and start killing all these monks? If he'd arrived, kept his head and his mouth shut, and got on with praying and self-flagellation and all that other monk stuff, we might never have found him.'

Proudfoot glances over her shoulder. Feels the shiver down her back. 'But the note?'

'Aye, the note,' says Mulholland. 'That's it, isn't it? The note. Written in Barney Thomson's handwriting, found on Sheep Dip, and as incriminating as you can get. It points right to the guy. It makes him centrefold, cop-killer of the month. But it just doesn't feel right.'

'So, what are we saying? That there's someone else hiding in the rafters? Or do you think that one of these clowns is the killer? I wouldn't have thought any of this lot could kill a bug.'

Mulholland shakes his head again, stares into the trees.

'You never know, though, do you? What brings a man to a place like this? It's bloody awful at the moment, but do you think it ever gets any warmer within these walls in the middle of summer? What kind of life must you have had in the past to want to come to a place like this? This lot have got to be the weirdest-fuck bunch of weird bastard weirdos I've ever met. I wouldn't put it past any of them to turn out to be the supreme loopo.'

Proudfoot takes another furtive glance over her shoulder. Edward and Steven prepare the food; Martin and Raphael are in low conversation; the Abbot sits alone. A broken man, a man who has now lost everything, for where is God when they need him the most?

'Which one, then?'

Mulholland shakes his head. Doing a lot of that. 'That's what I've been standing here thinking about. Which one? Absolutely no idea. Having said what I just said, this lot seem like a normal bunch of sad people with no lives. They're all pissing in their pants. I know we can't expect our serial killers to all wear hockey masks, but there's nothing about any of this crowd to make them stand out. If it's one of them, I'd only be guessing. We really need to sit them down and talk to them for a couple of hours, but we haven't got the time for that.'

'So, you think there might be someone else loose in the asylum?'

'Very possibly, Sergeant. Very possibly. Or maybe Barney Thomson's our man after all.'

'If we can't come up with any other explanation for the note he left Sheep Dip, then we have to assume it's him, don't we?'

He pauses. Contemplates, but his mind will not think clearly.

'Aye. Aye, I suppose you're right.' He turns round and looks at the band of unhappy thieves who mince around the great hall. 'You see, Sergeant, this is where we could do with a decent, relevant *Blitz!* article. "How to Tell a Serial Killer by the Length of His Cock."'

'I know where I can lay my hands on the issue with "Gretchen Schumacher on Why She's Shagged Her Last Detective".'

'Gretchen Schumacher's shagged her last detective, eh?' says Mulholland, beginning the short walk back into the midst of human sadness. 'And there was me thinking I still had a chance.'

'She's too thin,' says Proudfoot.

Their eyes meet; they know what the other's thinking. Nothing said, for this is not the time.

'Right,' says Mulholland, turning to the demented and tortured few. 'We should be getting on. We need to get as far as we can before nightfall.'

They look at him with little enthusiasm. Even Brother Steven, the philosopher-bard, has no emotion. Nothing to say, despite the quote from John Wilkes Booth nestling neatly in his subconscious.

'Where's the camping stuff you talked about, Brother?' Mulholland says to the Abbot. But the Abbot stares mournfully at the floor; if he hears the words he ignores them, for there are others who can answer the question. His time for speech has passed.

'A bit all over the place,' says Steven. 'There's some of it in Herman's room on the second floor, and some of it in the cellar. With Brother Ezekial and Brother Solomon.'

'Right.'

Mulholland looks at the floor. How are they going to do this? All seven of them trooping around the monastery, dragging the poor bastard of an Abbot along with them? It could take hours. It'll be bad enough to cajole the bloke into walking quickly enough, so they can get to Durness before Christmas.

And so he takes the decision to split the group; and there will be more blood shed.

'Look, we need to get on. We sort out what's where, and we go and get the stuff.' He hesitates, looks around the room. Unknowingly decides who will play on, and whose part in the match is coming to an end. 'Right, Proudfoot and I will go to the basement. Edward, Raphael and Martin can go to Herman's room, and Steven can stay here and look after the Abbot.' Knows as he is saying it that he and Proudfoot should split up; but, given what happened to Sheep Dip, would that make any difference anyway? Barney Thomson, or whoever it is, is no respecter of the police. And besides, there is no way he is letting her out of his sight. Not now.

'You happy?' he says, and regrets the word the second it is out of his mouth. The monks nod and raise their tired, worried, pathetic bodies from the cold wooden benches. All except the Abbot, who stays where he is, wallowing in his pain.

'No more than ten minutes, if you can, all right, you three?'

Edward nods. Raphael and Martin troop along behind.

Mulholland thinks about saying something to the Abbot, but there are no words. If he thought about it for a hundred years, he would have no words.

'Look after the bloke,' he says to Steven.

Steven blinks.

'This is a bad day, Brother.'

No reply. When you wake up on the wrong side of the bed, your car breaks down on the way to work and your team gets knocked out of Europe by some mob from Latvia that night – that's a bad day. This? There isn't a word for it.

So thinks the Abbot, and he does not answer Brother Steven. Steven drums his fingers. Watches the Abbot. A lamentable figure in brown. Head down, drowning in the vomit of his own self-pity.

'Heard a rumour,' says Steven. A small smile comes to his face. The Abbot does not look up. This time the words do not even register. He has no need for conversation. Steven drums his fingers.

'Enter Rumour, painted full of tongues,' he says in a low voice; the smile stays there, then is suddenly gone. The eyes cloud over. The Abbot does not respond. The fingers stop.

'Not interested in rumours, Brother? You should listen to them sometimes.'

Slowly the Abbot raises his head. The tone of voice, more than the words. The words haven't registered.

'Brother?' he says. He has never had much time for Brother Steven.

'I was saying that I'd heard a rumour,' says Steven.

'A rumour?'

'Yes. Like a curse from the gods.'

'The gods, Brother?' says the Abbot. 'I thought we only had one. Although I have my doubts about Him now, as well.'

'Oh, there are lots of gods, Brother Abbot. Whispering

299

gods. Whispering rumours.'

The Abbot looks into the depths of Steven's eyes, but sees nothing there. He might have done at one time but, like Brother Satan before him, he has lost the ability to see the true hearts of men.

'And what is this rumour of which you speak?'

The smile returns to Steven's face. He lifts a finger, moves it in time with his talk.

'They're saying that all this, all this murder, is about revenge.'

'Revenge? Revenge for what?'

Steven pauses. For effect, but it is lost on his audience. Too confused to be impressed.

'Two Tree Hill,' he says. Awaits the response.

The Abbot shakes his head. 'Two Tree Hill? What do you mean?'

'Two Tree Hill, Brother Abbot. Where the late Brother Cafferty was disgraced and expelled from the Holy Order of the Monks of St John. Condemned forever to walk the streets of normal men, condemned forever to be apart from the God whom he loved.'

The Abbot is even more confused. Tries desperately to think of Two Tree Hill, and it returns under a hazy fudge.

'The small hill at the foot of Ben Hope,' he says.

'Yes,' says Steven.

The Abbot waits for something more, but Steven glares through narrowed eyes.

'I don't understand, Brother,' the Abbot says.

'Not just any hill, Brother Abbot,' says Steven, spitting the name. 'The last hill of all. A very Calvary of the north, where a man might meet his destiny.'

The Abbot stares at him, his eyes widening. Trying to recollect the last time they were there; but it was so long ago. Slowly it returns, however, and the memory comes back through the mist. An ugly incident, a man alone, cast from their midst. A ruined man . . .

The Abbot's head still shakes; he looks at Steven in wonder and confusion.

'You are saying that Brother Cafferty is back among us, and is taking his revenge for that? That is absurd. Cafferty is dead. He lived an unhappy life in Edinburgh with a woman he never loved and a son who came to noth . . .'

Realisation dawns. He notices the eyes at last. The similarities. Because, for all the time that it has been, he still sees Cafferty's face; the anguish and the dismay. And in the eyes of Brother Steven, he sees Brother Cafferty. Steven's father.

The Abbot's mouth drops. 'But, Brother. You cannot be serious.'

Steven stands up, slowly drawing the knife from within his cloak as he does so. Prods the end of the blade with his finger; draws a little blood.

'I can be serious, Brother, and I am. You ruined his life. It is time for my father to be avenged.'

'You killed them all? You, Brother? You killed gentle Saturday and Morgan? Ash and Herman, Adolphus and Ezekial. Gentle Brother Satan. Brother Festus? . . .'

'Oh, not Festus,' says Steven, glad of the chance to interrupt, impressive though that list sounds to him. 'I had nothing to do with Festus.'

'I don't understand.'

'I can't be sure, but I think God took care of the big man. The man was a pervert, after all. Don't tell me he never regaled you with one of his three-breasted, cocaine-snorting fantasies? God hates that stuff.'

'But, Brother?' says the Abbot, and his voice is filled with wonder and incredulity. Slowly he raises himself from the bench, the better to accept the knife which awaits him. For he knows he is to die.

'This does not make sense, my son,' says the Abbot.

Steven's teeth grind; he takes a step forward.

'Don't you call me that, you bloody bastard. You must have been there. You were part of it. He was unjustly punished by a collective of bigots. His objections were more than merited but as a result of them you expelled him from the abbey. The man was never the same.'

The Abbot spreads his hands. Looks like he's appealing to a referee.

'But, Brother, it was nothing. No one cared about it. Your father made a mistake. If he'd accepted it, it would have been forgotten ten seconds later. But instead, he confronted the Abbot Gracelands from Burncleuth Abbey. He punched the man, for goodness' sake. Punched him, Brother. It was an abomination. We had no choice.'

Steven shakes his head. Stands poised with the knife. His anger with the Abbot has gone. The speech he has had prepared for years no longer seems worthy; or relevant. They are all going to die, and now it is nearly over. They deserve what has come to them, each and every one.

'Choice? White shall not neutralise black, nor good compensate bad in man, absolve him so: life's business being just the terrible choice,' says Steven.

'Oh, for God's sake, Brother,' says the Abbot, 'will you stop quoting all that nonsense! Can you not say something for yourself for once? I simply cannot believe this.'

The handle of the knife twitches in Steven's fingers. Another victim approaches. And he cannot be long about it, for the police will be returning soon; though he does not want to finish them off just yet. And he has something to do with the good Brother Abbot after he has killed him.

'It's just how you see it, Brother, isn't it? It's all just words, my friend, and they either mean something or they mean nothing at all. It's like the Bible, it's like the Apocrypha; it's like any words that anyone has ever written or said. We think them, we write them, we say them, but they're nothing. It's deeds that matter, Brother Abbot, deeds are the thing. Words aren't cheap, they're lower than that. They're nothing. It's deeds which are the thing, my friend, deeds are where that whole psychic thing pokes its dysfunctional head out of the womb, kicks off the umbilical cord of avarice and jealousy, and starts to breathe the good clean air of truth.'

The Abbot looks from Steven to the six inches of cold steel he holds in his hand.

'For God's sake, Brother, there you go again. If you're so full of contempt for words, why do you come out with so much bollocks?' The Abbot has lost himself, indeed and truly. 'This is the most absurd thing I've ever heard in my life. You've committed nearly thirty murders because of a lie, because that's what your father must have told you. A lie!'

'It was not!'

'Brother, dear Brother, it bloody was. I was there. Right was seen to be done. Your father had no leg to stand on. He lost his temper for nothing. It was a tragic over reaction, and one which merited admonishment.'

'Hah!' says Steven. He has heard all this before. From his father, Brother Cafferty. 'I know what it was all about. It was the politics of the abbey at the time. There was a power struggle and there were some of you just looking for a way to get rid of Cafferty. I know it to be true!'

Brother Steven exclaims the last remark. Getting ever more forceful; especially since he is now not so sure.

Enough people have said it now; maybe his father had made a mistake after all. Maybe he shouldn't just have killed twenty-six of them. Twenty-seven including the Dipmonster. Although that guy had deserved it anyway. Maybe this great rash of murder and death has just been a pointless waste of time. Great fun, but a waste of time.

However, the Abbot hesitates. It is all coming back. Brother Steven is right. That is exactly why they had Cafferty expelled from the abbey. Politics. The man was way too much of a liberal. Didn't approve of hairshirts; couldn't stand self-flagellation; didn't approve of sandpapering your testicles to cleanse the mind. Of course, these Caffertyisms had come into vogue over the years, but the time hadn't been right. He had had to be silenced.

And Steven sees the hesitation, sees the look in his eyes. So he does not hesitate. The knife is thrust forward; the Abbot has every intention of receiving it – now that he has nothing for which to live – and within seconds he lies bleeding on the floor, close to the death which will inevitably follow.

And Steven stands over the body; the smile comes to his face as the adrenaline pumps wildly through his veins and he gets the massive rush that comes with murder. He watches the eyes of the Abbot close and he knows him to be dead.

But he still holds the knife in his hands, and he bends over the Abbot and lifts the arm of his cloak out of the way. And then once more his knife pierces the skin; cooling blood is drawn, and the Abbot's tortured soul can do nothing but watch.

For Steven is not finished with his body.

Chapter 29

Carnival of Death

If the truth be told, Barney Thomson is going a little mad. Not stark raving, never see the sense of day, screaming loony mad, but a gentle slide into insanity which can still be arrested. But soon. It will have to be soon.

He had woken early from the happiest of dreams – there he was again, back behind his chair, his magical fingers creating a magnificent Bill Clinton Post-Monica Groping Session – the very latest in millennium proto-chic – with mercurial panache, engaged in idle discussion of the origin of the Turin Shroud – *Experts have now decided that it was first worn by one of the Bay City Rollers on a tour of Italy in 1975*, he was saying – while a queue of placid customers waited upon his golden hands – to crash frighteningly into the world of living night-mare.

More death, more murder, more bloodshed, more stained floors. If he ever gets his job back washing the stone, it's going to be a nightmare. And so finally, all these months after casually handling pound after pound of frozen human meat, he is being toppled over the edge. Not over some vertiginous cliff, where the bottom is a long way away but reached quickly nevertheless. This will be a slow slide down a grassy bank. But there's still manure at the bottom, no mistake.

Barney is mad. He spends the morning in his dismal haunts, looking through holes, watching what is going on. Eyes wide, yet stumbling into pillars and walls in the dark. He doesn't view the full carnival of death, but he gets to see most of it. A bit like the Bible, he thinks at one point. There's a lot of it, but you don't have to read it all to get the picture.

At some other point he drifts off into a waking dream. Stands six feet away from a wall, imagines there is a customer sitting in front of him facing an imaginary mirror, and his hands automatically work the thin air, the pretend scissors clicking in the dark. Giving a Harry Houdini. Smooth yet ruffled, elegant yet rakish.

For ten minutes does he stand like this, lost in this nether world. Such is the state of his mind after this latest catalogue of death. Murders of biblical proportions. Murders of which the God Formerly Known as Yahweh would have been proud. Barney is mad.

He doesn't know what it is that drags him from the trance, but he escapes it. Goes about his business, sometimes focused, sometimes lost.

Until now.

He lies on the floor above the great hall. Watches through a hole as Brother Steven stabs the Abbot, Brother Copernicus, through the stomach. Cannot hear what is being said, their voices low and muffled, but he sees everything. The repeated stabbing; and then, as the Abbot lies dead and bloodied on the floor, Steven lifting the Abbot's sleeve and firmly and swiftly severing his left hand from the wrist and leaving it lying on the table.

This is new. Barney squints into the hole, trying to look a little closer. Until now there has been no mutilation. This reminds him of his mother. One of those strange flickering thoughts go through his head to the effect that perhaps Brother Steven and his mother were in cahoots. Is not so mad that he can't dismiss it. And then . . .

Brother Steven lifts the right sleeve of the Abbot, and swiftly, precisely, neatly saws the hand from the wrist, then places it on the table beside the left. It is a bloody mess, Steven himself covered in it. He's not going to be able to pretend now, thinks Barney. And as he wonders what Steven's next move will be, so does he discover it, as the killer monk begins to drag the body of the Abbot from the hall, bloody stumps and bloody stomach wrapped in the confines of the thick brown cloak, so as not to leave a trail of blood.

Barney looks down in wonder. Two hands removed in under a minute; could his mother have been so efficient? And he doesn't move. Not for a second does he think that Steven might have been aware of his presence – and he is right – and so he looks with awe on these two hands which lie on the table.

Slowly the eyes and mind of Barney Thomson begin to work in tandem. The hands begin to take shape. The fingers; the hair; the thumbs; the nails; the wrinkles and the moles; the blood and the shredded skin where the knife brutally cut them apart from the body. Not such a clean cut on closer inspection.

A pair of hands. They lie silent. As hands do. Particularly when they are both left hands. Funny that, thinks Barney.

Bloody hell!

He presses his eyes closer to the floor, a millimetre closer to the hole, looks with greater concentration at the detached appendages. Two left hands! They are two sodding, no questions asked, absolutely thumped in the bollocks left hands. And he saw them cut from the arms of the Abbot. No wonder the sneaky old man never showed his right hand in public. It was the wrong way round. And he's had everyone thinking he'd lost it at Arnhem.

Barney pulls away. Two left hands. How would you tie your shoelaces? Or undo a bra strap? Or hold a golf club? Or give someone a Jack Lemmon? And Barney has a fleeting glimpse of why the Abbot found himself at the Holy Order to the Monks of St John. But he is not interested in that, and his thoughts move swiftly on.

Not so swift, however. This is Barney Thomson, not Sherlock Holmes. He'll do you a Sherlock Holmes cut if you like – both pre- and post-Reichenbach – but he won't pretend that he can think like him. And so he waits and watches, knowing that the others will soon return.

When they do he can more clearly hear their voices, because they have no need for the low tones of the conspirator. He hears their footsteps before they are in his line of vision; then the footsteps stop. He imagines them staring at the table; hears the muted exclamation from the woman.

Then Mulholland comes into view, and he stands over the table and stares at the severed hands. Stares for a minute or two. Doesn't say anything. The other three monks return, and halt in the doorway. Sense immediately that something is wrong, although Barney cannot see the looks on their faces.

'Two left hands,' says Mulholland.

'Do you think they might still be alive?' Barney hears

the woman ask; can see Mulholland shake his head.

'No, no I don't.'

Mulholland turns around, takes in the presence of the other three, then looks back at the human refuse on the table.

'Why, then?' says the woman. 'Why not just leave the bodies in the hall?'

He shakes his head again. 'Don't know. Christ.'

From where he lies, tense, bemused, slightly odd, Barney can hear the deep breath exhaled.

'So what are we saying?' Barney hears Proudfoot say. Almost a minute later, the silence absolute. Although somewhere in the monastery, Brother Steven must be dragging the body of the Abbot noisily along a stone cold floor.

'What are we saying, Sergeant? We're saying that this fuck-up, this Barney Thomson came in here the second we all left – which means he was watching us, listening to everything we were saying – came in here, killed the Abbot and Brother Steven, and for some reason best known to his own warped head, cut the left hands off each of them and left them as a calling card. That's what we're saying, Sergeant. Just the sort of thing his mother, or he himself, did last spring.'

Barney watches. Incredulous. Of course they're going to think it's him, but he still hadn't been expecting it. His meagre thought processes finally catch up with those of Brother Steven. A brilliant frame-up. He must have known all along about the Abbot's disability. His weirdness. The Amazing Double Left-Handed Boy, he must have been called at the circus. And somehow Steven had known all about it. And for the frame-up to work, Steven must be confident that Edward, Martin and Raphael do not know.

It wasn't me! he wants to shout through the hole, but he doesn't. So he lies, surrounded by the dark, unaware of anything going on around him. And if this happens to be the room where Steven decides to hide the body of the Abbot, he will come across Barney and Barney will never be aware; not until the knife slices into his back. Barney is beginning to take another roll down the hill of temporary madness. He watches Proudfoot come and stand beside Mulholland; they look at the hands.

'What about someone else being loose in the monastery?' she says.

Mulholland continues the head-shaking, which has become a permanent feature. There are all sorts of reasons to shake your head.

'Don't think so. If it wasn't Thomson, I thought it might be one of this lot. But this proves it. These two idiots are dead, and those three stuck together.'

'Maybe it's all three,' says Proudfoot, but at last the words are lost to Barney as the voice is lowered; and neither does Mulholland's negative reply reach up to him.

Anyway, he has lost concentration. He is imagining cutting hair with two left hands. It would be tricky, obviously, but once you got used to it, it might be all right. In fact, he thinks, sliding deeper into the fantasy, seeing himself behind the chair, two left hands working away, maybe it would make him even better. It would certainly be distinctive. Something else to help draw the crowds to his shop, on top of his awesome abilities.

Barney is lost, oblivious to the dark room around him and the scene of gruesome murder below. Deep in his fantasy, the contented smile forming around his face. Imagination can never be said to be as good as the real thing, but it is up there. When it feels real, it is real. That's what the mad Barney thinks.

And so wrapped up is he in the phantasmagoria of his delusion that he doesn't hear the door partially open behind him; he doesn't see the shaft of light which pokes its way into the darkened room; he doesn't hear the laboured breaths of Brother Steven, nor the faint whooshing sound of Brother Copernicus's body being dragged along the floor; he sees nothing and he hears nothing, while his mind wanders off and he can smell and feel and breathe the inside of a barber's shop.

Barney is a little bit mad.

Chapter 30

Barney Thomson must Die

'What now?'

Mulholland looks at her. Too shell-shocked by all this death to make a sarcastic comment. What now? Nothing has changed. They are about to leave and get to safety as quickly as possible. However now, for the first time, he feels the spectre of death lurking behind him. He hadn't come here to die, and no matter how miserable he was, he certainly didn't want to. But at last the import of what is going on here, all this carnage, is beginning to hit him.

Strange, that; there can be so much death but he hadn't thought for a second that it was going to affect him. Suddenly, standing over two left hands on a bloody table, he realises that he and Proudfoot are on the menu, just the same as everyone else in the place. And there are only three of them left. He shivers. Senses the weight of foreboding which makes him want to turn and look behind; not only that, it makes him want eyes on every side of his head.

'What now? Now, to quote no end of movies, we get the fuck out of Dodge, Sergeant. Saddle up the horses, get these three cowboys to get their backsides in gear and let's get going.'

✄

Barney Thomson watches from above, but he is no longer paying attention as Mulholland and Proudfoot move away from his line of vision and start distributing orders to the three lamentable surviving monks. Instead, his fingers twitch in time with his waking dream.

And all the time, unlike Mulholland, he does not feel the spectre of Death at his shoulder; even though, in his case, Death is right there, in the flesh, manoeuvring the corpse of Brother Copernicus into the little-used store-room. Death quietly closes the door, then continues to pull the body farther into the room. He does not light a candle and does not try to open the shutters. Death, as a rule, is not afraid of the dark. Tough bastard, Death, no mistake.

Had Barney just been dreaming he might have heard by now. But this hallucination goes beyond that. He's sliding down that hill; madness beckons, in all its glorious uncertainty. Everything can be as you like it in madness. You want to spend your life working in a barber's shop, never killing anyone and never being suspected of mass murder? No problem, you can be there any time you like. And stay for ever. And at the end of your day, you don't have to go home to your own wife, you can go home to any woman you like; and before this fantasy has run its course, Barney will go home to Barbara, the sexiest sister-in-law on this planet; and he won't have to construct a place for his brother, because in this perfect dream-world his brother won't exist.

Barney closes his eyes, but sleep is a long way off. Why sleep, when you can have everything you want? And all the while Death goes about his business behind, opening a cupboard door and moving the leaden, de-handed body of the Abbot inside. He closes the door; there is a quiet murmur of a hinge, but no more. Barney would have heard it in other circumstances.

Brother Steven ensures the door is closed properly, although it will be some time before anyone will come looking here. The adrenaline rush has slowed, and now he has that wonderful post-stabbing afterglow to which he has become addicted.

His eyes have become accustomed to the light.

He notices Barney.

He thinks. A body on the floor, and not of my doing? And he looks at it with some curiosity. Too dark to see who it is, and so he takes a tentative few steps towards it, bending low to better identify the suspect.

'Well, help m'boab!' he says upon realisation; for it is inevitable. If you are going to spend your life reciting the words of others, eventually you will quote Paw Broon. 'Barney Thomson; the great killer himself.'

The words are spoken quietly, but not so quietly that Barney should not hear. But Barney is mad – at the moment. And so Death approaches, then kneels down and looks at the face of Barney Thomson from no more than a few inches. The eyes are shut, the breathing even and regular.

Brother Steven fingers the knife which has once more been stashed inside the confines of his great cloak. This could be the easiest of the lot. One sweep of the arm and the knife will be embedded in Barney's back.

He is fascinated. Brother Jacob. Seemingly mild-mannered and innocent. And yet, the talk has been about nothing else between the monks since they learnt of his true identity. The Great Glasgow Serial Killer, they were calling him. Brother Jacob; couldn't hurt a fly.

Brother Steven has sometimes wondered if his exploits will be remembered. Once all this becomes known, will people talk about it for generations? Sometimes these things capture the imagination of the press and public and sometimes they don't. Jack the Ripper, the great example. Five victims. Good medical work, stacks of blood, a city held in the grip of terror, a whole bunch of movies and an episode of *Star Trek*; but small potatoes in the serial killer game. There have been others who have done much more for their art, but who only received a tenth of the renown. There was just something about Jack the Ripper.

So how will it be with him? Will he get the kind of acclaim now being enjoyed by Barney Thomson? What was it? Seven or eight deaths? He has now done that fourfold. Of the two, he is much the greater headcase. Of these two princes of the serial killer game, he is the man who should be king.

He hadn't started out thinking like this. He had initially, of course, intended to frame Brother Jacob. But that was back then, when his plans were small. Somewhere along the way, when the blood and the excitement began to infest his mind, he became consumed with the immensity of the whole. Of what he is achieving. And now he thinks of something for the first time; only now, when Barney Thomson lies in front of him, do all the threads come together to make a Balaclava of unease.

When this is out, when all these great events at the Abbey of the Holy Order of the Monks of St John become known, when the magnificent revenge for Two Tree Hill has been revealed and popularised and turned into a Hollywood movie with Anthony Hopkins and Sean Connery, will they not all think that Barney Thomson is the killer? How, in fact, will Two Tree Hill become known at all? The press and public, those ravenous fools, feasting on mistrust and misconception, will think it a continuation of Thomson's Glasgow rampage. Will the truth ever be out?

Barney's eyes remain closed; his face lies still above the hole to the world beneath. He has moved on to a Madonna ('Like a Prayer'), just a really weird haircut to give to a bloke, but in his mind his hands weave their magic and the drier blows hot air like breath from a sun-kissed Mediterranean island.

Bastard, thinks Brother Steven. He will steal my thunder, my name, my infamy. This bastard will steal my place in history.

Steven breathes deeply; an angry sneer invades his face, his lips curl. Suddenly he hates Barney Thomson as much as he has hated all those morons who drove his father from the true path of his life. It is bad enough to steal a man's possessions or to steal his wife; it might be really bad to take a man's life from him; there are plenty of bad things to take from a man; but nothing to match that of taking his name and his reputation, of stealing the honour of having committed the deeds for which he is known. From Alexander the Great pretending that it was he who had conquered the known world, and not his half-brother Maurice, to Milli Vanilli achieving fame on the back of Pavarotti's early studio work, history is replete with those living off the deeds of others.

He, Steven Cafferty, cannot allow this to happen. Before he is done, the world will know who he is and what he has achieved. Men will bow before him; presidents will drink from the poisoned chalice of his vision; kings and queens will bow in honour of his accomplishments; God himself will pay homage to him in celebration of his munificence. But, most of all, before he does anything else, before he walks down any other road, before he continues his extraordinary peregrination around the world of revenge, before he sinks his teeth into the apple of retribution, Barney Thomson must die.

The knife hovers in the air above Barney's back. Steven's grip is light but steady; he can feel the blood meandering limply through Barney's veins, he can smell it and taste it, and the flavour is honeyed. This death will be sweeter than the murder of Herman, sweeter than the murder of the Abbot. This will be sweeter than chocolate sauce over profiteroles with chocolate ice cream filling, covered in chocolate syrup and a chocolate coulis with chocolate ribbons, on a bed of chocolate, with a thick topping of chocolate chips and chocolate marshmallows, and a brushing of grated chocolate, washed down with an expensive Sauterne and a steaming mug of hot chocolate, with extra chocolate.

He can smell it, while Barney does not move. And so the knife begins its pungent plunge towards the waiting spine of Barney Thomson.

Chapter 31

A Walk in the Hills

They set out on the walk from the Abbey of the Holy Order of the Monks of St John to Durness. Twenty miles across fields and glens and hills of the deepest snow. They must wade through it at some points; at others they plough through drifts nearly five feet high; everywhere the snow is at least two feet deep and the going is painfully slow. Proudfoot is at the back, walking in the cleared paths of the others. This is indeed an incredible journey; of the octopus, lion and snake variety.

Mulholland, Proudfoot, Brother Martin, Brother Raphael and Brother Edward. The monks have discarded their robes, so that this looks like any normal collection of seriously deranged hikers prepared to go out in all weathers. The sort of people who would be best booking mountain rescue in advance.

They will do well to get a third of the way through their journey before nightfall, Brother Raphael having delayed departure further by insisting on praying; in the end, he had only reluctantly left the abbey, being more than prepared to die and meet his maker. *God will take care of us*, he had said. He's not done much of a job so far, Mulholland had thought, but said nothing.

Martin leads the way. He had sat and prayed along with Raphael, not wishing to upset his brother, but that was for the last time. When he gets to civilisation, if he gets to civilisation, he intends throwing off the shackles of the cloak for ever. If he lives through this, the first thing he's going to do is get in touch with one of the tabloids, sell his story – 'I Was Too Cool to Die, Says Monk Hunk' – then go on a world tour, taking large quantities of drugs and alcohol and whatever else there is on the planet to dull, remove or pervert your sensibilities; while at the same time sleeping with everything – woman, man, animal, inflatable or cardboard box – he can get his hands on. Strange that only one week ago he had had it in mind himself to murder Brother Herman, for the man was a bully who deserved all he got. He had thought of using Barney Thomson's scissors, little knowing that that was exactly what Barney had had in mind himself. Stupid that he went to see Barney to threaten him to keep his mouth shut. Ironic.

Funny how life pans out, thinks Martin, as he leads the way through the snowfields.

Raphael slots in behind. A man with an unshakable belief in God. When it had become apparent that the killer's agenda included everyone in the monastery, he had been the only one not afraid. The test of true faith. When Death is near, or an inevitability, are you afraid of what comes next, for if you truly believe in the Lord, then you need not be afraid. The ultimate test, and one which all of the brothers have failed, even Copernicus, as this demon has laid waste to the complement of the monastery. All have failed, except Brother Raphael. The man's faith is unyielding. He faces the prospect of Death

319

with certainty and he knows that should he survive this fantastic ordeal, one day he will return to the abbey to start afresh.

All this, of course, does not mean that he hasn't decided to sell his story to the papers. Any one of them will do; *Life and Work* if necessary. He can use the money to get the monastery restarted. And as he walks, he makes his plans for the future – not knowing that his future consists of little more than five hours' ploughing through snow. A refurbished monastery, spartan but comfortable. They will attract tourists, who can come and see life as it was in simpler times. People fall for that stuff all the time, he thinks. A brilliant idea. They'll get all sorts of tourists wanting to go for it. Prince Charles for a start, and then the Americans will come in droves. Women too – they could accept them. They would get all sorts of Scandinavian Uberchicks, like the lassies in Abba, only with sensible hair. They could have mixed saunas, with Gregorian chant playing over the Tannoy; messages; all kinds of things. The investment opportunities are endless; for why can't money and religion mix? The Vatican has been doing it for centuries. They could get production companies in to make movies and stuff. They could steal Cadfael from whomsoever has it at the moment; they could get the *Name of the Rose* follow-up; maybe some entirely new monk detective scenario; then, of course, there'll be the Barney Thomson biopic with Billy Connolly; or, if the worst comes to the worst, they could always fall back on the Nordic connection and get sleazy low-budget Scandianavian porn flics, with names like *Swedish Nympho Nuns Go Sex!* and *Lesbian Monastery Bitches Get Ugly*. And so, the longer he walks, the more Brother Raphael is lured by Mammon, and the further he gets away from the abbey – in more ways than one.

Brother Edward faces the inevitability of the future. This business has merely confirmed what he already knew – that the life of a monk is not for him. He must return to the real world and deal with the demons which await him. If it means that he has to sleep with hundreds of women, casting them aside like so much chaff to the winds of fate, then so be it. If his life is to be one long inferno of endless sex and bitter retribution from long-distance telephone boxes, then that is how it must be. Perhaps he will even be able to do it for a living. Gigolo Ed, working the holiday resorts in the south of France, escorting the old and infirm to casinos and restaurants, then slipping from their beds while the night remains young and they lie snoring; making off with their jewellery, maybe – although that is another game altogether – then ending up with some young Mediterranean floozy at two o'clock in the morning, knee deep in sangria and pubic hair. It is a black future and lies heavily upon his shoulders; he knows, however, that there will be no escape.

Mulholland; still in some sort of daze. He would like to be consumed by determination to get them all to safety and to bring Barney Thomson to justice, but he is sapped of enthusiasm to the point of capitulation. He wants Proudfoot to escape, but no longer cares about the other three. The sense of duty will drive him to protect them, but what does he care now? For, as he walks, he surveys the battlefield of his future, and it is barren and laid waste. His life is Flanders Fields.

Melanie has gone, who knows for how long. Possibly for ever, and in his heart he couldn't care less whether she returns or not. He tries picturing her in the arms of some bloke from Devon, but the image induces nothing in him. No anger, no jealousy, no pain. And what of the o? What is his future to be in the police after it is revealed that approximately three hundred monks have been murdered under his nose? Dispatched to catch Barney Thomson, and instead the man goes on a mass murder spree while Mulholland sleeps.

And so his thoughts turn to what else he could have done to ensure the safety of this pathetic band. Should he have kept them all together in the main hall from the minute he arrived? Made sure they went to the toilet in sixes and sevens? What else could have kept them safe? Not the twos he had suggested. Even then, he repeated his folly this morning with the Abbot and Brother Steven.

He hadn't imagined glory when he'd set out on this investigation; hadn't imagined much of anything. But that it will come to this: in future years this will be taught in police colleges as a perfect example of an investigation gone wrong. How not to handle a murder inquiry. How not to protect the public. How not to chase a serial killer across country. From now on, whenever an officer makes a hash of a case, they'll be said to have done a Mulholland. *Hear about Jonesy staking out the wrong house and arresting the Chief Super's daughter? Aye, mate, the daft bastard did a Mulholland.*

The monks all think about women, in their way; and like Mulholland, Proudfoot is dazed. She hasn't encountered this much death since *Die Hard II*, and while that may be a seminal piece of film-making, it just hasn't prepared her for two left hands lying on a table, warm blood still oozing. That, and everything which has gone before.

So, as she walks, Proudfoot does not think about the future. Her mind is concentrated on two left hands on a table. And as she watches them, mostly they sit still, but sometimes the fingers twitch; sometimes there is no blood, and sometimes the blood still pulses from them; sometimes they look inanimate, not human in any way, as if they never had life, and sometimes they move around; they walk on fingers, they dance, they cavort, they fight. It's not the worst that she's witnessed in these past two days, but it has captured her imagination. Imprisoned it, so that it holds her mind captive to the vision. Two amputated hands are all she sees. As she walks, twice her feet slip into freezing streams, twice she bangs her knees on rocks, but nothing fazes her. The walk through the snow is slow and tortuous, but she barely notices. Proudfoot's mind is on those two left hands. Occasionally she escapes the vision, but only to wonder in a detached way – as if it isn't her at all – why it is that they hold such an entangling grip on her mind, and why Barney Thomson would do something so bizarre; because that's what it is. Everyone who commits murder has their reasons, but why two left hands? Very eccentric behaviour. And so she contemplates the criminal mind, but only briefly, before she is returned to those two hands on the table. Sometimes still, sometimes animated, sometimes in conversation. *'Here, Billy, give us a hand, mate.' 'You make that so-called "joke" one more time, you moron, and I'll kick your head in.'*

In her way, Proudfoot is also going slightly mad; just not as mad as Barney, and with a much greater chance of recovery. She walks at the back; occasionally Mulholland turns to enquire after her wellbeing and she finds the words to answer, and she doesn't notice the cold and the snow and the blue skies turning to grey.

✂

It is slow going, but they do not stop until darkness is almost upon them; by which time they are a little over a third of the way through their journey. Martin stops ahead of the others, some fifty yards in front, and waits for them to catch up. He is in a small area of flat ground, the snow some two feet deep. As they approach, they can heard the sound of a small river somewhere underneath, and they all walk with trepidation down the line of Martin's footfalls. The skies are grey, turning darker, and were it not for the brightness of the snow, the light would have completely disappeared.

The four struggle up almost as one, none of them happy. Raphael's fantasies have given way to tiredness and cold; Edward is numb, mentally and physically; Mulholland is numb, trying to retain some semblance of authority; Proudfoot is numb, two hands dead in front of her. They arrive a sorry bunch, and Martin does not waste much time.

'I don't think we should go on much farther in the dark. Who knows where we could end up? If we clear away the snow from around here, it'll probably be flat enough to put the tent up.' And as he says it, he pulls a spade from his backpack, as if he is pulling a rifle from its holster, and immediately gets to work on an area in the middle of the flat ground.

There are two more spades among the party, and these are taken up by Mulholland and Edward. Raphael chooses to pray, while Proudfoot thinks about two detached hands crawling up her chest and tightening around her neck.

✂

Brother Steven watches from close range, lying in the snow – suitably attired in white, becoming one with the snow – behind a hill. Darkness has fallen, the clouds have returned. There is the hint of snow in the air again, the first faltering flakes, but there is no wind and there will be no blizzard tonight. No drifts, no swirling tumult, just another few inches onto the layer of snow already covering the ground.

He had benefited from the snow, and now he suffers by it. The Lord giveth and the Lord taketh away. All that stuff. The blizzard had kept the desperate horde from fleeing the abbey in the first place; now it stops him stealing stealthily across the ground towards the tent and the two figures on watch, huddled around the fire. They have positioned themselves well, chosen their location wisely. It will be difficult for him to make an approach unseen; not until one of them falls asleep.

He could just shoot them, of course, now that he is in possession of Sheep Dip's gun, but that is his last resort. Guns are so unnecessarily vulgar. To be any fun, he has discovered, the poison being a valuable lesson, murder must be hands-on. The feel of the victim's blood on your skin, warm and delicious; the sudden relaxation of their muscles at the moment of death; that last breath, so much richer and deeper and fuller than any other. Like a Château Laffitte '29.

So the gun will be his final option. If it looks as if the police might make it to Durness, then he will do what he has to do. Otherwise the gun stays tucked away.

Brother Steven lies and watches and waits. It must be tonight, for if they set off early enough in the morning they will make Durness by nightfall tomorrow; but it is not yet midnight and there are many hours of darkness ahead. Steven settles further into the snow, his eyes narrow, and he waits.

✀

It is cold, and the two figures huddle close to the fire, although not close together. Erin Proudfoot and Brother Edward. An explosive combination; at least in the eyes of Brother Edward. For now he is a man alone, free of the confines of his cloak and of his vows before God; a man alone with a woman, a possible contender for his first boat trip down the river of mistrust.

Proudfoot stares into the flames, trying to concentrate the warmth of them into her bones; while all the time she thinks about two hands dancing on a table, like Fred Astaire and Gene Kelly. Has no thoughts for Brother Edward, despite his assumptions. If she turns away from the flames it is to look around the field of snow in which they sit, but she knows that their position makes a surprise attack difficult. Her main concern is staying awake, and at the moment that isn't a problem. Fred and Gene are making sure of that.

'So, you're in the police, then?' says Edward, breaking the silence. It has taken him nearly an hour to work out his best opening line, and in the usual way the one he has chosen was the first he thought of. Uninspiring, certainly, but better than "What's a stunning bit o' crumpet like you doing in the police?" or "If we're quick we could probably get a sausage session in before this Thomson bloke knows what we're up to".

'What?' she says, some half a minute later; Edward beginning to think that he was going to get the same reaction he once got from Wee Betty Barstool in first year.

'The police?' he says. 'You're in the police.'

She nods, still distracted. She can talk and think about Fred and Gene at the same time.

'Aye,' she says. Why is it that every single bloke on the planet who hits on her has to express surprise that she's in the police?

'Right,' he says. One-word answers, he thinks; this might be tricky. Still, he's fried tougher fish. Something like that. 'Must be hard, you know, a good-looking bit of stuff like yourself. Must be hard sometimes with these criminals, you know.'

'How do you mean?'

'Well, you know, a good-looking bird. It must be hard getting respect from criminals and all that, when they probably just see you as a bit of tottie.'

Fred and Gene briefly vanish and she switches on to ex-Brother Edward. Is strangely fascinated that anyone would try and hit on anyone else at a time like this; before, all too soon, the dancing twins come waltzing back.

'If you're looking for a shag, forget it, creep,' she says, before disappearing once more into the void.

'Oh,' says Edward. She must be gagging for it, he thinks.

There is a movement behind and they both turn quickly; instant adrenaline, instant fright. Mulholland emerging from the tent. They relax. Proudfoot loses herself once again; Edward accepts defeat.

'Couldn't sleep,' says Mulholland. 'If either of you want to go in, it's all yours.'

Edward waits a decent interval of a few seconds, hears nothing from Proudfoot, then stands up to accept the offer. And so Mulholland takes his place at the fire, as Edward disappears back into the tent. Thinking as he goes. Would have had her then if that idiot hadn't appeared. Will add her to his list in any case; it'd been close enough.

'You all right?' says Mulholland after several minutes of looking at the grey landscape.

She shrugs her shoulders and he senses the movement without looking at her.

'Don't know,' she says. 'Can't get the image of those two hands out of my head. Stupid, I suppose.'

'It's not stupid.'

'I mean, given everything else we've seen in the last

couple of days, that was hardly the worst of it. But I'm haunted by them. I've even given them names.'

He turns and looks at her. The cold face, with lips full and warm. Sucking him in.

'Names?' he says. 'Mr Left and Mr Right?'

'Fred and Gene,' she says.

'Oh.' He continues to look at her; she stares into some indistinct patch of snow. Red cheeks, lips a delicious purply-red, that glorious air of vulnerability and the chance to protect her. I'm never letting her out of my sight, he thinks.

Something which he will be forced to deny within five minutes.

'Fred West and Jean ... I don't know, somebody loony?' he asks.

'Astaire and Kelly.'

'Right. I don't think I want an explanation for that.'

'I don't know,' she says, 'maybe there's some weird psychic thing going on. Trying to tell me something about those two hands. Like there might be something strange about it.'

'What? You think there might be something strange about two left hands lying on a table? Bloody right there is, Sergeant. It's way strange.'

'That wasn't what I meant.'

'You mean Fred and Gene are embedded in your subconscious for a reason? Your inner detective self is trying to tell you something?'

'Aye, I think so.'

'Don't buy any of that stuff, Sergeant, I'm afraid. You know what you know in this job. When you start relying on some loony sixth sense, you're usually desperate.'

She looks round at him for the first time since they started talking. Something of an ironic smile on her face.

'Of course. And at the moment we're not even remotely desperate. There are still plenty of us left to kill. Won't be any need to panic until there's at least another ten dead.'

'You know what I mean.'

'Well, what's instinct, then? We all rely to some degree on instinct.'

Mulholland stares at the white landscape, wondering where Barney Thomson hides in its midst. Wondering if he is out there at all. Wondering if within himself there should be some gut instinct telling him the answers to all their problems. He finds no inspiration, but realises that he is looking at the snow through more snow. Large white flakes drifting down in straight lines, increasing in intensity as he watches. Christmas snow, of the type which ought to be accompanied by Bing Crosby and Frank Sinatra, sleigh bells ringing, children singing, reindeer, Nat King Cole, presents, chestnuts roasting on an open fire, the peal of a bell and that Christmas-tree smell, turkey, mistletoe and mulled wine.

'Fuck.'

'Aye,' says Proudfoot. 'Fred and Gene don't seem to mind, though. They're still dancing.'

'Oh, that's what they're doing.'

'What did you think?'

Another noise from the tent behind, and the former Brother Edward reappears, pulling his jacket on as he comes, shivering noisily. Mulholland turns; Proudfoot doesn't even bother.

'Sorry, I'm dying to take a slash,' he says. 'I'll just nip over here.'

'Don't go too far,' says Mulholland, thinking that he really ought to accompany him, but having no intention of leaving Proudfoot alone for even half a minute. With a killer like Barney Thomson, that could be all he needed.

From a short distance, the white-clad figure of Brother Steven notices Edward's appearance. This could be the distraction he has been looking for. A chance. Immediately his blood boils, his heart begins to thump, hormones gallivant triumphantly around his body. He begins an unseen crawl towards the campfire, an expectant smile beginning to come to his face, already tasting splattered blood on his tongue.

'One of us should go with him,' says Proudfoot.

Mulholland watches him go as Edward walks off twenty yards and starts looking for a decent place to pee in the snow. Like a dog.

'We can see him from here,' says Mulholland, knowing she is right. But there is a conundrum with it, of course. 'One of us goes after him, it means there's one of us left on our own at the fire.'

'I can take care of myself, Chief Inspector, just as I'm sure you can.'

'Just as you're sure Sheep Dip could've.'

'Well, I'll be fine, but if I go after him he'll think I want to have sex. On you go.'

Mulholland looks at her; has his doubts. A few minutes ago he was never letting her out of his sight again. He looks round at Edward, who has decided on the right place and is now trying to wrestle the business end of his genitals free from fifteen layers of clothing. Thinks about it; knows his duty, but also knows that every other decision he's taken since they left Glasgow has been wrong.

'Right,' he says eventually, standing up. 'But the first sign of anything and you scream your head off. You got that?'

She nods without looking at him. Somewhere in her confused head she recognises his concern for what it is

330

but, having finished the conversation, she now goes back to watching the dancing all-stars.

His mind made up, another bad decision, Mulholland walks quickly over to where Edward stands with his back to the campfire, tackle bared to the elements, making his mark.

And so, Brother Steven sees his chance. It has fallen kindly for him, for Edward has moved to the other side of the campsite, away from him. The chances of him being able to get around there in time, undetected and in this snow, were impossible. Now he has a clear path to the middle of the camp, where Sergeant Proudfoot sits alone, her mind elsewhere, easy prey for a killer.

Proudfoot stares into the fire, occasionally prodding at it with a stick, stirring up the embers, moving wood. She doesn't look over her shoulder at the two men to her right, one doing a tremendous Matterhorn of a pish, and the other doing his best to watch the man, but not what he's doing.

Brother Steven creeps ever closer. Like a lizard he crawls through the snow with tremendous speed, his nose scything through it, knife gripped commando-like between his teeth, with only a few inches of his body visible; and that blending with the snow on the ground, and the thick, heavy flakes now coming down in a wall. Proudfoot is looking in the opposite direction anyway; Mulholland is constantly scanning the surroundings, watching for a sudden attack, but in this white-out, white falling against a white background, he does not see the figure in white advance upon the fire.

Proudfoot's instinct is overloaded by the presence of the two hands. There is no sixth sense to tell her that her killer approaches from behind. No warning, no alarm bells, nothing to tell her that the frigid steel of death is

331

about to be ripped across her throat.

Mulholland scans again, as Edward goes about the business of re-establishing everything where it is supposed to be. His eyes go around the camp area in a quick circle, but these are eyes trained to spot a drug dealer in a nightclub, not a man dressed in white against a background of white; and so he misses the creeping figure of Brother Steven as he scurries over the final few yards towards Proudfoot.

Steven transfers the knife to his hand; his eyes sparkle in the dull light; his body heaves; he begins to rise above the snowline. He can taste Proudfoot's blood; he wishes he had time to linger over this, his first female victim, but he must be quick. Doesn't want to get into a bun-fight with the other four.

Ten yards become five. The snow passes in a rush. Too late, Proudfoot suddenly senses the danger behind her. Mulholland watches the snow and has vague thoughts about football games played with orange balls.

There is another movement in the night. Steven is on top of Proudfoot as Brother Raphael staggers blindly out of the tent, bleary-eyed, in some need of answering the Lord's call. As Steven hangs in the air over Proudfoot, waiting to bring the knife plunging fully down into the back of her neck, his distracted eye catches that of Raphael. Raphael's eyes ignite; and Steven's mind is made up.

A flurry in the snow. Proudfoot swivels round, leaping to her feet, crying out as she does so. Mulholland is finally alerted to the predator. And Steven stabs the knife viciously through the inadequately raised defences of Raphael's arms and into his face. Another thrust, and Raphael falls, the knife embedded.

Steven stares down at his latest victim, catches sight of

332

Mulholland pounding, Edward floundering through the snow towards him. Feels Proudfoot about to pounce from behind. Does not turn; no thoughts of tackling everyone at once – murder should be measured; slow down – and he quickly takes to the snow again, in lizard-like fashion. Proudfoot pounds after him, is almost there; but she is trained to chase burglars up busy streets; she slips, her head is buried in the snow. And by the time she lifts herself up and Mulholland stands beside her, Brother Steven has vanished behind the vertical wall which descends upon them.

'You all right?' says Mulholland, breathless, kneeling beside her. Doesn't care about poor Raphael, knife in his face.

She doesn't answer, but stares towards the snow where Steven disappeared. Barney Thomson, as she assumes. Eventually she nods. 'Aye, I'm all right. Don't know about that poor bastard, though,' she says, indicating the wretched Raphael with her head.

They both turn and look at him, and they watch the blood go cold on his face. Edward arrives, panting and scared, and sees the knife in his brother's face.

'Bloody hell,' is all he manages. But it is heartfelt.

There is a noise from the tent, then Martin's head protrudes into the cold.

'Would you lot keep the sodding noise down out here,' says the monk. 'Some of us are trying to get a bit of kip.'

Chapter 32

Hall of Fame

Brother Steven – for he still thinks of himself as Brother Steven, and maybe intends to find some other monastery to grace when all this is over; having not thought of the difficulties of that when linked with the hoped-for serial killer mega-stardom – lies in wait. Heart still thumping, even though it is now three hours since he sent Brother Raphael on his way, red-carded, to the great changing room in the sky. Or down below – that's where he thinks he's sent Brother Raphael. All that praying crap was a cover.

The four remaining victims-to-be are sat around the fire, as at last, everything they could find to burn having been burned – including the clothes off the woebegone Raphael's back, including the tent, as Mulholland has decreed that they take no covered shelter, that none of the four take their eyes for one second off any of the others, or the surrounding area – it begins to dwindle and die. Still some five hours before daylight, and Steven remains the most alert, the most stimulated by this feast of death.

And all the time he watches, all the time his thoughts

change. He still has no intention of letting any of them get to Durness, but the odd death after the arrival of daylight might be fun. Everyone prefers light to darkness, and we serial murderers are no different, he thinks. He has begun to consider that maybe he might use the gun after all. Shouldn't do any harm to his reputation. Can't see Bundy turning to Dahmer in hell and saying, 'What a woose; used a gun.' Not now, after all this carnage.

And besides, he can imagine the torture they are currently going through. The cold; the fear; the waiting. That'll be the worst part for them. Not knowing when he'll attack next. Having to be on the edge, adrenaline pumping, for second after second, into minutes and hours, all through the night, when daybreak must seem years away. And he takes as much pleasure from the thought as he does from the fact that eventually they will all die by his hand. There are stalkers and there are super-stalkers. He, Steven Cafferty, is the first mega-bumper, super-deluxe, thirty victims for the price of one, going all the way to Madame Tussaud's on an abattoir of desire, no doubt about it a definite Hall of Fame stalker.

And this part of it, this endgame, has been the best of the lot. Like a hungry wolf, he thinks, then changes his mind. Like a sated wolf, but a wolf who just kills for the hell of it. And he is destined to spend the next few hours smiling; smiling and going nowhere.

✂

'I cannot believe that you burned the tent down. It's three o'clock in the sodding morning, it's not going to be daylight for another gazillion years, it's absolutely bollock bloody freezing, and we've got no shelter, because you've gone and burned the sodding tent.'

Mulholland stares into the dying fire. Has been wondering for some time now how effective it would be to place Raphael's body in it, but knows that it is not an option. If the only reason he is to live is because of that, he doesn't think he wants to. Barney Thomson might have killed the equivalent of half the population of Belgium, but if he, Mulholland, places one dead body in a fire, the news will be all about him.

'I thought you were supposed to be a monk,' he says to Martin, looking up at last.

'Bugger the monk thing,' says Martin. 'I want to talk about you burning the sodding tent. What were you thinking about? It's snowing like bollocks.'

'I didn't hear you protesting at the time,' says Mulholland.

'I assumed you knew what you were doing, being the polis 'n all, but it's pretty bloody obvious you've no idea. It's snowing like fuck, the only shelter we have is a tent; what should we do? I know! Let's burn the bloody thing. Jesus Christ.'

Mulholland turns his aching, cold, exhausted limbs to face Martin. On a quick list of ten things he could really do without at the moment, this would be up there at the top, along with toothache, haemorrhoids, and Japanese viral encephalitis.

'So what do you think, heid-the-ba'? That we should all just have hung out in the tent? No one on watch, so that Barney Thomson could come charging up here and torch us where we huddled, or whatever? He could see us, and we wouldn't have been able to see him.'

'Oh, and that's different from what we have at the moment, is it? Don't you call me heid-the-ba', you stupid bastard. You see Barney Thomson at the moment? Well, do you? Well, I'll tell you this, mate; that bastard can sure as fuck see us.'

'If we were in the tent we'd never see him coming.'

'You didn't see him coming the last time, did you, Mr Smartarse Wankstain. Brother Bloody Raphael didn't see him coming!'

'That's 'cause I was watching this eejit taking a piss.'

'Don't bring me into it,' says Edward, aroused from cold slumber by the raised voices. 'What, you're saying that I should just have pished in my breeks?'

'Oh, shut up, you 'n all,' says Mulholland. 'The snow's falling, so there's cloud cover, so it's not as cold as it could be. We're all wrapped up well enough, and there's no reason why the four of us can't make it to Durness tomorrow.'

'Aye there is,' says Martin. 'There's one bloody good reason why we're not making it to Durness tomorrow.'

'Not if we're careful, not if we don't take our eyes off each other, and not if we stop the fuck arguing.'

'What? You think I'm going to trust you? I wouldn't trust you with my sister's tits.'

'Oh, for God's sake!' says Proudfoot, finally joining the fray. 'Would the lot of you just shut up. However close he is, Barney Thomson is probably watching us and killing himself laughing at you lot. He's taken the absolute pish, something rotten. So can we all just shut the fuck up, stay awake, and keep a good lookout for something moving quickly over the snow at a low level?'

A few deep breaths are taken; a few words thought about; but nothing said. The words 'away and shite' are on the tip of Martin's tongue, but this is life and death here, not some pointless argument in a pub after a long night's drinking.

Silence descends.

✂

But, in her way, Proudfoot is wrong. Barney Thomson is not watching them and pishing himself laughing. He lies no more than twenty yards away, low behind a small rise in the ground. He hears every word, but has not made an effort to look at them, knowing that they will not be going anywhere until daybreak. He has seen the drama with Brother Raphael, he has heard the raised voices, though not the subdued. He doesn't know the whereabouts of Brother Steven; indeed, does not know that Steven's knife hovered no more than two inches above his back before the killer decided at the last second to spare his life; however, he knows Steven does the same as himself, watches the small group around the dying fire, and he is constantly aware of being crept up on from behind.

At times since they all left the monastery within fifteen minutes of each other, he has been aware of Steven; he has followed him, as Steven followed the others, but since darkness fell and the snows returned, Steven has been lost to him. But all this time he has been waiting for something. The same thing which so miraculously transformed his fortunes all those months earlier.

He has been waiting to come up with a brilliant idea. He's done it once before, so he assumes he should be able to do it again. A bit like Jim Bett; played a good game once – although no one can remember who it was against – and everyone waited for him to repeat the performance. It just never happened. Barney has never heard of Jim Bett; he is not aware of the analogy, but he thinks he can create another brilliant plan.

He knows he can't just barge into the middle of this little group, reveal all and expect everyone to believe him. The lynch mentality would probably take over. There's been too much said about Barney Thomson for everyone to readily believe everything he says. Or anything he says. Honest, Chief Inspector, the Abbot had two left hands. . . Not a hope. Unless he can think of some brilliant and spectacular plan, he's stuffed. Condemned to be on the run for ever more. Of course, he'd been on the run even before he got to the monastery, but that was another matter. That'd take a different plan altogether.

The group goes silent for a while, then Barney can hear low voices starting up again. No arguments this time, so they're not clear enough for him to hear. He lies on his side, pulls his topcoat more closely to him, and settles down. He is tired, but there is little chance he will fall asleep. Too many things to think of. Or only one thing to think of, but it's a big one.

A brilliant plan; Barney needs a brilliant plan. And if he didn't keep going slightly mad every now and again, imagining he is in a barber's shop, he might be getting on a lot better.

✂

'What happened to the monk in you?' says Proudfoot. The snow falls around her and she can feel herself giving in to tiredness and to the cold and to desperation.

Both Edward and Martin look up, then Edward drops his head when he realises she isn't speaking to him. I'm not much of a monk either, he wants to say.

'What's the point?' says Martin. 'The Abbot, Herman, Saturday, Steven. All these guys with their God, it hasn't helped them. Look at Raphael, the poor bastard. What did he get for believing in God? A knife in the chops. Hallelujah, I don't think.'

'You must have believed some time, or you wouldn't have gone there,' says Mulholland. Despite the argument, despite being called a wankstain and not reacting by either a) arresting the bloke or b) kicking his head in, he has the same need of conversation as the rest.

Martin grunts. He would have reacted more favourably if the question had come from Proudfoot. Sees the opportunity for his first post-monastic conquest; knows there is stiff competition to come from Edward.

'I don't know, I suppose. But everyone who goes there has to have a reason. You don't shut yourself off from the world and its temptations if you're not seriously messed up in some way in the first place.'

'Ha, ha,' says Edward. 'The man's on the ball. You've just got to look around at the sorry collective. Too many weird guys with secrets to hide. We all went there with them, but they'd all come out in the wash eventually.'

'Yep,' says Martin, beginning to warm to Brother Edward, a monk he has barely spoken to in the past. 'Herman's a great example. The stern, deeply religious monk and all that. Mince. The guy killed a man once, you know. Committed murder, and ended up at the monastery on the run. I suppose he felt he had to stay there for a while, and eventually just got used to it. His true home, bullying weirdos and secret-keepers like himself.'

'Adolphus, ridiculed out of his home town for cross-dressing.'

'Common enough these days,' says Proudfoot.

'You think? He was cross-dressing with donkeys. Used to walk around the town centre at two in the morning wearing nothing but a nosebag and a harness.'

'But you see,' says Martin, 'it's not just the idiosyncrasies, it's the men who had them. Sure, some guys are delighted to be put in nappies and get breast-fed when they're thirty, like Brother Jerusalem, but some folks just can't handle it. The shame or whatever. Drives 'em nuts, so that they end up at places like that monastery.'

'So, you're saying that everyone there was a total

340

pervert of some description?' says Mulholland. Fully prepared to believe it, too.

'No, no,' says Edward. 'You have to give some of these characters their due. Frederick's been there since the Great War, the poor guy. Driven there by shellshock. There are a bunch of us sent by women in some way or another; nothing wrong about that. Festus went just because he couldn't be accepted anywhere else. A bit weird, but not any kind of a loon. But you see, that's the point; maybe we weren't all perverts 'n all, but we did all have some serious mindset problems which drove us there. Drove us away from society, you know what I mean?'

'The lad's talking a lot of sense,' says Martin. 'Not all perverts, certainly, but a bigger bunch of social screwups you couldn't hope to find.'

'So what was your thing?' says Mulholland. A bit sadistically, he must admit, hoping that it still upsets the man.

'Doesn't matter,' says Martin, which is certainly true. 'It was a long time ago. It was a woman that did it, though, a bloody woman. No offence there, miss.'

'None taken,' says Proudfoot.

'And what about the Abbot?' says Mulholland. 'Until just before the end there, he seemed like a reasonably normal bloke.'

A look passes between Edward and Martin, then is lost in the snow.

'No one was really sure,' says Martin. 'There was a guy with secrets that no one could uncover. Sure, there were all sorts of rumours and stuff, but nothing any of us could ever get to the bottom of.'

'It might have been something to do with the right hand,' says Edward.

'Yep,' says Martin. 'That was the big one. The big rumour.'

'What do you mean?' says Mulholland. 'What about his right hand? I didn't notice anything odd about it.'

'That, Chief Inspector, was because you didn't see it. I thought you police were supposed to be observant?'

'What do you mean, I didn't see it?'

'Think about it,' says Edward, and Proudfoot gets to it before Mulholland, although the man is not far behind.

'Right,' she says. 'He kept it tucked away in his cloak the whole time. I just presumed he was cold.'

'Right,' says Mulholland. It had registered at the time, then moved slowly into that part of the brain from where thoughts are rarely retrieved.

'None of us knew what the score was. There were a hundred guesses, but no one knew the right answer. Webbed fingers, a claw, a talon. . .'

'A third eye on the end of his thumb. . .'

'Exactly,' says Martin. 'Who knew? The guy could have had anything up there. It could have been something onto which he screwed stuff, like drills and razors and electric toothbrushes. But whatever it was, it was way weird, and that's why he was at the monastery.'

Fred and Gene, who had vanished with the near-attempt on her life, suddenly dance across the front of Proudfoot's vision; and then, before she can pin them down and ask them why they've returned, they are off again.

'So I reckon he was toying with us, this Barney Thomson character,' says Edward.

'How come?' asks Mulholland. Stupid question, he thinks. Barney Thomson has been toying with the police since the very first time he was interviewed by MacPherson and Holdall.

342

'The hand thing. He knows every one of us was dying to know what the Abbot's right hand was like. So what does he do? He taunts us. He cuts off the bloke's left hand and leaves it lying there.'

'Some sort of weird Freudian thing,' says Martin.

'No,' says Edward, 'I'm not so sure. I think it was more of a subtle irony kind of a business. Freud didn't do subtle irony.'

'Get out of my face!'

'Yeah, all right. Maybe it was Sigmund Freud, maybe it was Ziggy Stardust. Whatever, the guy was taunting us. Messing with our minds, even more than he's messed with them already. And it's the jouissance of it all, the sheer revelling in barbarism. Really cool in a way, but not when it could happen to us.'

'Cool?' says Mulholland.

'Aye, well, cool, aye, sort of,' says Edward.

'You people are even more bollocksed in the head than I thought.'

'But you can see his point,' says Martin, warming still to Edward, despite the gentle frisson over Freud. 'He's been killing monks with general alacrity all over the shop, leaving the evidence for everyone to see. Tied to one another, propped against a tree, burned to a crisp, whatever. Then, suddenly, he changes his method. For no apparent reason, rather than leave the two bodies lying around, he only leaves the hands. The left hands. We know they're both dead, and yet the bodies are missing. And mixed in with that you've got the symbolism of the left hand, when he knows full well that Ed, Raphael and me would love to see the right. If that ain't cool, Chief Inspector, what is it?'

Mulholland stares at him, his mouth slightly open. A snowflake lands on his bottom lip. He doesn't blink.

Turns his head slowly to look at Proudfoot, and she stares back at him, the same look on her face and in her eyes. At last, for the first time since they set out on their journey to find Barney Thomson, they are beginning to think like detectives. Something doesn't sound right; something demands an explanation; and it is staring them in the face. Fred and Gene lie dead on the table in front of Proudfoot, while the same vision comes to Mulholland. Two left hands. Different sizes, but the same colouring.

Killers don't just change their methods overnight for nothing. And Barney Thomson is no killer. There is always an explanation.

'This right hand of the Abbot. Any other suggestions as to what it was? Were any of the rumours stronger than the others?' asks Mulholland. Not really concerned with the answers, just giving himself more time to think. But already he feels the fear beginning to creep up his back; the hairs on the back of his neck slowly lift against the collar of his jacket; a shiver cascades across his body. The knowledge that Barney Thomson, the harmless killer, has not been murdering these monks, knowledge that he had had all along, and which has been denied by the evidence, makes a late entrance to the party of the investigation.

'There were a stack-load of other things,' says Edward. 'Some said he had a cloven hoof, and you can guess why he'd want to hide that. Some said it was a gangrenous stump, some said leprosy, some said he had two left hands, some said he had a pincer. There were all sorts of things. All sorts. Don't know that any of them . . . what?'

Mulholland and Proudfoot stare at one another. Immediately they both take quick looks over their shoulders and around the unprotected, vulnerable field of snow which marks their territory. Suddenly the enemy has become much, much more dangerous.

'What?' says Edward. Martin says nothing, but his eyes squint at the two police officers, his mind slowly beginning to catch up. 'What?' says Edward again.

'Two left hands,' says Martin.

Mulholland stands up and takes a more solid look around the area. Vulnerable doesn't cover it. They are sitting ducks. But then there are four of them and one of him, and as long as they stick together and keep their eyes open. . .

'No,' says Edward, 'no way. That was just about the weirdest of the lot. How can you tell? Just because his left hand was there and so was Brother Steven's . . . Oh.' Edward thinks. A slow process. 'Steven? Steven? What are you saying?'

'What do you know about him?' says Mulholland, directing his question at Martin. He can ask Edward stuff some time in the future, when his brain is in the same time zone as the rest of them.

'Not sure,' says Martin. 'He always played the straight man, you know. Knew a lot of stuff, was quite literary. Used to quote stuff all the time, philosophers and that, but that was it. I suppose none of us knew the guy. He seemed to be friendly enough with Brother Jacob, mind you.'

'In it together?' says Proudfoot.

Mulholland shakes his head. 'We're not making the same mistake twice. Barney Thomson isn't killing anyone. In fact, I'd bet your gran's arse that the bloke's dead already. Shit, we've been stupid.'

'How were we supposed to know that the Abbot had two left hands? How could we know that?'

'Not just that,' says Mulholland, 'it's everything, right

345

from the off. We both knew it wasn't Thomson. It had to be one of the monks, and we never investigated it properly.'

'Wait a minute, wait a minute, wait a minute,' says Edward, voice slightly fevered.

'What?' say Proudfoot and Mulholland in unison.

'Are you saying,' says Edward, 'that those two left hands both belonged to the Abbot, and that it was Brother Steven who killed him rather than Barney Thomson?'

'Brilliant, Brother,' says Proudfoot. 'Well caught up. The rest of us realised that about eight minutes ago.'

'Help m'boab,' says Edward. 'Help m'fucking boab.'

And the words disappear into the snow, and nothing else is said for some time. Mulholland stands and looks at the snow, moving in a slow circle. Wondering where Brother Steven lies, wondering what advantage they will be able to put this new knowledge to, and not being able to think of anything.

While fifty yards away, Steven lies and watches, toying with the possibility of taking Mulholland out where he stands with a single shot. But that he decides against, and instead he ponders what it is that has suddenly brought him to his feet. That, and why they've been so stupid as to burn their tent.

Chapter 33

Getting Very Near the End, and We'd Like to Thank You All for Coming

Inevitably the day dawns. Low, cold skies, the snow no longer falling, the white on the ground reflecting dull grey with the clouds. The four of them are still huddled around the fire, although it has long since extinguished; a strange clutch at a straw of comfort. Edward is asleep where he sits, cross-legged, hands clasped as if in prayer in his lap, his head hung. Martin is in exactly the same position, but his eyes are open, staring at the circle of charred wood and black ash which is all they have left to cling to. Proudfoot is sleeping in an uncomfortable position, her legs splayed, her arms tucked, her head in Mulholland's lap. And only he sits alert, constantly on the lookout for Brother Steven. The new threat.

Occasionally he wonders what has become of Barney Thomson, but it is an irrelevance. Suddenly it is no longer about him, and their situation appears all the more perilous. Regardless of how many had already perished at the hands of the killer, when he had assumed it was Barney Thomson there was still something unlikely about the whole thing; he still held the firm belief that if it came to it he'd be all right because there was no way that the miserable barber was doing anything to him. Murderer or not, he has it in his head that Barney is a big girl's blouse.

However, now the goalposts have been shifted. In fact, not so much shifted as transported to a different pitch for a different sport on a different planet in a different universe. It's like being 5–0 down with twenty minutes left, thinking you're playing Sprackly Heath Ladies' Over-60s Dominoes XI, and that you'll be able to come back no problem; when it turns out that in fact you're playing the 1970 Brazil team, and that not only are you not coming back, you're about to get pumped even more.

Mulholland's mind is rambling.

He looks down at Proudfoot, her face cold and blue; at ease, nevertheless. He could just never move; he could sit there for days, with this cold face in his lap. But he must be willing. He has almost totally failed in his duty to protect these monks, but he can at least make sure that she makes it back to safety. As for himself, does he care anymore? Wife gone (good riddance), job down the toilet (good riddance), and that is all there's been in his life up until now. Can he go and start from scratch?

This whole thing is getting near the end. He feels it; he knows that Steven must make his move before they reach Durness. It seemed like they were ambling through the Highlands one day and the next plunged into confrontation, death and terror; a confrontation that is screaming towards a conclusion. And the weight on his shoulders that is the manifestation of this thought drags him farther and farther down, so that he no longer cares. And yet the fear is still there, so from where does that emotion come?

He shakes Proudfoot's shoulder, immediately feeling her muscles tense; the eyes open and she sits up. A moment's hesitation, then she looks about her, sees the dawn of the day, feels the embarrassment of having fallen asleep on his lap and moves away from him.

'We should get going,' she says.

'Aye,' he replies. He turns to Edward and nudges his ribs. 'Come on, we've got to move.'

Edward's head lifts slowly up, the eyes open and wrinkle, a low groan escapes the back of his throat. He immediately thinks of Brother Raphael, and avoids turning his head to where the naked body lies covered with snow.

'Right,' he says, and is the first person to stand up. The quicker they move, the quicker they can return to civilisation, the quicker he can get on with his life. Not for a second does he allow himself to think about death. Death happens to other people, and not to him. Not for a long time yet. That's what he thinks.

As the others stand up, brushing themselves free of snow, starting the painful, uncomfortable process of getting their muscles moving and the warmth charging through their bodies, Brother Steven watches from afar. He has backed off some since dawn poked its uncertain head into the day. Disappointed that the night has not presented further opportunities, but murder is a waiting game. Everyone knows that.

He could probably have managed to take them on with two of them sleeping, but why bother? He's come so far, achieved so much, why risk everything now? His plan: to give it another couple of hours, see if he is presented with any more propitious moments, and, if not, bring out the Colt. And he has another, altogether more exciting plan for that. And so, let them taste the bittersweet tang of hot lead; let them feast on the brutal pungency of a steel bullet; let them enjoy the festival of punishment that manifests itself in the searing heat of the monster which is spewed forth from the gun; let them wallow in a cauldron of ballistic Parmesan and let their heads drown in a plate of bloody ordnance.

Steven's mind is also rambling. But he watches closely, preparing to move. He will track them all the way; if they slip, if they stray, if they wander slightly from the course, he will pounce. And if they don't stray, he will shoot them.

A bloody good plan.

And as the four shake themselves down and prepare to start the final long haul to Durness, and as Brother Steven watches every move, Barney Thomson is still far from coming up with that brilliant plan. In fact, Barney sleeps. Soundly, eyes firmly shut, mind not even dreaming, head lodged in the pillow of a cloak, he sleeps. And as the others move off and Steven shadows them as closely as he can, Barney lets it all pass him by.

✂

Progress is slow. Men who walk through snow for a living, if there are such men, would have trouble with this terrain. And as the morning progresses, Mulholland begins to doubt that they will reach Durness that evening. But he also knows they cannot stop and be sitting ducks again. Whatever the weather and whatever the light, they must limp on until they reach the safety of the town. He knows, however, his beating heart and his fevered mind tell him, that they will not even get close to Durness before they have to answer the challenge. It is imminent. He can feel it. Everywhere.

As for how much ground they are covering and their exact location, he has no clue. Brother Martin leads the way, claiming to know where he is going; and Mulholland must trust him, for he himself could not be more lost. Visibility isn't bad, but it could be a hundred miles and it wouldn't make any difference. When everything is white, it's white.

He makes his way past Edward and comes up behind Martin, who he can tell is only grudgingly waiting for the rest of them.

'Martin!' he calls out from some fifteen yards back to save the final effort of catching him up. Martin turns slowly and waits for him. Plucks himself from the dream of a Swiss chalet in winter; snow outside, a roaring fire and a strumpet of naked women inside.

'You know where we are?' says Mulholland.

'No problem,' Martin says. He points to his left without looking. 'That's Ben Fleah over there' behind it is Beinn Achrah.' Made-up names, but he knows Mulholland isn't going to know any better.

Mulholland looks into the impenetrable white, one snow-covered physical feature pretty much blending into another.

'How can you possibly tell?' he asks.

Martin shrugs. Behind them, Edward and Proudfoot trudge slowly along their footfalls. Heads down, dreaming or depressed, their minds on other things. Neither of them looks up, or behind; and so Proudfoot does not notice that she is becoming detached at the back, and neither does Edward. Brother Steven notices, however. Brother Steven notices everything.

'Just can,' says Martin. 'I know these hills pretty well. When you're living with a bunch of goons like that mob, you like to get out sometimes.'

'To the town?'

'That would've been totally awesome, but I could never do it, you know? A guilt thing. Masochistic too, because I always teased myself. Allowed myself the

351

chance to get there, but didn't do it. I don't know what that was all about, but I wasn't the only one doing weird stuff.'

'Well, you can do it now,' says Mulholland.

A large smile begins to spread across Martin's face. 'You're right about that,' he says. 'Bloody right.'

Despite the tension, and his cement-mixer stomach, Mulholland laughs. Relief. Another clutch at a straw of comfort.

'So, what are you going to do, then?' he says. 'What's first on the list?'

The smile remains plastered to Martin's face. 'Sex,' he says. 'Stacks and stacks of sex.'

'Available in Durness, is it?' says Mulholland.

'Don't care. I'll get it somehow. There's sex to be had in most places, and I'm gagging for it. So that's first, then I'm going to get steaming pished out of my face, then I'm going to have some more sex, then get a decent night's sleep in a warm, comfy bed, then I'm going to get up, have the fullest breakfast they have to offer, then I'm going to have stacks more sex.'

'Fine words for a monk,' says Mulholland, the smile still on his face. 'Think I might join you in getting pished out of your face, but I don't know where you're going to find all these women.'

Martin indicates the back of their line with a role of his eyes. 'Might try that wee bit of crumpet you've got there, mate, if you don't mind.'

Mulholland stops smiling. Takes another couple of quick steps and is alongside the man. Lowers his voice. 'One word, one suggestion, one anything in her direction, I'm ripping your nuts off and stuffing them down your sodding throat. You got that, monkbrain?'

Martin also stops smiling. But he nods his head and

immediately switches off. Typical police, he's thinking, but he doesn't really care. Erin Proudfoot's all right, but there'll be plenty more babes in the Sango Sands Oasis in Durness; even at this time of year.

Mulholland gives him another few seconds of hard looks, then gives up when he realises that Martin isn't interested. So he turns round to check on the back of the line, looking to see that Proudfoot is all right. And that is how he comes to notice that Proudfoot isn't actually there.

Chapter 34

The Bloody, Bitter End. Almost

Mulholland immediately turns and starts heading back, struggling through the snow. He nearly falls over a couple of times, the snow suddenly seeming a foot deeper. Edward stares at him as he approaches, steps gingerly out of the way as Mulholland reaches him and pushes past.

'Proudfoot!'

Again he nearly falls. All this death he has encountered, but suddenly his heart beats like it hasn't for years. Fear? What he has felt earlier, running this gauntlet, was not fear. This is it, bloody and raw, and his chest heaves, his breaths come in uncomfortably tight spasms. He looks wildly around the grey-white blur, hoping that she's merely stepped from the path, modesty having got the better of good sense, but he knows she wouldn't be that stupid; and he has the gut-churning, sick-to-the-teeth feeling of the certain knowledge that this is serious. This is it. For all the build-up, they have suddenly, brutally, come to the bitter end.

Brother Steven waits.

Mulholland comes to the point in their path where the snow is blurred and trampled to the side; tracks lead away behind a hill; enough of a disturbance in the snow so that it is apparent she has been dragged off, rather than walking off quietly for a quick sandwich. He turns back to Martin and Edward, who are staring at him with only vague interest. He breathes deeply, knows that the only way is to be calm. There is no blood in the snow; Proudfoot's body has not been left dismembered where she was accosted; it might be that she is not yet dead. Steven has been toying with them since they arrived; maybe he intends toying with them even more.

'You two come on,' he shouts back, the words muffled and dying under the weight of cold and snow and low cloud.

Martin holds his hands out at his side, in that 'Referee!' gesture. 'Accept it, Chief Inspector,' he shouts back, 'she's already dead. Steven hasn't been messing with us. You go off our track and you're walking straight into his trap. What's the point? If we keep going, if the three of us stick tog. . .'

'You two get the fuck up here right now, or if he doesn't kill you, I'll arrest you, you stupid bastards! Do it'

But these are two liberated ex-monks, men who have only just shaken off the shackles. They are free, and that freedom rests gloriously on their shoulders, and tastes sweeter even than Steven's revenge. There is no way they are taking orders from anyone.

The three men stare at one another, long and hard. An eternity of a few seconds.

'Right. Fuck it,' says Mulholland. 'Get yourselves killed.'

He turns from the path they have made and begins

following the marks of commotion through the snow. He knows he is walking exactly where Steven wants him to walk, but he has no option. He could try another route, try sneaking up on the bloke, but this is no time for trickery. He has run long enough; he has been uninterested or worried, and a minute ago he had been frightened. Now it is time to confront the enemy.

Edward watches him go, is prodded by guilt. He should go with him; especially if he wants to lure Proudfoot to his bed. Of course, the woman will probably already be dead, so it doesn't make much of a difference.

'Come on,' says Martin to him, 'we don't need the guy. It's not as if he's protected any of us so far. It's me who knows the way anyway, so we don't need some sad, sexually deprived eejit to look after us.'

Like every other sound in this winter landscape, the sharp crack of the gun is muffled by the snow. In its way, the dull thud of the bullet into Martin's forehead is as impressive a noise as the muffled, crumpled thump of his body as he collapses, dead, into the snow. A clean shot, immaculately into the centre of his brow.

Brother Steven has never fired a gun in his life, but a man possessed has the aim of the gods.

Instinctively, Mulholland and Edward dive into the snow, no thought for the pointlessness of their action, for they are totally exposed. Edward covers his head with his arms and breathes ice; Mulholland looks in the direction of the gunshot, but there is nothing to see but the wall of white. He gives himself another five seconds on the ground, then slowly lifts himself up. He knows; if Steven had been going to kill him, he would have done it already.

He stands open and unprotected, looking at Steven's palisade, vague outlines of slopes and edges, behind any of which the man could be hiding. And hopefully Proudfoot too, held captive. Mulholland breathes deeply once more; calm. The sort of moment that gives you the willies to think about; but when you are in it, you swallow your fear, you forget the other guy has a gun, and you get on with it.

'Come on, you,' he says to Edward. 'We're going up this bank and looking over the other side.'

'No chance,' says Edward, from the ground. 'I'm staying right here. At least, until I start heading towards the town.'

Mulholland starts tramping through the snow. He has wasted enough time on these pathetic bastards. 'Suit yourself, Edward, but you've just seen what he did to your friend. You want a bullet in the napper, you stay right there. You're not just walking out of this, monk.'

Edward deliberates for a further half-second, then is out of the snow, catching up, and then a pace behind Mulholland as he heads up the hill; although the pace becomes three as they near the top.

It is a time to be cautious, but Mulholland is not for that. He has stepped away from the fight for long enough. His nerves are settled, his mind is set; and if he is to die in the next half-minute, then he will have done it looking out for one of his fellow officers, and he will have stared death in the eye.

'Very fucking noble,' he mutters to himself, and five seconds later he is at the top of a small ridge, and down below, in the dip, not more than twenty yards away, they await them.

Proudfoot on her knees, roughly bound and gagged; eyes open, staring wildly up at him, as Edward joins him on the ridge. Brother Steven behind her, gun at the back of her head. Proudfoot looks scared, although the frantic

357

eyes are screaming at Mulholland to get away while he can; Steven looks serene. His job almost done, just the dénouement to come. The last of the Holy Order of the Monks of St John; and a couple of hapless police officers to boot. The perfect end to a perfect crime of retribution.

He has not yet faced the great unanswered question of what life holds once a long-held burning ambition has been achieved; the question which haunts everyone who has the misfortune to achieve all their dreams.

'And then there was one. . .' says Steven, looking Edward in the eye. He has enjoyed toying with Mulholland, fevered blood sweeps around his body at the presence of Proudfoot on her knees before him, but this has always been about these monks.

Edward trembles; his resolve does not stiffen. He would like to tell Steven to let the woman go if all he is interested in is him, but the words do not make it all the way from his determination to his mouth. At least he does not immediately turn and run, because he accepts that this has to be faced. But still he is incapacitated by fear.

'Let her go,' says Mulholland. 'If this is just about the monks, let her go and the boy and I'll sort it out with you.'

'Come on, Chief Inspector, you'll have to do better than that, gallant though it may be. You don't seriously expect me to relinquish one of my weapons, do you? This is some karmic game of chess we're at, Chief Inspector, and I'm not about to throw away my queen.'

'Very deep,' mutters Mulholland. 'But before you talk any more shite, you want to tell us what this is about? Did they make you pray more than you wanted, or not enough maybe? You a religious zealot or an out-of-place atheist?'

Steven toys with the idea of their immediate future; a

bullet in the back of Proudfoot's head, followed by a couple of quick shots to take care of Mulholland and Edward; or a more drawn-out climax, as he has planned. The 'bad guy in a Bond movie' climax, taking the time to explain himself before the execution.

Of course, it has to be the latter. No fun in expeditiousness.

'You'll never have heard of Two Tree Hill, Chief Inspector,' he says. Statement rather than question. Mulholland shakes his head; Edward narrows his eyes. Mild confusion.

'Two Tree Hill is a place of such abomination, of such hideous repugnance and shame, that it eats at the hearts of men like some insidious cancer. It is a place where the veracity with which men decry was at once naked in our vengeful Lord's undying light. It speaks of fear and loathing and shouts to the very insouciance which separates the faithless from the godly. I know that my redeemer liveth, and that he shall stand at the latter day upon the earth: And though after my skin worms destroy this body, yet in my flesh shall I see God. Indeed, Chief Inspector, Two Tree Hill is about that and much more. It's that whole life-blood thing – the battle of concupiscence against frigidity, unethical materialism against the rejection of immorality, the ignoble plagiarism of convention against the gemmiferous spontaneity of requited vehemence. It is a great Mahabharata of disenchantment, carved into the path of righteousness. Two Tree Hill is in everything; it is in this snow, it is in the hills, the air that we breathe, the gun I hold at your able sergeant's neck, the clothes we wear, the Abbot's two ridiculous left hands. It is all around us; it holds us and binds us and sucks us into its persecuted province.'

The damning words sit in the air; they beg the snow to

fall, the ground to soak them up. They haunt and possess, they taunt and tease.

'I thought Two Tree Hill was a football match?' says Edward.

Steven does not immediately answer.

'What?' says Mulholland.

'I've heard the guys talk about it. There was some football match at Two Tree Hill. That was about it, wasn't it?'

'A football match?' says Mulholland. 'A sodding football match? Well, was it? All that shite you've just been spouting's over a bloody game of football? No one ever spoke like that when Thistle got relegated to the second division.'

The gun trembles slightly in Steven's hand; Proudfoot feels it against her skull.

'It was more than a football match, Chief Inspector. It was about injustice and oppression. It was about one decent man's obfuscation, his descent into a Hades of women and shattered aspiration.'

'Would you stop talking shite,' says Mulholland, 'and tell us what actually happened at this Two Tree bloody Hill?'

Steven seethes; the gun twitches in his hand. He could fire right now. Be done with the ridicule. How can any of them hope to understand?

'It was a game of football,' says Edward. 'In the seventies, some time. Way before I got there. Anyway, our mob were playing a crowd over from Caithness somewhere. Twenty-two guys in robes kicking a ball about a bit of a field. Their abbot was refereeing the game. Near the end it's still nothing each, or something like that, when one of our mob sticks the ball in the net, or whatever it was they had for a net. In the middle of

the bloke's celebrations, with no one else really bothering, this abbot guy chops the goal off for offside.'

'It was never offside,' says Steven.

'Whatever. The goal is chopped off, and our guy goes
ape-shit. Attacks the ref, does the whole pissed-off player
thing. This fixture's been getting played for over three
hundred years, and your man becomes the first player to
be sent off. So, everyone's a bit embarrassed, the game
gets abandoned, and the guy not only gets his marching
orders from the match, he's sent packing from the abbey
as well, head hung in shame and all that. A bit like
Christopher Lambert in *Highlander* without the physical
abuse. And the fixture's never been held since. In fact, I
don't think we've spoken to that lot in years. It's a bit
like England and Pakistan at cricket after that Mike
Gatting business, except it's still going on.'

Edward shrugs. The tension has eased from him with
the explanation. It almost seems normal again; to be
having a discussion about football. Sort of football.

'And?' says Mulholland, still searching for the thing
that would incite a man to murder.

'That man was my father,' says Steven.

'Which man?'

'The man who scored the goal.'

'What? The offside one?' says Edward.

'It wasn't offside. Don't you fools see that? It was a
perfectly good goal, and they ruined his life over it. He
was never the same.'

Mulholland waves his hands in front of him, trying to
shake away what has just been said. His head shakes in
time, his shoulders shrug.

'Wait a minute, wait a minute, wait a minute. Wait a
minute. Wait a minute. You're telling us that you've just
murdered over thirty men because of a bad offside call?'

361

'It wasn't bloody offside!' sats Steven.

'I heard it was a mile offside,' says Edward.

Steven lifts the gun and points it at him.

'Fuck it!' shouts Mulholland. 'I couldn't give a shit if it was offside or if there were fifteen fucking monks standing on the sodding goal line. You're saying that you've just murdered all these bastards because of a refereeing decision? Over thirty men dead for that? Are you serious? Are you seriously serious? Are you really serious, you weird-as-fuck, stupid, ignorant, cretinous moron? You numpty, brainless, twat-faced, shit-brained, heid-the-ba'd, twat-brained, shit-faced, couldn't-piss-in-a-blanket Spam-head? I've eaten fish suppers with more brains than you. You can't honestly be saying that you've just killed more people than live in the suburbs of Shanghai because of a bad offside call. That would just have to be the most ridiculous, fuck-witted piece of stupid fuck-headedness I've ever heard of.'

Steven does nought but frown. He should have known they wouldn't understand. Such is the abuse that the enlightened must face.

'It was a really, really bad decision,' he says.

Mulholland doesn't know what to say. This is stupid. Most crimes are stupid, but this is up there in the top one of really stupid crimes he's investigated. This is beyond stupid. This is the Real Madrid 1960 European Cup-winning side of stupidity.

'Well, why didn't you go after the referee?'

Steven smiles, lowers the gun from his aim on the shaking Edward and rests it once more against Proudfoot's head. 'I did, several years ago. But it was this mob I really wanted. It was them who drove my father away from the place he loved. It was them who ruined his life. It was them who forced him to die a

362

broken man, and it was on his deathbed that he told me about the injustice of Two Tree Hill. I knew then that he must be avenged.'

Mulholland is still aghast; and aghast at himself for even indulging in conversation about it.

'So why kill them all? If it was in the seventies, a lot of this lot couldn't even have been here.'

Steven shrugs. The gun is raised then comes back down to rest on Proudfoot's head. She had wondered if Mulholland would manage to effect her escape, but she has now resigned herself to the bullet in the back of the head. Someone this insane will not spare her.

'I took my time. I tried to find records of the day to see who was here at the time, then I was going to take them out. Spare the innocent, you know? But, of course, they had long ago binned any record of their day of shame, so there was nothing to find. And none of them would talk about it, of course. Then I was discovered in my searches by Brother Saturday. I had to kill him and that kind of opened up a bit of a wasps' nest. Got rather carried away, I have to admit, but I tell you, it's been one hell of a ride. Anyway, when I realised you lot were coming, I thought I'd better get a move on. Otherwise, I'd have lingered a lot longer over it.'

Mulholland still shakes his head. Staggered. He's used to stupidity, but this is unbelievable.

'But a bad offside decision?' he says, still incredulous.

'That's the point,' says Edward. 'It wasn't a bad decision. Everyone says he was a mile offside.'

'Hey, you can think what you like, Brother Shagger, but the fact is, I know it was a good goal, and I know that your lot deserved to die.'

'What about Sheep Dip?' says Mulholland.

'That idiot? Just stumbled into him in a corridor,

363

thought I might as well take him out. He was dangerous, you see, so I had to get rid of him when I had the chance. You two? I stood over you two nights ago as you lay sleeping, and I decided to leave you alive for a while longer. I wasn't that bothered about whether you died or not, and to be honest, there's no way you were ever going to catch me. So, I might kill you now, and I might not. Who knows? There is one thing I want from you first, though. You do this, and I might let you and your girlfriend here live.'

All stupidity aside, it had to come to it eventually. They weren't going to stand here for ever, discussing bad offside decisions and their consequences – although the thought crosses Mulholland's mind; if people were like this every Saturday, the only people left in Scotland would be a few rogue forwards looking for someone else to complain about linesmen to.

'What can I possibly do for you?' he says.

Steven smiles. He lifts the gun from Proudfoot's head, waves it at Edward, and then lowers it again. This time he ostentatiously exercises his trigger finger and pushes the gun harder against her scalp.

'You can kill him,' he says.

'What?' says Edward. 'What are you talking about?'

Mulholland glances out of the corner of his eye at him, looks back to Steven. 'What's the point?' he says.

'Oh, I don't know, Chief Inspector. Just having a bit of fun. I'm curious to see how keen you are on your girl-friend here, you know? Just how much are you prepared to do for her?'

'She's not my girlfriend.'

'Aye, all right, whatever. But you want her to be, it's pretty bloody obvious. So, let's just find out how much. You want her to live, you kill sad little Brother Edward.'

'Wait a minute,' says Edward.

'She's a police officer,' says Mulholland. 'She knows I'm not going to do it. She's prepared to die in the line of duty. It comes with the job.'

'Yes, Mulholland, but are *you* prepared for her to die in the line of duty? Think about it, my friend. If you don't do it, all three of you are going to die anyway. But you kill Edward here, I might well let the two of you go. In fact, I *will* let you go. And I'm a man of my word. All you have to do to get your freedom is put your hands round the boy's neck, squeeze for two minutes, kill someone who is as good as already dead, and you and your friend are out of here.'

Mulholland looks into Proudfoot's eyes. Pale blue and frightened. His mind races through the alternatives. The distance between himself and Steven, the time it would take for a blind charge; how to communicate to Edward the possibility that Steven's plan presents – that Edward can feign death; the alternative of doing as Steven suggests, keeping him talking until something else comes to mind. His mind is a mess, but whose wouldn't be when faced with such choices? And not once do his eyes stray from those of Proudfoot. Scared and nervous, but something about them which says that if this is it, then so be it. You've got to go some time, and rather this than a car crash or a debilitating illness. A bullet in the back of the head in the line of duty. She wriggles, wishing that she were free so that she could taunt Steven about being such a total moron; at least get a good sneer in before he brings the curtain down.

'Can't decide, eh?' says Steven. 'The clock ticks, my friend. Ten seconds and your girlfriend gets a bullet in the brain.'

'Leave her out of it, for God's sake.'

'Eight . . . seven . . . wasting time, Mulholland.'

He takes a step towards him, his mind in confusion. He turns and looks at Edward; maybe if he could just fake it, but will Edward know to play along? He tries doing something with his eyes at the man, but Edward stares back, frightened. Contemplating a dive over the other side of the hill. It'll be a job to run away, but how many bullets is the man going to have left?

'Four seconds, Chief Inspector.'

Proudfoot closes her eyes. Will she die instantly, or will there be some sort of sensation before she goes? Searing pain? Heat? Epiphany?

Mulholland hesitates. Three seconds, two seconds. Makes his mind up, but only on an attempt to buy more time. He turns towards Edward. Hands around the throat, look him in the eye as he strangles him, and hope the guy works it out before he has to kill him. Feigning death is the only way.

'One second. . .' says Steven, intending to drag that second out a little longer, to increase the agony.

Proudfoot takes her final breath; Edward sees Mulholland coming and goes with instinct. It makes sense. If either way he stays here he is going to die; he might as well make a run for it. Feigning death does not occur to him, and at the sight of Mulholland turning he is gone. On the back foot, then he turns, sprints heavy-legged through the snow the few yards until he can disappear over the other side of the ridge.

The gun cracks its subdued explosion; a firework of blood sprays across the snow.

Mulholland turns back to Steven, heart thumping again; mouth open; ears singing. The bullet having sung past his head on its way into the late Brother Edward's back. And by the time Mulholland turns, Steven once more holds the gun to Proudfoot's head.

'Hey, Chief Inspector, I didn't think you were going to play. So, what the hell. They're all dead now. Bastards.'

Mulholland calms down, though he can yet hear the bullet. His eyes engage with Proudfoot's once more, and they are now more settled. She has already faced the inevitability of death, and it has passed her by. When it comes for real in the next few seconds, she will be ready.

Mulholland knows he is going to have to run at them, he knows he is going to be too slow, he knows that he will be shot and then so will Proudfoot. And the game will be done. He can try talking to gain more time, but what use is more time?

'Right then, dick-face,' he says, 'get it over with.'

Steven twitches. The gun shakes in his hand. About time, thinks Proudfoot.

'What do you mean, "dick-face"? I'm the one with the gun. Who are you to call me "dick-face"?'

'I'm the guy who knows that you're a dick-face, that's who.' Mulholland smiles – might as well go down verbally fighting; on another level, try to get the loony annoyed and distracted, standard police stuff – and waves his hands a little. 'I mean, what am I supposed to call you? You've spent all your life planning to avenge some crap refereeing decision when, as far as anyone can tell, it was right. Your dad was just an idiot, and you're an even bigger idiot. What kind of sad, pathetic moron spends his life planning to avenge a lousy refereeing call? I'll tell you what kind. The dick-faced kind, that's who, dick-face.'

All the time he takes slow, mincing, invisible steps towards them. Pointless words, but if he can keep it up, get the balance between keeping Steven interested and getting him so annoyed he shoots him instantly, he might get close enough. But it's a long twenty yards, which has become a long fifteen yards, and it's still too far on a good surface, never mind with this snow between them.

Steven twitches again. Sees Mulholland coming. Debating with himself whether or not to let him get nearer so that he can answer these outrageous taunts. But no, the closer he gets the more chance there is of him making a move. Why mess around when five seconds from now his job could be complete and he could be walking away from here and getting on with his life?

He lifts the gun, hand steady, perfect aim. One and a half centimetres above Mulholland's right eye. Get them there and they'll twitch; he read that in a book once. Proudfoot can watch it, and then she can get hers.

Mulholland hesitates, recognises the look. Saw it once from a moron in Hyndland who came at him with a knife. This is it.

One last look at Proudfoot – the eyes say everything – and mouth open and screaming, he charges towards Brother Steven.

Chapter 35

From nowhere he comes. Dressed in white, invisible to all until the last second, a man possessed, Barney Thomson springs from behind Brother Steven, his hands reach his shoulders before the finger squeezes the trigger, and when the gun goes off the bullet flies harmlessly away into the low cloud.

Proudfoot falls forward into the snow; Mulholland races towards her. Barney pushes Steven under him, grabbing at his right wrist to stop him manoeuvring the gun. He has the benefit of surprise for a few seconds, and so Steven wilts, but he is the stronger man. Barney struggles, manages to avoid the knee that Steven tries to thrust up into his groin.

Steven pushes back at him, raises him up, then pushes him over onto his back. Still Barney grabs at his wrists, still Barney struggles to remember what about this particular plan was brilliant. Steven's forehead comes accelerating down, but Barney spots it and takes the blow to the side of his skull rather than to the bridge of his nose. Steven reels for a second, hurt as much as his victim.

Mulholland undoes the restraints around Proudfoot; they watch no more than two yards away. A strange fascination. Then suddenly the realisation that he has to do something. Too late.

The gun is brought down into the midst of the wrestling match. Barney screws his face up; Steven tries to steer the gun into Barney's stomach, muscles tense.

But Steven is a man who has lived his dream; a man whose time has come and gone; and a man who suddenly doubts his entire life. Barney is a man who has not come this far to go down like this.

The gun goes off as Mulholland is on top of them, another muffled thud. Sometimes it is not always the one who doesn't care who loses. . .

He pulls at them, and nothing yields, then slowly Steven's shoulder gives in, and his body falls away from that of Barney Thomson. There is blood on them both, but the blood is Steven's, and when he falls into the snow, the gun still clutched in his hand, he doesn't move.

Barney Thomson looks up at Mulholland, chest heaving, breath coming in short, desperate bursts, and manages to say a few short words. He knows he is looking at the police; he knows this will be the epitaph to his years of freedom. He knows that these very words might dictate the course of the rest of his life.

'It wisnae me,' he says.

An Ordinary Man

They have moved back over the hill, away from the final scene of bloody carnage, and far enough away from Martin's body that it is out of sight. They have a vague idea in what direction they should be heading; they have retrieved Martin's compass. One day they will get back to a road, or one day their bodies will be found on a hillside.

370

The clouds are still low, but they do not promise more snow and they are stopping the temperature plummeting. So they take a rest before they set out on the final road, and sit in a small circle eating some of the food which they have aplenty now that most of their party are dead.

Barney has said nothing since he killed Brother Steven. Still cannot believe that that had been the extent of his brilliant plan. How do you make yourself look innocent of murder? Run out and kill someone, then say 'It wisnae me'. That'll convince anyone. Perhaps the circumstances will have helped, but you can never tell with the polis. Bastards, most of them.

'How did yese find me?' he says, deciding that it is time to get it over with. The temporary madness which afflicted him in the monastery has gone. The tiredness which allowed him to fall asleep while watching them is gone. He has tracked them by their footfalls, he has brought everything out in the open, and now he must face the future.

'Accident,' says Mulholland. 'We knew you were in Sutherland somewhere, but we only came to the monastery because of the other murders. How did you end up in a place like that?'

'Naewhere else tae go,' says Barney. 'Ah knew Ah had tae go some place that nae one would've heard o' me. How wis Ah supposed tae know that there'd be some murdering eejit there 'n a'?'

'Just like your mum?' says Proudfoot.

Barney nods. 'Yese know about her, eh? I thought yese might have worked it out. Does the press know, 'n a' that?'

Mulholland shakes his head. 'Don't think so. We've been stuck out here so long, who knows? The press have probably moved on by now, anyway. You know what they're like. We just couldn't work out the story with the other two. Wullie and Chris.'

Barney Thomson draws a deep breath. This is it. No more running; no more lies; no more fantasies. He might as well tell the truth, and face the music. Maybe he'll get to cut hair in prison.

'Ah know yese're no' gonnae believe me, but they were baith accidents. Yon Wullie slipped oan some watter and fell intae a pair o' scissors Ah wis holding. A couple o' days later, that eejit Chris confronted me aboot it, we had a fight, an' he fell an' cracked his napper. Ye know.'

Mulholland bites into a stale sandwich. Proudfoot drinks some water. Barney plays with snow.

'That true?' says Mulholland.

'Aye,' says Barney, without any pleading in his voice. 'Stupit, but true. No' as stupit as yon eejit Steven, mind you.'

'So why didn't you just go to the police after the first one? If it was an accident, what did you have to fear?' says Proudfoot.

Barney shrugs slowly, shaking his head. How many times has he asked himself that in the last few weeks? If only he'd gone to the police in the first place. . .

'Don't know. Ah wis just stupit, like Ah says. Stupit.'

'And what about the four polis at the lochside? D'you have anything to do with that?'

'Talk about stupit. Ah wis there, an' a' that, ye know, but they a' just shot themselves. Don't know whit they were on.'

Mulholland stares at the legendary and infamous Barney Thomson from close up. An ordinary man. If the press and public who so vilified him could see this. . . This is the great killer. Just a wee bloke, sitting in the snow looking slightly bemused and eating some cheese

372

which has not been well served by the journey.

How will they take to him when they get back? How will he and Proudfoot fit into the whole Barney Thomson story when they are disclosed as the ones who caught him?

He shakes his head, looks at the innocent in the snow. Caught him? What is he talking about? Barney Thomson just saved their lives. They no more caught him than they caught Steven. If they have finally found Barney it is because he wanted to be found. He trailed them across the snow, when he could have gone in the opposite direction. He's given up his chance of freedom for them. How should he repay that?

'You'd better get going, then,' he says.

Both Proudfoot and Barney look at him. Barney has cheese crumbs on his lips.

'Whit d'ye mean?'

Mulholland sighs heavily. Looks at Proudfoot but, initial surprise aside, she knows what he's thinking.

'You saved our lives. You're no more a killer than either of us two. The real evil in this is dead, and it was you who did it. If we take you back you never know how you're going to get treated. You might as well just disappear. Go and make a life for yourself somewhere, if you can.'

'Ye serious?' says Barney, standing up.

Mulholland nods. 'Aye, I'm serious.'

Barney Thomson stares down at the two police officers. He never knew that the police could be like this. Bloody hell, he thinks; and wonders again if it would have been this easy if he'd confessed right from the off.

'Can I take some food for the walk?' he says. 'I don't have much left.'

'As much as you like,' says Mulholland. 'We've got a stack-load.'

And Barney sets about loading up his rucksack, a sack which contains a torch, some firelighters, some matches, a compass, a change of clothes, and his scissors and a comb. Everything a man needs when he is on the run.

Suitably laden with food, his heart lighter than it has been in many weeks – and if he is honest with himself, possibly lighter than it has been in years – he looks down at Mulholland and Proudfoot for the last time.

'Thanks,' he says.

'You saved our lives, Barney,' says Mulholland. 'Thank you.'

'Aye, right. Whatever.'

'Where'll you go?' asks Proudfoot.

Barney draws a deep breath. He takes a quick look over his shoulder at the snowscape which awaits him.

'No' sure,' he says. 'Just somewhere Ah can cut hair, Ah suppose. Some place that they need a barber. Wherever there are men in search of a steady pair of scissors; wherever there is injustice against the noble art of barbery; wherever there is evil being perpetrated in the name of hirsutology; wherever men are forced to grovel in the pit of abomination in order to receive what every man deserves, you will. . .'

'Barney?'

'Whit?'

'If you don't shut up I'm going to arrest you for talking shite. Now fuck off and get going. I've heard enough people talking mince in the last week. So you've got twenty minutes and then we're moving, so you'd better git a shift on 'cause I never want to see you again.'

'Oh. Right then.'

And so, with a wave of the hand, the world's last

remaining barber surgeon takes his leave of the police officers who were sent to bring him to justice. Rucksack over his shoulder, boots sinking deep into the snow, Barney sets off on his way. The world ahead is clean and white and untouched and, as long as he does not look back, there is no one else within sight. He is free.

They watch him go for a few minutes without a word, until finally he is lost in the snow and the grey gloom. They turn and look at one another, but no words are said on the matter. Barney Thomson is gone. Proudfoot wants to tell Mulholland that he's done the right thing, but the words don't come out. They both see the tiredness in the other; they both feel it in their bones. But there is nothing that will stop them getting back to civilisation, although who knows what awaits them there. An entire colony of monks have been wiped out before their eyes.

'Right,' says Mulholland, beginning to move. 'It's over. We should get our stuff together and get going. We might still be able to make it back tonight, even if not before it gets dark. Then, who knows, we can have a fun-filled few days doing paperwork and talking to pissed-off chief superintendents.'

Proudfoot stands up, realises that her legs are weak. She has faced death; she is exhausted. But she will make it back to civilisation, no question. There are things to be taken care of.

'When we get back to the hotel, before we announce our return or complete any paperwork. . .' she says, starting to move necessary items from Edward's rucksack to her own.

'What?' he says.

'Fancy a shag?'

Mulholland stares at her across a ham sandwich, which he has been contemplating taking a bite out of before storing it away. Their eyes disappear into one another, and he bites erotically into the stale bread and dry ham.

'Aye, no problem,' he says.

The Long Midnight of Barney Thomson

The hilariously funny debut novel by

Douglas Lindsay

Black humour. Bloody murder. And no kissing.

Barney Thomson's success as a barber is limited. It's not just that he's crap at cutting hair (and he is); it's because he has no blather. He hates football for one thing. He hates most people. He hates his colleagues most of all, and the glib confidence with which they can discuss Florence Nightingale's sexuality or the ongoing plight of Partick Thistle.

But a serial killer is spreading terror throughout the city. The police are baffled. And for one sad little Glasgow barber, life is about to get seriously strange...

The very best of Piatkus fiction is now available in paperback as well as hardcover. Piatkus paperbacks, where *every* book is special.

The prices shown above were correct at the time of going to press. However, Piatkus Books reserve the right to show new retail prices on covers which may differ from those previously advertised in the text or elsewhere.

Piatkus Books will be available from your bookshop or newsagent, or can be ordered from the following address:
Piatkus Paperbacks, PO Box 11, Falmouth, TR10 9EN
Alternatively you can fax your order to this address on 01326 374 888 or e-mail us at books@barni.avel.co.uk

Payments can be made as follows: Sterling cheque, Eurocheque, postal order (payable to Piatkus Books) or by credit card, Visa/Mastercard. Do not send cash or currency. UK and B.F.P.O. customers should allow £1.00 postage and packing for the first book, 50p for the second and 30p for each additional book ordered to a maximum of £3.00 (7 books plus).

Overseas customers, including Eire, allow £2.00 for postage and packing for the first book, plus £1.00 for the second and 50p for each subsequent title ordered.

NAME (block letters) _____

ADDRESS_____

_____

I enclose my remittance for £ _____

I wish to pay by Visa/Mastercard   Expiry Date:_____
